This book is fiction. The characters, properties, and dialogues are from the author's imagination and are not to be construed as fact.

Real people with dialog have been used by approval.

www.hoofbeatsinthewind.com

ISBN-13: 978-1-7339528-0-4

Hoofbeats In The Wind

The green light turned red. What just happened? I blinked once, then twice. It was red when I stopped so I must have sat through the whole green light. I was surprised no one honked.

The light turned green again so I moved forward and was stopped again at the next light.

Why would Jodi have an affair? I didn't even know she and Greg were having issues. Greg was handsome, nice, and was a president at one of the local banks so he had a great income. Their sons were teenagers now so why not just divorce? Why have an affair with a married man? Did she know he was married? Would it have mattered?

The green light turned red.

Son of a bitch! I did it again.

The window of my truck was down and my elbow was leaning on the door with my chin resting in my hand. An old orange Ford pulled up next to me. Just from the fender and hood, I could tell it had to be at least 50 years old.

"Hey!"

I turned to the voice and saw an older man leaning over the seat of his truck and looking through the passenger side window at me.

"What?"

"Aren't you Lauren Conners? Didn't you use to rope?"

I leaned up in the seat and looked at him trying to decide if I knew him. I didn't.

"I am and I used to." I finally answered.

"I'm headed over to practice…team roping. Want to come?"

I stared at him in surprise. "What?"

"You have anything better to do?" He smiled.

"I have to clean bricks." I shook my head to get my mind clear. Roping? Why in the hell would he ask me that?

"Can it wait?" He asked. "It's only a couple blocks away. It's a perfect sunshiny day to rope a steer. There are five of us, we could use a sixth."

I stared at him through the haze. Huh…it was…and I had to go back to that empty house and Dave's blood on the bricks.

"Yeah," I heard the word come out of me.

"It's the club arena on 4th. We rent it out to rope when we can."

"Who is we?"

"My grandson and some friends. Turn left at the next corner."

"I know where it is."

"Alright," He grinned. "I'll follow you over."

I nodded as the light turned green again then drove to the arena as a moth would fly to a flame.

ACKNOWLEDGMENTS

A huge thanks to the following ladies for their support and willingness to share their knowledge and their love of rodeo.

Tracy Hammond
Kim Grubbs
Rylee Potter
Crystal Longfellow
Sydney Berquist
Janey Reeves

Hoof Beats
In
The Wind

CHAPTER ONE

Now what the hell was I supposed to do?

I stood at the patio doors of my house and stared at the dozen people talking or just lying in the summer sun while they enjoyed the company barbeque. I turned back to my laundry room door that I had just shut to block the sounds of the couple having sex in the small bathroom inside.

Curious to know who it was that would do such a thing at my party, I scanned the faces of my guests. I first searched for my best friend Andrea Richards and her husband, Stan. I was relieved to see him flipping the steaks on the grill and Andrea at the back of the yard. She was standing next to the pasture fence running a hand down the nose of my one of my horses while she talked to her brother, Greg Lawson. Logical progression…I looked for his wife, Jodi. Twice, I scanned each face. From the brick patio to the built-in grill to the large swing hanging from an oak tree and back to the horse pasture. She was not in my backyard. A queasy foreboding set into my stomach.

I searched the other 12 faces of my friends and co-workers. The ball of acid in my stomach began to bubble when I realized who was in the bathroom with Jodi. It was my boss, Dave Armstrong.

"Ugghhh," I groaned and looked back at his wife, Sheila, who was talking to Stan at the grill while he flipped a large steak.

My best friend's sister-in-law and my boss were having an affair. I had no idea that Jodi and Dave even knew each other.

So, now what the hell was I supposed to do?

I always kept the laundry room door shut and the only reason I had stepped in there was to retrieve another roll of paper towels stored in a closet. Damned paper towels; if it wasn't for them I would be blissfully unaware and wouldn't have heard the moans, giggles, and panting.

Unless I made a scene, I'm not sure anyone would believe me. Was it even my place to say anything? Would I be destroying two marriages if I did? No, they were destroying their marriages, not me.

I pulled my phone out of my pocket and turned on the recorder. With a deep breath and quivering stomach, I slowly opened the door of the laundry room and set the phone on the shelf so it would record the door. That way I could confirm that it was Dave and Jodi before I said anything at all…if I said anything at all.

To my full displeasure, I could hear the woman squeal and moan, "Oh, oh, oh…"

"That's it…yeah…there we go…" The man's voice was barely audible.

I was almost 100% sure it was Dave. The sound and the image made me shudder. Although he was tall, fit, and handsome, he was still my boss that I had worked for the last two years. No matter how much time went by, I would never forget the 'there we go'. It would haunt me.

Jodi owned a chain of fitness centers and was a Pilate's instructor. She was extremely fit with long brown hair and today she was wearing a tiny, barely covering her 'nether regions' yellow dress. The tanning beds didn't go unused either.

I shut the door, picked up the paper towels, and scurried to the backyard.

"Lauren! There you are," Andrea laughed. Her eyes twinkled with too much alcohol and innocence of the situation. "We were just thinking of breaking out the ring toss game."

"Oh, that sounds fun," I smiled to cover the nausea in my stomach. "We can set it up to the side of the swing."

The game pieces were in the small shed to the side of the large yard, so I kept my mind busy by helping her set them in the expanse of green grass. It was deep green, thick, and well-manicured in preparation for the party.

Out of the corner of my eye, I could see Jodi smiling innocently as she walked out the double French patio doors of the house. With a pep in her step, she walked to the small group of people gathered at the patio table that sat next to the pasture gate. Within moments, Dave walked around the side corner of the house. He strolled over to his wife at the grill and nodded to Stan. His eyes flickered to Jodi who had her back to him.

The nausea rose again when he slid an arm around his wife's tiny waist and kissed the top of her head. He whispered something into her ear that made her grin and nod then he casually joined the conversation. That just made me sick, angry, and I had the urge to tell everyone to leave so I could burn down my bathroom or at least use a long mop and wipe it down with a gallon of bleach.

At that moment, I knew I was going to quit my job. There was no way I could work for a loathsome asshole that would do something like that.

"Lauren? What's up?" Andrea's voice drew my attention back to reality.

Her long blonde hair was in a loose braid down her back, the bright blue dress she had on made her look like she was in her twenties, not forties like me. I looked into her brown eyes and tried to decide what to do but it was no use. I had no idea.

"We need to talk. Can you stay after everyone leaves?" I whispered.

"Is everything OK?" She whispered in return.

"No…" I walked back to the shed to retrieve the whiteboard and easel we used for keeping score.

I had it set up and turned to ask who was going to play. Greg was standing right behind me.

"Hi," I gasped…the fear that I may blurt out 'your wife just screwed my boss in the laundry room' ran through me and I clenched my teeth together.

"Didn't you say on the invitation there would be a karaoke machine?" He asked.

"Yes, it's just outside the patio door behind the buffet table. I forgot you were in a band in high school." I smiled but I felt cold and physically shivered. It was 98 degrees outside. We were in the shade so the heat wasn't so bad…but still…I shouldn't be shivering. "Do you take special requests? I'd love to hear you sing that song from your high school prom."

"Sure," He said as he turned. "As soon as I play…" His voice trailed off as he walked away.

I'm not even sure he finished the sentence because my eyes went to his hand…that was holding my phone.

"Son of a bitch…this isn't good…" I closed my eyes tightly then opened them to see Andrea standing in front of me with wide eyes.

"What?" She asked.

The whine of the karaoke machine rang out and drew the attention of everyone in the yard.

The acid in my stomach ate the lining and my hand covered it.

"Oh, Greg! I love to hear you sing!" His wife laughed.

He turned and looked at her with a bored expression as he fiddled with the settings on the box. Then the microphone went to his mouth as I stepped back and cringed.

"What?" Andrea's voice was tight as she turned to follow my gaze.

"Testing," Greg said and his voice was barely heard. He adjusted the knobs and turned back to the awaiting crowd and repeated, "Testing…"

My nearest neighbor was a half mile away but I had no doubt they would be able to hear it.

Well, I certainly didn't want that.

"No…" I started and took a step toward him.

His eyes shot to me with a bland 'fuck you' look then he placed my phone on the top of the karaoke machine and tapped the front of it.

"Oh, oh, oh…" Spewed from the speakers and everyone froze in place.

"Oh!" Rang out from the patio table and there was no doubt it was the same voice saying both.

I turned to Jodi. Her eyes were wide, one hand to her stomach and one to her mouth.

I turned to Dave as the "That's it…yeah…there we go…" echoed from the machine.

His wife's shoulders rose and her face turned white. Dave stared hard at Greg.

"Yes…yes…" Jodi's voice panted.

"You sweet little flower," Dave panted.

No one moved as the voices continued so I took a deep quivering breath and walked next to Greg.

His body was rigid and eyes staring at his reddened wife.

"We have to get to the party…" Jodi panted then a low moan vibrated from the phone.

My hand trembled as I pushed the stop button on my phone. I made no move to pick it up. The last thing I wanted was everyone to know that I had recorded them.

The yard was silent; everyone waiting for someone else to make the first move.

That move came from Andrea as she walked to her brother. Her husband joined them and without a word, the three of them walked into the house.

I'm not sure that any of the 14 people left in the backyard beside me, Jodi, and Sheila knew it was Dave on the recording but when his wife stepped forward, grabbed the two foot long barbeque fork and turned with lightning speed and a force beyond her petite frame and jabbed the three-inch tines into his chest there was no doubt.

There was no sound from the shocked crowd as his hands went to the fork with his wide eyes looking at her with a 'what did you do?' question. He slowly dropped to his knees.

Jodi screamed as Sheila turned and walked away.

Dave slid to the ground as the world came alive with people rushing to his side.

"Call 911!" Someone yelled.

I picked up the damning phone and made the call.

CHAPTER TWO

"How far away were you?" The detective asked.

I turned and looked at him with a 'what the hell?' expression.

"I have to ask," He blushed slightly.

"You told us all to go stand where we were when it happened," I said. "So, I'm standing right where I was when it happened and you can easily see the blood pool right there."

My mind was still trying to process the events by continually looping the vision of Sheila, the fork, and Dave. Having to point to the blood that was half in the grass and half on the patio bricks did not help. The paramedics had already left with a conscious Dave twenty minutes before.

"So…twenty feet." He said and wrote it on his notepad.

"What did you say your name was?" I asked. He had already told me at least three times. This time, he took a card out of his pocket and handed it to me. I read the name then looked up at him. "Well, Detective Malone, that man over there is measuring and taking pictures. That one over there is videoing everyone and, if I'm remembering correctly, someone said they were recording Greg because everyone thought he was going to sing. It's all on video. Why can I not go tend to my guests that are having problems?" I glanced at the house. "I'd very much like to go talk to Greg and Andrea."

"They the people that went in the house just before it happened?" He asked.

"Yes," I sighed. I'd told him twice already.

"They left about ten minutes ago."

I turned and looked at him in surprise, "What?"

Andrea left? Of course, she would have taken Greg away. I turned to look for Jodi. She was across my wide driveway, sitting in her car; a police officer blocking her from view.

"They didn't witness what happened so their statements were taken and they were allowed to leave."

I turned back to him…wondering what he was talking about when I remembered I'd asked about Andrea and Greg.

"Oh," I looked around at the seven guests that remained. They were all the ones that were the closest to what happened and they were all my co-workers from the mortgage company. We all reported to Dave.

"Have you heard how he is?" I asked.

"The victim? Nah…"

He said it as an afterthought…like I asked him if he wanted a cup of coffee.

My eyes went to Nadine, the finance specialist at our company. She was sitting at the patio table. She and another co-worker, Mark had tried to help Dave and their hands and clothes were covered in blood. Her body was shaking from the sobs as Mark's hand lay on her shoulder as he stared, pale-faced, out into the pasture. Lydia, Dave's assistant, was in another chair…she looked like a statue with her eyes staring at her car as if it were her salvation. The other four co-workers were also silently staring into the distance as they stood where they were "when the incident happened."

"They all need to go home, Detective Malone," I said.

He looked up at me with a huff then turned to look at my guests.

"Let them go home and deal with this," I whispered. I didn't know how I was going to be able to deal with this…how were they? "You have video…you have everyone's statements…please let them go home to their families that can help them."

My voice was low, pleading…nearly begging him.

"Yeah…yeah…" He mumbled then turned and waved an arm in the air. "Thank you, everyone, for staying and giving us your statements. If we need anything further, we'll contact you. Please take care."

No one spoke or looked at each other as they nearly ran to their cars. Within minutes, all the guests were gone, including Jodi.

Two police cars and the detective's car remained. Somewhere down the road were K9 police cars that had dogs out searching for Sheila.

I looked around at what remained of my summer party. The party that was supposed to help me get my life back after this last year…since my divorce was final. As Andrea and I called it; "the year from hell…that was preceded by the second year from hell…which was preceded by the first year from hell". It had been a very long three years. A year of dealing with my husband leaving me for another woman, then a year of fighting his outlandish requests in the divorce papers, then this last year where my twenty-one-year old daughter had also abandoned me. That, unfortunately, was mostly my fault, not his…sort of.

"I can give you the name of a company that will come clean up the blood, ma'am." I turned to a large well-seasoned officer. "Mullins…Officer Mullins." He said.

"No, thank you…" I sighed and looked blankly at the bricks. "It's just a portion of the patio…a few bricks…I'll try…"

"It's Sunday but they'll still come out if you want." He smiled politely.

"No…no…I don't want to ruin anyone else's day." I sighed again and looked at the pool of blood. My boss's blood. I closed my eyes just to have the vision of Sheila swinging around with the fork in her hand and plunging it into his chest.

My eyes opened to stop the vision from continuing.

"I'll at least wash down what I can then." he said.

I'm sure he could see I was still a bit dazed.

"There is a spot remover…one of those meant for pet stains that you can buy if the brick stains." he said.

"It can stain?" I whispered in dread.

"It's pretty porous." He nodded and walked to the hose.

I watched him until the first spray of the water hit the bricks and the blood splattered. My body shivered and I turned away.

Tables full of food were spread out on the porch. Three steps up from the patio and I glanced at the potato salad, macaroni salad, and four other salads that led to baked potatoes, deviled eggs, fruit trays, veggie trays, pies, cupcakes…so much food. Andrea and I had worked days…weeks preparing for this party and it had barely started.

A glass had tipped over on a table with the red punch spreading out over the white tablecloth. It looked like blood too. I turned and looked at the bricks the water was still hitting then looked back at the punch. I now knew that red punch looked nothing like blood.

My hand reached for the paper towel roll at the end of the table. My fingers hovered over it as I thought of the moment I opened the cupboard to retrieve them…the moment I heard Jodi's 'oh' and Dave's "That's it…yeah…there we go…"

I shuttered and picked up the damning roll.

Before the 'years from hell' began, I used to host horse riding clinics and play days in the multiple arenas and horse stable. Many times I would have food left over and so I had a supply of the plastic food containers you would see in stores. I retrieved them from the back of the pantry and started filling them with all the food…including the steak that was still on the now cold grill.

There were empty cardboard boxes remaining from our shopping spree at Costco so I retrieved those and filled them with the food containers. Without a word to the officers still remaining, I carried the first box to one of their cars. They silently carried the rest of them for me. Evidently, this wasn't the first time they had taken food home from a crime scene. Why should it all go to waste?

It took six boxes of the containers to empty the tables, kitchen counter, and refrigerator of party food. After helping me fold down and store the tables on the porch, they all thanked me for the food and left.

I stood on the porch and watched them drive away then turned to the patio which showed no evidence of a party. It was washed down, swept, and even the grill was cleaned and the lid shut. The only thing that remained was the blood stain on the bricks.

"Oh, son of a bitch…" I whispered as the tears stung at the back of my eyes.

The inside of the house was another story. The kitchen was a complete mess but before I tackled it, I sent a text.

Text to Andrea: How is Greg, how are you?

I expected a quick reply, like normal, but there was no response.

I turned back to the kitchen and began washing dishes, pots, pans, glasses, silverware, and bowls until I was sweating and exhausted. I even dried them and put them away since I had nothing else to do.

No text response from Andrea so I went out to feed the horses.

When I returned, I picked up my phone from the kitchen counter and found a message from Detective Malone. Dave was in surgery and they still had not found his wife.

At 10:00 at night there was still no response from my text to Andrea so I shut off all the lights, locked the doors, and went to bed.

The house was silent. It was silent every night but this was different. It was the silence that makes you look around…look in corners…I had the strong urge to look under the bed and in the closets. I resisted until my eyes closed.

I woke up at least a dozen times to the image of Dave falling to his knees then to the ground…Jodi screaming. People rushed to him to try to stop the bleeding…then the sirens…the ambulance…medics running into the yard…police cars …people yelling…crying…the questions.

Then finally watching him be lifted onto a gurney and wheeled to the ambulance where he disappeared. The ambulance lights turned on and siren blared. They were a half mile from a neighbor…a half mile from the first road…a half mile of pastures, trees, and farmer's hay fields.

At four o'clock I tired of the images and rose from the bed. There was still no message from Andrea so I slowly walked down the stairs and headed for the office…to the computer. I searched the internet for anything related to Dave.   Nothing had changed; the last report was of him in surgery and no location of Sheila.

I sat in the office chair and stared out the window. I watched as the horse pastures, barn, corrals, and arenas brightened as the sun rose.

Text to Andrea: You awake?

I felt detached from the world and really had no idea what to do besides get ready for work like any other day. My autopilot kicked in and I showered and dressed. A tired haze engulfed my dark brown eyes making them seem wide…bigger than usual. No amount of makeup helped nor could it hide the dark circles under my eyes. I brushed my waist length hair and captured it into a high ponytail. It looked black until the sunlight touched it then you could see the auburn highlights. I was ready at the normal 7:25.

Text to Andrea: Call me

I drove to the office and walked to my desk in a haze. It was if the world was moving at triple speed around me and I was disconnected from it.

A few people spoke to me but I wasn't sure what they said so I just smiled politely and nodded…then walked away before they tried to draw me into a conversation.

I set at my desk and turned on the computer and stared at the image of the company logo on the background of the monitor. It was yellow and green and for the first time, I wondered if the owners of the company were Green Bay Packers fans.

"Lauren?"

I heard the word but it was somewhere in a dream behind me.

"Lauren?"

I slowly turned to see if I could see where the word was coming from.

"I'm right here. In front of you."

I turned back and looked up. Patricia Evans, the owner of the company was standing right in front of me. She was not called Pat or Patti, she only allowed the whole Patricia. She was an older stern woman and now her eyes were drawn together in concern.

"Are you a Packers fan?" I asked.

Her eyebrows moved up in surprise then back as the concern returned.

"Let's go in my office." She said and turned away.

"OK…but I really should check my email."

"It will wait." She said over her shoulder.

"OK, but since I was off Thursday and Friday to get ready for the party it's probably really full of messages."

She stopped at her office door and looked back at me, "Like I said, it will wait."

I rose slowly and followed her into her dark green and burgundy decorated office. She sat at her large desk then leaned her arms against it and toward me as I lowered into a chair.

"I read the official record of what happened in the paper this morning." She said with a low almost a whisper voice. "You are the only one that was at the party that came to work this morning and I heard they still haven't found his wife."

"Last night she was still missing and he was going into surgery." I sighed.

"Lauren, I received a call about 30 minutes ago and obviously you haven't heard."

"What?"

"He died."

I stared at her as the vision of Greg gave me the "fuck you" look and started the recording…the words…Jodi's gasp.

Silence echoed in my head. He died…

"Lauren, are you OK?" Patricia asked. The image of Sheila twirling around with the fork and plunging it into Dave ran through my mind and it was as if they were standing right in front of me.

"Yes, I should go check my messages. I should…"

"No, don't worry about the messages. Cindy is going to handle them for a while."

"What? Why?" I asked as he fell to his knees with that 'what have you done?' look on his face.

"I'm giving you some time off."

"You're firing me?" I gasped as he slid forward onto the ground.

"No, just giving you time off to deal with this."

"But I don't want to…" Sheila slowly turned and casually walked away.

"You don't have a choice. Mandatory 30 days and human resources will assist you in getting counseling." Sirens echoed in my head.

My vision cleared and the realization of what she was saying became clear.

"What?" I gasped. "30 days?"

"Yes and an all-clear from the counselor."

"But, I…"

"You deal with sensitive information and you have to have a clear head. Thirty days and counseling."

What the hell was I going to do for 30 days?

"Do you need a ride home?" She rose.

"No…I drove here."

"Which probably shouldn't have happened in your mental state."

"I'm fine," I growled then stood.

"Go home and I'll have HR call you." She said sternly but there was compassion in her eyes.

"But, what am I supposed to do?"

"Get your head straight, give it time. Find someone to talk to."

I don't remember the drive home or walking to the swing in my backyard. I slowly lowered onto the bench seat and just started swinging my legs. The swing had comforted me for twenty-one years; ever since my uncle had the house and barns constructed. He built the swing as a surprise when I brought my daughter home from the hospital.

My eyes went to the back patio…to the grill…to the ground where he had fallen.

He was dead. The haze was joined by a numbness that tingled through my body.

As a boss, he had been strict, humorous at times, and loyal to the mortgage company we worked for. He reported directly to the owner and I had reported to him as the mortgage manager. It was a fun job…most of the time.

I had no idea he was a moral-less ass hole. He was always professional in the office to all of the women. Not once had I heard a rumor that he was having an affair or ever had an affair.

I had met his wife, Sheila, on numerous occasions when she came to the office. I had never seen her outside the office…nor him. Which was why I was so surprised he wanted to attend the party this year. He'd initially declined so the work staff wouldn't feel restricted by having a boss in attendance but he changed his mind. Now I know why. He must have found out that Jodi was going to be there. But how did they know each other and why in the hell did he bring his wife?

I called Andrea. Maybe she would have some answers from Jodi.

Two rings and the call went to voicemail so I left a message; "Call me…I need to talk."

As the sun rose high into the sky, I called her again. No answer. Should I just go over there? She only lived ten minutes away. She and Stan had bought a house close to my ranch since they knew Andrea spent most of her time with me riding horses and raising her sons and my daughter. There was no doubt we had saved thousands of dollars in fuel with them being so close. Stan and Greg also loved fishing and their house was close to the river.

Text to Andrea: I'll be over in 10

Immediate text back: No, I will come there

Oh, finally. I sighed in relief.

My phone rang out an alert that someone was at the gate to my property. The ranch was just fifteen minutes from downtown Boise, but it was so remote, my uncle had installed the gate for privacy and for protection he installed a motion detection camera. In the last few years, I added a video camera so I could watch who was at the gate. It wasn't attached to the gate like the other camera. It was hidden in the trees that ran alongside the fence. The trees continued from the gate and around the full 3500 acres which was a mixture of irrigated pastures, farm ground, and rolling tree covered hills. The trees were there to hide the view of the ranch from anyone standing at the gate.

I looked at my phone to see a news van stopped at the gate and two men standing in front of their vehicle. It looked like they were in a serious conversation with the man with the camera shaking his head as the other man, who I assumed was a reporter, motioned over the gate. I just stood and watched as they argued then finally the reporter stood in front of the gate and talked while the cameraman videoed him.

After five minutes they loaded in the van and turned around. The camera went dark after thirty seconds of no motion.

I hadn't thought of reporters. I guess it was logical they would want to come to see the scene of the crime…the murder? Would it be considered murder when it was such a sudden act of rage? What else could it be called? Just a crime of passion? But that was still murder.

I sighed and stood to walk out to the barn. I had no idea why; all the horses were grazing at the far end of the pasture. I opened the gate to the arena and walked through. The arena was built at the same time as the house. My uncle was a team roper and many an hour had been spent in this arena. Hours of sweat, laughter, work, and practice. It felt like home to me. It felt…safe.

It was a habit to walk across the mixture of sand and soil to pull weeds and pick up rocks that seemed to appear out of nowhere. It was something I did to relax…to escape.

This time, I was escaping the reality of Dave's death. He was dead…it couldn't really be true but there had been so much blood…it had to be true. The vision of Sheila turning white…then red…starting to walk away but turning…so damn fast…so damn lethal.

I stood in the middle of the arena and closed my eyes to let the hot sun's rays absorb into me. Maybe they would melt the haze…melt the reality. Sweat beaded on my brow and slid down my spine. When I opened my eyes, the haze…the numbness was still there.

What the hell was I going to do for 30 days to make this go away?

My phone vibrated twice letting me know that someone had driven through the gate. Only three people had the transmitter in their vehicle to open the gate without keying in the code. Me, Andrea, and my daughter Jamie.

I knew it wasn't Jamie, she hadn't been here for a year so it was Andrea arriving. She would help.

I stayed in the arena and waited for her. She must have seen me since her blue truck drove straight to the barn. Her door flew open and slammed shut. What was that about?

CHAPTER THREE

Andrea walked through the gate with long strides and an unreadable expression. She was normally quite open with me…I haven't seen that glare in years.

"Why out here?" She asked coldly.

"Did you hear?" I exhaled. "Dave died."

"Yes," She stopped with hands on hips, blonde hair braided down her back, and brown eyes looking…pissed. "We were called…or I should say Jodi was called."

"Really?"

"Yes, she was in a relationship with him. Remember?"

I was taken back by her tone. "Yeah…it was her, not me so why are you ripping my head off?"

"Because it's all your fucking fault."

And there is was…said out loud for the first time by my best friend of 32 years.

I stared at her with no idea what to say. That thought…that inkling had been slowly making its way out of my gut…out of my heart…out of my brain. I recorded it. I made the affair real…known. I had started the motions that ultimately killed my boss. It was my fault that my boss was dead.

The haze in my brain became foggier. The one person that was supposed to me helping me just drowned me in the accusations and the guilt.

I just stared at her with my body tingling in disbelief.

"Greg and Jodi are both distraught," Andrea growled. "Greg is tearing himself up because he blames himself for playing the damn video."

"I…" I barely uttered the sound.

"The fucking video that you did! Damn Lauren! Why did you do that?" Her whole body was vibrating in anger. "How could you be so fucking selfish? Didn't you think of anyone else? Didn't you think of what…?"

"No…I didn't do it for me." I interrupted as the accusations wore through the haze. "I wasn't going to do anything with the video besides make sure of who it was."

"So you could show Greg?" She screeched.

"No…no…just so I would know." I shook my head in defense. "I was going to talk to you after the party to…"

"Why?" She stomped a foot and her hand flew out to the side. "So you could get ME involved in this…this…what was it? Blackmail? Were you going to blackmail your boss?"

"No," I cried out in disbelief. "I wasn't sure it was him…or Jodi…that's why I…"

"I can't BELIEVE you would do something like that," Andrea growled then her eyes narrowed with a bit of a snarl making her lip curl. "You've changed in the last few years and last year's episode proved that and this…THIS…you wouldn't have done this before. You're not the same person."

"What the hell makes you say that?" I gasped. "I haven't changed who I am. Last year was just me getting fed up with…"

"It was wrong and you know it." She glared.

"Where it happened, yes. What I said, no." I countered.

"I don't agree."

"Well, that is your right but I am not Jodi and I did not screw someone else's husband. You cannot stand there and blame me for Jodi having an affair and Greg getting hurt."

"If you hadn't put that phone…"

"I didn't do it for any other reason than to know exactly who was in there…not that I was going to show it to anyone…least of all Greg!"

"I don't believe that Lauren. I have no doubt you were going to show that to Greg so he and Jodi would get a divorce and you could finally have him."

"What?" I gasped. "Are you kidding me? You've known me long enough that you should know I would never do anything like that! Least of all to Greg…who I am NOT interested in 'having'."

"That's a lie and we both know it." She growled. "You've wanted him for years."

My chin dropped in utter shock, "I have not! My crush on him was in high school and you damn well know that. Well before I was married. I have not been interested in him since."

"You've pined away for him for years to the point that Blake couldn't take it anymore."

I stepped back in surprise, "That's bullshit. Where in the hell did that come from?"

"We had dinner with Blake and Bette. He said…"

My spine straightened. "YOU! My best friend for 32 years had dinner with my ex-husband and his new wife? The man that treated me like I was nothing and the woman that he cheated on me with for three years? You were by my side helping me through the divorce. You know what that did to me."

Her face reddened, "I didn't intend to tell you that but since you're standing here lying to me what difference does it make?"

My heart hurt. I looked at her like she had just ripped it out of my chest.

"When did this animosity toward me start?" I whispered.

"Don't stand there and look at me so injured." She spat. "You have no right after what you did with me and Austin."

I took another step back in shock. "What does this have to do with my uncle?"

"You know damn well that when you were crushing on my brother, I was crushing on your uncle and he followed through on it."

"What? That was high school!"

We were only sixteen! Every memory of my uncle began to shatter as I imagined him sleeping with her. There was only a nine-year difference but that would have made him 25 to her 16.

My heart had hurt before…but now it was breaking.

My hand went to my stomach as it swirled.

"My God, Andrea…you never said anything."

"You were too busy with Jamie to even notice."

I gasped, "You slept with him from high school to when Jamie was born? Five years?"

She rolled her eyes as if I was stupid.

"We did not sleep together when I was in high school. It started while you were pregnant with Jamie."

Relief and anger flooded through me.

"You just made it sound like my uncle was a fucking pedophile."

"He had more class than that." She smirked. "You, of all people, would have known that."

"I did!" I so wanted to call her a bitch. "But I also have trusted you for 32 years so why would I doubt what you are saying?"

She just stared at me like she didn't know how to answer.

"You slept with my uncle while I was pregnant," I said as the realization swept through me. "Why didn't you ever tell me?"

"Because he asked me not to. When he broke it off he said he would deny it and you would believe him over me."

"And since you obviously think I caused the breakup why would that have mattered to you?"

"Because we were friends and had been for years and I didn't want to lose you or miss out on what he was doing."

"What was he doing?"

"Lauren, while you were pregnant he started building this place for you to raise Jamie."

My eyes widened in realization, "So you remained quiet about the affair with my uncle and remained friends with me so you could come here? To the ranch?"

She just stared again, probably realizing what she admitted and how cold that sounded.

"No," She finally said. "We were friends…"

"You basically lived here the first couple of years with me and Jamie when Uncle Austin was away," I stated. "You joined in all the events, clinics, and special occasions as if you were the hostess…like this place was yours."

"It should have been!" She yelled with her neck and cheeks turning red. "Austin and I should have stayed together and this damn place should be mine!"

I gasped, "So you're jealous!"

"You're damn right. I buried it because I loved you and Jamie."

"…and coming here." I shook my head. "So, when Uncle Austin got married and built the ranch in Texas? Was that supposed to be yours too?"

"His whole life was my life," She cried. "If we had stayed together we would have had both and maybe he wouldn't have died."

"How would that have changed his death?"

"Things would have been different." She flung a hand to the side. "He shouldn't be dead and I should be his wife and this place and the place in Texas should be mine."

I never saw this coming. How could I have truly known her all these years and not see this coming?

"Well, I'm sure Stan would love to hear that."

She glared at me. "You want to record that too?"

I sighed, "Of course not…I'm just at a loss for why you're saying all this when you're happily married."

She took a deep breath and looked into the distance. "I'm happy with Stan and my kids." She turned back to me. "It's not the life I chose, it was the life I had to play out."

"Why have you never said this to me before? After all these years of friendship and I didn't know all this," I whispered.

"Because…just like Austin said. You wouldn't have believed me." Her voice was low and accusing. "It was him…always him for you. Well, it was for me too. You were just too fucking selfish to see it…and now Greg. He sees himself as a killer now, thanks to you, he'll never be the same again. My brother is broken and your boss is dead because of you." She started to turn away then looked back over her shoulder. "I want nothing to do with you."

She turned and walked away. We had been friends for nearly all of our 42 years but I knew we never would be again.

With every step she took, a part of me left with her. My last chance of holding onto any part of my life was walking away. It felt as if my soul…my essence was leaving with her.

Her car door slammed shut and I fell to my knees in the middle of the arena. The engine roared to life and I slid to my hip. The car moved down the road and my body melted into the dirt. When the sound of her car faded away, I rolled onto my back; legs and arms splayed out as if I was going to make a snow angel. I stared at the blue sky as the hot sun burned at my skin.

There was no sound around me, but the smell of dirt and sweat invaded my senses.

Visions of our childhood played in the sky as I lay there…unmoving…barely breathing.

A compression in my chest…squeezing tighter…lungs stopping…heartbreaking. I lie on the sand and dirt arena floor and stared at the sky as my life passed by. My father leaving when I was three, my mother abandoning me with his brother when I was twelve and Austin was only twenty-one. My uncle became the best surrogate father anyone could ask for until he died at only thirty-six years old. A part of me died that day but I kept it together with the help of my husband, daughter and my best friend. They were all gone now; betrayal, disgust, and jealousy. Their lives continued. My life was fading away in the middle of a dirt arena.

The blue sky turned black with millions of twinkling stars in the sky. I envisioned each star as a human. How could there be that many people in the world yet I was lying alone and dying of a broken life in the arena? I couldn't take the loss, the loneliness, and the despair that was slowly killing me. My eyes closed to hide all those stars.

I began willing every shallow breath to be my last.

A breeze swept up small particles of dust and they floated over me. A stronger breeze blew sand in the air. I lay focusing on the feel of the tingles of the sand hitting my skin when a large gust of wind swirled around me. It lifted my hair and it too fell over me. More dust swirled up and slowly drifted to cover me.

I could hear the sway of the long grass in the field next to the arena as the wind waved it back and forth. I concentrated on it and the dust.

Then I heard it. My senses honed to it. It was a rumble that was growing closer and closer. A whinny danced in the wind then another and another as the horses neared.

Hoofbeats in the wind.

My eyes slowly opened as I listen to the sound approach. They ran by the arena and I could feel the vibration through the ground until they disappeared. I lay quietly staring at the sky and listening for them again.

Hoofbeats in the wind.

They ran by the arena again; the vibration seemed to wake my body as I slowly sat up and turned to the pasture to see them but they had already disappeared into the darkness as if they were ghosts.

I slowly stood and looked out into the night, waiting for them to return. A whinny danced on the wind just before the rumble…the thumping…the heartbeat returned…hoofbeats in the wind.

I crossed the arena as the horses ran to the fence. They were panting for breath, pushing against each other and excitedly looking at me for grain.

"I guess I missed your dinner," I whispered to them as a few gave me a split second to run a hand down their noses before they disappeared to the barn and took their places in the stalls.

I walked through the gate and into the barn to pour grain into each of their feeders before turning off all the lights and slowly making my way to the large house.

As it had been the last year, it was silent…quiet…absent of life.

I turned off the lights, slowly made my way up the stairs and fell onto my bed fully clothed and covered in dust and sand.

CHAPTER FOUR

The alarm woke me at 6:00; my normal time to finish chores and make it to the office by 8:00. I knew there was no way I was going to get back to sleep so I rolled out of bed.

I felt like someone had pulled the drain on my energy. Every movement made my body ache.

The pale blue comforter was covered in dirt so I pulled it off the bed as I walked out of the room. It trailed behind me down the hall, across the loft, and down the stairs to the large washer that was in that laundry room where the pantry was; where I innocently went in and fetched the damned paper towels.

I stuffed the blanket in the machine, started it, glanced at that damn bathroom then walked out the back door of the house.

The quiet of the ranch seemed to be magnified. The horses were on the far west side of the pasture. No cows or dogs were on the property and the farmers had not yet started harvesting in the fields across the road. I couldn't see any of the 5 barn cats.

There was only the rustling of the leaves in the trees as the slight breeze danced through them.

To the eye, the day was beautiful. It was a day every horse person dreamed of. With the slight breeze, the temperature was just brisk at 6:30 in the morning for a promised warm day. Blue sky as far as I could see; my guess was an afternoon with 80-degree weather. Just perfect…normally.

Today it just seemed to amplify the solitude of the place. When Uncle Austin was alive and even a couple of years that followed, the ranch would be full of horse trailers, riders, and horses. Life…he had built the place for life and friendship and days like today.

But, today, it was dead…a perfectly dead day.

I sighed heavily as my eyes went to the horses. They didn't need more grain after their late dinner but I needed something to do. I walked out the door, across the porch, and down the steps to the patio. I stopped next to the blood stain on the bricks. I remembered one of the police officers mentioning a cleanser but couldn't remember what he said so I Googled it.

Tuesday morning's mission became a trip to town to buy brick cleaner. I altered my path to my truck.

On the drive I received a phone call confirming my first session with a counselor was the next day. Knowing I would forget, I keyed in a reminder into the phone.

I was stepping out of the truck at the ranch store when I realized I hadn't even looked in the mirror after lying in the arena. A quick glance down, I brushed off what dust didn't land on the bedding then looked in the mirror. My long black hair was in a loose, messy and now bedhead ponytail. It was covered in a sand and dirt mixture so I finger brushed it back and pulled a cowboy hat from the back seat and hid it.

There wasn't a speck of makeup left on my face and I really didn't care. I turned to the store.

The Googled article said a pet cleaner would clean the brick and I found it quickly. As I read the directions on the bottle, I heard a sound that brought back the memories of my daughter laughing as a child. I closed my eyes and pictured her smiling face as a six-year-old. Every spring we would come here and buy a dozen baby chickens. The chirping of chicks lifted my head as the tears invaded my eyes which I opened slowly.

How could we go from being so close, almost inseparable, to not speaking for a year? My heart hurt to go along with the tired muscles. I set the bottle back on the shelf as the chirping of the chicks pulled me down the aisle and around to the other side.

A woman with a white cardboard box in her grocery cart was looking at lawn mowers. The chirping came from inside the closed lid that had multiple holes cut into it.

"Isn't it a little late in the season for baby chicks?" I asked her. "Are they still selling them here?"

She turned and looked at me with a smile. She didn't have makeup on and her boots and jeans were dirty too. I felt right at home.

"Not here," she said. "These are from my hens and I was meeting a lady here that was gonna' buy 'em but she didn't show up. Too chilly in the truck so they got to go shopping with me."

We both chuckled.

"Can I buy them?" I asked with memories of Jamie and I picking out the perfect chicks out of the large bins each spring ran through my mind.

"Yeah," She nodded and pushed her cart to me. The chirping inside the box increased. "They are only a couple of days old so they'll need a heat lamp."

"I have a couple. How much do I owe you?"

"You don't even want to see them?" She asked.

"No…I'll trust that they are healthy if you brought them into the store. You wouldn't want anyone seeing you with sickly chicks."

She laughed, "You're right there. That would give me a reputation that I'm not interested in."

I gave her the money then walked my little noisemakers to the feed section. The ranch chicken coop was good sized and I knew the feeders and waterers were stored inside so I bought bedding and feed…and a spare bulb for my heat lamp just in case. I surely didn't want to freeze the little noisemakers the first night.

I set all the supplies in the bed of the truck then the box of chicks on the passenger side floor.

Not having seen them yet, I slowly opened the top of the box and peeked in.

"Well, son-of-a-bitch," I gasped.

I expected five or six but there had to be twenty little chicks shoved in the box. They had a little room to move but not much. I hurried home before any of them suffocated.

The chicken coop was a replica of a red gambrel roof barn with two shelves on the inside and a large wired run for them so they could roam outside without fear of a coyote or dog getting to them. Uncle Austin had helped Jamie and I build it when she was four. It was still in good shape even though it hadn't been used in three years.

I spread a good layer of bedding in the warming box. It was the inside corner of the coop and was sectioned off by 2 x 6 pieces of lumber. Just tall enough to keep them from wandering and small enough that they had room to move but not too far from the lamp. Thankfully both warming lights worked so there was plenty of room for the little herd. After filling a feeder and waterer, I sat on the ground and slowly lifted each little chick out of the box and set them under the lights.

There were little black ones with lighter colored feathers which I knew were Barred Rock chickens. The golden ones I guessed were Rhode Island Red or Buff Orpington; they were good egg laying chickens. It really didn't matter to me what they were…they brought life and noise to the ranch.

For an hour I watched them wander around the little warmer box.

Memories of sitting in the coop with Jamie made my eyes glisten again. I pulled out my phone and took a picture of them. I hesitated for a moment before sending it to her. I'd sent numerous texts, tried phone calls, and even emails. No answer…not even at Christmas. Refusing to spend the holiday by myself, I'd flown to Texas for the week and spent it with Uncle Austin's widowed wife and her new husband and four kids; the two oldest were my uncle's sons. Charlene was an absolute joy to be around and worked very hard at keeping me busy and entertained during the visit. During the day it worked well but at night I missed my daughter so much I cried myself to sleep.

I pushed the button and sent the picture of the baby chicks to her. She had cut ties with me but I didn't with her so I'd just keep trying.

An hour later, there was no answer from her and the chicks were sleeping in their new home so I finally rose and walked to the house. My stomach rumbled so I dipped a spoon in the peanut butter jar and shoved it in my mouth like a lollipop.

I stood at the side window of the living room and looked out to the pasture. The horses were lying in the middle sunning themselves.

The second the alert on my phone rang out I was digging into my pocket for it.

Text from Jamie: So you resorted to buying friends.

The tears were instant. The energy the chicks had given to me flooded out. I lowered into the closest chair and cried.

For the last year, I had used the office and work to keep me busy. I'd even bring work home so when I wasn't riding and training my horses I would have something to do.

Now…nothing…and no desire to even walk into the horse pasture. Thousands of hours were spent with Andrea and Jamie with the horses. With them gone, I just couldn't find the will to ride.

When my mind came out of its haze, the sky was dark. I walked out to the chicken coop to check on the chicks. They were fine so I fed the horses then sat on the couch and stared at the television. My mind looped between Jodi's voice in the bathroom during her sex romp, Dave's wife, Sheila, spinning with surprising speed and shoving the fork in his chest, and Andrea's tale of sleeping with my uncle. All the years she held back the anger and jealousy and not once had she mentioned it.

At some point, my eyes closed. The alarm woke me again. I really needed to turn that off.

I drug myself off the couch, dipped another spoon into the peanut butter and walked out toward the chicken coop. I stopped on the patio next to the stained bricks. Damn…I had to go back to the store.

I walked to my truck and when I stepped up I saw the dirty jeans covering my legs. Three days just wasn't presentable so I turned back to the house and forced myself to take a shower.

I slid on clean jeans, an old Wrangler t-shirt, and boots. No makeup and hair back in a braid down my back. The end just touched the top of my jeans. I shoved on the hat again and drove to town.

My phone alert went off just as I drove into the ranch store parking lot. It was alerting me to my scheduled mandatory counseling meeting with the therapist, Aubrey Olsen. A deep sigh and I turned the truck around and drove to the office.

"What am I supposed to say?" I asked her after settling down into the chair next to her desk.

It was a bright room with dark green furniture, tan carpet, and maroon and navy blue accents; very earthy and comfortable.

"Whatever you want," She answered.

I didn't want to say anything…so I didn't. I sat looking at the landscape pictures she had on the wall for 50 minutes. I thought of the baby chicks, the barbeque fork, sex panting, and Andrea's demeanor the last time we spoke. My heart hurt again at the pure jealously she emoted.

The therapist wrote on a pad on her desk with an occasional look to me.

"All right," She stood and opened the door. "I'll see you Thursday morning."

"Same time and place," I nodded and walked to the door.

"Let's be a little chattier next time if you want to get back to work," She smiled and shut the door behind me.

Back to work…where my boss wasn't there to greet me because he was dead…because I had decided to record the fucking bathroom door…because of those damned paper towels. My mind became numb again and my body ached…the energy drained.

As I drove back to the ranch store, the voice on the radio reported about a stabbing at a weekend barbeque. The victim had died at the hospital during surgery and the suspect, the man's own wife, had disappeared. There was a report that it was a lover's quarrel. The radio station would alert us to the search for the wife and they did not believe the general public was in danger.

Huh, I thought. There was no quarrel involved.

I thought of Greg as I drove into the store parking lot. He was a year older than Andrea and me. After his tall gawky teenage years, he had grown and matured into a handsome man.

I stepped out of my truck and walked into the store.

I never told Andrea that Greg and I had spent 15 minutes kissing in his car one night while she was busy with choir practice. In those 15 minutes, we realized we would never be more than friends. There was absolutely no chemistry between us. I thought of him as a big brother and he thought of me as his sister's friend.

Maybe if I had told her, then she would have known I wasn't interested in him…that I wouldn't have tried to break up his marriage to Jodi. Maybe Dave wouldn't have died. His shocked face flashed in my mind…then he slowly fell to his knees with his hand grabbing at the fork.

The sound of my truck door closing brought my mind out of the haze. I was back in the truck. I looked down and saw the bottle of cleaner in my hand. Thankfully there was a receipt with it.

I set it on the passenger seat and drove toward home. I stopped at the first red light and my mind wandered to Dave and Jodie and Sheila. If he invited himself to the party to hook up with Jodie, why would he bring Sheila? Why did he cheat on her? Sheila was a tiny woman with pretty blonde hair that she kept swept back away from her face. It was just long enough to cover her long elegant neck. She was a genuinely nice woman…who ended up stabbing her husband.

The green light turned red. What just happened? I blinked once, then twice. It was red when I stopped so I must have sat through the whole green light. I was surprised no one honked.

The light turned green again so I moved forward and was stopped again at the next light.

Why would Jodi have an affair? I didn't even know she and Greg were having issues. Greg was handsome, nice, and was a president at one of the local banks so he had a great income. Their sons were teenagers now so why not just divorce? Why have an affair with a married man? Did she know he was married? Would it have mattered?

The green light turned red.

Son of a bitch! I did it again.

The window of my truck was down and my elbow was leaning on the door with my chin resting in my hand. An old orange Ford pulled up next to me. Just from the fender and hood, I could tell it had to be at least 50 years old.

"Hey!"

I turned to the voice and saw an older man leaning over the seat of his truck and looking through the passenger side window at me.

"What?"

"Aren't you Lauren Conners? Didn't you use to rope?"

I leaned up in the seat and looked at him trying to decide if I knew him. I didn't.

"I am and I used to." I finally answered.

"I'm headed over to practice…team roping. Want to come?"

I stared at him in surprise. "What?"

"You have anything better to do?" He smiled.

"I have to clean bricks." I blinked a couple times to get my mind clear. Roping? Why in the hell would he ask me that?

"Can it wait?" He asked. "It's only a couple blocks away. It's a perfect sunshiny day to rope a steer. There are five of us, we could use a sixth."

I stared at him through the haze. Huh…it was…and I had to go back to that empty house and Dave's blood on the bricks.

"Yeah," I heard the word come out of me.

"It's the club arena on 4th. We rent it out to rope when we can."

"Who is we?"

"My grandson and some friends. Turn left at the next corner."

"I know where it is."

"Alright," He grinned. "I'll follow you over."

I nodded as the light turned green again then drove to the arena as a moth would fly to a flame.

CHAPTER FIVE

The arena was built with white panel fencing with a smaller warmup arena on the opposite side of where the older Ford parked next to a newer four-door Ford. That truck was attached to a trailer with four horses tied to the side. A four-door white Dodge pulling another trailer was on the other side of it. Three horses were attached to it. Backed up to the cattle pens was a large stock trailer that had hauled the two dozen steers that were milling around in the pen. The leather head wraps were already tied around their horns to protect them from the rope.

Four men were riding in the middle of the larger arena.

By the time I stopped my truck and my foot hit the dirt, the older man was already walking to me. He was slender and just an inch or two taller than me with well-worn brown cowboy boots and jeans. A heavily sweat-stained straw hat hid nearly all of his grey hair. The green and white plaid shirt he was wearing looked like it had been washed over a thousand times.

A mostly grey mustache graced his well-tanned face. It was full across his upper lip then dipped down the side of his mouth and seemed to drop off at his chin. He had to be in his seventies but seemed very fit.

"Welcome to our playground, Lauren," He said and stretched out a very tan and wrinkled hand. His blue eyes were happy and welcoming.

My motion of shaking his hand was automatic.

"My name's Pete Weston," He continued. "I'll introduce you to my four comrades then we'll pick you out a horse."

"I'll just watch from the bleachers," I said and looked out at the pen of cattle.

"All right," He nodded. "Let's go on over so you can meet the crew."

I didn't really want to. I just wanted to sit on a bleacher and watch but it would be pretty rude if I didn't at least let him make the introductions.

I followed him to the arena gate and we stepped into the dirt. All four riders trotted up to us and stepped out of their saddles. I looked at each of them with a forced hint of a smile. I don't think there was a doubt with any of them that I was being forced to be introduced.

"This is Lauren," Pete said. "We'll start with my grandson, Kade Weston."

He nodded to the man in a new straw hat that didn't quite cover dark brown hair. He had at least a two days' growth of whiskers over a strong jaw.

His large hand engulfed mine when we shook hands. There was no welcoming smile, just questioning eyes as he looked from his grandfather than back to me.

"Nice to meet you, Lauren." He said in a deep voice with a southern accent. I just nodded.

"This is Marty Hammond," Pete said. "We met about thirty years ago and started roping together…couldn't seem to shake each other after that."

Pete and Marty both chuckled.

Marty was younger than Pete but not by much. He had a mustache too but it stopped at just the edge of his lips. His face was rounder, smile wider which created deep creases along with dimples. The twinkle in his eyes confirmed he was a pretty happy guy. He wore a darker straw cowboy hat with a dark green button-up western shirt. I had no doubt that it was his usual 'uniform' of every day.

My hand automatically went to Marty's as we both just nodded to each other.

"Then this young bandit is Jess Corday," Pete nodded to the tall slender cowboy to my left.

"Ma'am," Jess said. He too had a couple of day's growth of whiskers over a long narrow jaw. His dark hair just covered his ears and was covered by a black baseball cap with the "Go Rope" logo on the front of it and he was wearing well-worn Wranglers with a black button up, short sleeve shirt tucked in at the waist. I shook his hand with a nod.

"And this is our young pup, Ryle Jaspers." Pete grinned and earned a smile from the three other men as Ryle glared at him.

"I'm twenty-one," Ryle shook his head. "I'm not a pup."

But he looked young with anxious eager eyes and a youthful energy about him. Longer black hair was covered with a "Go Rope" baseball cap that was well stained with days, weeks, if not months of use. He was a handsome cute…the type of guy I would have chased after when I was his age.

"You are compared to our not 21." Marty teased with his eyes twinkling mischievously.

I just wanted to go sit down and tucked my thumbs in my pockets and looked back over at the steers.

"I'm just gonna watch for a while." I turned away and stepped through the gate before any of them could speak.

I wasn't stopped and no one said anything as I made my way to the shade at the top of the bleachers. I sat on the top seat and put my feet up on the bleacher in front of me. Elbows resting on knees I watched the five men remount and ride in circles around the arena to warm up the horses.

The day my mother left me with my uncle we had been sitting on similar bleachers watching him and his friends team rope. We had never done it before and I had been surprised but very happy to be around all the horses and cowboys. It was much better than staying in the apartment by myself watching TV.

"Stay here," She had said to me and I hadn't even watched her go. I just watched Uncle Austin riding his horse and throwing his rope at a steer. His rope captured the horns and he turned the horse quickly so the other cowboy could rope the back legs. I didn't understand what they were doing but the men seemed happy and that made my heart race.

My uncle was tall with broad shoulders and kept himself in shape. We both had nearly black hair, dark brown eyes, and angular features so it was easy to tell that we were related. I had only met him a couple of times but never at an arena or around horses.

He looked like a western movie star to me and I was fascinated with the whole thing of horses, lariats, and cowboys. I watched every movement, every ride, and every throw; my body would twitch as they threw the rope. The horse's hooves striking on the ground made my heart pound harder in my chest.

After the last steer had been set out to pasture, my uncle had walked up the bleachers to me with a big grin. There had been something about him that drew people to him. Everyone loved him unless they were jealous of him. He was very rarely without that grin.

"Where's your Mom?" He had asked as he sat next to me.

I shrugged and looked out in the parking lot for the old white sedan, "She left a little while ago and told me to stay here."

"Well, what would you like to do while we wait for her?"

"Can you show me how to do what you were doing?"

"Roping?"

"Yeah, can I throw a rope?" I asked hopefully.

"Sure," He grinned and we made our way down the bleachers.

I was nearly dancing down them.

"First thing," He said as he opened the gate. "We were team roping. That's where two of us rope the steer."

"It's a steer, not a cow?"

"Technically a cow," He chuckled. "We use steer, with horns, for team roping and calves, without horns, for calf roping."

"What's the difference?"

"Calf roping is one person roping the calf then stepping down from the saddle and running out to flip the calf onto its side and tie its legs together. Team roping involves two ropers. Let's start with the basics."

We walked up to the metal fencing where the steer had run out. My heart raced in excitement.

"The steer comes through the ally and is loaded into the chute…this is the chute," His hand rest on the metal rails.

"OK, so it's a chute and not a cage. I saw that while you guys were roping."

"You were watching pretty closely."

"It looks so fast and exciting."

"It is…very…gets my heart pumping." He laughed. "It's a bit addicting…gets in your blood."

I stopped and looked up at him with wide eyes, "But a good addiction? Not like what…?" My words fell away.

He stared at me a moment, his eyes locked onto mine as if searching for answers but I gave none. He turned away and nodded, "Yes, it's good and healthy for you. It keeps you outside with animals and friends."

"OK," I nodded. "So how come you were always riding your horse on this side and the other guy was over there?"

"Excellent question, Lauren," He beamed proudly and my heart had swelled. "I'll teach you the basics…real basic so you have a general understanding then we'll build from there."

"Ok!" The dirt was seeping in through the holes in the sides of my tennis shoes but I wasn't complaining or telling him because I didn't want him to stop.

"This is called the box," He said and walked into the area next to the chute. "The header is always in the box to the steer's left side, the heeler is on the right side. You know why they are called headers and heelers?"

"Because you roped the horns at the head and he roped the cow…steer's back feet…his heels."

"Very good," He grinned again. "Now the header watches the steer to make sure it's looking straight ahead so it will come right out and hopefully make a straight run for the end. When the header is ready, he nods to the guy that is opening the chute."

"Aren't horses faster than the steer?"

"Damn, you are a thinker aren't you?" He chuckled.

I grinned proudly because no one had ever called me that before.

"There is a rope tied to the chute and around the steer's neck. The steer gets the length of that rope as a head start. It has to break off the steer before the roper can break their barrier which is stretched out in front of the header's box."

"What happens if they do?"

"If you break the barrier it's a ten-second penalty."

"Wow…that's seems long since it doesn't take you ten seconds to rope the steer."

He nodded, "On good days."

"So then you rope the steer's horns."

"Yep, follow me."

He walked out of the box with his hand swinging in the air as if he had a rope, "I'm going to come out and as soon as I have a good angle, I'm going to throw to the horns." His arm flew forward. "Once it's around the horns I'm going to pull back the slack so the rope tightens around them and I will then wrap the rope around the saddle horn to hold him."

"Slack?"

"It's all the extra rope that is loose between the steer and my horse. A tighter rope means I have better control over where the steer is going."

"OK, then what?"

"Then I have to make the steer turn to the left so it presents the back legs to the heeler." He jogged to the left but at an angle looking over his shoulder. "I have to watch my heeler so when he throws and traps the heels then I have to turn around real fast..." He spun around and trotted backward. "My heeler has stopped, pulled back his slack, dallied, then backs up if he needs to so the rope around the steer's back legs is tight. As the header, I'm backing up and our horse's heads have to be facing each other to stop the clock."

"Ok...," I frowned. "But what is dallied?"

"Another good question," He smiled. "Dally means taking the rope and wrapping it around the saddle horn as fast as you can to hold the steer so he can't run away."

"Oh...OK,"

"You get in the heeler box and I'll get in the header box and we'll run one out."

Without hesitation and with more dirt filling my shoes I ran to the right box and leaned against the fence in the back...because that's what the ropers did earlier.

Uncle Austin looked at me proudly then turned in the box with his arm held high as if he was holding a rope. I matched his position and concentrated on his every move.

"I'll nod, the chute is opened then steer runs. You run out and as soon as I throw and turn then you throw. Ready?"

"Ready!" My heart was racing in excitement and all we were doing was riding pretend horses as we pretended to catch a pretend steer with pretend ropes.

He nodded then ran and I followed. His arm twirled then threw the imaginary rope and he turned sideways as he pretended to wrap the rope around the saddle horn.   I twirled my pretend rope and threw just like him. I stopped and dallied then took a couple steps back as he turned and stepped back too.

"We got him!" Uncle Austin cried out. "A 3.3 world record run!"

I laughed as we ran to each other and we high-fived in the air.

"Can we do it with real ropes now?" I asked excitedly. "Can you show me how to rope?"

"Can't see a reason why not," He said and started walking back across the arena to his trailer. "It'll give us something to do until your mother gets back."

He retrieved two ropes and a plastic roping steer then we walked back into the arena.

"First things first," he said. "…how to coil the rope to build your loop."

My fingers wrapped around the rope he gave me and my stomach fluttered. It was harder and rougher than I thought it would be. I gripped it so hard my knuckles were white.

For an hour he taught me about the rope and throwing: the tail, honda, spoke, tip of the rope, swinging the rope, and rolling the rope. Then, using the ropes in his trailer tack room, he showed me all the different ropes; from super soft, extra soft and soft for headers and medium soft, medium, and medium hard for heelers.

When I didn't think there could be anything more, he started on the horses. Head horses were usually a little bigger, powerful and they had to be fast. A heel horse was usually a little smaller but had a great stop.

There was so much more than just throwing a rope at a steer!

My head was spinning with all the information but I had hung on every word and asked questions and imagined the answers if he didn't have an example. Not one day in school had I ever absorbed so much, paid attention so much, or asked so many questions.

I was extremely disappointed when we had to stop because the sun was setting and there were no lights at the arena.

"Well, we can't stay here all night." He had said. "I'll call your mom and see what time she's coming back."

I very happily followed him to his truck and while he walked the lariats and calf dummy back to the tack room of the trailer, I sat on its wheel well and removed my shoes. I didn't think it was right to take that much dirt into his truck.

I dumped out each shoe then shook them free of any remaining dirt. I wasn't wearing socks so I wiped my feet off the best I could with my hand then slid the shoes back on. As I wiped my hands on my shorts I looked up to see him watching me with a frown as he slid his phone back into his pocket. I just smiled.

"Your mom didn't answer," He said then looked at me thoughtfully. "Who cut your hair?"

I laughed, "That was Mom. She did it with a knife."

"A knife?"

"Yeah, she had me lay down on the floor and she stretched it way out the top of my head then cut it where she thought it would come to my shoulders." I laughed again. "Well, the top part doesn't go all the way down to my shoulders but the bottom part does."

I grinned because it really had been funny at the time but he just frowned back. Not knowing what to do I looked up at the horse that was standing quietly in the trailer.

I stepped up on the trailer, just in front of the wheel well and looked at the horse.

Round brown eyes looked back at me. They were warm and curious as they watched me. His body was a dark red and his mane and tail were black.

My hand slowly rose as the urge to touch the horse became overwhelming but my fingers hesitated just outside the opening.

"You can touch him," My uncle had whispered. "His name is Mitchum."

I watched the horse's eyes as the tip of my finger touched the fine hairs of his round jaw. There was something about the touch that filled something deep within me. That empty space…that lost space…the horse filled it as my hand flattened against his cheek. He was warm and felt like silk. I inhaled his sweet scent and for a moment there was no one else in the world but just me and the horse. I closed my eyes and inhaled deeply trying to capture the moment.

"Do you think…?" My eyes slowly opened. "Maybe…someday…I could sit on him like you do?" In a haze, I turned to my uncle. "Maybe…someday? Or maybe I can just…give him a hug?"

My uncle stared again…looking for those answers in my eyes. I wasn't sure…but I thought I had seen a bit of a glisten on his.

"We can do that now," He said softly.

"Now?" I gasped.

"Sure…"

Without another word he opened the back of the trailer and led the horse out. I stood with my body trembling, heart racing, and eyes filled with tears of joy.

He stopped the horse right in front of me and the Mitchum's long nose reached out to touch my stomach…then my hand. A tear slid down my cheek as my hand slid across his jaw, then just under his soft brown eye, then down his nose to that soft spot right on the end. I stepped around his head, tucked myself under his neck, and wrapped my arms around his chest the best I could. His warmth filled my soul…I didn't feel lost anymore.

I don't know how long we stood there but when I finally stepped back I took a deep breath and wiped my face with my dirty hands. I slowly looked up at my uncle but he was looking away.

"Thank you," I said softly.

He turned back with a nod, "Let's get you on top."

My heart nearly exploded.

"Put your left foot in my hands and I'll hoist you up."

He cupped his hands together then lowered so I could reach them…within seconds I was flying onto the horse and my heart was flying with me. I gasped as I landed with a leg over each side of the horse and my hands grasped at the only thing to hold onto…the horse's mane. I was leaned forward on my belly; scared to move.

Uncle Austin chuckled as he looked up at me, "Just lean back as if sitting in a chair."

I did as he said and once up, my whole body relaxed. I wasn't even scared when he started to walk.

When he helped me slide down off the horse I couldn't stop my arms from going around his waist and hugging him tightly.

"Thank you so much," I whispered. "I will remember this forever."

His hand came to rest on my shoulder and he patted it gently.

"Well, like I said, we can't stay here all night. I'll take you home and call your mom to let her know. Go get in."

I walked around the corner of the trailer and at the last second, I looked back at him. He was pulling his phone out of his pocket again as he took a deep breath and slowly let it out.

I opened the passenger side door and crawled onto the seat but he didn't appear so I just relaxed and thought of the roping and horses. It was literally the best day I had ever had.

When he appeared, his arm was reaching for an envelope that was tucked under the windshield wiper of his truck.

CHAPTER SIX

I silently watched him read the letter until his hand gripped it tightly then slowly lowered to his side, his eyes went to the horizon, and his shoulders slumped.

When he finally turned to me, his expression was thoughtful and he stared for the longest time.

He would later tell me he was trying to figure out how he was going to keep me from going to a foster home and being taken from him. He knew immediately that he would take care of me forever.

I never saw the letter again and he never told me what it said.

The metal clanging of the cattle chute jolted me out of my past.

I looked out to the arena to see Pete pushing a steer into the chute then pulling the lever so the two younger men could chase it. The other older man and Pete's grandson were on their horses and backing into the box to take their turns. They took turns for the next couple hours as I sat on the bleachers and silently reminisced about the first months living with my uncle.

The first thing he did was buy me my own lariat, cowboy hat and boots then he took me to get my hair cut in a big pretty hair salon. He had an older mare that he had grown up with and she became my horse. It was the beginning of summer when my mother left, so I spent the next couple months traveling with him to rodeos and jackpots until school started.

It wasn't until October that the school realized that my mother was no longer around. The year before, with the help of Andrea, I had been a bit of a hell-raiser in school but I was an angel in school that year. The teachers and principal had seen how much difference my uncle had made in my life. They helped Uncle Austin become my legal guardian.

"Rover, shut the fuck up."

My mind came out of the past and looked down at the voice. The one that had called me Ma'am was talking to a black and white border collie that was standing in the back of his white truck. The dog's tongue was hanging out and he was looking at the approaching man with eyes that beamed adoration.

All the men were walking their horses to the trailers.

I stood and slowly made my way down the wooden steps and toward my truck. Figuring it would be extremely too rude to just drive away, I walked to Pete. He was tying his horse to the trailer that was attached to the newer four-door Ford.

He turned to me as I approached.

"Thank you," I said quickly before he spoke. "I appreciate the invite."

"We're here tomorrow at 10:00 if you'd like to join us." He said with a welcoming smile.

"I have some free time," I said. "So, I might."

"You're welcome to bring a horse or ride one of mine." He said. "This is Berry."

I looked at the red roan horse he had just tied to the trailer. "Again…thanks for the invite."

I shook his hand then drove away.

It was 4:27 when I drove into the driveway. I walked to the barn but the horses were at the far end of the pasture and ignored me. Two of the five barn cats made an appearance but they ignored me too. The chicks all huddled under the heat lamp as I changed the water and added more feed to the feeder. They basically ignored me too.

Walking into the house, I dipped another spoon into the peanut butter then sat on the couch and turned on the television.

My mind went back to the letter my mother had left my uncle.

I called Charlene, his widow.

"Lauren! Nice to hear from you."

"It's really good to hear your voice." I sighed. She always made me feel better.

"Is something the matter?"

"I've been reminiscing a bit, and I was wondering if you could tell me…" I hesitated. Why bring up the past?

"What?"

"Did Uncle Austin ever tell you about my mother leaving?"

"Well…yes." She said hesitantly.

"Did he tell you about the letter?"

"He just said that she left a letter."

"He never told you what was in it? What it said?"

"Lauren? Are you alright?"

"Yes, I've just been thinking about that day and how he didn't get angry or try to find her. He just took care of me." I said. "Did he tell you if he looked for her?"

"No, Hon…he said he never wanted to see her again. He didn't think she deserved you and since you were a minor he didn't want any chance of her taking you back."

"Oh…yeah, he told me that's why he didn't look for my father." I sighed. My father was his brother and they hadn't talked since my father had abandoned me and my mother.   "Did he ever tell you what the letter said?"

"No, but he did say that he destroyed it on your 18th birthday…when you weren't a minor anymore."

"Oh…"

"Lauren, what's this about? What would make you reminisce about that day?"

I fell back against the cushions and stared out the window, "I watched some ropers today that made me think of him…that first day."

"You're alright then?"

I didn't feel alright but I also didn't want her to worry about me, "Just one of those days."

"So, Jamie hasn't come home yet?"

"No…still wants nothing to do with me." And neither does my best friend, I wanted to add but didn't.

"She'll come around," Charlene said decisively. I could almost see her nodding as she said it.

"How are all the boys doing?" I asked. She had two with my uncle and two with her new husband.

"Taylor and Ace are tearing up the rodeos this year," She said proudly. "They definitely take after their father. Monte and Liam take after their father too…as in only wanting to ride dirt bikes. I don't know how I ended up with a guy that was into motorcycles instead of horses."

"Both horsepower," We said again…just as we had dozens of times before. We both chuckled.

She talked about her sons for another hour before we finally ended the call.

I spent the rest of the evening staring blankly at the television and thinking of the months leading to my mother driving away without me. She was seventeen when I was born and twenty-nine when she left me. I had been a terror in school, one of the biggest bullies…with Andrea, of course. It couldn't have been easy on my mother since she was pulled away from work once or twice a week to come to the school.

The summer I was eleven, I stayed home in a small apartment by myself while she went to work at a convenience store. There were times I wouldn't see her for a couple of days but she always made sure I had plenty of food and the cable TV paid before she would leave for a long period of time.

The first time she left was scary because I didn't know if she was ever going to come back and I wasn't sure what to do if she didn't. It got easier each time.

The first night with my uncle was awkward. He lived in a small one bedroom apartment at a stable where he took care of horses and cows. He only had chairs in his living room and just the one bed, but he did have an older living quarters horse trailer that had two beds. Not wanting either of us to sleep in a chair we had slept in his horse trailer instead. It was a bit scary listening to him snore through the night but after our first full day together, I was more comfortable. Although we were still getting to know each other, we had fun all day with him teaching me how to ride. I practiced roping everything while he rode with his friends.

The trailer would become our home until school started then he found a small two bedroom apartment that we moved into. That would be our home for three years as we traveled the rodeo circuit and he became more successful. Then he bought a house. We were there until he qualified for his first of seven trips to the National Finals Rodeo. Then we moved to a ranch where we raised and trained horses together. When I became pregnant, he began building his dream ranch so I could raise my daughter there.

Although I was married, Blake had not complained at all and had worked with my uncle during the construction.

Blake…my husband or ex-husband now. I closed my eyes at the memories and drifted off into a restless night of sleep.

When I woke, I felt like I hadn't slept. I rose from the couch and automatically walked out the door to check on the animals.

When I arrived at the arena, all the riders were circling the horses to warm up. I silently made my way halfway up the bleachers and sat with feet on the one in front of me and elbows on knees.

I looked at the different horses they were riding then looked out to the ones I could see tied to the trailers or hitching post. You can tell the quality of a rider by the quality of their horses; and these were quality, well legged up horses. Even just standing, the conformation in their bodies were well defined.

But one horse stood out above the others. It might have been because of his golden hide and white flowing mane and tail that were well groomed and swung around in dramatic fashion. I was surprised they weren't in protective braids.

The "pup" as Pete had called him was riding him. My uncle would have approved.

"If you're a roper or a racer, you'll get nowhere unless you have a horse that matches your dreams. Doesn't mean how much the horse cost you, because a horse doesn't know how much you spent. It's the heart, willingness, and athletic ability the horse has for what you're doing." He had said that more than once throughout the years. His horses were top breeding, treated like royalty, and very well acknowledged as teammates. Five of his and his partner's horses were with him when the accident happened. Four of the five perished with him. The fifth, now twenty-two years old, is retired in my pasture. The mare was scarred down her legs and neck but she wasn't in pain. There is no physical reason she hadn't been ridden in the sixteen years since, but there was a very deep emotional one.

I thought of Andrea who had been one of the few people to actually ride the horse. She had begged me and Charlene to sell the mare to her but we both said no. The horse would be retired. I didn't understand at the time why Andrea had been so upset. Now I knew she was trying to hold onto something of my uncles.

My mind went back to all the memories I could find of her and Uncle Austin together. She had a schoolgirl crush but I never saw the woman in love with the man...or vice versa. It was truly a case of being blindsided.

Somewhat like Dave being blindsided by the barbeque fork being angrily shoved into his chest...into his heart...by his still missing wife. In a not so literal way, Andrea had done the same thing to my heart and I had nearly died from it.

My uncle, best friend, dead boss and his wife disappearing ran through my head. The pressure behind my eyes increased and I swore the memories and dreams were rushing through my blood as my ears began to ring.

I lowered my head into my hands and tried to rub them all away. Over and over I rubbed my forehead, temples, then finally the whole dirt gritty face.

The clanging of the chute brought my head up and out of the haze.

The youngest of the ropers was chasing a steer on the stunning palomino horse. It took him half of the arena before he finally got around to throwing.

I tried to remember what his name was. The rope twirled around the steer's horns then popped off when he yanked his arm back to tighten the slack.

He trotted back down and all four of the other men gave him advice on coming out of the box at a different angle, flattening out his hand more, when to throw, and even moving the horse differently.

After the fourth miss in a row, he was shaking his head in frustration and began coiling his rope as he trotted the horse back across the arena in front of me.

"Hey!" I called out to him.

His head jerked around in surprise. No doubt he had forgotten I was there.

"Ma'am?" He asked.

That made me feel ancient.

"I appreciate the manners but if you call me that again I'll come down and knock your ass off that horse." I stared hard but lifted my lip in a smirk. "My name is Lauren."

He smiled with a nod, "Lauren…"

"You Kyle or Josh?"

His smile widened, "I'm Ryle and his name is Jess."

"How long have you been roping?"

"Since I was eight," He answered.

"So, what the hell is the matter with you?"

"What?" He gasped with wide eyes.

"You're sitting on one of the nicest roping horses I've ever seen." I nodded to the horse. "And I've seen a few."

"Thanks, ma'…Lauren," He quickly corrected himself with a smile.

"Between the horse and your years of roping…what the hell is the matter?"

"What do you mean?"

"You're roping like hell," I stated bluntly. "With that horse, it means you're taking this seriously."

"I am," He sat straighter in the saddle. "I turned 21 this year so we're working toward the World Series Roping in Vegas this December."

"Then stop letting those four fill your head with so much crap and just go out there and throw the damn rope. You know what you're doing…you're just trying too damn hard to do everything they tell you that you're forgetting just to throw."

He stared at me with his brows drawn together as if thinking about what I said.

"Don't think so damn hard," I said. "Go throw the rope like you're ten years old again."

"Alright," He nodded then pushed the horse into a trot toward the chute.

He didn't say anything to any of the men. He just backed up into the box, rolled his shoulders, took a deep breath…and a grin spread across his face.

A nod and the palomino burst out of the box with Ryle already swinging the rope. Barely four strides and the rope was flying through the air and wrapping the horns of the steer. Ryle yanked his arm back to pull up the slack then dallied the rope. The horse seemed to be watching the steer and turned just as the rope tightened. Jess was throwing and the rope trapped the steer's hind legs and Pete called the catch.

They all five hollered as I just smiled. Sometimes…you just think too hard.

Maybe…just maybe that was becoming my problem.

Ryle turned with a grin and nodded to me.

He roped three more in a row. He had stopped thinking so hard…maybe it was time for me to do the same thing.

When I stood, all five men turned and looked at me. They watched as I walked down the wooden steps of the bleachers, down the fence line, and through the gate. I didn't say anything nor even look at them as I walked by the horses giving a pat on the palomino's neck. I stepped up to the chute and threw the lever so the next steer could advance out of the ally and into the chute. I gripped the lever tightly and looked up at Ryle as he backed into the box.

"His name is Silas," Ryle said of the palomino then nodded his head.

I threw the lever and Silas carried Ryle out of the box for another successful throw…Jess missed this time.

I spent the next two hours moving steers and throwing levers. By the time I was sliding onto the seat of my truck, I had energy pumping through me again. I was even a bit muscle tired.

"So, what the hell did you say to him?"

I turned and looked at the older man that wasn't Pete. I couldn't remember his name.

"I'm Marty." He nodded in understanding.

The other four men were standing with their horses behind him and looking at me. I looked at Ryle to see if he was going to answer…he didn't. He just smiled with a bit of an embarrassed blush.

I started the engine of my truck and looked at Marty.

"I told him to quit listening to all the crap you four were filling his head with and rope like he was ten years old again."

I put the truck in gear as their laughter erupted. I drove away with a smile on my face.

The next day, I arrived at the arena at 10:00 like I had before but now there were trucks and horse trailers covering the parking lot. I sighed with a true sense of remorse that they wouldn't be practicing there. I pulled into the arena grounds and turned the truck around. Now what was I supposed to do for the day?

A familiar old orange Ford pulled in front of me to block my path out of the parking lot. I felt a spark of hope in my gut.

Pete waved and slowly stepped out of his truck and walked up to my truck window.

"Mornin'," I nodded.

"Barrel race today," He said and looked out at the arena full of riders then back to me. "I realized after you left last night that we didn't tell you we wouldn't be riding today. Kade is driving Jess and Ryle to Elgin for the rodeo tonight, then off to the next."

"Well, that makes sense," I sighed.

"Can I take you to breakfast?" Pete smiled.

I just stared at him.

"You have anything better to do?" He chuckled at the familiar question.

I smiled and shook my head, "I'll follow you this time."

He slapped the fender on my truck as he made it back to his truck. I hadn't noticed before that he had a slight limp. I guess you couldn't get to his age riding horses and not expect a limp or an ache. I did, however, notice that his old blue shirt looked like it had been washed at least a thousand times.

Considering I was in jeans I had worn for three days, an old grey t-shirt, no makeup and a well-worn straw cowboy hat covering my finger-combed hair; I didn't really have much room to make a fuss over wardrobe.

I followed him to a small diner on the edge of town. It was one of those Mom and Pop places that served breakfast all day.

He was out of his truck and next to my door before I had a chance to grab for the handle.

"Thank you," I smiled as he shut my door.

"Used to bring the wife here on our 'dates' before she passed away," Pete said as he opened the door to the café for me.

"I'm sorry to hear about her passing," I said and looked around at the dozen tables that were only half occupied.

"Back in the corner," He pointed. "…out of the sunlight and it's quiet."

The waitress was right behind us as we slid onto the chairs.

"Late morning, Pete," The older woman with dark brown hair pulled back in a bun smiled at him. She wore blue jeans with a white shirt which was covered by an old-fashioned apron down the front of her. It was bright blue with tiny flowers embroidered around the bodice. She pulled a pen and order pad from the apron's pocket.

"Had to wait for my date," Pete nodded to me. "Cathy this is Lauren."

"Good morning," I smiled politely but suddenly felt like going home and my stomach began to ache. I looked at the door longingly.

"Welcome to the diner," She nodded. "Usual biscuits and gravy for Pete and for you?"

"Just toast and coffee," I answered.

She nodded with a concerned frown but walked away.

I turned to Pete and spoke before he had a chance. "How long have you been roping?"

He looked at me thoughtfully then sighed. It was clear he wanted to talk about me and not him.

"Since I was little," He answered, obviously not wanting to give the number. "Pops always told me I was born with one in hand." He chuckled. "Can't really remember a day without horses and roping."

For a solid two hours, he told me stories of growing up on a ranch in Texas. I escaped my own world and lived in his childhood. I even found myself laughing and not once did I look at the door as an escape.

"And when did you start roping?" Pete asked.

Mood plummeted and my eyes went to the door.

"When I was twelve," I said and pulled my phone out of my pocket to check the time.

"My son bought a ranch in Texas just before Kade was born," Pete said quickly.

I glanced up at him. "That explains his southern drawl but how did you end up in Idaho?"

"Met my wife when she came down to Lubbock to visit family," His grin was full of memories. "She was there for a week and I was hooked. I followed her back here and never looked back."

"What about your family ranch?"

"My brother and his family took it over and bought me out so I could pick up a little place for me and the missus after we got married."

"How did Kade end up here?"

"He came to visit, fell for a girl and got married here."

"Sounds kind of appropriate…following his grandfather's example." I smiled.

Pete shrugged, "It lasted about ten years and two kids. Don't think he ever considered moving back to Texas away from his kids even though his son moved back down to work on the family ranch last year."

I didn't really want to talk about Kade…my eyes went to the door.

"So I'm a great grandfather," Pete said loudly to pull my attention back to him.

I just nodded and looked at my phone. No messages, no calls, and it was 1:30. How depressing…

My whole body jumped when my phone rang. It was Detective Malone.

"I'm sorry," I said to Pete and he nodded thoughtfully.

"Hello?" I answered with my eyes going to the door.

"Lauren Conners?" He asked.

"Yes."

"This is Detective Malone…we spoke last Sunday after the incident at your party."

The incident…the image of Sheila turning and jamming the long fork into Dave's chest played in my mind…the silence then shattering scream as he fell to his knees. That was an incident?

"Yes?" I leaned back against the chair and sighed.

"I was updating the paperwork for the investigation this week and realized no one has called to update you."

"What is it?"

"Well…basically nothing," He admitted. "We still have no leads on Sheila Armstrong's location. We've contacted her entire family but Tuesday she was officially indicted on second-degree murder."

"OK," What was I supposed to say?

"The funeral is Monday morning and we'll have people there looking for her."

"OK," I glanced at Pete; he was watching people walk into the diner.

"Well…that's it really," he said. "I just thought you should be updated. Let us know if Mrs. Armstrong contacts you."

"I will," I ended the call and stared at the phone.

Why in the hell would she contact me? I had only met her a couple of times before the party and there would be nothing she would need from me…or vice versa.

It seemed like a total waste of a call…it just brought reality back with a jolt.

I looked up at Pete and smiled with a sigh, "I hate it when people answer the phone while we're talking. I truly am sorry."

He just nodded and watched me closely.

"Anything you need to talk about?" He said softly.

"No," I stood from the chair and looked at the door. My hand went in my pocket.

"You're my date. I'll be paying for this one."

He stepped between me and the table and tossed cash next to the plate holding the untouched toast I had ordered.

We walked out of the diner and to my truck in silence.

"Jess, Kade, and Ryle are headed up to the Cheney rodeo in the morning. They won't be back until late tomorrow night." Pete said as he opened my door. "The barrel race is still at the arena tomorrow."

"So, no roping," I was so disappointed.

"No…but I'd enjoy your company tomorrow for breakfast again." he said. "It's pretty quiet without Kade around."

"You live together?" I asked in surprise.

"No, he has his place for him and the kids. I have a place not too far away."

"Oh…he has custody?"

"He and the ex get along pretty good," Pete nodded. "But no custody anymore, they are nineteen and twenty-one but his daughter stays with him every once in a while…son is in Texas."

I nodded.

"Oh…we'll just be roping on Monday and Tuesday this week," Pete added.

My heart sunk. "Why?"

"Arena is in use from Wednesday through the weekend."

"Oh…OK…" I stared out the front window.

"So…I'll see you here tomorrow at 9:00?"

I slowly turned to him. "Why not? I don't have anything better to do."

He chuckled and my mood lifted until he nodded, waved, and walked away.

I drove under the speed limit all the way home then walked to the barn instead of the house. The horses were laying in the sunshine in the middle of their pasture again. I could see four of the five barn cats so I walked to the chicken coop. All chicks alive and accounted for so I slowly walked to the quiet house…giving a wide birth around the stained bricks.

Three more weeks without work then I go back to where my boss won't be. My mind went to a haunted house Andrea, Jamie and I had once visited. It was eerie and left my stomach hollow…that was how I felt just thinking about going back to that office.

As I neared the porch, I heard a very distinctive sound. I stopped and took a few steps back and listened. There was another and another little mew, mew, mew. I followed the sound to the edge of the porch and looked underneath. Barn cat #5, a dark grey with green eyes, looked out at me.

"Mew, mew, mew," She said and looked at me expectantly.

"Well, little one, what do you have here?" I knelt on the ground and wiggled under the porch next to her.

Curled into her side were five little kittens that were only a few hours old. There were two white and grey babies and three dark grey.

"Mew, mew, mew," Momma cat looked up at me.

It was hot and dusty under the porch and my already dirty jeans would now be considered filthy. I had never appreciated a cowboy hat more than now as it was blocking any spiders or bugs from crawling into my hair from the bottom of the porch floor.

"I'm glad you had your babies here," I said to the momma and slowly reached out to touch a kitten. She had never had a litter before and wasn't overly friendly to start with so I wasn't sure how she would react. Of course, I'm sure she was just as confused. "We need to get you to a better home." I told her and picked up one of the tiny babies that barely filled half my palm.

I checked on each baby as the momma cat fussed over each one as I tucked them back into her.

"They all look healthy but you need some water and food," I told her and slowly reached out to her.

As my hand neared, she rubbed her head up and down my wrist. I sat quietly enjoying the moment until she stopped and went back to the babies.

"Alright, I'll be right back."

I wiggled out from underneath the porch to her constant mewing.

"I'll be right back," I promised as I brushed imaginary spiders from my shoulders and back then flipped my hat in the air to make sure nothing was on it.

For an hour I worked on moving the empty dog house next to the porch, filling it with bedding, then adding a dish of food and water.

When I lowered the food dish into the dog house the momma kitty appeared with a mew and started eating. I carefully moved the five little kittens into the dog house. I just hoped she accepted the new home and didn't move her kittens back under the porch. I was relieved when she finished eating and curled into the back of the dog house and began nursing the babies.

She purred softly as I ran a hand over her head and down her back. She was healthy, barely a bone to be felt.

I sat with her until the sun lowered and the sky began to darken.

After dipping a spoon into the peanut butter and shoving it into my mouth I walked upstairs to take a much-needed shower.

Sunday morning, still lying in bed and using my phone, I searched for the results of the Elgin rodeo. Jess and Ryle were second in the team roping by three-tenths of a second. I had a flicker of happiness for them.

I barely knew the two men yet they had brought me more happiness in the last week than anyone else in my life…except for Pete…who I barely knew.

I stood and walked to the window that overlooked the back porch, patio, chicken coop, bunkhouse, barn, arena, corrals, and pastures. The horses were standing next to the barn and staring at the house. I had no doubt they had seen me in the window as their heads had raised.

I dressed in clean well-worn jeans, a "Go Rope" t-shirt and slid my feet into tennis shoes for the day since there was no roping. Still no makeup and I touched up the braid down my back without actually undoing it. I just hid it under a baseball cap this time then stepped out the door.

Mew, mew, mew greeted me. Peeps from the chicks could be heard and a few whinnies from the barn called out.

That was better than the dead silence. I glanced out to the bricks of the patio that were still stained from Dave's blood. The bottle of cleaner set on the grill waiting to be used.

Mew, mew, mew kept me from that job as I looked in at the momma. She had stayed in the dog house.

"Good momma," I whispered. "I guess we can call it a cat house now."

I took a picture of momma cat and babies and sent it to Jamie. I didn't expect a reply back so I wasn't completely disappointed when I didn't receive one. I would keep trying so she would know the door was always open for her.

I took care of the animals and headed in for another breakfast with Pete. Marty and an older woman were in the parking lot with him when I arrived.

My stomach ached and I nearly turned around but they had seen me and waved. I would give it 30 minutes then go back home.

I was there for three hours as Marty and his wife, Sarah, joined Pete in entertaining me with stories of roping jackpots, rodeos, horses, and parties.

Sarah gave me a strong embrace in the parking lot before Marty assisted her into their truck. Both he and Pete nodded their goodbyes and I stepped up into my truck.

The beep from my phone alerted me to a message and I silently prayed it was a good and positive message from Jamie but it wasn't from her.

It was from Greg. I fell back against the truck seat as the energy from the morning melted away. I pushed play for the voice message.

CHAPTER SEVEN

"Lauren, I was calling to see how you were doing. I'm not sure what's going on between you and Andrea but she says she hasn't talked to you since the party. Anyway, I know Dave's funeral is tomorrow and you'll probably be going so I was wondering if we could meet Tuesday morning. Text me if you can meet at Hyde Perk Coffee House at 7:30 before you go to work."

My head fell back against the seat and I stared out the window to the passing traffic.

Dave's funeral…I'd worked for him for two years so it was logical to think I would be going to his funeral but I just couldn't. I closed my eyes and heard the panting from the bathroom, the "there we go" from Dave and the "oohs" from Jodi. Why in the hell did I record it? Why in the hell didn't I put out enough paper towels so I wouldn't have needed more? How different would our worlds be now? I'd still be working…Dave would still be alive and Sheila wouldn't have disappeared and be on the run from a murder charge. Her swinging around and shoving the fork into his chest replayed in my mind over and over and slower each time until it was in slow motion as the fork penetrated his chest.

His eyes widened as he stared at his wife then his eyes lowered to the fork as his hands grasped at it.

Jodi screamed…he fell to his knees then slowly to the ground.

Why?

I have no idea how long I sat in the truck staring out to the street but I finally realized there was no answer. I started the truck and slowly drove home again.

After checking on the new kittens I stood on the back porch and looked at the bloodstained bricks.

Andrea told Greg we hadn't talked since the party. Why did she lie to him? Maybe she hadn't told him she was in love with my uncle. She and Greg were pretty close, always had been. Closer than most brother and sisters so I was sure she had told him.

I walked over to the swing and sat down as the whole party played out in my head. It was almost as if I could see each person standing on the patio and porch as Jodi walked out the back door of the house and Dave walked from the side door to his wife. He looked out to Jodi whose back was to him when he slid an arm around his wife's waist. He said something to Sheila that made her smile then he turned to Stan at the grill.

The scene skipped ahead to the voices over the karaoke machine and Jodi's 'oh' from the patio. My eyes went back to the visions at the grill…Sheila's face turning white then she took a few steps, grabbed the fork and twirled.

I saw blood…blood pouring onto the bricks.

I shook my head to rid my mind of the vision…but the blood stains were still there.

I stood and walked into the house and fell onto the couch and turned on the TV. I couldn't get my body to move all day.

Monday morning started with a counseling session. I walked into the earthy comfortable office and sat on the couch. I stared at the landscape pictures again for the first ten minutes.

"Tell me something that you've been doing this last week." The counselor finally said.

I turned to her as if in slow motion, "I bought a bunch of chicks and my cat had kittens." I turned back to the landscape pictures.

Another five minutes of silence.

"I read your boss's funeral is today," she said.

"Yes…it is," I said.

"Since you're in jeans and a t-shirt, I would guess you're not going."

I looked down at my clothes that I had put on the morning before. "No…this wouldn't be appropriate," I said and looked out the window. I was so damn tired I just wanted to close my eyes and disappear.

Minutes ticked away in silence as I thought of Pete and his childhood ranch stories. My body began to relax.

When she stood, I stood.

"You need to talk, Lauren." She said with a concerned frown.

I just nodded and walked away.

When my mind came out of the haze, I was sitting in the bleachers of the arena waiting for the five ropers to show up.

Ryle and Jess were the first to pull into the parking lot. Jess was on the phone and remained in the cab as Ryle waved when he stepped out of the truck. I nodded to him and watched as he first walked Silas, his palomino, out of the trailer then a sorrel. The last out was a black horse that Jess rode and a grey gelding.

Ryle saddled the sorrel and trotted into the arena where he stopped right in front of me.

"How did you do over the weekend?" I asked before he could speak.

His eyes and grin beamed with pride, "Second in Elgin then third in Cheney."

"Good job," I said as Marty's stock trailer appeared.

"I'm gonna help him unload," Ryle said and trotted back across the arena.

Jess joined him as the steers were unloaded. Pete and Kade arrived, saddled their horses and made their way into the arena and they all rode in circles to warm up the horses.

I sat and watched as the first steer was loaded into the chute and was ready to go.

All five riders sat on their horses in front of the chute and looked up at me.

I hesitated…wasn't this why I came here? To move forward, to busy myself so I didn't think so hard?

I slowly rose and made my way to the chute. Kade gave me a curt nod while the other four smiled happily with a warm greeting. I responded with a nod to all of them then turned to Ryle who was the first in the box.

He stared at me a moment with furrowed brows but I just stared back; patiently waiting. His shoulders lowered then his body rose in anticipation of the ride, he nodded and I pushed the lever.

After an hour of working the chutes for the five of them and avoiding all conversations my body began to come out of its protective shell and I started to feel alive again. Another hour and Pete cracked a joke that I laughed at and I became human again.

Another hour later the horses were walked to the trailers and I helped Marty load the steers back in the cattle hauler.

"Lauren?" Pete met me as I opened my truck door.

"Yes?" I turned back to him.

"Are you OK?"

I stared at him and tried to decide what to say. I was better at that moment than I had been in the last week…but I didn't think it would be classified as OK.

"You're still in the same clothes you wore to breakfast yesterday," He pointed out. "So…are you OK?"

I had no idea what to say.

"Lauren, if you need someone to talk to…" He said softly.

I just shook my head. There was no reason to add my misery into his happy life.

"I'll see you in the morning," I said and stepped into the truck.

"Lauren…" He placed a hand on the open window of the truck.

I turned and stared into his narrowed concerned eyes. There was true caring there. I felt it and the tears began to rise…I turned away quickly and just nodded as I put the truck in gear.

As I drove away, I wondered how it could be that a man I had known for only a week cared more for me than my daughter and the woman I had called my best friend for over 30 years.

The fuel light blinked on my dash drawing my attention so I pulled into the first gas station I came to. As the fuel pumped, I pulled out my phone and searched for information on Dave's funeral. I wasn't going to go, I just wanted to know.

The graveside service was at 2:00. In fifteen minutes. It would take me twenty minutes to get there if I was going…but I wasn't going.

I replaced the fuel nozzle onto the stand and screwed on the cap. With a quick flip of the hand, the cover snapped shut. I wasn't going to go I told myself again.

When I pulled out of the parking lot, I turned left instead of right…which was the way home. My gut told me I had to go but I would just sit in my truck at a distance and pay my regards my way. Just because I was there, it didn't mean I had to talk to anyone. There were dozens of vehicles parked along the narrow one-lane road that meandered through the cemetery. I would guess at least a hundred people were standing next to the black coffin that was covered in white flowers. I stopped the truck at the end of the first line of cars and turned off the engine.

I scanned the area around me and saw a man standing at a distant headstone but watching the funeral. He would occasionally look around him as if looking for someone. No doubt, he was watching for Sheila. I couldn't imagine she would show up at the funeral after being in hiding for the last week. Why would she?

Maybe she wasn't even in the area anymore or even alive. Would she have committed suicide after realizing what she had done? Or had she escaped the country somehow? There were endless possibilities so I just turned back to the funeral. A man in a black suit was talking to the crowd. His right hand held a book and his left hand occasionally swung out to the people to put an emphasis a statement.

I looked at the people. Everyone that worked at the mortgage company was there, even the seven that had witnessed the…murder? …incident? …act of rage?

My window was rolled down but I was parked too far away to hear anyone. The minister's voice was just a low hum as he spoke. I sat there, unnoticed, for a half hour watching people stand and the minister speak. My body relaxed back in the seat and I thought back to the years, months, weeks, days that I had worked with Dave. Memories of morning hellos, evening goodbyes, arguments over an approval or decline of a loan, personnel discussions…the memories were so vivid. But they didn't include anything personal, never about women or relationships, and not once did I get the feeling he was anything but professional; never an inclination that he was unfaithful to his wife.

Why did he take Sheila to the party knowing that Jodi was going to be there?

The crowd around the casket began to move toward the vehicles. I quickly started the truck as I watched them depart. Just as I put the truck in reverse, my eyes focused on two people still standing with the minister.

Ice flowed in my veins as the tears began to rise. Molly and Ethan Armstrong; Dave and Sheila's teenage children. Not once had I thought of them. Their father was dead and their mother, if found…if alive…was going to prison. The peanut butter I had eaten for breakfast began to rise.

"Lauren?"

My eyes moved from the two teenagers to, Patricia, the owner of the mortgage company that was standing in the middle of the narrow road. Patricia; the woman that forced me away from work for 30 days.

Without even a blink of a response, my foot rose from the brake and I slowly backed away from her. She stood standing and watching until I turned around and drove away.

I drove back to the arena and sat in the parking lot as I thought about the emotional turmoil Molly and Ethan were going through.

Memories of them coming into the office surfaced and I had to admit they weren't the nicest or friendliest of teenagers but they surely didn't deserve this ending. For the rest of their lives, they would have to live with the fact their mother killed their father. Would they wonder too if they could have done something different? Did they know their father was having an affair with Jodi…or anyone else? Was Jodi his first? How did they meet? Why did he invite himself to the party and why in the hell did he bring Sheila?

It was a company get together; more than half the people he worked with were at the party and knew he was married so why invite himself when he knew Jodi was going to be there?

So many questions and not a damned answer…especially for the one I really needed an answer for. How could I turn back time for Molly and Ethan and not need those damned paper towels?

I drove home to the baby chickens and kittens, a spoonful of peanut butter and the couch. I stared at the television until my eyes burned. It was still on when my eyes opened at 5:30 the next morning.

I took a long shower then slid into a simple blue summer dress and sandals. I did my hair as if I was going into the office after meeting with Greg at the coffee house. I couldn't get the energy to apply makeup. Maybe he wouldn't notice.

One spoonful of peanut butter calmed my nervous stomach. I tossed the spoon into the sink next to a dozen other spoons.

I parked a half block away and walked to the front of the building. Greg was already sitting in one of the small tables on the sidewalk in front of the door…and so was Jodi.

CHAPTER EIGHT

Son of a bitch…my stomach ached. I stopped and started to turn when his eyes connected with mine and he nodded a hello. His expression and movements as he stood and pulled a chair out for me were grim.

"Lauren," Jodi looked at me timidly. She is a strong woman to be married to a corporate executive and raise two boys.

I nodded in return as I sat and wrapped my hands around the white coffee cup Greg shoved toward me.

We sat in silence for a good two minutes before Greg spoke. "I'm sorry this happened."

"Me, too," Jodi whispered with a glance to Greg then an unsure look to me.

"Yes…well…we all are." I leaned back in my chair and looked down the road.

"I never…in a million years…would have thought she was going to do that." Greg continued. "I wasn't really thinking of her."

"Lauren?" Jodi whispered.

I turned to see tears glistening in her eyes.

"I'm so sorry I did that in your house. You trusted me for years…I just can't imagine how that made you feel. I was just so…" She quickly wiped a tear away and glanced at Greg then to me.

I had no idea what to say so I just looked between the two of them. They seemed so different than the last twenty years. Even though their marriage had changed, they had remained loving to each other but there was a distinct coolness between them now.

"How did you know him?" I finally asked.

She didn't even look at her husband this time.

"I met him through a friend from the gym. We went out for dinner one night and he was there and she introduced us." Her hand reached out and grabbed my wrist. She squeezed tightly. "I had no idea he was married…no idea…he said he was divorced."

My eyebrows shot up, "But YOU are married." I pointed out with a look to Greg then back to her.

Jodi shook her head and finally looked at him with a question in her eyes.

I looked at Greg with raised brows.

"We got a divorce two months ago," Greg said.

My whole body shivered, "What?" I whispered.

"Andrea wanted to keep it quiet until after your party since you were trying to get your life back to normal…as normal as possible anyway."

I just stared at him in disbelief. "Then playing the video was what?" I asked numbly.

Greg set back in his chair and shook his head, "I was fucking pissed that she would do that at the party…with everyone…including his wife in the backyard."

"I had no idea he was married or that she was there," Jodi added quickly.

I stared at her trying to decide if she was being honest. There was really no reason to lie anymore. I'd known her long enough to know when she was lying but the last couple months they had been divorced and I didn't know that. But, I hadn't seen them for a while; unlike Andrea who I had talked to daily and seen multiple times a week.

"How did he know you knew me and that you were at the party?" I asked.

"He told me where he worked and I said you worked there too." she said. "Everything was so normal…so what I would consider typical dating in the last couple of weeks. We went out for lunch or dinner a couple times a week and talked every day. We spent last weekend together. I told him that we couldn't interact at the party because you thought I was still married to Greg." She sighed and shook her head. "Now I know why he was so obliging to that."

"You didn't see Sheila?" I asked.

"No, I had no idea she was there or even who she was…or that she existed. I wasn't introduced to her when I got there. I walked directly into the house and he came in behind me and pulled me into the laundry room." Her cheeks turned red. "He was going to wait a couple minutes then come up with an excuse to leave." She shrugged slightly and looked at me apologetically. "I was going to leave a few minutes later and we were going to meet at a hotel."

I lay my face in my hands and rubbed away the disbelief. If it wasn't for the damned paper towels.

"I truly am sorry," Jodi whispered.

I looked up into her eyes and saw the remorse; there was no doubt she was.

"I have to go…I have to get to work." She said and looked from Greg to me.

I just nodded and looked back down the street as she stood.

"If you need anything..." Her voice trailed off.

I had no words so I just watched her walk away.

"What's going on with you and Andrea?" Greg asked. "She blaming you for this because of the recording?"

I huffed and rolled my tired eyes, "She's blaming me for everything bad in her life."

"What's that mean?" He leaned forward and placed his elbows on top the table.

I looked at him, "Did you know she had an affair with Uncle Austin?"

He huffed this time and fell back against the chair, "She finally told you about that?"

"Yes," I said softly…waiting for his answer.

"I don't really think you can call it an affair." He chuckled with a bit of a sneer.

I stared with questioning eyes.

"They both got drunk at one of the parties at your place and ended up in bed together." Greg shrugged.

"One night?" I gasped.

He shrugged a shoulder. "He left the next morning and the week he was gone she acted like they had been together forever and were getting married. The next weekend, one of the roping weekends at your place, a little blonde was hitting on him and Andrea nearly took her head off…literally." He sneered. "Austin took her aside and told her that they weren't going to have a relationship because he wouldn't do anything to hurt you."

"Yes…" I whispered. "She did tell me that part."

"He'd also met Charlene a couple weeks before and really liked her. They had spent time together while he was gone that week." He added then looked thoughtfully at me. "But Andrea said an affair?"

I nodded slowly and looked back down the street. "Around the time Jamie was born."

"Yeah…sounds about right."

"You and Uncle Austin were good friends." I looked back at him.

"Yeah…pretty good. All except the fact his world was you and horses and I don't like horses." He smiled.

"Did he ever tell you about my mother?"

His brows rose in surprise, "No…just that he hoped to never see her again…or his piece of shit brother."

"Anything about the letter?"

He shook his head, "No, never mentioned a letter."

"Hmmm," I guess I would never know.

"I saw Andrea yesterday and she didn't seem like anything was wrong. Maybe, after a couple weeks…?"

I shook my head, "No…not after Dave."

"What's he got to do with you two?"

"It was my fault," I felt the tightness in my chest and my hand went to cover it. "She said that it was all my fault because…"

Greg exhaled slowly and leaned against the table again. His eyes connected with mine, "I played the recording because I was pissed at the two of them. The audacity of that jackass…alive or dead…he's a fucking jackass to do that. But who knew his wife would do something like that? It's my fault, Lauren. Not yours."

I brushed away a tear and shook my head. "No, I'm just…I'm trying…to move on with my life."

"Have you heard from Jamie?"

"No," I whispered and stood. My whole body was tired and it was everything I could do to get it to move.

"Yeah, you're going to be late for work." He said and I didn't correct him.

He walked me to my truck in silence. I slid onto the seat then rolled down my window to look at him. I had known him for thirty years. Although we had no romantic feelings for each other, we'd always been good friends. He'd always been a good big brother to me.

"I'm sorry about the divorce."

He shook his head, "That's been coming for a long time. We knew it and so did the kids. They're fine. We WERE all happier for the last couple of months."

"It will get better," I told him and internally told myself the same thing; I wasn't really believing it though.

"Yeah," He nodded and sighed. "Time…it just takes time."

I turned the key and the engine's roar stopped the conversation.

He walked away and I drove to the arena to wait for the ropers to get there. I used the bleachers and my truck to block anyone watching and changed into my jeans, t-shirt, boots, and baseball cap. I twisted my hair into a messy braid then slipped it through the opening in the back of the hat.

I had just parked the truck in the normal spot by the gate when I heard a truck enter. I turned to see Ryle and Jess arriving. Ryle waved with that happy grin.

I walked over to help them unload the horses.

"Mornin' Lauren," They said in unison.

I forced a nod and a smile but remained quiet as we unloaded four horses.

"I'll ride Silas first thing, Dexter is the wide blazed sorrel, then I have Gus back at the stable. The black, Warlock, is Jess' main horse, Zeb is his backup and Casper is his young one. We're working on building solid horses for our run for the NFR next year." Ryle informed me and continued to chatter about the horses and then the upcoming rodeo in Nampa; the Snake River Stampede. It was the largest in the area.

"We roped in the slack there yesterday," Jess added. "We're sitting second and rope again at the performance Friday night."

"You should come watch," Ryle grinned as he tossed his saddle onto the palomino.

I could tell he was trying really hard to fill the silence I was giving him.

"No, but thanks for the offer," I said and turned to see Marty arrive with the steers.

"We're only here today then we'll just be conditioning on the trails the rest of the week," Jess said. "You want to come riding with us?"

I swallowed hard. I really didn't want to be alone at my house for the next week. My stomach hurt with rising anxiety and a pressure pushed against my eyes. I shook my head then walked to help Marty with the steers. As usual, Kade and Pete arrived together.

I stood with the steers as everyone rode to warm up their horses. The first steer in line was a shorter black one with long horns. I slowly ran my finger up and down the horn as memories of working the chute for my uncle and his friends ran through my mind. They had been such great years; so much laughter and love. It seemed so long ago…a whole lifetime before.

"Roll them through," Ryle hollered as he backed the horse into the pen.

I pushed the lever and the first steer ran out of the chute with the rest of the herd following him. All five men trotted after them. I could hear a low rumble of laughter from the men as Kade stepped from the saddle and herded the steers through the gate then ran them back up the alleyway.

What was I going to do without them distracting me for a couple hours each day? They gave me something to look forward to…now I'd have nothing.

Since they had their backs to me, my eyes went to each one of them. Ryle's happy grin, Jess' bad jokes, Kade hadn't said more than a dozen words to me the last week but he clearly adored his grandfather…then Marty's laugh and dancing eyes…then Pete. What was I going to do without Pete trying so hard to cheer me up? I don't know why he kept trying but most of the time he succeeded.

What was I going to do without them keeping me grounded? Keeping me sane?

The tears threatened to rise as the men trotted back so I lowered my gaze and concentrated on pushing the first steer into the chute. I took a deep breath to calm my trembling stomach and looked up at the rider that backed into the header box. It was Pete…damn… He was smiling down at me like he was happy to see me and I knew he truly was.

The tears quivered on the edge of my aching eyes.

"Are you alright, Lauren?" He whispered as his smile faded.

I turned away from him and my hand reached for the lever. After a deep breath, I slowly looked over my shoulder to watch for his nod. He hesitated then looked at whoever was in the heeler box…then back to me.

He nodded and I pushed the lever.

The steer bolted with both horses in pursuit.

Pete swung the rope but didn't throw.

"Tired already?" Jess called out as he laughed and rode into the heeler box.

Ryle rode into the header box. He looked down at my glistening eyes and he hesitated…his eyes narrowed.

"Why don't you come to the rodeo Friday night and watch us?" He asked with clear hope dripping from his voice.

"I'll watch online," I promised.

He sighed, "Not the same."

"Yeah!" Jess said excitedly from behind me. "Come with us Friday. I promise we won't keep you out too late."

I shook my head and pushed the lever without the nod. Both horses bolted with neither rider ready.

"Not fair!" Ryle hollered as he pulled Silas down from a run to a trot.

The other three men laughed. Marty was grinning down at me this time when I looked up at the rider.

"You keep those young pups in line," His eyes twinkled and dimples increased.

My stomach trembled and the pressure behind my eyes made them narrow to the point I could barely see. My fingers went to my temple.

I heard Pete and Kade talking to the two riders as they joined them next to the fence.

What was I going to do without them?

I looked up at Marty as if I was a lost dog looking for a new owner. His eyes changed from joy to worry. I turned and looked out at the four riders who were now looking at me with concern in their eyes too. My heart was pounding as my stomach swirled in anxiety.

"I have an arena at home," I blurted out. The thought of inviting them to the ranch had never crossed my mind, but I couldn't imagine surviving a week without them.

"You do?" Ryle gasped.

"Yes," I nodded in rising desperation. "You can go there and ride this week." My eyes were pleading with them and the desperation was hanging on every word.

"You sure?" Kade drawled.

I looked at him…his brown eyes bore into mine. He was suddenly very intense and my stomach trembled again. He'd never been overly friendly to me so I looked to Pete. He was smiling as if pleased I'd asked.

"Yes," I said to Pete. "If you want…when you get done here…we can go look at it. See if you want to come out the rest of the week."

"Is the arena big enough for roping?" Kade asked.

Without looking at the arena or him I answered the question to Pete, "It's twice the size of this one."

"What?" Ryle gasped.

I looked to him…his eyes were wide and eager.

"You want to come see it? See if you want to ride there?" I asked him.

"Twice the size as this one?" He huffed. "I want to go now."

My stomach trembled in hope and I looked anxiously at Jess then to Marty. They both nodded so I looked at Kade. He just stared at me so I looked to Pete.

"I think we should at least go take a look," Pete nodded. "Then you can decide if you really want this crew at your home."

I sighed in relief and smiled at him which made his smile broaden.

"Let's get some steers roped then we'll head out," Marty said and backed into the box.

He nodded and I threw the lever.

It only took a half hour of riding and roping before Ryle finally trotted up next to me.

"Twice the size? Can we go now?" He chuckled.

"Whenever you're ready," I nodded eagerly.

Ryle turned in his saddle to look at Marty and Pete.

"I was wondering how long you'd hold out." Pete chuckled.

"Let's get the horses and steers loaded." Marty turned and looked at the other men. "I'm not too eager to leave them here unattended."

Within fifteen minutes I was driving out of the parking lot with the two trucks and Marty's cattle hauler behind me.

CHAPTER NINE

As I turned off the highway and onto my private road, I began to wonder what they were going to think when they saw the iron gates. I smiled to myself and looked in the rearview mirror as we approached them. I could see Pete and Kade in the first truck and their heads swung to each other then back to the gates. I wished I could see the others. I'd have to look at the security videos later.

As I drove down the hill to the ranch, I watched in the mirrors as their trucks came to a complete stop about halfway down. It was at the spot where you could see the whole estate through the trees that shaded the house.

I continued down the driveway and drove straight to the barn instead of stopping next to the house like normal.

I opened the door and the echo of whinnying rang out from the pastures followed by the rumbling of horse hoofs hitting the ground. Answering whinnies called from inside the horse trailers as the men drove down the driveway.

My older horses were in one pasture with the younger horses in another but they shared the same fence line down the driveway which they were currently running next to.

The trucks were parked side by side then the men stepped out with heads swinging around at all the different corrals, arenas, and buildings.

"Damn, Lauren!" Ryle yelled as the five men stopped in front of the vehicles and looked around then looked back at me.

"This place is huge!" Jess added with wide surprised eyes.

"That arena was built for roping," Marty said with narrowed eyes and a tip of the head. "And now I remember that brand on the gate. 3.3…Conners?"

"Yes," I nodded. "Austin was my uncle."

"Austin Conners?" Kade's eyes were wide in disbelief.

"THE Austin Conners?" Jess asked. "Seven-time NFR qualifier?"

"As in, the World Champion Roper, Austin Conners?" Ryle exhaled.

"Yes," I grinned proudly. "This was his Idaho home and he also had one in Texas."

They just stood in stunned silence.

"Would you like a tour?" I asked with a bit of humor because I knew they wouldn't turn it down.

"Uh, yeah," Jess nodded just as my older horses ran down the edge of the fence behind the barns then back to the horse trailers and younger horses that were bucking and rearing in the far pasture. "Those are your horses?" He asked.

"Yes," I nodded then turned toward the barn.

The thundering sound of boots hitting gravel followed me.

There was a normal size door to our left that led into the building but I led them to the large double doors instead and pushed open the left door that led into the barn. Some people would call it a stable instead. A twenty foot wide, brick floored breeze way greeted us. The interior of the building was made of the same rough cut pine as the outside of the main house and bunkhouse. The wrought iron rails above each stable door were twisted into my uncle's brand; a circle with 3.3 in the center.

I stepped into the building but bypassed the first closed door to our left. I wasn't ready for them to see that. I may never be ready for them to see behind that door.

"To your right are a dozen horse stalls split by a wash rack. Each has a small outdoor run that leads out to the large pasture where my horses are." I said. "To your left is the feed room, two more indoor only stalls, then tack room, then three more stalls with small outdoor runs, another washroom, then another feed room, then more stalls."

I turned and looked at the men. They were still silent except the occasional gasp.

"The hay is upstairs and dropped down into chutes to the feeders in the stalls," I said and continued to the back of the barn where I pushed open another tall wide door.

Kade helped with the last few feet.

"Thanks," I smiled at him. "It sticks sometimes."

He just nodded and his eyes rose then widened.

"There are two corrals here for catching stubborn horses," I continued with the tour. "Then the pasture for my band." Twenty acres of irrigated green pastures stretched out to a row of pine trees in the far distance. Another twenty acres were to our left.

I walked around the edge of the barn that led to the outside runs for the stalls in the barn.

"There is a 60-foot round pen here," I pointed to the obvious pen then to the next obvious pen. "Then a covered 120-foot round pen."

The paneling on both pens were the rough cut pine with dark shake roofing over the covered larger pen.

"There is a warm-up arena on the other side of the round pens but the ground is a bit hard and weed invested right now," I admitted.

We walked back to the front with the large arena was to our right, their trucks in front of us, and to the left were my horses standing patiently at the fence trying to see into the trailers.

"There are restrooms over there," I pointed to the side of the barn. "We didn't want all the corners of the fences and buildings saturated with cowboy urine." I chuckled and received grins back.

I turned and looked at Ryle. His eyes were wandering over the entire large arena then stopped at the cattle alleyway and chutes.

"Your chute and cattle pens are covered." He whispered.

"Yes, Uncle Austin was pretty insistent on that." I chuckled. "It helps keep the cows fresh and happy for roping. There are a dozen outside stalls back there for resting horses and a couple tables and chairs for the riders."

It had been a long time since I had introduced the estate to someone new...or even a group of people. It was fun and heartwarming to see Uncle Austin's dreams come alive in their eyes.

I led them to the bleachers that sat mid-way down the arena.

I turned to Pete then to Kade, "I'm not sure it's quite twice the size but I think it's pretty close."

Pete just grinned and Kade nodded.

"Yeah, I think it's big enough for roping," Kade said.

"I'm surprised you don't have an indoor arena," Jess said as his eyes wandered the property.

"That was next on the list until he met Charlene. They bought the place in Texas to stay close to her family and the mass of rodeos there." I answered.

There was a pause as they continued to look around.

"So, you guys want to rope here this week?" I asked innocently.

They all five laughed and the sound calmed my nervous stomach, filled my energy, and gave life to the property. My nerves still tingled with the knowledge I needed to tell them about the party.

"I want to rope here forever," Ryle said softly with his eyes wandering over to my horses. "Austin Conners…"

"Austin Conners…" Jess sighed while slowly nodding his head.

I looked between each of them again and suddenly wanted to share more of my uncle. If anyone would appreciate it, these five men would.

"Alright, more of the tour," I said eagerly. I would show them this first then tell them about the party. "Follow me."

I walked toward the house with the thunder of footsteps behind me.

"Tread lightly so you don't scare my cat. She just had kittens yesterday." I said and gave the dog house a wide birth.

My eyes landed on the stained bricks but I pushed the memory down deep and walked by it.

I opened the patio doors and stepped into the house with the crew following.

"Nice…" Marty nodded.

The others were silent as their eyes took in the cathedral ceiling over the large great room then the wood and stone kitchen to the long mahogany dining table that was a feature in the room. Across the house from it was the large stone fireplace with the mahogany mantle covered in picture frames and wooden horse statues. My uncle had collected those from his travels. Dozens of horses from large to only one inch tall covered the mantle.

"To the right are the stairs that go up to the bedrooms and a loft sitting area that overlooks the great room," I said. My arm swung out to the right. "Laundry room…" I hesitated at the memory of Jodi and Dave's voices and sounds flashed in my memory. I shook it off and continued. "First room down this hall is the office…or travel agency, as I used to tease Uncle Austin." I chuckled and continued walking. "His bedroom is on the right behind the stairs and under the loft area." I didn't open his bedroom door but continued down the hall. "Then there is the last stop on the tour."

My hand gripped the handles of the double doors then I hesitated again.

"You OK?" Pete asked.

"Yes," I nodded then turned to look at each of the men. My eyes stopped on Ryle then moved to Jess. "Not many people have seen this room." I smiled as their eyes widened. "Take a deep breath…"

I opened the double doors and took five strides in to rest my hip against a large dark leather sofa. I leaned against it and turned to the men that had stopped just inside the doors.

Their eyes feasted on the trophy room of a National Finals Rodeo World Champion Team Roper. Buckles from every stage of his career lined the walls. Posters of his magazine covers framed in dark leather were placed chronologically on the walls. Pictures of him with celebrities, athletes from every sport, and fans were framed and placed on dark oak tables that matched the hardwood floors. There were trophy saddles throughout the room.

A large rug with the Texas star was on the floor between two large leather sofas and in front of a rock fireplace.

On the wall to the left of the door, centered and framed in leather was the world champion gold belt buckle.

"On each side of the champion buckle are the buckles he won throughout the year that led to the Thomas & Mack," I said softly. "Just under the champion buckle are the three gold buckles he won the nights of the finals…and of course the saddles he brought home that week."

To each side of the collection of buckles was a large picture. The first picture my uncle was standing with his NFR finals jacket on and he was holding up his #23 back number. The second picture he had his left arm around his wife, who was beaming proudly, and his right arm around me. I was beaming just as proudly.

The memories of the night of his win filled my heart…filled my soul…it fueled dreams. I looked at Jess and Ryle who were standing in front of the champion buckle and the tooled saddles. Their eyes were bright with the dreams, desires, and drive my uncle had throughout his career…all the way to the day he died.

I left them in the room and wandered to the refrigerator to grab six bottles of water. They had barely moved when I returned and handed them each one.

Pete was standing in front of the fireplace looking at a large framed print that was sitting on the mantle. He turned and looked at me with a raised questioning brow.

I smiled…I was the header pulling the steer away from my uncle so he could rope the back legs of a black steer.

"I was thirteen," I said wistfully. "We won that district rodeo and those two buckles to the right were our prize." I pointed to two small buckles that looked so insignificant next to the wall of gold but they held the brightest memories. "It was my first gold buckle."

"Son of a bitch," Ryle exhaled and looked at me with a new light in his eyes. "I never would have guessed and I'm so damned jealous."

"That was just the beginning…" The words fell away as I looked around the room again, "Most of this was in his house in Texas. When he died and my aunt remarried she sent it here for my memories; mine and my daughter's."

"You have a daughter?" Jess asked.

"Yes," I answered and felt the warm memories fading as the more recent cold ones took over.

"Where is she?" Kade asked.

I glanced at him, "College in Idaho Falls."

"Aren't they on summer break?" Ryle asked.

"Yes," I nodded and took a long drink of water and walked to the door.

The men glanced around the room then slowly walked out.

I led them back out the door and toward the horse trailers and trucks.

"You want to rope here this week?" I asked again.

"Yes," They all answered in unison.

"OK," I sighed and fidgeted from foot to foot as I looked at them. My eyes went back to the patio then to the ground. "So…you've seen the good…the dreams of this place, but I need to tell you…"

My stomach swirled and the pressure behind my eyes caused my hand to rise against my temple.

"You OK?" Marty asked.

I didn't answer him, I just took a deep breath and looked up at Pete. He was the easiest to talk to. I'd just pretend the others weren't standing there.

"I need to tell you what happened here a couple of weeks ago," My hand went to my temple again. "I had a party and there was a…"

"This the one on the news?" Marty asked. "That's where I saw that gate before."

I nodded and continued to look into Pete's eyes; judging their reaction to the news by him.

"Some lady stabbed and killed her husband," Kade stated matter-of-factly.

"Yes," I exhaled and looked to the patio. "Over there."

They all turned and looked.

"She disappeared," Jess said. "That's what I remember. Did they find her?"

"No," I answered and continued to look at Pete. He nodded in encouragement so I turned to the group. "So…knowing that…do you still want to rope here?"

Ryle looked at the men, back to the patio then back to me. "Why wouldn't we? You didn't kill him."

I huffed in disbelief…in a way I did but I didn't say that out loud.

"I have no problem with it," Jess added.

"Me either," Marty said.

I looked at Kade since he was always so standoffish toward me. He was staring at the patio and when he turned his head he looked at his grandfather with narrowed thoughtful eyes.

"You have a problem with it?" Pete asked him.

"No," He said and looked at me. "I appreciate your honesty and letting us know, but I don't see how that woman stabbing her husband should stop life from going on here."

I internally gasped and my eyes widened as I looked at him. That was a fear hidden deep within me.

I tried to hide my reaction by turning to Marty and stammered, "If you'd like, you could leave the steers in the pasture on the other side of the arena and your trailer here so you don't have to haul it back today."

He grinned.

"I promise I won't sell them." I teased with a relieved exhale.

"Sounds like a plan," He laughed.

It took less than fifteen minutes to have the steers unloaded and the trailer backed up alongside my horse trailers by the barn.

As he pulled his truck away from the trailer my mood began to shift. Within minutes I was going to be left on my own again. Their chatter would cease and the conversation I had with Greg that morning would creep its way back to the top.

Instead of going to their trucks the men walked to my horses that were still next to the fence. I shifted my weight to the left then to the right. My hands dipped into my pockets then back out.

"You OK?" Pete asked as he walked up to me.

"Yes," I nodded anxiously.

His eyes went from mine to the horses then back.

"You ready to go, Granddad?" Kade asked.

We both turned to him. My stomach swirled, the pressure behind my eyes increased. I felt a panic begin to make my veins tingle.

"All fourteen are yours?" Ryle asked as he walked back from the horses.

"Yes…well one, the bay with the white star is Jamie's…my daughter…and the sorrel with the strip and snip…Andrea considered the horse hers because she rode her all the time but on paper she is mine, so all but one is mine." I knew I was rambling but the nerves were attacking my words.

"Who is Andrea?" Ryle asked.

I didn't answer. I just stared at him then leaned against the metal pipe of the arena fence. My eyes slowly moved to stare at the spot in the arena we had last spoken…where I had wished my life away.

There was a pause as they waited for me to answer then Jess' voice interrupted the silence.

"We'll see you tomorrow."

I just nodded and kept my glistening eyes focused in the arena.

Five car doors slammed and I could hear the tires on gravel as they drove away.

I rested both arms against the rail and stared at that spot where I lost my best friend.

The years Blake had betrayed me didn't compare to the years that she had by pretending to be my friend so she could come to this place. Never had I dreamed I would ever lose her friendship. Memories danced in my mind of the years of school, proms, graduation, our kid's births, riding, rodeos, laughter and now…the loss.

Greg's words from the morning's coffee made my headache. How could she have lied for all those years which led to the lies she told me just the week before? While standing in that arena?

How could she do that to our friendship? What I thought was our friendship but was nothing more than her desperately trying to hold onto the property and her obsession with my uncle.

The memories began to overwhelm me…my head hurt…my heart hurt. I leaned against the fence, lowered my head and let the tears fall into the dirt. My body shook as it released the pent-up emotions.

"Darlin', you alright?" Pete asked from behind me.

I gasped at his voice, then hiccupped when I tried to stop the tears.

"How can I help?" He whispered.

"I thought you left." My voice trembled.

"I just didn't feel right leaving…just wanted to check with you one more time." There was a hesitation before he spoke again. "Talk to me."

I took a few deep breathes to stop the tears but I remained against the fence for support. I didn't look at him. If I did, I knew that all the self-control that was left would dissolve.

"I was just thinking about the last time I talked to Andrea."

"Who is she?"

"She was my best friend for 32 years…since we were in grade school. She is the only one that knew me before I came to live with my uncle. After my mother left, he made arrangements so I could stay in the same school…so I had something familiar in my life. He thought it would be easier on me."

"He was a very good uncle to you," Pete said.

The tears welled again and fell to the ground. There was a large circle of dark moist dirt forming at my feet.

I sniffed and took another deep breath.

"When I was twenty and pregnant, he built this place for me to raise Jamie. Andrea basically lived here with us."

"Where is she now?"

I shrugged, "I don't know…probably home with her husband and boys."

"When was the last time you talked to her?"

"Two days before you stopped me at the stop light."

"Why?"

Another deep breath and the tears stopped and my voice stopped trembling.

"Evidently, everything that is bad in her life is my fault. Her brother Greg…well, his wife was the one having the affair with Dave…my boss…the man that died at my party."

"And…that was your fault?"

"Because I recorded the door so when they came out, I'd really know who it was. I had no idea what was going to happen…no idea that Greg would find my phone and see it. He played it for everyone to hear…I didn't want that but Andrea thought...well..." I sighed and looked back out across the arena. "But that isn't even the worse part…well for Dave and his wife it was, but not between me and Andrea."

"What happened?"

"I found out this morning…from Greg and Jodi his wife…or ex-wife now."

"They got a divorce because of what happened?"

"No…that's just it. They were divorced two months before the party. Andrea had convinced them to keep it quiet until after the party."

"That was nice…"

"NO," I spat in anger at her. "She didn't tell me because I was single too and she didn't want me to have Greg…who I didn't and don't want anyway."

"She was hiding his divorce to keep the two of you apart?"

"Yes, and the whole fucking thing…the whole son of a bitching thing?" My eyes went from the arena to the blue clear sky. "If I had known he was divorced, then it wouldn't have mattered if it was Jodi in the bathroom screwing my boss. It wouldn't have mattered so I wouldn't have recorded it."

"And Greg wouldn't have found it and played the video at the party," Pete sighed.

"And Dave's wife wouldn't have gotten enraged and stabbed him on my patio with a barbeque fork."

I heard his deep sigh as I looked out at the arena in time for the wind to create a dust tornado that swirled and danced.

"I still haven't dealt with the loss of her friendship. Now, it's her jealousy over this ranch, Uncle Austin, and

Greg…and how all that ended up getting my boss murdered by his wife."

A large gust of wind pulled at my hair and shirt. It dried any remnants of tears on my face. I heard a whinny in the distance and turned to see the horses begin a run around the pasture.

"I'm just so…lost," I whispered.

"Close your eyes," Pete said.

My eyes were so tired and aching I had no problem doing as he said.

"Now what? You're not going to try something are you?"

He chuckled and the sound made me smile.

"What do you hear?" He asked.

"Wind."

"And?"

"Horses."

"Now just listen to the wind," He whispered.

I heard the rustle of the wind in the grass and whistling its way through the barn. There was a whinny, then again, then the pounding against the ground of the fourteen horses as they ran by the fence.

"Now what else do you hear?"

"Horses."

"What specifically do you hear?"

"Hoofbeats." My mind went back to the night Andrea had walked away and I lay on the ground wishing for my last breath. The wind and hoofbeats had brought me back to life.

"Listen to the wind then focus on the hoofbeats." He whispered again.

Like that night, I listened to the pounding, remembered the vibration through the ground, and the hoofbeats creating a heartbeat.

"You can't control life any more than you can control the wind. The hoofbeats are your heart beats." Pete whispered.

How could he have known?

"You are a person that runs with the wind, not one that hides from it in the barn or behind trees waiting for it to pass." he said. "When you choose to run with the wind, there is a point when all hooves are off the ground and you're at your most vulnerable. That's where you're at right now, Lauren. Anything that comes along is going to knock you over because you don't have the ground…you're just kind of floating above it right now."

A gust of wind whipped my hair around me and slid against my skin. I concentrated on the sound of the horses. I imagined them running and their legs all tucked under them as they flew in the air. Yes, I did feel that way.

"We're here to help you. Let us be that first hoof on the ground to help you get to all four." Pete whispered.

I took a deep breath as another gust swept through, the horses whinnied, and their hoofbeats danced in the wind.

I nodded.

"Go with us to the rodeo this weekend and we'll start from there."

I nodded again and opened my eyes to turn to him. His eyes were full of concern, honesty, and hope.

"Alright," I stepped back away from the fence. "I'll go as your date."

He sighed in relief.

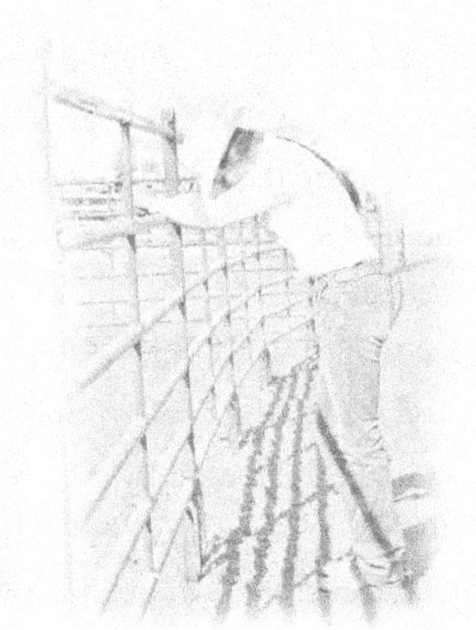

CHAPTER TEN

I spent the evening by myself on the tractor working the arena dirt so it was ready for the riders the next day. It had been weeks since the arena was worked so I spent extra time preparing the ground. Then, with a can of WD40 in my hand, I made sure the chute opened easily. I double checked every gate.

At 10:00 at night I was at the grocery store buying bottles of water and ice for the cooler I pulled out of the tack room and set up in the corner by the chute.

Fully clothed, I fell onto the bed at midnight but was up again at 6:00 to work the arena one more time then filled the coolers with the water and ice. I turned on the radio by the chutes so the music would play as they roped.

My heart was racing when they arrived for their first practice. My hands trembled.

I stood with the men as they saddled their horses.

"So, how did you two meet and become partners?" I asked the younger pair.

Ryle grinned, "We were just drawn together."

I rolled my eyes at the corny joke.

"We both went to an open draw competition in Idaho Falls a couple years back," Jess said as he tightened the cinch on his grey horse. "There were 101 riders and 210 teams."

"We were drawn twice together," Ryle chuckled.

"Progressive…four rounds," Jess nodded.

"We made it to the final round together…both draws," Ryle added.

"Impressive," I nodded.

"And Ryle made it with another roper," Jess said and grinned at his partner proudly. "There were fourteen teams in the fourth round and he was in three of them."

"How did you do?" I asked.

"We came in first and sixth." Ryle grinned at Jess then back to me. "Then I also came in fourth with the other guy."

"We talked all day while waiting for each ride and just hit it off." Jess shrugged while sliding the bridle on the horse. "He was young, only 19, but he impressed me."

"We decided to go to a jackpot together the next weekend and we won third out of 114 teams." Ryle added.

"Been roping together ever since." Jess said and stepped up into the saddle.

"And they've been doing pretty damn good," Marty said as he rode by.

"Road warriors for Cowboy Christmas," Kade walked by. "Won enough money that they rose ten places in the Columbia River Circuit and now they're leading the ICA."

Pete rode by and added, "…by a good margin."

It was very obvious Marty, Kade, and Pete were very proud of the other two.

I opened the gate for all of them to enter the arena for this first time. I stood by the chute watching them with memories of the thousands of times I'd done the same thing with Jamie and Andrea. Then there were the thousands of practices with Uncle Austin and his dozens of friends that would come out to ride. We had hosted dozens of clinics and play days.

Memories…dreams…laughter…friendships…all in this arena. Life…in this arena.

When their horses were warmed up, I opened the gate to the field so they could ride out to round up the steers. I didn't realize just how much seeing cowboys out riding with the steers was going to mean to me. The history of the ranch…my uncle and all his friends…my friends…the years we rode the exact ground they were riding.

I had to take deep breaths to keep the tears away.

I shut the gate behind the steers and pushed them down the alley. I had done this very thing hundreds of times for my uncle and his friends. Hell, even for myself.

As I worked the chute for the men, I thought of my past in the arena.

Even after my uncle died, I continued to team rope with friends. That is until my husband persuaded me to quit so I wasn't hanging around with a bunch of men each week. He convinced me that just doing breakaway roping and barrels with Jamie would be enough. That's what a good wife and mother would do. Uncle Austin had told me to be more compromising in life and I was young and stupid and wanted to please my husband. At least I still had the rope in hand and could teach my daughter to rope too.

I was a High School National Champion team roper…my uncle would have expected nothing less and helped me fulfill my dreams in the arena as he made his own come true.

Jamie and I worked hard to make sure she qualified for high school finals too. She was the state champion her senior year in barrels and breakaway roping. She even qualified for nationals in goat tying. She became the High School National Champion in breakaway and placed third in barrels which led her to college on a rodeo scholarship.

For the local rodeo association and clubs, the two of us had even team roped together and won a number of gold buckles and prizes.

Roping was a huge part of our lives…with Uncle Austin and after.

I have not picked up a lariat since the day Jamie walked away.

"Lauren."

I looked up and came out of the memories to look at all five men looking down at me.

"What?" My eyes went to each one of them.

"Where did you go?" Marty asked.

I smiled timidly, "Sorry, I was thinking of the hours here with my daughter since she was born. This was her playground until last year."

"She go off to college?" Jess asked.

"Yeah, a couple of years ago…she's going into her last year in August." I hoped anyway. I hadn't heard that she'd dropped out. It had been a year since I had signed onto Facebook to see any updates from her college rodeos. It just got too painful to see it and not be a part of it.

"Is she coming home for summer?" Ryle asked.

"No," I turned and walked back to the cooler. "You guys thirsty? I have water."

"Sure," Jess said. "That's handy."

I handed him a bottle and smiled, "This cooler is so old, I think Uncle Austin actually bought it."

"That is so fucking cool," Ryle grinned.

The other four men looked at him with disapproving looks.

"Sorry for the language," Ryle smiled at me.

"Trust me, I've heard worse." I laughed.

"I'm gonna go get Dexter." Ryle rode away to switch horses.

"Thanks for getting the arena worked for us," Jess said. "It looks like you've been pretty busy since we left last night."

I just nodded to him. I didn't want to admit I had absolutely nothing else to do and appreciated the distraction.

"Where's your dog?" I asked him.

He shrugged, "Left him at home. I was worried he'd chase your new momma kitten…you were pretty protective of her."

"Your dog doesn't leave your truck," I smiled. "You can bring him. My cats are used to dogs."

"How come you don't have a dog?" Marty asked.

"I did," I answered.

All four turned and looked at me.

Ryle trotted in and stopped in front of us. He looked at me, to the four men looking at me then back to me, "What?"

"We're waiting for her to tell us about her dog," Kade said.

"You have a dog?" Ryle's eyes shot around the property.

"I did," I repeated.

His shoulders lowered. "Did…"

"When did he die?" Pete asked with a sigh.

"What makes you think it died?" Marty asked. "That ex coulda took it."

Pete looked at me to Marty, "This is Lauren Conners we're talking about."

I sighed, "She died a couple months ago."

"You are just about every sad country song all rolled up into one." Jess shook his head.

We all chuckled.

They rode for another hour then came back in for more water and to visit the restroom in the barn.

"So, besides roping, what do you do?" I asked Jess after he returned from switching horses.

"Nighttime inventory manager," He answered. "I work all night then rope all morning then sleep in the afternoon when it's hot outside."

"I work as a night stockman at the same company," Ryle said. "But in another store, so we don't have to see each other so much."

The pair grinned at each other.

I turned to Marty.

"Retired ranch store manager," He answered. "Also the small ranch with my wife."

"Retired attorney," Pete said.

I turned to Kade.

"I'm an architect and make my own hours since I work out of my house." He grumbled.

"His office is in the daylight basement of his house so there is a separate business entry. The living portion of the house is upstairs." Pete said proudly. "It's a very nice place."

"Don't you have a job?" Kade asked me with narrowed eyes.

"Yes, I've just been given some mandatory time off," I answered.

"You piss someone off?" Ryle grinned.

"Time off instead of firing? Why?" Kade asked.

"My boss died," I reminded him. "On my patio…twenty feet away from me."

They were quiet a moment, each looking a bit taken aback. Obviously, the 'incident' wasn't at the top of their minds like it was mine.

"Damn, did you work for him long?" Marty finally asked.

"Two years," I answered.

"Did you like him?" Pete asked.

"Up until the last 20 minutes," I answered and my eyes went to the back of my house. To the laundry room window where Jodi and Dave had their sexual encounter. Jodi's 'oh's' and "You sweet little flower," from Dave made my stomach sour.

"Who wants the stocky red one?" I turned back to the steer in the chute.

I was amazed as they loaded the horses into their trailers how calm my nerves were. Having them at the ranch and knowing they were coming back the next day gave me a sense of ease. It just seemed so natural.

"I'll see you tomorrow," I said to them as they stood at the back of the horse trailers.

"We'll be here," Pete smiled with a mischievous twinkle in his eyes. "But don't worry about dressing up for us."

My eyebrows shot up in surprise…then I slowly looked down to my clothes…that I had worn the day before while working the dirt and preparing the chutes. My hand went to the braid falling down my back…it felt and probably looked like a cat had used it as a play toy. At least my 'not so clean' baseball cap hid the top of my head.

I looked back to Pete's twinkling eyes then turned to each one of the men. Marty's dimples were deeper, Jess was chuckling with a quick shy glance at me, Ryle had a grin on his face but was looking out at my horses, and Kade was looking at the ground, his hat covering his face.

I looked back to Pete, "Smart ass."

They all laughed and walked to their trucks.

I spent the night getting ready for their arrival again. This time, it meant an hour in the shower shaving my legs and deep conditioning my hair. Then I put my long tresses into large curlers to dry overnight.

I opened my large walk-in closet and went to the back corner. To the clothes I hadn't worn since before Uncle Austin had died.

I pulled out a dress bag and a boot box and found myself giggling to myself all night in anticipation of the roper's arrival. I woke early to give myself time to get the kittens, chicks, and horses taken care of then a quick glance out to the resting steers.

Then I not only fixed my hair but I also put on makeup for the first time since the party. Large black curls bounced down my back and over my shoulders but I left my sweatpants and t-shirt on and took the clothes and boots out to the barn to put on. I didn't want them to get dirty from the walk.

I was ready for them 10 minutes before my phone alerted me to their passing through the gate. I hid in the tack room and peeked out the window as I watched them all park and step out of their trucks.

They gathered in front of Pete's truck and all looked back at the house…no doubt looking for me.

Their expressions became concerned so I put my hand over my stomach to quell the giggles and stood straight and walked out of the barn.

All five heads turned to me, ten eyebrows went in the air, then grins and laughter erupted.

During the National Finals Rodeo, a large party is held to award the contestants their back numbers for the week. It was very formal and Charlene and I had taken the opportunity to go 'all out'. My husband just about died when I bought the dress and boots; not because of their style but because of the price tag…even though he didn't pay for them.

The gown was deep royal blue velvet with a low neckline that just covered the bust and barely gave a hint of a cleavage. Cap sleeves dangled over my shoulders and were more for decoration. From the bust down to the hips was skin tight then a waterfall of blue velvet fell to the ground behind me and just to the top of the boots in front. The cowboy boots were black with blue stitching. I had worn a black cowboy hat in Vegas for the party but today I was hatless and my long curled hair shimmered in the sun to let the auburn highlights glisten.

I grinned as I sashayed out of the stable to stop in front of the men and looked at Pete.

"This better, Smart Ass?" I purred.

"Oh, my God, Lauren," Pete gasped with a hand over his chest. "I think I'm going to have a heart attack."

"Damn!" Ryle gasped. "I sure wish I would have taken a picture yesterday so I could do a comparison." He lifted his phone and I gave him a hip popping, head tilted back, chest out pose.

"I think yesterday's is burned in my mind," Jess laughed. "And so is this one."

"Isn't that the one you had on in the picture with Austin in his trophy room?" Marty asked. "From Vegas?"

I was surprised he noticed.

"Yes, it is," I said and did a turn for them.

"You going to work the chute in that?" Pete laughed.

"Sure," I grinned. "Why not?"

Kade hadn't said a word. He had just given me the normal blank look. I was a bit surprised when he walked by me and into the tack room.

I looked at Pete but he didn't seem to notice.

When Kade returned, he was carrying a dummy roping steer under one arm and had a lariat in the other.

He tossed the dummy in the middle of the driveway then turned and held out the lariat to me with a slight smile of a challenge.

The other four men laughed and circled the steer at a safe distance.

I had not picked up a lariat since before my daughter had left telling me she didn't want anything to do with me. My heart had left with her and any desire to rope or compete was gone.

I stared at the rope…bright green…Cactus…the ridges calling out for me to touch them. The coil was loose and needed tightened…my mind told me to fix it. My hand slowly reached out to the lariat and Kade dropped it into my hand.

Muscle memory…I'd roped since I was twelve until the year before when I was 41. The only day, in all those years, that I did not throw a loop was the day after Uncle Austin had died. I had even thrown the day Jamie was born and the day of my wedding.

Today, my fingers wrapped around the coils and slid slowly across the rough ridges. I flipped the rope out then coiled it back up…I did it again…then again then built the loop. Muscle memory…I flipped it out, coiled it up, then twirled it to my side again. As if a day hadn't passed, I whirled the loop over my head and looked at the dummy steer. I felt a slight twinge in my shoulder as I whipped the rope over the head of the steer. It didn't catch the horns but it went around the neck. I flipped it off the dummy, coiled the rope, and threw it again…this time wrapping the horns.

As I coiled the rope after the third throw, I came out of my haze and remembered the dress and the men. I looked up a bit flushed and my heart feeling at home again.

Ryle had his phone up again and I grinned at him.

"Looks kind of natural," Marty smiled.

"It is," I sighed. "All except the dress…that's not quite so natural."

I continued to throw as they saddled their horses, stopping only when they were trotting the real steers towards the arena pen.

The dress just touched the ground but I stomped through the dirt in my fancy boots and watched the dust rise and settle over the blue velvet of the hem.

I looked across the arena. I needed to water it down so it wasn't so dusty…then work it again for the next day.

Ryle was chuckling and had his phone out videoing me as I worked the chute the first time. Pete and Marty burst out of the boxes and chased after the steer.

"No posting or sending that anywhere," I told Ryle.

"Ok," He shrugged and slid it into his pocket. "It's a classic…something to remember." He chuckled and backed Silas into the box and looked down at me. "You have the prettiest hair…"

"…when it's clean." I finished for him.

We both laughed as he nodded and I pushed the lever.

Even though it was hot and I was sweating up a storm, I wore the dress for the whole day and actually had fun…it had been a long time.

When they walked their horses to the trailers I looked over at Ryle and Jess. "When do you leave next?"

"We have the Stampede in Nampa on Friday and hopefully the short go on Saturday. Then the second round in Ogden on Monday." Jess answered.

"Well," I looked at the five men. "If you want, there is a pasture just behind the steer pasture that your horses can stay in. So you don't have to take them back and forth…it's up to you…I'll understand if you don't want to…but I promise I will take care of them."

"They'll just be grazing anyway," Marty said thoughtfully and looked out across the arena to the pasture.

"Man," Ryle exhaled. "I sure love the thought, but trying to catch Silas on a pasture that size? I don't know…it could take a week and we have to be at the Idaho Horse Park tomorrow afternoon."

I chuckled and gave him a reassuring look, "Uncle Austin had a horse that was tough to catch too. That's why we have the corral system out back where we can capture them."

They were all quiet as I looked around them, "It's OK if you don't want to. I understand."

"You could try it overnight," Pete said and nodded. "We'll all help catch him if we have to."

"I'd like to ride the fence first…check the ground." Kade said blandly. I seriously don't think the man likes me.

"OK, I understand. My horses have been in there without a problem but I understand you need to check for yourself," I nodded. "Just go down to the end of the barn and through that corral and to your left. My herd is in the right pasture…just close that gate. There is more than enough feed out there for them."

Kade, Ryle, and Jess remounted and rode out of the barn.

I turned and looked back at Marty and Pete.

"That was a nice offer," Marty said. "I'll take ours home…Sarah would be upset if I didn't."

"Where are theirs normally stalled?" I asked.

"Mine and Kade's are at Marty's," Pete said. "Jess and Ryle's are stalled at a small place in town with indoor stalls and a decent outside run."

"It has an arena there but lots of people use it," Marty said. "I don't have an arena, just pasture and corrals."

Ryle and Jess came back with smiles and nods in agreement. Kade just silently nodded.

"It may take us all day tomorrow to catch Silas but I sure would love all three to have a good day of pasture and running," Ryle said.

"Mine could use it too." Jess nodded.

"Do you want me to put them in stalls at night?" I asked.

Ryle laughed, "I don't think Silas will let you."

"I don't ride him so he may trust me," I shrugged. "There is a creek that runs through the east pasture my horses are in so I don't have to worry about them. But for the West pasture, we have the stock tank in the corrals. If he gets thirsty enough we can trap him when he goes in to drink."

"Let's put him in there for a bit so he knows where the water is," Pete said. "Then I want to see all of them run out into that green grass."

Ryle's three horses and Jess' three horses were led through the barn and into the corral with the water tank. Once the halters were removed, they bucked and snorted then all six went for the water.

We waited another ten minutes until they settled down, then Ryle climbed up on the corral fence and held up his phone to record them as they were released.

I thought of climbing up next to him…but I was still in the blue velvet evening gown.

"I can't wait to see the pictures from the photo shoot," Ryle said to Jess.

"What shoot?" I asked.

Jess turned to me, "Ryle and Silas were asked to do a cover for The Team Roper's Journal."

"That's great," I turned to Ryle who was grinning sheepishly.

"It was more for Silas," Ryle said. "He's pretty flashy…they did his mane and tail and he looked pretty damn good."

I smiled at his humbleness, "I have a feeling you had something to do with it too."

He shrugged, "The article is about the younger horses that have been making names for themselves so far this year."

"You're on top of him when he's 'making a name' for himself." Kade chuckled.

Again, Ryle just shrugged.

"Well, get your camera ready," Marty said. "Let's let them loose."

Ryle and Jess stood with phones ready to record the release. Marty opened the gate and all six horses trotted out twenty feet and stopped with noses to the ground and teeth ripping at the grass.

"That's it?" Ryle laughed then climbed down from the fence. "Watch this." He said to me then walked out to his horses. His sorrel and bay let him slide a hand down their backs and pat their shoulders then he walked toward Silas.

The palomino watched him as he approached and just as he got within arm's reach the horse walked away then stopped when Ryle stopped. Three times the horse waited then at the last second he walked away. The fourth time, Silas didn't even wait. He took off at a dead run across the pasture. His mane was braided but his white tail flew like silk behind him. The other five horses took off as if a bolt of lightning had struck them.

All six stopped at the far end of the pasture and put their heads down.

Ryle turned with a wry grin, "Pain in the ass."

Ten minutes later I was standing on my porch in the blue velvet gown and flowing curled hair. I was alone again…looking out at the six roping horses then over to my fourteen horses, down to the twenty chicks, then down to the doghouse that held momma cat and five kittens. Then the couple dozen steers in the pasture. Somewhere by the barns and corrals were four other cats.

This was better. I may not have another human around me but life was coming back to the ranch.

My eyes landed on the bloodstained bricks. It was 2 o'clock in the afternoon and it was the first time all day that I had thought of the party, death, blood, guilt.

I needed to get that blood stain gone but not while I was wearing a velvet gown…which was damn hot. Why the hell was I still wearing it with the sun beating down on me making me sweat?

I turned into the house.

After showering and putting my hair up into a ponytail I slid on a t-shirt, shorts and tennis shoes then walked out to the pasture to check on the new ranch occupants. They were in the middle of the pasture now and all six heads went up when they saw me. None of them moved any closer as I climbed the fence with phone in hand.

I took a picture of the six of them all huddled together eating peacefully on twenty acres of green grass with pine trees in the distance. With the blue sky and white puffy clouds, it really was a serene image. I sent it to both Ryle and Jess.

I watched the horses for a while then my curiosity got the best of me and I walked out into the pasture toward the horses. I tried to remember all their names…besides Silas and Dexter, Ryle's sorrel horse with the wide blaze. I couldn't do it. I knew one of Jess' was Zeb…or was that

Ryle's bay? There was a Casper too but I didn't know which one he was.   I needed to pay more attention.

All but Jess' big black gelding and Silas let me walk up to them and run a hand across their backs. It took a few minutes but the big black finally stopped moving and let me touch him.

Silas let me approach then walked away. Four times he did it then on the fifth I walked at an angle away from him. His head went up and he watched me walk a complete circle around him. I took two steps toward him then turned quickly before he could. I did that three times before he took a step toward me. Then I walked toward the corral that held the water tank.

Silas and Jess' grey horse followed me. I walked to the complete opposite side of the corral and waited until they joined me. They stood calmly and watched me for a couple minutes until I moved then both their heads rose in anticipation. I turned my back to them and walked backward along the fence and toward the gate. They just stood and watched until I got to the gate and closed it.

Silas was captured. I smiled and nodded.

"I got you," I chuckled then walked around to the gate that led into the barn.

I retrieved a pink bucket and scooped a small portion of the grain Ryle had left behind. I tossed out two heavy rubber feed tubs and poured just a small portion of the grain in them as a reward to the 2 horses for coming into the corral.

The other horses were still grazing out in the middle of the pasture so I opened the gate so Silas and the grey could leave when they were ready. I walked back to the arena and climbed the fence and waited.

Within minutes I heard the pounding of hoofbeats and turned to see the horses running out of the corral and to their buddies. I started the video on my phone and recorded the four in the middle joining the run of freedom. My horses joined in on the other side of the barn. The run lasted a good five minutes but I only recorded the beginning.

I lowered the phone and just watched until they all settled back down to grazing. I would give anything to have Jamie with me watching the horses. I considered sending her the video of the run but didn't. She wouldn't understand who they were. I sent it to Ryle and Jess…and Pete since I had his number too. I didn't have the phone numbers for the other two.

On my way back to the house, I stopped and looked at the trailers just to make sure the windows were closed. All the tractor work and riding in the arena kicked up a lot of dust and I always made sure to close the windows in the living quarters horse trailer so it didn't get filthy. The windows were closed so turned back to the house then stopped.

The roping dummy that Kade had placed in the driveway was still there. The rope was hanging on the end of the hitching post. It called to me and I spent the next half hour throwing the rope.

It was dark outside and I was back in the house staring blindly at the television when I received the first text. I removed the spoonful of peanut butter from my mouth.

Text from Ryle: Just woke up, thanks for pics and video, off to work

Five minutes later;

Text from Jess: Just woke up, love watching them run, thanks. Conditioning in the morning, no cows then off to rodeo

No response from Pete.

CHAPTER ELEVEN

Friday morning all the horses were at the far sides of the pasture. The ground inside the water trough corral was covered in hoof prints so they had already been in for water. No chance of capturing them with that trick.

The ropers arrived at 7:00…my next counseling session was at 10:00.

Pete and Marty saddled their geldings and rode out to herd in the six horses. Five trotted their way into the corral. The gorgeous blonde palomino kept darting away and held back in the middle of the pasture watching the riders and horses. The five were captured in the water corral then herded into the second corral and held there until Silas was caught.

With me on the ATV, Marty, and Pete on horseback, and the other three on foot we made our way out to capture the elusive golden palomino. It took over two hundred swear words, ten 'let's just shoot him', twenty 'I just give up', one suggestion of a tranquilizer gun, and at least fifty thrown dirt clods before I finally went to the barn and retrieved the pink bucket.

I gave Kade the ATV and then I stood at the entrance of the corral shaking the bucket filled with enough grain and small rocks to make a loud rattle. Silas' head went up and he stared at me as Ryle approached him from behind. Just as Ryle was lifting the rope to put it around the horse, the damn gelding bolted…which gave way to another round of swear words from each man in the pasture.

I just stood and shook the bucket and silently chuckled at them and swore at Silas.

The horse stood ten feet outside of the gate and stared at me while he pranced. I turned my back on him and walked into the barn. After a short questioning whinny, the horse calmly trotted into the corral looking for me. Two men ran, two horses ran faster, and the ATV roared to life to block the gate before our prize escaped. Silas just walked to one of the black tubs and waited for me to pour the grain then pick out the rocks.

With a mouth full of grain, Silas' head rose and he gave the exhausted men the 'what?' look.

They all caught their horses and walked them back to the trailers.

"Grrr…"

Jess' dog was standing in the bed of his truck staring back at the horse trailers and barn. His ears were back and the low growl continued.

"Rover, knock it off," Jess called out.

"I have four other cats," I told him. "I'm sure they are teasing him that they are free and he isn't."

"Yeah, he's not much of a cat lover," Jess said. "But he won't come out of the truck."

I shrugged. I wasn't too worried about the cats…they were pretty tough.

"So…let me guess. You have the washboard abs with the hip-V and the tats that drive all the women crazy." I smirked at Ryle as he set his saddle on the horse's back.

He grinned with a one-shoulder shrug, "I have the abs but not the V. Kade's the one with the ink."

I turned to Kade who was already mounted on his horse…as was everyone else while waiting for Ryle.

He shook his head, "I didn't get them for the girls. I got them to honor my dad and the ranch I grew up on."

"Oh…OK," I said. "But…can I see them?"

"They are on my back, chest, shoulder and around my bicep." He answered.

"OK, but…can I see them?"

"You want me to take off my shirt out here?"

"You bashful?" I teased.

"Come on Kade," Pete said. "You've taken off your shirt to show them off before. Let her see."

"Yeah, let me see." I grinned up at him. He didn't like me much so he just gave me an irritated glare.

"Yeah, come one Kade." Marty laughed. "Take off your shirt."

"I'll show you mine," Jess said and started unbuttoning his shirt. "I ain't bashful."

"Yours for the girls?" I asked and walked to him.

He rolled the shirt over his right shoulder to show the typical barb wire wrapped around a bicep but this one had a rattlesnake entwined.

"Nah, got it for myself," He grinned. "Me and some buddies had a paycheck to burn."

I chuckled and turned to Kade. He was still just glaring at me; no move to remove his shirt.

I looked over at Pete and Marty. "Tattoos to share?"

Marty shook his head with a grin, "Don't like needles."

Pete nodded, "Just my wife's name over my heart."

My eyebrows shot up in surprise, "You were that confident it was going to work out?"

He shook his head and opened the shirt just enough we could see 'Miranda' written in curly script, "Did it after she died."

"Oh," I stepped back. "I'm sorry…but that's a wonderful thing to do for her."

"Ain't no more women for me. She was my one and only for 55 years. Lost her three years ago." Pete said.

"I'm glad you had a good life with her," I said then looked at him a moment while I calculated his age. "I'm guessing 77 then?"

He chuckled while the other four laughed.

"And still roping," Kade grinned proudly. "Hope I still am when I'm your age."

They all four turned to him.

"You ain't going to make it that long if you're so damn delicate you can't even show her your damn tattoo," Pete growled with a smirk.

Kade shook his head, "It ain't like I can just open a button or two…I have to take the whole damn shirt off."

"Then take the damn shirt off," All five of us told him then looked at each other and laughed.

Kade shook his head with a growl but wrapped the reins around his saddle horn and started unbuttoning his shirt.

Ryle started it…then we all joined in and serenaded Kade to a striptease beat as the shirt came off. His glare turned to laughter by the time he whipped the shirt off and swung it around his head like a Chippendale dancer.

Of course, Ryle and Jess were standing in their stirrups with hips grinding and shoulders bumping to the rhythm.

My laughter ended with a gasp at the full sight of the tattoo. "Wow…that's some work!"

I walked closer to him and stood on tiptoes to get a good look at the art. I had to walk completely around the horse.

The skull of a longhorn steer covered his wide left shoulder and down to his elbow. The left horn stretched across his chest while the right horn went across his back. They nearly met at the tip of his right shoulder. Barbwire was tangled around the length of the horns and beyond to meet on the right shoulder creating a circle. In the middle of the circle was a brand; ‾KD.

"Bar KD?" I asked.

"Yes," He nodded. "That's where I got my name."

"KD…Kade…" I nodded. "Makes sense…and this is really outstanding work."

I walked around him twice to see it all until Pete started chuckling.

"Did you get a good look?" He asked with a roguish grin.

I stopped and looked up at him then back to Kade's tattoo…which covered his wide bare chest and back…which were quite tan and muscular. His stomach was covered in a fine layer of black hair…it wasn't washboard but it was flat and there wasn't a hint of a roll over the top of his belt. I looked up into Kade's eyes and felt the blush run up my neck and to my cheeks.

His right brow rose as if silently asking me the same question.

I turned to Pete, "Damn, Pete. What did you have to go and do that for? I was just appreciating the art."

They all laughed.

"Some people consider a man's well defined muscular body as art too." Pete teased.

"Yes, well…" I looked from the tattoo to the chest…back …shoulders and abs then looked back at Pete. "I appreciate both."

Kade slid his shirt back on as I turned to motion down my driveway.

"Go to the left down the road," I pointed. "The road ends at the end of my pasture. There are trails through the trees then it opens to hay ground. I don't have to tell you guys to stay out of the hay field."

"That your field?" Pete asked.

"On paper, mine," I answered. "I get the 1st cutting, he gets the second and some years we can get a third. I take more if I need it then he gets the rest."

"Nice system," Marty nodded.

"Saves one hell of a lot of money when you run up to twenty head of horses," I nodded.

"Why don't you go with us if you have that many?" Jess asked.

I looked out at the horses then back to the arena where Andrea had walked away with my heart and my desire to ride.

"Just don't get lost," I said and waved them away.

They rode for an hour and a half while I ran the tractor around the arena to work the dirt again.

"Let's just put him in a stall with hay," Ryle grinned as he walked the pain in the butt palomino into the barn.

"Choose a stall…any stall," I chuckled. "I'll get a couple bags of shavings."

Ryle handed me the lead rope and shook his head, "I'll get the bags while you choose the stall."

"Fine," I smiled and pointed to the room that held the bedding.

The rest of the men had their horses put away by the time Ryle was ripping open the shavings then kicking it around the stall. He released Silas into the enclosure and opened the back door so the horse could get to the small outside pen.

"There," Ryle said. "Now we can catch you easier. We don't have time to chase your butt tonight."

"What's tonight?" I asked.

"Snake River Stampede," Jess answered.

"Oh," I exhaled. I'd forgotten about the rodeo…that I had promised Pete I would go as his date.

As soon as the crew left, I walked to my truck and drove to the counselor's office.

"Good morning," She said and closed the door behind me.

We sat quietly as she wrote in her book and I stared at the landscape pictures. I thought of the rodeo; it was one of the first rodeos that Uncle Austin had taken me to. He won the calf roping that night and came in third in team roping with his partner, Carl Mercer. They were partners until the year before my uncle won the Championship at the NFR. That year he had roped with Barry Wilder. Carl had willingly stepped aside for my uncle to partner with Barry. He knew they were a better fit for a run to get to the Thomas & Mack Center in Vegas where the NFR is held.

I had been to the Snake River stampede every year until last year when Jamie was no longer with me. Andrea had tried to get me to go with her and Stan but I just couldn't. I had taken Jamie every year after my uncle died. Without either one of them, I just couldn't find the will to go.

This year, I had promised Pete to go during one of my lowest moments. Would he understand if I didn't go? I didn't think so.

So now I had to go. My stomach soured at the thought and my skin moistened to the point sweat slowly trickled down my spine and little beads of moisture formed on my brow. I wiped them away and the counselor turned to me.

"Why are you sweating?" She asked.

I exhaled, "I have to do what I don't want to do and it makes me nauseous thinking about it."

Her eyebrows shot up in surprise, "That's the most you've said in here. We're making progress."

I sighed and fell back against the chair.

"We all have to do things we don't want to do, Lauren." She said thoughtfully. "What is it you have to do that's making you so nauseous?"

"Go to the rodeo," I whispered.

"You don't want to but you're going to, aren't you?"

"Yes, I promised I would so now I have to."

"You don't, you're a grown woman and can say no."

Say no to Pete? After he had done so much for me? I was a grown woman…but I was lost and he was trying so hard to help find me. There was no way I would back down from my promise.

I didn't respond and we sat quietly for the remainder of the appointment.

"Are you going to go?" She asked as we stood at the door.

"I promised I would," I answered and walked away.

I stopped at the store on the way home and bought another jar of peanut butter.

I drove into my driveway and parked in my normal space behind the house, facing the patio. The swing was to my left between the truck and house. My eyes landed on the bottle of cleaner sitting on the barbeque grill on the patio.

I was already sick to my stomach so I might as well get those damned bricks cleaned.

With a deep breath, I walked straight to the bottle, turned the nozzle knob to stream and pointed it at the blood stains. I could not get my fingers to squeeze the trigger.

I just stared at the stain until my arm slowly lowered to my side. All I could see was the image of the blood pouring out of Dave and the blood-soaked towels being pressed into him by Mark and Nadine to try and make it stop. So much blood…how did he last long enough to make it to surgery?

The sound of tires on the gravel brought me out of my haze and I looked down the road to see Jess's truck slowly making its way to the house.

I set the bottle of cleaner back on the grill and walked away.

"You're comin' tonight…right?" Ryle asked as he shut the trailer gate with his Silas and Dexter and Jess's Zeb and Warlock safely inside. Gus and Casper, the two younger horses, were standing at the gate watching.

"I'll be there," I promised and tried to sound more positive about it than I felt. "Which horse are you riding?"

"Dexter," Ryle answered. "It's a big indoor rodeo…huge crowd. Dexter is more used to that and he did great Monday at slack. Silas is just his back up tonight and it gets him around big crowds."

"I'm on Warlock…both horses were great Monday and we're still in second," Jess grinned. "We'll get em' tonight then hopefully make the short go tomorrow. We'll rest the horses Sunday."

"Then off to Ogden." Ryle nodded.

"Ropin', ropin', ropin'…" Jess sang to the Rawhide TV theme song.

"Get your butts going and I'll see you tonight." I smiled encouragingly until they drove out of the driveway…then my smile fell.

I stood in my underwear and stared at the mirror. What to do with my hair? I couldn't remember a Snake River Stampede that I didn't go to with my hair straight down or in a braid down my back. But tonight I created two braids then twisted them together in a stylish chignon at the back of my neck. Then a little makeup because…well…thousands of people were going to be there. It was also close to 100 degrees. I slid on a black sleeveless tank dress then added a pair of black dress cowboy boots and a black cowboy hat. The chignon was tucked under the rim of the hat so it looked like I had short hair. The last touch was black and silver hoop earrings. My black hair with the black dress and the black hat…I looked dark and gloomy. I added a bright red, wide western belt to lighten it up a bit.

Definitely not the normal way I would have dressed to go to the rodeo. Maybe no one would recognize me.

Then it hit me…that's why it made me so nauseous to go. I didn't want to be around anyone that knew about the party…Dave…his death. I didn't want anyone else accusing me to my face that I was responsible for Dave's death. It was bad enough that I knew I got him killed without anyone else besides Andrea telling me to my face.

My body sighed. Knowing that fact didn't make me want to go any more than I already didn't want to go but, I had promised Pete. Moving forward…letting them help me get four hooves on the ground instead of flying in limbo. My team roping crew were most definitely that first hoof. They made me feel stronger. I nodded to the image in the mirror. I can be stronger with them at my side.

I heard a truck drive by the house…bring it on…I thought as I swooped my phone from the bedside table and slid it into the dress pocket. With determination, I walked down the steps of the house and to the back door.

Marty and Sarah were waving from the front seat of the truck with Pete walking toward the house.

"I see you brought the limo and driver," I teased as I walked out of the house and set the security code.

He laughed and I felt stronger.

"You are lookin' all kinds of snazzy tonight," He held out an arm for me to wrap my hand around.

"Snazzy…" I chuckled. "You aren't looking too bad yourself."

He was in black jeans, old cowboy boots, newer, not so sweat-stained cowboy hat, and a red shirt that looked like it had only been washed a dozen times. He was also clean shaven except for the mustache that dropped across his lip then down off his chin.

He opened the door of the truck for me with a wide grin.

"Been years since I've had a date," He chuckled and leaned in to pick up a small clear plastic box. "This is for you."

I gasped. It was a simple wrist corsage of tiny white roses with a blue ribbon. I proudly held out an arm for him to attach it too.

"I just love it," I giggled as he helped me into the truck.

"I used to buy them for Miranda on her birthday," Pete said after he slid into the truck.

"Now, that is special and I am honored," I smiled warmly then turned to the happy couple in the front seat. "Double date…we'll have fun." My stomach swirled in anticipation…or dread.

With a goodhearted man like Pete at my side, I could face this night. Hopefully…

CHAPTER TWELVE

I gripped his arm tightly as we walked to the ticket gate of the Idaho Horse Park.

"Where are our seats?" My voice trembled.

"We're going to have a good night," he said and patted my arm. "We're right behind and above the alley and roping chutes."

"So, I could spit on one of them if I wanted?" I laughed nervously.

"Keep the humor up tonight," He chuckled.

I kept my head low as we walked through the crowd. Unless they saw my face, I doubted anyone I know would recognize me with the dress and hair tucked away.

"You look like you just walked off a Western Magazine," Sarah said as we took our seats.

I sat between her and Pete with Marty just on the other side of her.

"Thank you," I smiled and relaxed a little. "And you are just beautiful tonight."

She wore a black ankle length skirt, white blouse, and a massive turquoise necklace and dangling earrings.

Her hand went to the necklace. "My 30th wedding anniversary gift…had it 12 years now."

"Ya done good," I teased Marty. "Can't wait to see the 50th."

Marty grinned proudly.

"The first time I brought Miranda here…" Pete started another story to keep my mind occupied.

As I listened, I could not get myself to stop looking around and looking at faces. We were in the first row behind the chute so it was only to the side that I could see people clearly. I knew dozens of people but didn't make eye contact with any of them. I kept my hat low.

I looked down to the chute to see the men checking the gates, and even caught a glimpse of Kade.

"I was wondering where he was," I said to Pete.

He turned and looked down at his grandson.

"He's pushing the steer for them," he said. "And keeping them calm…or trying to."

The announcer's voice rang out over the loud hum of the crowd.

"Can I get you something to eat or drink?" Pete asked.

My hand instantly went over my stomach, "No…thank you."

"Big crowd tonight…looks like a full house," Marty said.

My eyes went back to the crowd…across the arena and to the section I usually sat during the Stampede. I knew Andrea and Stan were there…probably with their boys. I stared…trying to see them. I don't know why…maybe to break my heart just that little bit more. The tears pushed their way up and I slowly lowered my hat to cover my face and silently wipe them away.

"Come back to me," Pete said softly and patted my arm. "Have you shown your flowers to Sarah?"

I tipped my head slightly to smile at him. It was a sad smile, but at least I was trying.

"Yes, she loved them as much as I do," I answered.

The opening ceremonies began and we sat quietly and watched the rodeo until the team ropers began to gather below us.

Ryle and Dexter walked to the back of the chute and looked out…then disappeared again.

"What's Kade's phone number?" I asked Pete.

I typed it in and sent him a text.

Text to Kade: Ryle looks nervous…btw, this is Lauren

Text from Kade: He is and Dexter is feeling his stress. Was doing good until Brazile, Smith, Masters, Driggers, Begay…the big dogs showed up.

Text to Kade: How is Jess and Warlock?

Text from Kade: Starting to feel Ryle's nerves.

The steer wrestlers appeared below us and we silently watched each run.

I looked down as the last steer wrestler bolted out of the chute. Kade was standing along the side looking up at us with a mean glare. Our eyes connected and we just stared at each other. There was no doubt this man did not like me, but I didn't care…I didn't particularly like me either.

I turned away and watched for Ryle and Jess.

"What number are they?" I asked no one in particular.

"Third out," Marty answered.

The first pair of team ropers walked through the back of the boxes.

My nerves peaked and I leaned over the edge to see Begay was right below me.

They bolted out…hooves and arms flying, ropes whizzing.

"5.7…" Was called out from the announcer.

Patrick Smith rode into the heeler box then Trevor Brazile rode in across from him. The memories of Trevor and my uncle competing against each other, practicing together, and just laughing together made my heart warm. The memories would always be there and there were days they made me happy and days that cut me to the core.

I held my breath as Trevor nodded and the chute clanged open…the steer ran but the rope was faster.

"4.4…" Was announced.

"Puts them in the lead and easily into the short go tomorrow night," Pete sighed.

I typed a text to Kade as fast as I could and hoped he read it in time.

"The next team of Jess Corday and Ryle Jasper…" The announcer called out and all four of us leaned over the edge to catch the first glimpse of our crew. Jess appeared first…followed by Ryle. Jess walked into the heeler box then backed into the corner; rope in a perfect loop and tucked under his right arm, eyes on Ryle.

"He looks cool as a cucumber," Marty whispered.

Ryle walked into the box with his head down…chin on chest.

"Damn, he needs to relax," Sarah whispered.

"He's a bit star struck," Marty said.

Kade was at the chute and turned to look up at Ryle. He said something but we couldn't hear it, then Ryle looked up…right at us.

His eyes connected with mine.

"What's that 10-year-old doing in the header box?" I called out and received a smile…his shoulders lowered. "You sure you're old enough for this rodeo, Cowboy?"

His shoulders shook from the laughter.

"Yes, MA'AM, I am," He called up to me with a smirk.

"Well, show me what ya got then," I smiled to reassure him.

Ryle nodded then turned to back Dexter into the box. The rope whizzed over his head then down at his side and he readied from the run.

He looked down at the steer then over to Jess with a grin. Jess nodded to let him know he was ready…then Ryle's eyes went back to the steer. He hesitated until the steer was straight in the chute and looking down the arena.

Ryle nodded.

My hands went directly to Pete and Sarah's as Dexter launched himself out of the box. One whirl of the rope and my lungs filled with air and held it until the third whirl danced around the steer's horns. Ryle's arm flew back to take in the slack then dallied quickly as he and Dexter both looked at the steer then Ryle turned to Jess. One…two…three turns…palm flat…flip of the wrist…rope mixing between steer legs and the ground…the trap was set and the steer stepped in. Jess's arm flew back to take in the slack then he dallied as Warlock skidded to a halt. Dexter twirled and faced them with both of the steer's back legs up in the air. Heads turned to the judge's flag that was already going down then to the box in search of a penalty flag…there wasn't one.

Our eyes flew to the clock as the announcer gave us the time, "4.3."

"Damnation!" Pete called out.

"Heart attack in 4.3 seconds," I laughed.

"They are in the short go tomorrow night!" Pete slapped his knee.

Ryle and Jess rode to each other for a high five then trotted down the arena to follow Ryle's rope that tethered him to the steer. Ryle turned in the saddle and looked at me. His fingers went to the tip of his hat and he nodded. I grinned as he turned back.

"Now that was something," Sarah exhaled as she wrote down the time on the day sheet in her lap. "I just love those two boys and I am so proud of them."

I exhaled the joy and pride that had built up in me and made my skin tingle. Yeah…I remembered that feeling from watching my uncle compete and oh how I had missed it.

"Where does that put them?" Marty asked.

"Second behind Brazile and Smith in the average but in the lead tonight," Sarah answered. "But we have more ropers to go."

Sarah kept track of every run and averaged them out as she went. Ryle and Jess won the night and remained second in the average. It was a great night for them.

My feet bounced in excitement with my head raised looking out at the crowd as their focus moved to the other end of the arena for the saddle bronc riding.

My phone buzzed and I nearly jumped.

Text from Ryle: Thanks Ma'am

I giggled.

Text to Ryle: Keep that up and I'll come out there and knock you off that damned horse

I smiled at Pete and showed him the message.

"He's a good boy…big future ahead of him," Pete nodded then looked up at me. "It's good you were here for him."

"Ah, thanks, Pete," I grinned with a sigh.

We turned to the first horse bucking its way across the arena.

I relaxed back into the seat without hiding my face and enjoyed the rest of the rodeo.

My heart was in my throat the whole time as the barrel racers turned the cloverleaf pattern. Someday my daughter would be down there…I just hoped to be involved with her when she was.

My head dipped down again as I thought of Jamie and the years we had watched and dreamed of racing in this rodeo together.

"Those boys are going to have a hard time sleeping tonight," Pete said loudly. "It's also a good paycheck for them to add to their savings for next year's run."

I turned my focus back to him and the announcer screaming over the speakers as he announced the first bull rider. I personally knew two of the bull riders. They were in high school rodeo at the same time as Jamie so I had seen them grow through the years. I couldn't have been prouder of the pair to come as far as to compete in their hometown rodeo as professionals. Roscoe had earned the title of the NFR Bull Rider Rookie of the Year in 2016. I held my breath and silently cheered for both. It was Roscoe that placed 3rd for the night.

"From the look on your face," Pete said when the standings were announced. "You know one of them."

"Roscoe Jarboe," I answered with a proud grin. "He's from New Plymouth and was competing in high school rodeo the same time as my daughter. They went to the High School National Finals together. I also know Brady Portenier; he's from Caldwell."

"Well, that was fun," Sarah said as they announced the end of the rodeo.

"I agree," I nodded and stood.

We huddled together as we made our way out to the parking lot.

Halfway there we walked under one of the large outdoor lights.

"Lauren?"

It was said behind me and in surprise. My heart dropped and my arm tightened around Pete's.

We slowly turned to Stan's voice…was Andrea with him?

CHAPTER THIRTEEN

I had stopped breathing by the time I saw Stan, my heart was pounding in my chest and the ringing in my ears grew louder. I did not want to see her accusing, jealous, betraying eyes. I leaned against Pete when I saw it was just Stan; no Andrea or their sons.

"It is you," Stan gasped in surprise.

I took a deep breath and tried to calm my racing heart, "Hello, Stan."

"I don't understand," He muttered with brows drawn together in confusion. "Andrea said you flew down to Texas after the party."

I was stunned and just stared at him as I slowly shook my head. "No…I've been home."

Stan looked from me to Pete then to our entwined arms.

"What the hell is going on?" He demanded. "Why in the hell would she tell me that and who is this?"

"This is a friend of mine," I said and left it at that.

Neither Pete, Sarah, nor Marty spoke although Marty slowly made his way to my side opposite of Pete. My crew was surrounding the wagon…that made me feel stronger.

"I don't know why she did," I answered. "You'll have to ask her that. I haven't spoken to her since the day after…the…party."

He shook his head in disbelief, "Just a little while ago…she told me it wasn't you I thought I'd seen on the big screen behind the team ropers."

I had no idea what to say to that so I just slowly shrugged.

"Lauren, if you were coming tonight, why didn't you sit with us as we have done for the last twenty years?" Stan asked.

"Pete asked me to go with him so I did," I answered. Stan looked at Pete then me, Pete then me again. Classic case of getting caught in the middle but I had no idea why Andrea lied to him. "You need to talk to Andrea," I said softly.

He nodded with clenched jaw and eyes narrowed, "Oh, I will." He huffed. Then he exhaled roughly and his shoulders lowered. His eyes fixed on mine and grew calm…worried…questioning. "How are you?"

"Honestly," I said as the energy and fear gave way to the nausea. "I've had a very rough time."

"Yeah…" His whole body seemed to shrink. "I've had a number of talks with Jodi and Greg."

I stared at him a moment then just blurted it out, "Why didn't you tell me they had gotten a divorce?"

His back straightened and his eyes narrowed, "You didn't know?"

"No, not until I talked to Greg last Tuesday," I answered.

"Son of a bitch," He growled and looked from Pete to Marty, Sarah, then back to me. "I thought you knew. It never crossed my mind to say anything to you. I don't think we've seen each other but a handful of times since they separated in April."

"No, between your work and fishing…Andrea and I weren't competing…so…no we haven't," I agreed.

"Lauren," He stared hard at me. His brown eyes were angry and worried. "What the hell is going on? Why would Andrea not tell you? Why did she lie about you being in Texas and why in the hell are you here tonight with this guy and not us?"

Pete's arm tightened around me and I looked back at Stan with compassion but he needed to get the answers from his wife.

"I'm sorry, Stan," I said. "You have to ask Andrea."

His eyes closed and his chest rose as he took in deep breaths.

"Alright," He said as his eyes opened, his voice calmer. "That's between me and her…but…between the two of us, who have been friends for that twenty years…how are you? Can I help you in any way?"

Tears rose and my eyes glistened at the true love and honesty that radiated from him.

"Thank you, Stan," I whispered and stepped out of Pete's arms to be wrapped in Stan's.

He squeezed tighter then lowered his head to whisper in my ear, "Don't blame yourself, Hon. It was Dave's own fault by taking his wife to the party he was attending with his girlfriend. He lied to everyone. It's his fault he drove his wife to that point…literally." He was taller than me so when he leaned back he looked down into my shimmering eyes. "I've told Greg and Jodi the same thing. This is his fault…no one else's."

"Thank you," I smiled up at him.

"This sounds odd," He sighed. "But I talked to Sheila for about ten minutes before it happened. She was really nice…sweet."

"Yes," I said. "She was always that way when she came in the office…always nice and pleasant to talk to."

Stan nodded slightly, "It had been building in her…this wasn't just a get mad onetime thing. He had been driving her to the brink and…well, she must have been pretty mortified to have a dozen people know what he did just before joining her on the patio. I can't imagine how she felt."

"Me either," I whispered and my stomach swirled as a new feeling of sorrow for Sheila started in my heart. "With Blake, he never made it public until he was out of the house but still…"

"I've said it a dozen times," Stan's arms dropped from my sides and his lips twisted in a scowl. "You and Jamie are better without him…something happened a long time ago that changed him. He's not the same man that you married."

"Yes," I nodded slightly in agreement. "But it still hurts to know that he was…" I hesitated. "I never had their affair thrown in my face like Dave did to Sheila."

"You remember that," Stan ordered gruffly. "This is his fault. She may have swung the fork but he drove her to it. It's his own fault."

A loud laugh next to us brought back the reality that we were standing in the middle of the parking lot with my friends behind me and hundreds of people walking by.

I looked around at all the smiling faces then turned back to Stan.

"Thank you," I whispered and hugged him again. "I need to go."

Stan's eyes went to my trio of friends then to me, "You let me know if you need anything, even just someone to talk to."

I smiled warmly then turned away. Pete's arm instantly lifted and I wrapped my hand around his elbow.

We were quiet until we were in the truck and Marty started his slow path out of the lot.

"You're OK?" Pete asked softly.

"Yes, thank you," I took a deep breath. "I bet Ryle and Jess are living the dream right now."

They all three laughed.

"They need to savor this one," Marty smacked a hand against the steering wheel.

"First time against some of the big dogs and they won," Sarah said proudly.

"I hope the photographer got a good shot. I'll buy some copies for them." Pete said.

"I always bought the pictures of Jamie," I relaxed back into the seat. I noticed Pete relaxed too.

We chatted comfortably the rest of the way to my ranch where I said my goodbye to Marty and Sarah before Pete walked me to the door.

"You think of Ryle and Jess tonight," He said as I punched in the key code on the security system.

"I will," I smiled warmly at him.

"And you have my phone number if you need someone to talk to."

"I do."

"And you'll call."

"Yes, I promise I will call but I don't believe that I will need to. I had a fun night with friends and am so excited for the boys."

"OK, good."

I pulled him into a thankful embrace. "Thank you."

"I'll see you tomorrow." He smiled as he stepped out of the embrace and to the truck.

"Bright and early before the heat sets in."

I didn't turn a light on until I reached my bedroom. I undressed and slid under the covers just to stare at the ceiling.

I went over every word that Stan had said.

I had no answers.

I woke with a headache and felt exhausted. I may have promised Pete to think of Ryle and Jess but I dreamt all night about Andrea and Stan.

To make up for it, I used my phone to search the internet for pictures of the pair at the rodeo. There were a number of really great shots of them. My favorite was the grin Ryle had on his face as he looked at Jess just before he nodded. That made me feel better. Looking at all of the pictures and videos of the run made my heart pound with memories.

I set my phone on the table and slid out of bed for a quick shower. It was early yet so I slid on a loose pair of yoga pants and an oversized t-shirt. My hair was still braided and twisted at the base of my neck so I just left it alone. I jogged down the steps of the house and was going to check on the kittens and chicks before the men arrived.

I opened the door to Dave standing in the middle of the porch.

I screamed and fell back against the door. My hand instinctively reached for the doorknob to keep from falling. I looked back up at Dave but it was Kade's scowl looking at me. I could hear my heartbeat in my ears and my lungs nearly burst.

"What the fuck?" I growled and had to take deep breathes to stop my heart from racing.

He just stood and glowered.

"How the hell did you get here?" I gasped with a hand over my heart.

"We drove here," He snarled.

I looked out at the barn to see Marty and Pete saddling their horses.

My hands went to my pockets, looking for my phone but it was still on my bedside table.

"My phone usually warns me when someone comes through the gate," I stammered and turned back into the house.

I caught a glimpse of him taking a step to the door but I had no desire for his attitude in my house and I needed to get my heart beating normally so I slammed the door in his scowling face and tromped up the stairs to my bedroom. Not being in any hurry to face him, I took a moment to look at the security image when they entered the code to the gate.

Marty was looking at the keypad with Pete in the passenger seat looking straight ahead. The truck moved forward so the second image was caught with Kade in the backseat of the truck. His face was void of any emotion. What the hell was his problem?

I was halfway down the stairs again when my phone vibrated. I stopped and looked at the image to see Jess driving and Ryle in the passenger seat. They were grinning at the camera.

My heart leaped for joy to see them and feel their energy. I hopped down the stairs and nearly ran for the back door. I expected Kade this time. He was still standing on the porch. I just bounded past him without actually looking at him and nearly skipped to the side yard.

Kade followed.

"You want to tell me what you're doing?" He said as he stepped up next to me.

I turned dramatically with hands on hips and glared back. "I don't know what the hell your problem is, but Ryle and Jess just arrived and they deserve a great welcome, not you glaring at me for no reason."

"I want to know…" He grumbled but stopped when the truck turned into the driveway with two big grins inside.

I ignored Kade and turned to look at the barn for Marty and Pete. They were leading their horses toward us and they looked so old-fashioned western that I couldn't help but take a picture with my phone. Then I turned and took a picture of the grinning pair.

They talked non-stop for nearly 15 minutes about how great the other ropers were and they had even been congratulated by Trevor Brazile, Patrick Smith, Coleman Proctor, Clay O'Brien Cooper and more.

Their energy was infectious with all of us and it was fun just sitting back and listening to them talk until they left to try to catch a nap before heading to the rodeo. The memories they stirred up in me made my heart warm…and beat faster.

The other three men took their horses for a ride in the hills and trees behind my property.

I filled the silence they left behind with the lawn mower then the tractor as I reworked the arena and even worked on the warmup arena and the round pens. A hundred times I looked over toward the bloodstained bricks on the patio but I couldn't get myself to even go near them.

I kept my body busy and my mind full of the rodeo, Ryle and Jess as I worked. I was sweeping out the barn when the trio returned from their ride. It was only 10:00 in the morning.

"We're headed for a late breakfast at the café," Pete said as he stepped off his horse. "Go change and you can go with us."

I gave him a raised brow and a smirk for the command but wandered into the house anyway.

They were nice enough to order me to breakfast the least I could do was show up clean. I released the braids in my hair and after a quick shower, I put it into a ponytail that started from the top of my head and fell down my back. Just mascara and eyeliner for makeup to coincide with the simple yellow sleeveless summer dress. I slid on sandals just before walking out the door.

"Well, look at you," Pete chuckled with laughter dancing in his eyes.

Marty's dimples were even deeper, "We were beginning to wonder what the hell was taking you so long, but I'd say it was worth the wait."

"Well, thank you." I smiled.

"My truck is a little dirty for your pretty dress," Marty opened the passenger side door of his truck for me and started to brush away the dust that had settled onto the seat.

Pete and Kade slid into the back seat together.

"It will clean," I said as I stepped into the truck.

When we arrived at the café, my stomach was still uneasy so I lied and said I had already had breakfast and came along for the stories. So Marty and Pete regaled us with stories for a good two hours. I disappeared into their past and thoroughly enjoyed myself. Kade was silent through most of the day with an occasional addition of 'truth' to the two men's adventures. I ignored him most of the time.

"Are you coming to the rodeo tonight?" Kade asked.

It was the only thing he had said directly to me.

"No, I'll watch them run from the live feed tonight," I answered.

"You're sure?" Pete asked in disappointment.

"Yes," I said firmly.

When they dropped me off at my ranch, I watched them drive away then looked around the property. What to do now? The rodeo wasn't until 7:30.

Two years before, Andrea, Jamie, and I had gone to the parade and matinee performance of the rodeo then the evening performance of the rodeo.

Last year, Andrea and I had taken the horses to the mountains to ride all day then she went to the evening performance with her family.

Today, I had neither of them. I wandered to the swing and fell back into the pillows and thought of all the memories the three of us had made over the years. Then there was the dream of us riding in the rodeo together once Jamie finished college.

Memories of my uncle and his friends at the rodeo filled me with sadness this time and I wiped away a tear.

I needed to get past these memories so I stood to walk into the house. My foot landing on the patio had my eyes darting to the bloodstained bricks. That whole day played like a movie. My head turned as I imagined Greg walking to the Karaoke machine and turning with the "fuck you" look on his face when I tried to get him to stop.

Sheila's face turning white…what had she thought? Felt? As Stan had said, it must have been mortifying for her to stand there and listen to her husband having sex with another woman…let alone to be standing with over a dozen people listening.

Why in the hell would Dave bring her to the party with Jodi there too?

A little whinny cried out from the pasture and I turned back to see the three foals running around their mothers, rearing up on back legs then bucking and kicking. The three mothers just grazed peacefully and ignored them.

I turned and walked across the yard and wide driveway. I not so ladylike climbed the fence in my dress and walked out toward the mares.

It was then that I remembered I was still in sandals.

I turned back and climbed up on the fence as the mares and their foals walked to me. I gave them as much attention as I could from my perch. All six of them looked fat and happy; just a few marks on the babies from their playful fighting but nothing serious.

I looked out to my older horses but they were on the opposite side of the barn and arena so I played with these six until they were bored of me. The mares went back to grazing and the foals plopped on the ground to take naps. I walked into the house to change back into shorts and a tank top.

I returned to the barn and pulled out every roping dummy we had…which was more than enough for clinics and play days I hosted in the past. Then I attached the plastic calf hocks to the trailer and pulled out a bale of straw and shoved in the spike attached to the plastic steer head. The last thing out was the first roping dummy Uncle Austin had bought me. It was an old Don Parsons Calf Tracker. It looked nothing like a calf but it had somewhat of the same shape. The blue paint was flaking off revealing patches of rust. I had roped the damned thing thousands of times and I loved it and the memories it held.

I had a couple dozen targets ready and with Johnny Cash, Sons of the Pioneers and Merle Haggard serenading me I roped for hours.

At 5:00 I was very surprised to receive a text from Kade. It was a picture of Jess and Ryle saddling Dexter and Warlock.

Text from Kade: Grandad wanted me to send this to you.

Text to Kade: Thank you to both of you

I hung my rope in the tack room and hurried into the house to curl into my office chair and turned on the computer to make sure the live feed worked. I watched the videos from the night before and searched for pictures of Ryle and Jess. My jaw dropped when I came across a picture of Ryle and Jess looking up at me just prior to their run. Although my hat was low over my eyes, I could tell it was me…I'm not sure anyone else could though. It must have been the shot that Stan had seen letting him know I was there.

I put the live feedback on the computer then thought over my conversation with Stan. Why would Andrea tell him I was in Texas?

Jess appeared on the live feed riding Warlock. I leaned forward looking for Ryle but he didn't appear. Jess disappeared.

I quietly watched the beginning of the rodeo and thought of all those nights…thirty years' worth of attending that rodeo.

The steer wrestling began and I watched the background for any sign of the ropers. I saw a flash of Kade then a flash of Jess and Warlock. Ryle appeared…he was riding Silas!

"Where's Dexter?" I gasped in surprise.

My hand reached for my phone.

Pete didn't answer and I didn't have Marty's number so I had to call Kade. He didn't answer either so I sent a text.

Text to Kade: Where's Dexter? What's wrong?

CHAPTER FOURTEEN

It was an excruciating 10 minutes before the alert rang on my phone.

Text from Kade: Something in his shoulder, Ryle didn't want to take a chance of hurting him.

My first thought was 'poor Dexter', my second thought was of Ryle. He was willing to risk losing time on a run in an effort not to risk his horse. That is a true cowboy. Money will come, but only if you have a healthy horse. There was no doubt Ryle was thinking of his horse more than the prize money.

I liked this kid…he reminded me of my uncle who had done the same thing.

Text to Kade: Thank you

There was no response.

I leaned back into my chair, every muscle tense and my eyes staring at the monitor.

The last steer wrestler rode and it was time for team roping.

I took a deep breath…my hands gripped the armrests tightly.

There were twelve teams to ride and the first team out the header's rope swirled off the horns…no time.

I wished I had gone to the rodeo and sat next to Sarah as she kept notes.

Second team out broke the barrier for an added 10 seconds on their 6.9 run.

Third team…no time with the steer jumping out of the heeler's loop.

Fourth team…6.4 run…put them in first place.

Fifth team…no time as the header missed the horns.

"Damn…" I mumbled my disappointment for them.

The sixth team came into the finals sitting into third place…they rode out with a no time.

"Damn…" I sighed for them.

The seventh came into the finals in fourth…5.2 run put them into second.

Three disappointing 'no times' later and the eleventh team of Trevor Brazile and Patrick Smith entered the box.

My heart was pounding, hands gripping the office chair, and eyes starting to hurt from staring so hard.

I took a deep breath and held it for the full 4.6 seconds of the run that put them back on top. I was elated for them but my stomach swirled for Jess and Ryle.

The black Warlock and golden Silas pranced into the boxes. I knew he was there but I couldn't see Kade.

Warlock stood as still as a statue in the back of the box, Silas' head was swinging from side to side as he looked around the arena. I couldn't see either rider's face and my fingers squeezed the armrests tighter. My heart was pounding as Silas twirled in the box then Ryle nudged him back into the corner then tucked the rope under his arm. Warlock was the statue as Jess stared at Ryle.

Silas was still…Ryle nodded…the chute opened…the steer bolted.

The rope in Ryle's hand was twirling as Jess held his to the side ready to go as they busted out of the box. Three swings and Ryle's hand flew forward, rope leaving his fingertips and swirling around the horns…his arm flying back to pull the slack then he turned the horse while dallying. Jess' rope was twirling above his head. The steer ran behind Silas with Ryle having to take the extra precious seconds to cue the horse over to make room for Jess to throw. Warlock brought Jess within throwing distance of the steer and the rope flew out of his hand and the black horse put on the brakes as Jess' arm flew back then swirled around the horn to dally.

Silas' golden rump twirled around so the horses were facing each other and the steer's back legs lifted from the ground.

"Yahh!" I yelled and jumped from the chair, my heart racing and skin tingling.

6.9 seconds…the steer's sudden dart had caused them the few seconds to keep them from taking the lead…and they lost one position as they came in third.

"Damn!" I screamed into the empty room.

Tears filled my eyes in a mixture of disappointment for them yet elation for them too. They came in third! There was no shame in that in one of their first major rodeos. It put money in the bank and memories in their hearts!

I watched the pair as they trotted down the arena to retrieve their ropes. Ryle was holding the rope and reins in one hand and patting Silas' neck with the other. Near the end, the camera showed the ropers clearly as they grinned at each other and high-fived. They were happy…I was impressed. Instead of focusing on the loss of first place, they shared the victory of third…of competing…of Silas' first big show…and their friendship.

I fell back in the office chair with a grin…yet exhausted.

Text from a number I didn't know: They did it!

I was nearly crying as I texted back. I guessed the number was either Sarah or Marty.

Text: Yes they did! So excited for them.

Text from Sarah/Marty: Damn steer, Silas did good

Text to Sarah/Marty: Yes he did, Ryle should be proud

Text to Ryle: Very proud of you, Silas was awesome

Text to Jess: You and Warlock are a damn fine team…magic to match his name

It was an hour before I received another text.

Text from Ryle: Thanks, excited, still shaking

Text from Jess: Coming from you, I take that with honor

Text from Marty: Kade and Pete are bringing horses over, boys staying at rodeo to celebrate.

Text to Marty: Dexter?

Text from Marty: Sore shoulder, needs contained.

Text to Marty: I'll get a stall ready for him.

I jumped out of the chair and hurried to the barn.

I was still in my shorts and tank top so by the time I had the stall ready, my legs, arms, and face were covered in sweat and dust but I didn't care. All I could think about was making Dexter comfortable.

When the men arrived it was all business until Silas and Warlock were pampered as congratulations to them then set out on the pasture to run. They didn't. Twenty feet out, their heads were at the ground ripping at grass with Gus and Casper happily at their sides.

Dexter was the last out of the trailer and he limped slightly as he was walked to his new indoor home.

"Any idea how it happened?" I asked.

"Halfway through warm-up he just started limping," Kade answered.

I ran a hand down the sorrel's neck. He wasn't paying much attention to anyone…his muzzle was buried into his nightly ration of grain and his eyes were looking at the hay in the feeder.

"Well, he doesn't look too worried about it," I ran a hand over his back and down his rump before leaving the stall. At the last second, I turned and took a quick picture of the content horse.

Kade latched the stall door then turned away to close the gate on the trailer.

I sent the picture to Ryle.

Text to Ryle: I have a Bemer we can use on him in the morning.

The electromagnetic system really helped with my horses when they were sore.

"We'll pick up the boys tonight then come over in the morning," Kade said.

"I will take very good care of him," I said as we walked to the truck. "Are they traveling tomorrow?"

"No," Kade answered. "Back to Ogden for their second run on Monday; he used Silas last week."

"They are in second still," Pete answered.

"Then we leave Thursday for a four-day road trip." Kade continued.

He was still terse with his words but at least he didn't seem angry in his manner.

"Sarah has decided to throw them a party a week from Monday so keep your calendar open," Pete said as he opened his truck door. He turned with a cocky grin.

"Very funny, Smart Ass," I huffed with a smile. "I'll try to pencil it in."

I heard him chuckle as the door closed.

I looked at Kade to see that blank look on his face. He nodded to me and then his eyes went to the mirror to back down the driveway. I turned back into the barn.

I was up late watching over Dexter then up early to check on him. His sides were covered with the bedding so I knew he had been lying down but he was up eating hay when I arrived with halter in hand. I set my phone on a table at the end of the aisle and walked Dexter back and forth as the phone recorded it. There was barely a limp.

I sent the video to Pete and Ryle.

Text from Ryle: Thanks, looks good. Barely awake…late night.

Text to Ryle: No hurry, I'll take care of him.

No response from Pete.

I walked out to the pasture to check on their other horses. They were out in the middle of the pasture grazing and didn't even lift a head when they saw me.

Silas and Warlock didn't look like they had been out celebrating their 3rd place win.

It was noon before the crew of team ropers and Sarah arrived.

Jess and Ryle were smiling through squinted eyes.

"Thanks for taking care of him," Ryle said as he stepped into Dexter's stall.

"Glad to do it." I placed the Beamer pads over his shoulder and down his back. The second it turned on Dexter's head lowered and his eyes closed. His lower lip began to quiver.

Ryle chuckled, "I think he likes it." He turned and grinned at me. "Thanks for being there this weekend and for this."

"You are quite welcome."

He saddled his young horse and worked him in the round pen. Jess was in the larger pen working his younger horse and the other three men and Sarah went for a ride.

It was a laid back day so I ordered pizza for them all and had it delivered. Slowly, throughout the day, it disappeared with not a piece left as they all went home for the night.

Monday morning as Kade, Jess, and Ryle left with the horses I followed them down the driveway and to my scheduled counseling session.

"You go to the rodeo?" Was the first thing she asked.

"Yes," I said and relaxed onto the sofa. "I went Friday night with some friends and stayed home and watched the live feed Saturday."

"Good," She seemed to be very pleased as she leaned back in her chair, slowly crossed her legs then leaned forward to me. "You look better today."

I was clean anyway.

"I'm going to ask you a very pointed question," She said with an intensity in her eyes that made my stomach ache. "I want you to answer with your first thought as quickly as you can."

"Alright," I said cautiously.

"On a scale of 1 to 10, 10 being highest…as for your bosses death at your party, where is your guilt level right now."

"10."

She leaned back in her chair and shook her head, "Have you talked to anyone about what happened?"

"A couple people."

"And what did they say?"

"One said it was completely my fault and the others said it wasn't."

"And the one that said it was your fault, do you trust this person?"

"With my life," I answered and realized that was the problem. Andrea was the only person that told me it was my fault and she was the only person that had always told me the truth.

"Could there be an underlying reason the person said it was your fault?"

"No, none at all."

"Lauren," She leaned forward again. "You did not swing that barbeque fork and stab your boss. His wife did. Therefore, it is all her fault."

I huffed, "Most people say it's his fault."

"There you go," She leaned back again. "It is not your fault. There is more to their backstory than what happened at the party. I'm sure she was devastated when she heard the recording played for everyone to hear, but that wasn't your fault either."

"If I hadn't…"

"Did you do it to hurt anyone?"

"No…just to be sure who it was."

"So you didn't record them for the wife to listen to so she would get mad and stab him?"

"No…"

"Did Greg play the recording to have her get mad and stab him?"

"No…it's not his fault. I told him that."

"Then why is it your fault if it's not his fault?" She leaned back again. "You only recorded it…you didn't play it in front of everyone."

I sat up straight and glared at her, "It's not Greg's fault."

"And it's not your fault." She glared back.

We stared at each other until I fell back against the cushions.

"1-10, where is your guilt level?"

I didn't answer this time. My eyes went back to the landscape pictures as my mind went to Andrea. If it wasn't my fault, why would she tell me it was?

We were quiet the rest of the session. I knew she was giving me time to process the conversation.

"I'll see you Thursday but you can call anytime when you want to talk."

I just nodded as I walked out the door.

The haze in my mind returned as I drove home. If it wasn't my fault then why did Andrea say it was? The last conversation with her played out in my memory as I turned off the highway and down the long driveway. Her angry glare… "I want nothing to do with you."

I topped the hill to my property and stopped. There was a car at the gate, pulled off just to the side as if they were waiting for me. My phone hadn't vibrated so they weren't close enough to set off the video system on the gate.

With my phone, I pulled up the video from the second camera that was hidden in the trees.

There were two people standing in front of the car. My stomach swirled and I had to force myself not to cry. Ethan and Molly Armstrong were in an animated conversation then their heads turned and looked up the hill where my truck was sitting.

As much as I wanted to turn around and drive away, I knew they deserved more. Their whole lives had changed because of what happened with their parents on my property. I slowly pushed on the pedal and drove toward them.

CHAPTER FIFTEEN

My stomach was in knots, tears threatening to escape, and my guilt level rising to 20.

I turned off the video on my phone as I neared their car. They walked to the side of the car as I pulled up alongside them. Neither of them looked like they wanted to be there either. So why were they?

"Lauren," Ethan said. He was seventeen to his sister's sixteen.

"Ethan, Molly…I'm…"

"No, don't say it," Molly huffed with glaring eyes. "Everyone is sorry but that doesn't do a fucking bit of good."

I took a deep breath.

"Is there…?" I started.

"NO!" Molly yelled. Her eyes filled with tears as her neck and cheeks turned red.

"Molly," Ethan placed a hand on her arm…she shook it off.

"What can I…?" My stomach ached so bad I thought I was going to throw up.

"Nothing," Ethan said with a tense but calm tone. "We had thought we wanted to see where it all happened but once we got here we realized it didn't matter. Dad is still dead and Mom is gone."

"And seeing your fucking place just makes it worse!" Molly cried out as the tears started falling.

I fought away the tears…they didn't need to see me crying when they were the ones hurting so much…so horribly so.

Molly turned into her brother's arms.

I didn't know what to do.

"We'll just go," Ethan said. "There really isn't anything that can be said or done because no one can turn back time."

I sat quietly and watched as he opened the door for his sister then walked around to the other side. Molly stared out the front window and did not acknowledge me again. Ethan nodded just before backing his car and turning it around.

I watched them in the rearview mirror until they disappeared over the hill then I drove through my gate.

I fell onto the couch and couldn't get myself to move. I thought I was passed this…I needed to be passed this but I couldn't get myself up.

I stared at the TV not seeing anything but visions from the party and Dave going to his knees. What was it going to be like going back to work? No matter what it was like for me, it didn't compare to those two kids having to take care of themselves. I had no idea if they had a family to take them in. Would they have to go to foster care?

When darkness descended, I pushed myself off the couch and drug my feet out the door and down to look at the kittens. Their eyes were almost open and they were moving around pretty well. The chicks' feathers were coming in and wouldn't need a heat lamp at night much longer. Dexter was fine…and the rest of the horses and steers were perfectly fine in their pastures.

I grabbed a spoonful of peanut butter and fell back onto the sofa. I woke to the sound of trucks driving by the house. Lying on my stomach, head buried in one of the pillows, I didn't move.

Five minutes later, I heard them talking outside the back patio door, then a tap on the door. I didn't move. I had no energy to go to the arena. I just wanted to lay there until I could figure out how to turn back time.

Another tap then nothing until a knock on the front door; I didn't move. My phone rang and I barely rose enough to push the answer button.

"I'm fine…just rope." I pushed the end button then fell back down with tired eyes staring at a man and woman talking on the television. The volume was down so I couldn't hear them.

There was silence until a head appeared in the window to the right of the television. It was Pete with his fingers covering his eyes…until the fingers slowly spread open enough to peep in the window. If I wasn't so tired I would have laughed.

He smiled at me then waved. I just stared.

His head disappeared only to be replaced by five heads. What a crew. They all stood there and looked at me with their lips moving as if in deep conversation…then they disappeared again.

There was a tap on the back door. I was just wondering if I locked it when I heard it open. It was behind the couch and on the other side of the kitchen and dining table so I couldn't see them.

"Good morning!" Marty's voice rang out. "Maybe you didn't notice we were here."

Couldn't they just give me a day?

"I did," I said to the television.

"Coming out?"

"No."

"OK, then…we're coming in."

"I'd rather…"

The thunder of cowboy boots drowned out my voice.

"You have breakfast yet?" Pete asked.

I didn't answer.

"What's with all the spoons in the sink?" Jess asked.

"Sorry…I didn't expect visitors so I didn't clean up." I mumbled.

"Spoons…with peanut butter," Pete said. "Is that all you've been eating?"

I didn't answer and felt the heat rise up my neck and into my cheeks.

"What's in the fridge?" Marty asked.

"Nothin' but eggs and milk…that's a start." Ryle answered. "But there's some steak in the freezer."

"Found some potatoes," Kade added.

It went silent as I heard them wandering around the kitchen. The microwave turned on…water…refrigerator opened and closed. I just gave up wishing they would go away and stared at the television.

"Hey, look at this," Jess whispered.

I had no idea what he was looking at. There were still a number of items in the cupboards and freezer that we decided not to make for the party.

I heard sizzling then the aroma of steak filled the house and my stomach rumbled.

"What ya watchin'?" Jess asked as he walked in and sat in the chair next to me.

"I don't know," I answered truthfully.

"I'll find something more interesting." He leaned over and grabbed the channel changer before I had a chance to say anything. Then he started clicking through the channels.

"Oh, sweet!" Jess turned excitedly and looked into the kitchen. "Blazin' Saddles is on."

"Love that movie," Kade answered as he walked in and sat in the loveseat on the other side of the room. Pete appeared and sat next to him; both had their legs stretched out comfortably and leaning on an arm as they watched. It was easy to tell they were related.

My eyes went to the movie. This was such a stupid movie. How could so many people like it? How did it become such a classic? Other than a few quotes…it was ridiculous.

"That horse reminds me of Silas," Kade said of the palomino that Cleavon Little was riding in the movie.

"He likes movies," Jess said. "He'd love this one."

There was silence except for the cooking in the kitchen.

I closed my eyes and tried to forget they were in the room. The food aroma made that pretty hard because my stomach kept rumbling.

"Breakfast is almost ready," Marty said from the kitchen…then there was a bit of a chuckle.

What was that about? I looked over at Pete and Kade. They were looking behind me with eyes crinkling in smiles.

I heard the door open then the echo of hoofbeats.

"You are not bringing that horse in my house!" I yelled from my lying position.

The hoofbeats drew closer and changed in tone as they moved from brick to wood.

"Ryle!" I yelled.

No answer just approaching hoofbeats.

"Damn it," I leaned up and looked over the back of the couch.

Silas was standing with his front hooves and shoulders in the house with his head high and he had the "what?" look on his face. I swear that horse would follow Ryle anywhere…after he was caught.

"Ryle…" I growled. "Do not bring that horse in here."

He grinned that happy grin that lit up his eyes…I could barely keep from breaking into a smile.

"But…he would love this movie." He whined through a grin. "It's a funny western."

"Not in my house," I repeated. I had no intentions of telling him it would not be the first time someone had brought a horse in the house.

"Fine," He sighed and backed the horse out the door. Marty shut the door behind him.

I fell back onto the couch and buried my face into the pillow. I had to admit they were doing a pretty good job of brightening my mood.

Within a minute, everyone was chuckling. I looked up to see Pete had opened the window next to the television and removed the screen while Kade turned the TV.

Ryle's head was peering through the window right next to Silas' which was all the way into his shoulders. The blonde horse was looking around at everyone then he turned and looked at the television.

"What in the wide, wide world of sports is going on here?" Marty quoted a movie line from the kitchen.

"See, I told you." Ryle grinned at me.

I shook my head and grinned back at him…how could I not? He was so freaking adorable, handsome, and just freaking funny.

The other four cowboys had their phones out and were taking pictures of the pair watching TV through the window.

"Damn team ropers," I grumbled and sat up.

"Breakfast is ready," Marty chuckled and walked back into the kitchen.

Although my stomach was rumbling, the thought of food made it ache. Steak, hash browns, and eggs were joined by biscuits and gravy and a large platter of brownies was waiting on the counter.

"I didn't even know I had brownie mix," I said as I slid onto my usual chair. Once down, Jess, Pete, and Kade joined me while Marty walked a plate to the window for Ryle.

We laughed as Silas' lips nabbed the biscuit off the plate before Ryle could react. He ate it then turned back for more.

"Damned horse," Ryle grinned.

Marty fed another biscuit to the horse and handed a couple to Ryle.

"If he ever gets loose, I'll just put biscuits in the window as a trap." I teased.

We laughed and settled down to watch the movie and eat.

I only managed to get a couple bites of eggs down before my stomach soured. I pushed the food around so they wouldn't notice then once they were all turned to the television I stood quickly.

"Thanks for breakfast," I said to Marty then began cleaning the dishes.

It was only 8:00 in the morning when the movie was over. Silas had watched for a while but once he began to get restless, Ryle put him in a stall and came to finish the movie next to me on the couch.

I wished I could enjoy this movie as much as they did…must be a guy movie…except I knew that Andrea and Jamie loved it too.

"Well…damn," Jess muttered.

My mind came out of the haze and I looked over at him.

"Silverado is next," He sighed.

I loved that movie and really enjoyed sitting in the living room with the crew. It had been almost two years since I'd had this much company…except for the party…which is why I had the damn party to start with…to get life back to normal. I sighed and closed my eyes.

"Who wants brownies?" Marty said loudly.

I opened my eyes and smiled at him since it was obvious he was interrupting my mood.

"I'll help." I stood and joined him in the kitchen.

The pan of brownies was cut in six chunks and I handed one to each cowboy. The brownies were all gone in less than two bites; except mine which was still sitting on the kitchen counter when I sat back down on the couch.

A half-hour after Silverado was over we were at the arena. I was going to be driving the 4-wheeler so they could take turns roping the dummy steer that was attached. The live steers would rest for the day.

I straddled the ATV as my phone rang.

Detective Malone…

Taking a deep breath I looked out at the men as they loped in circles…I would use them for strength.

"Hello?"

"Lauren?"

"Yes, Detective Malone."

"I was calling to let you know there was a lead on Sheila Armstrong's whereabouts."

Whereabouts? Who said that word besides the police?

"Have they found her?"

"No, but her cell phone was turned on and pinged on a tower."

"Where is she?"

"Chula Vista, California." He answered.

"Oh!" I gasped. "Wow…isn't that by the Mexican border?"

"Very close; looks like she went for the warmer border rather than the closer …but colder Canadian border."

"Do they know where she actually is to arrest her?"

"No, just that she is down there. We've alerted the border guards so they will be watching for her."

"Ok, then…" I had no idea what to say. I had no intentions of telling him that I had talked to her kids the day before.

"I just thought I would update you."

"I appreciate it. Thank you."

"Have a good day."

The call ended.

All five cowboys were on their horses and standing quietly watching me.

"Sheila Armstrong…the lady that stabbed her husband is down by the Mexican border," I explained.

The vision of Sheila swinging the barbeque fork at Dave played in my mind. The rush of blood that flew out…

"Lauren!"

My eyes jerked to Pete.

"Get that machine started and get moving." he said.

"Not too fast," Marty added.

"You don't want a speed challenge today?" I teased and my muscles relaxed again.

We played in the dirt until the sun was high in the sky and the heat became overwhelming for human and horse. The horses were bathed, watered, and let loose in the shade. The humans went back into the house to watch more movies.

"Let's go get loaded," Marty said and stood.

"You're leaving?" I asked in disappointment and stood from the couch. "I'm sure we can find another movie. I have some DVD's…"

"We don't have time," Pete said.

They walked out the back door.

"Oh…Ok," I sighed and followed them out to the porch.

Marty turned and looked at me with a raised brow, "You going to lock up the house?"

"What for?" I asked.

Kade, Jess, and Ryle were walking toward the barn, not their trucks.

"Where are you going?" I asked in surprise.

"To the jackpot," Pete said…as if he was reminding me about something he had told me about twenty times…instead of never.

"What jackpot?" I asked.

"Over in Star," Marty said. "Hurry up, we want to have time to warm up the horses."

I turned and looked at the door…the lock.

"Lauren, lock the damn door and let's go," Marty said and walked down the porch steps and across the patio.

I hesitated…looked back at the door…then back to Marty who was walking away.

"You have anything better to do?" Pete asked from the patio.

I looked at him…to the stained bricks behind him…then back to him.

I locked the door and followed him to his truck.

Kade, Jess, and Ryle sat in the back seat while I sat between Marty and Pete in the front.

"You said Star?" I asked as they drove out the property gate.

"Yes, you been there?" Marty asked.

"Lots of times," I sighed and thought of Jamie and Andrea. Barrel races and breakaway…yeah, we'd been there lots of times. "It's only 32 minutes away."

"You have it down to the minute?" Ryle chuckled.

I grinned, "Yes…Jamie was pulling one of her typical teenage drag your feet days and I kept telling her we were going to be late. She said we had plenty of time…thirty-five minutes to get there so we had plenty of time."

"She was off by three minutes?" Jess asked.

"She had no idea," I chuckled. "She just guessed to talk her way out of being in trouble." They all chuckled. "But we did time it on the way over."

"Thirty-two minutes," Ryle said.

"The last time we were there was for a lady's roping event." I smiled proudly. "She won the breakaway by beating me by two-tenths of a second."

"She's good," Pete said.

"She is," I nodded and thought of the last time I had seen her. I sighed heavily.

"Ryle and I came in third there last time," Jess said.

He told the story the rest of the way to the arena. I knew he was just trying to lift my mood again. These guys were really good at that.

On the far end of the building that held the arena, was an event center. There were dozens of vehicles in front of that area but we passed it and drove up to the top of the hill above the arena.

I stood at the back of the trailer as they unloaded and started saddling their horses.

"I'll see you inside," I said as they mounted.

Just to the left of the tall doors that led into the arena was a smaller door that led to the spectator area. It was just a large cement-floored area with no bleachers. I'd forgotten that part. There were a couple dozen people sitting at the few provided picnic tables and in chairs they had brought themselves.

I walked to the side and leaned against the wall. There were two little girls about 5 years old playing with a dozen little plastic horses in the dirt next to the arena fence. They reminded me of Jamie when she was little. She carried around a small galvanized bucket like a purse. It was always filled with plastic horses and cows.

"Lauren!"

I turned to see Pete in the arena on his roan horse. Marty was right behind him on his horse and he was leading Zeb, Jess's sorrel horse, who was saddled.

"What?" I looked between the two of them.

"Get on Zeb," Pete said.

My stomach clenched, "No."

"Lauren," Pete sighed. "You cannot even see the chute from there plus there is nowhere for you to sit."

"I'm OK…" I started.

"No, get your ass on that horse," Pete said with a glare. "Come over here and keep us company."

"I don't want to ride," I said firmly.

"You don't have to ride," Marty said. "You're just going to sit on him."

"Just like you would a chair," Pete added.

My uncle had said that to me the first time I had ever sat on a horse and the memory had me just staring at Pete as I thought of that fateful day.

"Lauren!" Pete growled and glared at me. "Get your damned ass onto that saddle and come over and enjoy the night with us."

"I…" I barely said.

"Lauren!" Marty growled this time. "Get over here."

I looked between the two of them then to Zeb. The memory of my uncle walking me around the parking lot of the old arena felt like it was just hours ago. I missed him.

I climbed the fence and slid onto the saddle and automatically tucked my feet into the stirrups. It felt natural but it didn't feel like home since it wasn't one of my horses. I reached for the reins in Marty's hands.

"No…you're just sitting there not riding a horse," Marty smirked and led me across the arena to the chutes as if I was a child.

"Damn, Marty," I chuckled and looked around me at the questions in people's eyes as they looked at us. "Let me have the reins."

"No," He said and stopped along the fence so we had a great view of the rider's coming out of the box and the wide arena to watch their run. "If you have the reins, you're riding and you don't want to ride a horse so you're just sitting on one."

Since I was in the spot that I intended to stay the rest of the night, I just shook my head with a chuckle, "Damn, team ropers."

I leaned back in the saddle and just relaxed as the jackpot began. For this jackpot, it was one chosen teammate and two drawn from a pot. Eight teams went through before any of our crew rode into the box. Kade and a guy I didn't know backed into the box and assumed the position. Kade's stocky bay horse stood absolutely still until the heeler was set then Kade nodded. They burst out of the box with lariats whizzing through the air. His throw was on the mark and the heeler caught one leg of the steer.

Kade was really handsome in his straw cowboy hat, bright red shirt, and the grin that he aimed at his grandfather. It's when he looked at me that his whole demeanor changed with eyes narrowing and his grin fading to a bit of a scowl.

"Well…they make it through to the second round anyway," Marty sighed then turned and looked at me thoughtfully. "You a header or a heeler?"

"Both," I answered automatically. I'd been asked that question thousands of times since I was twelve.

"What does your horse say about that?" Pete asked.

"He likes heading better," I answered.

"What's his name?" Marty asked.

"JW," I answered. "The big buckskin gelding in the north pasture. Bigger than a normal head horse but he is fast."

"You just a roper?" Marty asked.

I turned to him with a raised brow, "JUST a roper? Can anyone ever be JUST a roper?"

We all three chuckled.

"But no…I barrel race and JUST the roping includes breakaway." I answered.

"JW breakaway with you too?" Pete asked.

"I have with him but Marko, the big bay in the pasture is my main breakaway and my barrel horse is BlueDoc," I answered and since everyone always asked me why I told them, "We guessed he was going to be a blue roan and we had been watching Lonesome Dove. I've always liked the name Blue Duck but didn't want to name my horse after a psycho killer so he became Doc instead of Duck."

"Is he a blue roan?" Pete asked.

"Yes, it was either blue or red roan. He's out of Okanogan Blue from the Promised Land Ranch. He only sires roans." I chuckled. "I have a couple younger barrel horses but BlueDoc has been my main one for the last five years."

Kade walked up next to Pete with four of the small red and white checkered food vendor trays that each held a hamburger and a small bag of chips. After handing one to Pete then Marty he stepped next to me and looked up while holding the tray to me. There was no smile, warm greeting, or anything friendly. It was a bit of an impatient look…as if he was putting up with my presence because of the rest of the crew.

"No, thank you, I'm not hungry," I smiled politely but my eyes were on the hamburger. Andrea, Jamie and I always devoured the vendor burgers at competitions. We looked forward to them, they were usually quite delicious. The hamburger patty was larger than the bun and was thick and juicy…even the small part of the tomato I could see looked fresh and inviting.

"I'm not sure I believe that," He said blandly with his eyes narrowed slightly and his jaw tightening. "But, that's up to you. You can hold it so I can eat this one."

"Alright…" I took the small tray and balanced it on the saddle horn.

"Here go the boys," Marty said through a bite of his burger.

Jess and Ryle were standing next in line on their two younger horses, Gus and Casper.

"Casper will probably outrun the steer," Kade said and I looked down in time to see him take a huge bite of the really good looking hamburger. A small speck of ketchup remained on his lip and he wiped it off with his thumb.

My stomach rumbled and my mouth watered.

I turned away to look for Ryle and Jess. They were walking the horses into the arena and backing into the chute.

"First time out for Jess's gelding," Pete said.

I turned to him as he took a bite of burger…his lips were shiny from the hamburger grease. He wiped it away with the back of his hand.

My stomach rumbled again as I looked down at the small tray I was holding. The golden bun…fresh tomato…green fresh lettuce…and that juicy burger…the aroma was calling out to my stomach.

The sound of the chute opening brought me out of my food haze to see Jess and Ryle bolt out of the box. Ryle had the horns captured and pulling the steer to the left when Jess' gray nearly ran over the steer…he managed to move the horse to the side as he leaned down to throw the rope and capture the back hooves. The gray stopped and backed up perfectly. Ryle's horse turned so they were facing each other and the flag dropped.

"Not bad," Pete said. "Just needs to control that overrun."

I didn't look at him because I had no doubt he would be taking another bite of the juicy aromatic hamburger.

I looked back down at the burger balancing on my saddle horn. Damn, it looked so good. It reminded me of Andrea, Jamie and I patiently waiting in line at the different races and rodeos for our first bite. I don't think we ever left a bite unbitten.

I could handle just one bite to quell the stomach rumbling.

So, I took one bite…the sweet ketchup…savory hamburger…the tender freshness of the tomato…heaven…my stomach rumbled for more…so I gave it one more…then another…and another. Then there was the little bag of chips that took about two bites and they were gone.

"Huh, I thought you weren't hungry?"

I turned to look down at Kade who was looking at the empty tray then up to me.

I smiled sheepishly through the last bite. "Sorry." I wiped away the delicious hamburger juice and salt from the chips left on my lips.

"Want something to wash it down?" He asked and took the empty tray from me.

"I can get it," I started to dismount when he shook his head.

"Stay there, I'll get it." He turned and walked away.

He returned with four bottles of water and handed them out then remounted his horse.

Jess appeared with another small tray but it was filled with chips and golden liquid nacho cheese.

"That looks healthy," I teased.

He grinned and held it out to me…one chip wouldn't hurt. The tangy sweet cheese and crisp salty chip had me looking back at him and he held the tray out again. The third time, he just handed me the tray and turned the horse and walked out the doors.

"Here's Ryle again," Pete said.

We turned to watch him make his run.

"That horse is turning pretty good for such a beginner," I said.

"Yep, looked good. That boy is good at training as well as riding." Marty nodded, handed my horse's reins to Pete then backed up his horse to walk to the chute.

Jess rode in with three more nacho trays. He handed one to Ryle as they both joined us at the fence. The third tray was handed to me.

"I don't know…" I said as I took the tray and devoured the first chip.

Jess grinned as he shoved a bundle of chips into his mouth with the cheese dripping down his whiskered chin.

"Gross," I wrinkled my nose at him as I shoved more chips in my mouth.

We finished the chips just as Marty made his run with someone I didn't know.

Ryle disappeared and returned with a hamburger and chips. He tossed the chips to me and I didn't hesitate to open them.

Pete handed Marty the reins to my horse when he went to make a run.

"I can handle my own reins," I told Marty.

"We discussed that," He said flatly then turned to Pete and the chute.

"Damn, team roper," I mumbled with a grin and turned to watch Pete run.

They were near the end of the arena before the steer was caught.

"Looks like all five of you are on to round two," I said turning to the crew. Ryle wasn't there.

After twenty minutes of watching ropers try their luck at a throw with Kade and Marty both running again, Ryle reappeared.

"Here," He handed me a paper bowl with a plastic fork stuck in the middle of a piece of chocolate frosting covered chocolate cake.

"Where did you get that?" I asked as my hands automatically took it from him. The delicate red frosting rose that decorated the top was the first thing in my mouth.

"Down at the event center," Ryle answered.

Jess looked at him then to me, "Where's mine?" He grumbled.

When he looked back at me, I grinned then opened my mouth and stuck out my tongue that was covered in red frosting.

"That's for the cheese chin," I said and we both chuckled.

"Some lady was having a party and bought too much cake and had a lot of food left over so she asked if I wanted some," Ryle explained.

Jess turned to me with a wicked grin, "He's so cute and adorable that old ladies can't help but give him things."

I laughed and looked at Ryle who was nodding his head with a roguish grin. "Including their phone numbers a couple of times." A devilish giggle escaped him.

I had no doubt about that.

"When do you rope next?" Jess asked him.

"Twenty out," Ryle said.

"Come on…I want some." Jess said then turned back to me just as I was shoveling a big bite into my mouth.

We both grinned.

"You want more?" Jess asked.

My brows came together in a thoughtful frown as my lips grimaced, "I don't know." I said but couldn't keep the guilty desire for more out of my eyes.

They both laughed and rode away to return with bowls of cake for all the crew. All hands were lifting forks full of cake when I glanced at Jess.

My cake was white this time with a blue flower on top. His cake was white with a yellow flower.

"You know," Jess said through a smirk. "If you were my girlfriend we could have a lot of fun making green frosting together."

I snorted…and it was loud enough it made heads turn toward me. I nearly choked on the cake as we both laughed.

"Damn," Pete turned in the saddle with wide eyes. "Can't take you anywhere!"

We all chuckled…except for Kade who was watching a run.

Jess's phone rang. He looked down at the screen then whirled around to Ryle, "It's Crystal!"

"Who is Crystal?" I whispered to Pete as Jess answered the phone with Ryle nudging his horse closer to him.

"Rodeo secretary…" He started to answer.

"Longfellow? Edie's daughter?" I nodded. "I know them…great ladies."

"I'm guessing Crystal is working Ogden or just watching," Pete said. "Jess' mother married into their family when he was sixteen."

"Hell, yeah!" Jess hollered and grinned at Ryle. "We won Ogden!"

Pure joy shone in their faces and the rest of the crew. Once all the congratulations were given I sat quietly on the horse and watched the roping with Ryle and Jess to my right. Their chatter had turned from celebratory to business. I listened as they calculated the money they had won at the Snake River Stampede and Ogden and how many entry fees and expenses it would cover for rodeos over the winter and into the spring.

Another half hour of talking and watching the crew take their turns in the arena and Ryle was coming back with more bowls of food.

"Now what?" I asked.

He handed me a bowl full of strawberries that had been dipped in milk chocolate and decorated with white icing.

"Oh, hell," I sighed as my hand went out. "I love those damn things."

Within seconds of the first bowl disappearing, Ryle handed me another.

"Stop," I gasped. "I can't eat anymore." I shoved another one in my mouth.

"Like you weren't hungry for that first hamburger," Kade drawled.

"Or that first and second tray of nachos," Jess said.

"Well, you didn't say you didn't want cake and strawberries," Ryle said with a cocky grin.

We chuckled as I caught a glimpse of a rider walking my way. She was on a sorrel horse with a wide blaze. I knew who it was just from that horse. Kim Grubbs, one of the best ropers in the state and was always my finest competition when I was team roping.

"Lauren?"

I took a deep breath and smiled warmly, "Hi, Kim."

"I couldn't believe it when I saw you." Her grin was wide and there was an honesty in her eyes that made my nerves relax. "Are you back to roping?"

"Just watching friends tonight," I answered.

She looked to my companions, "Marty? Pete?" She laughed with a shake of her head to me. "How in the world did you end up with this pair?"

"I didn't drive fast enough," I laughed with a teasing look at Pete. He just grinned and winked at me.

"Kim, it's good to see you," Marty stretched out a hand to shake hers.

Then she turned to Pete to shake his, "I was expecting to see you guys tonight but really happy you hauled Lauren with you."

"Thanks," I smiled and my whole body relaxed.

I missed people like her. The honest ones with a true happy heart that always hoped you did your best against her so she could beat you fair and square…or say she lost to the best roper that day. It was the same way I tried to be and how I raised Jamie.

We talked until it was her turn to make a run then she leaned forward to shake my hand. It was the first time she noticed that Marty was holding my reins.

She looked at me with a raised brow, "There's a story behind that."

"Yes, there is." I chuckled and grinned at Marty and Pete.

"Well," Kim said and backed her horse away from the fence. "You call me when you're ready to host another play day at your ranch and you can tell me that story over a burger and drink."

"Oh, those were fun days," The memories filled my heart.

"Yes, they were," Kim nodded. "Get your girl home from college and let's play."

She tipped her baseball cap to me and walked across the pen and into the heeler box with her husband across from her.

It was a perfect run…I wouldn't expect anything else from her.

There were three rounds for this jackpot and all of the crew made it to the last round; Pete and Marty together for one and Pete and Kade together for another. Ryle and Jess made it as a team then each made it with another roper.

"Twenty teams in the final round and we have five covered." Pete grinned at me. "You must be our good luck charm tonight."

I rolled my eyes, "I have a feeling you've done that before."

"Couple times," Marty answered.

"Hey, turn around," Ryle said from behind us.

I had to twist in the saddle to look at him while the others turned their horses.

Ryle handed another roper his phone then rode up next to us to complete the line.

"Let me get Lauren turned first," Marty said.

"Damn, Marty," I sighed but didn't reach for the reins. "At least hide them between us so you can't tell in the picture."

He chuckled and did as I asked as the six of us smiled at the camera.

Ryle went forward to check on the pictures and Marty walked a large circle around the pen to lead me around and back to the fence. Everyone, that was still remaining in the arena, was watching us by the time he was done.

"You just couldn't help yourself…now could you?" I teased Marty.

He gave me a guilty grin back then snickered.

By the end of the night, Ryle and Jess came in eighth on their young horses, and Kade and Pete came in third. Kim and her husband won the night. Everyone was happy as we rode out of the building…or as I was led out of the building.

With horses loaded into Marty's truck, we all six slid into the truck with Kade, Ryle, and Jess in the back and me in the front between Pete and Marty.

Two turns from the arena the road dipped down a long hill. The first rumble in my stomach started as Marty came to a halt at the stop sign at the base of the hill. He turned left and had barely picked up speed when the next grumble hit. I took an inconspicuous deep breath then it rumbled again which made me grimace.

This was not going to be good.

CHAPTER SIXTEEN

"You need to find somewhere to pull over," I said to Marty.

"We're just getting on the highway," he said.

"No…you need to stop now." A fine layer of moisture formed across the back of my neck and my stomach grumbled with a growing pressure trying to get out.

"Lauren, we just got started," Pete said. "We're only twenty minutes from your place."

"Stop, Marty…" I said with a deep breath and a tight bubble moving through my stomach.

"Well…I'll see…" He started.

The bubble was silently released.

"Never mind," I said softly with a sense of foreboding that came out as a low chuckle. "But you may want to roll down the windows."

"Why…." Pete stopped as his hand hit the window button. "It's not going down fast enough!" He chuckled.

Marty's window was making its way down too…as he coughed.

"What the hell are you doing?" Kade asked from the back seat.

"That's windy…" Ryle started then gasped. "Oh, holy hell…what the hell is that?"

I could hear the back windows winding their way down as all five men started gasping for air.

I started giggling.

"Damn, Grandad," Kade coughed.

"I didn't do it," Pete leaned his head out the window.

"Marty?" Ryle asked.

"Not me either," He answered and leaned his head toward the window.

I chuckled again as my stomach grumbled again. "You may want to find a spot to pull over," I warned him.

"Oh, hell, Lauren," Marty coughed.

"I need a window!" Ryle cried out as he was stuck between the other two men. "And I'm right behind it!"

"Marty…I'm warning you," I said with a grin as the bubble started to make its way around my stomach.

"MARTY!" The other four men cried out.

"I'm trying," Marty laughed. "But I can't stop this thing on a dime."

I grimaced but the bubble escaped for another silent release.

"Never mind…" I snickered.

"Son of a bitch!" Pete took his cowboy hat off and was nearly crawling out the window.

Marty started gasping.

"Not again!" Ryle called out. "I am fucking trapped!"

We all laughed and gasped…the wind from four open windows seemed to fight and swirl in the middle to hold the aroma in the vehicle.

Marty finally pulled over and the doors were opening before the truck was stopped. I was the last out of the truck with a sheepish, guilty grin. I should be embarrassed but I just found it funny.

"You ride next to a window the rest of the way," Pete said.

"Yeah, so you can hang your butt out of it for the next one," Ryle chuckled.

"I can ride in the back with the horses." I offered through a giggle.

"I'm not putting Casper through that," Jess said. "That would be too much trauma for his first big outing."

We all laughed.

"You done?" Marty asked me.

I dramatically covered my stomach with a hand then paused as if I was contemplating another release. "No bubbles," I chuckled.

"You sure?" Pete asked with a smirk.

"As of now, yes," I answered. "But we should probably get to my house sooner than later."

Within minutes we were on the road again with me in the front between Marty and Pete again and no one rolled up the windows…which I thought was funny and couldn't help the low giggles.

"Burger, nachos, cake and strawberries…" Jess said.

"Don't forget the chips," Ryle added.

"That's one hell of a combination of food to create that smell," Kade said.

We all chuckled again as I finally felt the growing heat of embarrassment…and another stomach grumble. Damn it!

Marty turned off the highway and down my long driveway.

"Marty…" I whispered.

"What the hell you whispering for?" Pete asked loudly. "More sneak attacks?"

I laughed and the pressure from the clenching of my stomach let another bubble out.

"Well, at least the windows are down this time," I covered my face with my hand to hide just how funny I thought it was.

"DAMN IT!" Ryle yelled from the back seat.

I just laughed…which created a few little and silent bubbles to escape.

Then the pressure changed as my stomach swirled, my skin moistened and my lungs constricted to hold the food down.

"Oh…hurry," I said and placed a hand over my mouth.

My eyes started to water as he came to a stop and typed in the code for the gate.

I needed to get him a transmitter so the gate would automatically open as he approached. I concentrated on that as he drove down the hill to the house.

"I will say goodbye right now," I gasped through a gag.

"Do not throw up in my truck," Marty said flatly…with absolutely no humor.

He stopped right next to the house with Pete opening the door before it stopped and jumping out.

He gave me a hand to brace against as I slid quickly out of the truck. I nodded with wide eyes…then ran to the house. It was all I could do to hold in the vomit as I typed in the code to the house then ran down to the nearest bathroom with my cowboy hat tossed onto the floor.

Two flushes later, I was unzipping my jeans as fast as I could as the food decided to come out the other way. My phone fell out of my pocket and rattled against the floor as I kicked off my boots then slid the jeans off and landed on the cold seat. The shirt was next so I was just in my bra with the panties at my ankles as I tried to cool off and let the sweat dry.

Well, I felt better, I thought as I slid the bathroom window open.

My phone beeped and I picked it up.

Text from Marty: How you doing? Need anything before we leave?

Text to Marty: DO NOT ENTER THIS HOUSE

My giggles erupted into laughter until tears ran down my face and my arms were wrapped around my stomach as I thought of the five ropers and poor Ryle yelling he was "fucking trapped".

Oh, Lord, I should be embarrassed and I probably would be in the morning but, damn, it was just funny.

I finally made it upstairs and into the bathroom in my bedroom for a long shower.

I opened the windows to the room incase more bubbles released during the night then fell onto the bed and curled under the covers.

As I stared at the ceiling, I realized I had run to the bathroom where Dave and Jodi had their sex romp and I hadn't even thought about it.

"Well, I have fumigated the bad spirits from the room," I said out loud. "And I've fumigated the team ropers."

I laughed.

CHAPTER SEVENTEEN

It was 7:30 when my eyes opened. I couldn't remember the last time I had slept so soundly and for so long.

I sat up to the sun streaming in the window and fresh air filling the room from the window I had opened before crawling into bed.

I took in a deep breath of the fresh morning air that was full of pine trees and moisture from the sprinklers that had turned on in the middle of the night.

My whole body and mind felt better so I slid out of bed and walked to the window that overlooked the property. Horses and cows were all grazing peacefully on the green pasture and under the clear blue sky. It was a beautiful fresh morning.

The type of morning all horseback riders dream of. My phone alerted me to a message.

Text from Ryle: It was the picture taken the night before of the six of us.

I laughed at the sight of us all looking happy…even Kade since he wasn't looking at me. He was on the end leaning toward to his grandfather.

I thought of the day before with these damn team ropers invading my morning and not letting me lie in a depression on the couch. They kept me busy all day and into the night. It was fun, just like the old days with my uncle. He would have enjoyed these men.

These men that reminded me of my uncle and his dream…and Kim reminding me of the play days…full days of riding and eating and drinking…laughter and memories.

I pulled my hair back into a ponytail as I looked out at the property; arenas, barns, bunkhouse, corrals, and pastures.

It was going to be another hot day so I slid on a tank top. I was zipping up my jeans when I heard the trucks arriving.

I picked up my phone, looked at the picture of the six of us again, then out to the property. Memories and dreams swirled in my mind before I turned away.

I sent the picture to Jamie to let her know life was coming back.

They were walking toward the pastures when I stepped out of the house. My eyes went to the blood stains in the bricks and a twinge hit my heart but I pushed it away.

"How are you feeling this morning?" Pete asked as I approached. His light blue shirt today must have been as old as him.

"Much better!" I gave them all a guilty grin. "I should say I'm sorry but you guys fed me."

"I didn't," Marty and Pete said at the same time.

"And we got the worst of it," Marty added.

We all laughed then I turned to the youngest pair.

"Jess…Ryle?" Deep inside me, I knew this was the right thing.

"Yeah?" They asked in unison.

"I'd like to talk to you," I said and turned to walk toward the house. Ten steps I turned to see all five still standing and watching me. "…in the house."

"Really?" Jess said with brows together in confusion.

"Alright…" Ryle looked at him nervously.

"You leaving us out, Princess?" Marty asked.

I chuckled, "Princess? If anything, I'd go for Empress."

Marty and Pete laughed while the other three were looking at me curiously.

"You can all come in," I turned back to the house and left the door open as I walked in.

I walked down the hall to the back of the house with a thunder of boots behind me.

"We going to his room?" Ryle whispered.

I smiled. My uncle did that to people even when he was alive.

I opened the door and walked to the middle of the room and turned back to the group. All their eyes were wandering over the trophies, photographs, saddles, and the multitude of gold buckles.

I gave them a few moments to absorb the room before I spoke.

"I was very impressed with your rides at the rodeo and your composure Saturday night," I said to the two younger cowboys.

They both turned to me with a proud smile.

"You two are completely serious about rodeo? It's not just a part-time thing?" I asked and looked between the two of them.

"Oh, hell yeah," Ryle nodded. His eyes grew wide and I could see the excitement building in him. "We're saving everything we got to make a run for the finals next year."

I turned to Jess.

"Lauren, we're giving it everything we got," He added. "The savings account is growing and our horses are coming together nicely. We're going to do it."

I looked both in the eye then looked around the room at everything I had of my uncles.

"Use this room to inspire you," I said. "Anytime you want, you come in here and take in all that this represents; the hours…thousands and thousands of hours of practice, traveling, and sacrifice to make it this far."

They both looked around the room again and I could see the dreams come alive in their eyes.

"And if you both want, you can live in the bunkhouse and use this place as your training center."

Jess gasped and Ryle stared at me with jaw dropped, eyes wide and beginning to glisten.

"You can't make it to the Thomas & Mack without people who believe in you and support you any way they can." I continued. "I've seen you practice. I've seen you deal with the good and the bad and take both as a learning lesson to get better."

"Yeah…" Jess exhaled softly.

"I believe in you and so do the three men behind you," I said and looked between both of them. "So, I offer Uncle Austin's training facility as yours."

Ryle's chin began to quiver as the tears finally fell.

Jess stared until his eyes began to glisten too.

I looked back at Pete, Marty, and Kade. They were staring too with moist eyes so I turned back to Ryle and Jess.

"You have the rooms for free as long as they are treated with respect and kept clean. Horse pasture and stalls just as you have now. You can put some conditioning miles on the horses by helping with the fencing when needed, then putting the hay in the barn and anything else that might come up."

"Yes…absolutely." Jess nodded.

Ryle was just staring at me in open awe.

I smiled at both of them and took a deep breath as the reality of what I was doing began to set it.

"You stand on the floors a world champion stood. You walk the path to the barn a world champion walked. You ride on the dirt a world champion rode." Tears began to rise in my eyes. "Take his path…ride with the knowledge that he would have wanted you here too."

Ryle's lips rolled tightly; it was all he could do to keep from sobbing. Jess was staring at the ground and shaking his head.

"Do you accept?" I asked.

"YES!" They both shouted and Ryle began taking deep breathes to control himself.

"Well, you haven't seen the inside of the bunkhouse yet, so let's go look," I said and walked past all five without looking any of them in the eyes. My own tears were battling to get out. I had finally begun to rebuild my life and the life of the ranch…this was the beginning of rebuilding my uncle's dream that I had left behind.

The thunder of cowboy boots followed me back out of the house, across the patio, and to the bunkhouse.

There were three steps up to a wide porch that ran the full length of the front of the building. A few wood chairs and benches set across it. The building itself was made of a rough cut pine to give it the rustic feel. The main door had a keypad lock just like the house.

I told them the code as I tapped it in then opened the door.

"I have a lady come in once a week to sweep, dust, and vacuum the building so it's clean," I said.

"Here and the house?" Ryle asked.

"You don't do it?" Marty asked.

"No," I smiled. "I don't want to be in the house cleaning dust, I want to be in the arena creating it."

They all nodded and chuckled as we walked in.

"Just inside is a large common area so anyone living here could meet without having to talk in their bedrooms." I swept an arm across the room that held four leather recliners and two long sofas, a dining table for a dozen people, and the chairs that matched. A large TV hung from the wall and a small kitchenette set in the far corner. "The floors are real wood from an old barn that used to sit on the property."

"Those are cool," Jess exhaled softly.

"Back here," I walked down the hall. "There is one large room that has 4 bunk beds to hold 8 people. They were originally built for the kids but there was a cowboy or cowgirl that landed on them too." I could still remember the cowboys and cowgirls sprawled out sleeping…which some people would consider passed out. "Farther down the hall we have four individual rooms that aren't very big but not much was needed since the common room had the mini-kitchen and sitting area." I pushed a door open and the men pushed against each other to see into the room.

"That's bigger than my apartment." Ryle chuckled.

A large king size bed and a dresser ran along the wall. Each had their own private bathroom that had a shower, toilet, sink, and storage cabinet; no tubs.

"Each room is decorated in a different color," I said. "We would have cowboys call before an event out here and ask for the different color room."

"Who has been here?" Kade asked.

I turned and smiled at him then around to the other four men. "Just about every roper that has roped at the

Snake River Stampede while Uncle Austin was alive and a few rough stock riders. They would come here to play and practice before and after the rodeo. Some stayed here instead of the rodeo grounds."

"Damn…" Jess' eyes were wide.

"There is another large room in the back that has a treadmill and some fitness equipment," I said and pointed down the hall. "Not up to date but it still works. Uncle Austin believed in being as fit as he expected his horses to be."

They all nodded in agreement.

"Pick your room," I grinned at Jess and Ryle.

My new tenants walked through each room while the rest of us gathered in the common room. We didn't really talk, we just waited, but Pete patted me on the shoulder with a wide proud grin. It made my heart warm and it confirmed again that I was doing the right thing.

"When can we move in?" Jess asked as they walked back down the hall.

"Anytime you want," I answered.

He turned to Ryle, "We leave tomorrow for four days."

"Want to do it now?" Ryle asked.

They both turned to me.

"I'm fine with that," I smiled with the excitement building in me as much as I could see it building in them.

They turned to the other three men.

"Load up and let's go get your stuff," Marty grinned.

"Let's unload the horses then we'll have three trucks and the horse trailer," Kade said.

"We can make it in one trip then," Ryle nodded and started to walk out the door.

He turned and nearly ran back and threw his arms around me.

I laughed and hugged him back.

He stepped back with a bit of an embarrassed chuckle and Jess' arms wrapped around me.

"Don't squeeze her too hard," Pete chuckled. "There may be more bubbles from last night."

I slapped him on the arm but laughed right along with them.

My phone alert went off as I shut the door to the bunkhouse.

Text from Jamie: Your latest conquests?

Now why in the hell would she think I was sleeping with any of them? The only man I had ever been with was her father.

"Lauren?" Pete said from next to me.

I looked up with a frown.

"You going with?" He asked.

I looked up at the four men walking horses out of the trailer.

"No, I'll run to the store and buy them something for the refrigerator," I said then looked down at the phone…to her message. What the hell? Should I just ask her or just let it be?

"Well, I can be more helpful in a grocery store than carrying anything," Pete said.

The thought of shopping with him brought a smile to my face so I deleted her message and shoved the phone in my pocket.

By the time the two had settled into the bunkhouse and their refrigerator and cupboards were full, it was too hot to ride so we watched a movie in their new home. Kade had left for a meeting so the rest of us settled in for the movie and Jess making dinner.

He served everyone a bowl of spaghetti with an abundance of garlic bread then stopped next to the couch I was sitting on. His eyes narrowed and nose crinkled in a silent question.

"Oh, just sit down," I chuckled. "I'm past that."

"You passed a lot last night," Ryle chuckled then sucked in a noodle as his eyes twinkled mischievously.

We were all chuckling when Kade walked in the door.

"Dude…don't you know how to knock?" Ryle teased.

"On the bedroom door, because you never know what you'll see," Kade smirked as he walked to the kitchen to fill a bowl full of noodles then piled slices of garlic bread on top of it.

Jess and I sat next to each other with our feet up on the coffee table and devoured the noodles.

"Good job," I told him. "This is delicious."

"My mom is Italian, raised in Italy." He said. "She taught me how to cook pasta."

"Really?" I smiled. "You know Italian?"

"Sei una bella signora gentile," He smiled.

"Oooh," I gasped. "That sounds sexy. What did you say?"

"You are a mean woman." He grinned.

I laughed and slapped him on the chest, "I know bella is beautiful and signora must be woman."

"So…you think I'm saying you're beautiful?" His brow raised. "That's a little conceited isn't it?"

I laughed and elbowed him playfully.

"What's the temp outside?" Pete asked.

Four people picked up phones to look…none were Pete and Marty and we all grinned.

"Finally down in the double digits," Kade said. "Ninety-three when I came in; looks like it's down to 89."

"Finally," Pete said and stood.

A half hour later, they were saddled and I was on the ATV pulling the roping sled.

CHAPTER EIGHTEEN

"So, what are you going to name the baby?"

I turned to my uncle as I slid a hand over my enlarged abdomen.

"Well, Austin James Conners," I smiled. "Boy is James or girl is Jamie."

He grinned with a proud light in his eyes as he threw the saddle onto the horse's back, "And Blake is alright with that?"

I shrugged slightly, letting him know I didn't really give my husband a say in the name. "He understands how important that is to me and we compromised."

He crossed his arms over the side of the saddle and looked at me thoughtfully, "He gets to name the second one?"

"Yes," I gave him a sideways look…showing my guilt. He knew me well.

He chuckled, "You didn't exactly tell him you only wanted one baby."

I glanced around the people and horses by the new barn, in the new arena and back in the new corrals, then over to the new house construction which had at least six people wandering around it. It had another month to go before we would move in. Currently, we were sleeping in the living quarters horse trailers parked next to the barn. It reminded my uncle and me of our early days together. Needless to say, my husband didn't really appreciate the history and wanted to stay at a hotel until the house was complete. Of course, he wanted my uncle to pay for it. I said no, which meant the trailers.

No one was close enough to hear us so I turned back to my uncle.

"I've told him before…when we first got engaged. I was very clear on that." I shrugged again. "It's not my fault he forgot or thinks he can change my mind."

"You may change your mind."

"No, I won't."

"Lauren," He said softly. "You'll always be taken care of…you and that baby. You have me and Andrea…you're not alone."

Tears rose from the tenderness in his voice.

"You can have more than one child, we'll be here for you." He continued.

"I don't want more than one," I battled the tears.

"You are four years older than your mother was when she had you, and you have us…and Blake. You're not alone like she was."

I took a deep breath and shook my head, "No…that's not the reason…"

His eyes told me he knew I was lying…more to myself than to him.

I massaged my hand over the baby, "I've never been around babies…except Greg and Jodi's. She promised to help me, too."

"Good, she's always been a great mom."

"She is," I conceded. "But that doesn't change my mind. I only want one child. How many do you want?"

"Well, I once answered that question by saying I wanted three or four boys to rope with," He answered with a growing smile. "But, now, after you, I can now say I want three or four kids, boys or girls to rope with."

My heart warmed as we grinned at each other…memories of days of roping in the past and a bright future ahead of us.

"You have three or four too and we'll have a rodeo of our own here." He said.

"I only want one," I repeated.

He flipped the stirrup over the saddle horn then lowered to grab the cinch. "You have always done things your way and been strong-willed about it."

"Is that a bad thing?" I asked with a raised concerned brow. How he thought of me meant everything to me.

"No," He answered. "But you must be honest and compromise…but stay focused on what you want.

"I was honest. I told him I only wanted one child. I did compromise. If the unthinkable happens and I get pregnant again then he can name the baby. And! I am staying focused on what I want…which is naming this baby after you." I gave him a cocky, smart-ass grin.

He just laughed and tightened the cinch.

"I also compromised by not riding anymore," I reminded him.

"We both told you to stop." He said with a pointed look.

"Yes, so I compromised with both of you…I will stop riding but not roping." Another smartass grin was shot his way.

"Like I said…" He matched my smartass grin with his own. "Strong willed."

"I'm not going to be walked over," I countered. "You would want me to be a pushover?"

He stepped up into the saddle and adjusted his reins then leaned his arms on the saddle horn as he looked down at me. His dark eyes were serious.

"Don't let anyone walk all over you," He ordered. "One of the best ways to do that is to make sure you hold the cards and know the answers so you can stick up for yourself, your daughter, and this place." His eyes rose toward the road and I turned to see Andrea driving toward us. He looked back down at me. "There are times that will arise that you aren't sure what to do."

"What does that mean?"

"When you doubt decisions you've made that affect those you love…your daughter."

"…and you."

He smiled warmly. "And I do when it comes to you." His eyes rose to Andrea as she closed her car door.

"Good morning!" She waved; her smile beaming with happiness as she walked to us. "It's been 48 hours since I've seen you and you look like you've grown two inches in diameter." She laughed and her hand slid across my stomach.

"Thanks," I huffed. "This will be the only time in my life I will let you get away with that statement."

We all three laughed and he turned his horse toward the arena.

Andrea and I watched him walk away.

"I still hear grumblings about you two finishing the barn and arena before getting the house done." Andrea turned to me.

"I don't care," I said honestly. "Blake can grumble all he wants. It's not like he isn't taking advantage of that too."

He was currently galloping down the middle of the arena throwing a loop at a steer.

Andrea turned to me with a concerned look, "You're married…you're supposed to care."

I chuckled, "I do care about him…very much. I love him but sometimes he…well…"

"What?"

"He just gets jealous," I finally said. "I'm eight months pregnant and show every day of that, and yet he still gets jealous when a man talks to me. I love HIM. He should understand that."

"Men have been in your world since you were twelve because of roping." She nodded and watched him lope back across the arena while coiling his rope. "It's not going to change."

"You're right," I nodded and ran a hand over my baby. "He will just have to understand that it IS part of my life and will be with this baby…boy or girl."

We stood quietly and watched the men ride and chase steer until Andrea turned to the house.

"Good things will happen here," She whispered.

"Dreams…" I agreed.

Six years later we stood in the same spot watching the mass of cars and trucks slowly make their way out of the driveway and down the road. I stood with my uncle's one-year-old son, Ace, tucked into my shoulder and my daughter standing next to me with her arms wrapped around my right thigh; her eyes battling to stay open. Andrea stood to my right with my uncle's two-year-old, Taylor, sleeping in her arms. Charlene was to my left in a strong embrace with Barry Wilder, Uncle Austin's last team roping partner and longtime friend.

Charlene stepped back and looked up into his very sad eyes.

"Have you talked to them yet?" She asked.

"Yeah," He nodded with a deep sigh. "Walt Rosewood was the 16th header in the standings so he is moved up to 15th."

"He's good," I said. "Are you going to head with him or another qualifier?"

"I talked to Walt this morning. We'll meet up next week and start working together." He answered then glanced to his truck where his wife was patiently waiting for him. "Right now? I just don't even want…" Tears shook his voice.

"You will, Barry," Charlene said forcefully. "You will be there for him. Win or lose, you will be there for him…ride for him." Her voice quivered. "I don't care if you miss every damn throw or if you don't even throw but you just be in that arena."

"It's just raw right now," My voice shook when I spoke and my arm tightened around Ace. "You ride for all of us."

The tears fell down his cheeks and the back of his hand wiped them away. He nodded and turned.

There was no moving on for the next six weeks as requests for interviews and tributes were filmed in preparation for the rodeo.

The rodeo's tribute to him ran right before the team roping commenced. The entire arena was silent as Barry rode into the heeler box. Walt hesitated outside of the header box then after a deep breath rode in and backed himself into the corner. He looked at Barry. The close-up on the large video screen showed Barry's face. Tears glimmered in his eyes and his chin quivered. Twenty years he and my uncle had been friends. He had been in the arena the day my mother had abandoned me. They had also won the world championship together the year before.

Barry turned and looked at Walt. The men shared a silent thought and Walt looked down at the man holding the lever and he nodded.

The steer was released from the chute and neither man made a move to follow. That steer was my uncles.

Charlene, Andrea and I stood; the large monitor showing the tears running down our cheeks. The crowd rose to their feet and applauded as the men walked out of the boxes and across the arena to the gate.

The second night of the ten, Walt caught the horns but Barry couldn't get himself to throw. It was the third night that he was finally able to collect himself to make a good run; 10.4 it was well outside of the leaders.

On the last night, the two men ran the winning run. They won the gold buckles for the night to another standing ovation.

It was a very long two weeks in Las Vegas for the rodeo and we arrived home in time to check on the horses then I put Jamie to bed. She was happy to be home in her own room and fell asleep quickly.

Alone, I walked out of the house and across the quiet property to the barn then pushed both the double doors open. The sound of my boots hitting brick echoed as I walked into the barn. It was dark and silent except for the occasional scuff of a horse's hoof.

My heart had been on hold since my uncle's death but standing there alone knowing he would never walk out of a stall, step into the saddle, or smile at me with unwavering love and support…how could that happen?

"Uncle Austin?" I had cried out and the question returned in a hollow echo. My chin quivered, tears rose, and my heart trembled. "How could you be taken from me?" Another echo in return. "How is that fair? How is that right?" I cried out in an angry sob.

I stood in the middle of the barn as the reality, finality swarmed through me making my body shake. I fell to my knees and screamed my goodbye. "I love you."

My world was never the same.

My eyes opened to the first light of dawn filtering into the windows. My body felt heavy as if someone had sat on me all night. It was a struggle to sit up just as it had the night after coming home from Vegas.

It took all my strength to force myself out of bed and walk to that bedroom window and look out at the property. My heart hurt. Moving on had not been easy but I had Jamie, Andrea, and Blake helping me through.

My eyes dropped to the patio…to the stained bricks and I thought of Ethan and Molly. How were they going to move on? Their father dead and their mother on the run?

I just hoped they had a family to help them through.

I knew that I wouldn't move on as long as the stains were there so I turned from the window. In a loose t-shirt and yoga-pants I marched down the stairs and out the door. I stepped onto the patio and stared at Dave's blood stain. The vision of Sheila spinning with the barbeque fork in her hand and the shock of Dave's gasp played in my mind. So much blood covered him, the ground, and my co-workers as they tried to stop it…I had to get rid of the stains.

The hose was coiled at the side of the yard so I drug it over and attached a spray nozzle to the end then turned it on. I walked around the stained bricks to the bottle of cleaner that was still sitting on the grill then pointed the hose nozzle to the bricks in one hand and the cleaner bottle in the other. Both triggers ready to go but I couldn't get myself to squeeze.

"That's it…yeah…there we go…" Dave's voice through the bathroom door.

"Yes…yes…" Jodi's voice panted.

"Because it's all your fucking fault." Andrea, my best friend for over 30 years. "Because it's all your fucking fault."

Those words repeated over and over in my head until the pressure began to build behind my eyes. My hands trembled but wouldn't squeeze the triggers.

"Because it's all your fucking fault."

"Yes," I whispered and felt the tears rise.

The blood on the bricks was my fault. The memories continued with Mark and Nadine trying to stop the blood from pouring out of his chest…the medics running across the yard as the police moved people back.

How did Dave survive so long with all that blood on the ground, soaked into towels, and on Mark and Nadine?

As if they were standing in front of me, I could see the faces of my co-workers…staring…lost…traumatized. Because I recorded that damn door, they would never be the same.

A tear fell and I used my shoulder to wipe it away.

"Just pull the damn trigger," I whispered harshly.

Still, my fingers were frozen.

"Because it's all your fucking fault." Andrea had said. The angry look on her face made my breath shake.

Greg, Jodi, Stan, my co-workers changed forever. Sheila was on the run in Mexico and their kids…Molly and Ethan…forever without their parents.

More tears fell and I could feel the sob rising then escaping.

"Lauren?"

CHAPTER NINETEEN

My eyes slowly moved to Jess standing at the end of the patio. His eyes looked confused and concerned.

"Are you OK?" He whispered.

I just nodded and wiped another tear away.

"Can I help?"

"No…" I whispered and looked back down at the stain. "I have to do it."

"Do what?"

"Clean Dave's blood off the bricks." I pointed to them with the tip of the bottle and hose.

"Why?"

I looked up at him, "Why what?"

"Why do YOU have to do it?"

"Because…because it was my fault." I stammered.

"After we left here the first day, I read all the papers and watched the news," He admitted. "There was nothing there that said it was your fault. You didn't stab him."

My breath quivered as I took a deep breath to try and stop the tears.

"His wife did it. It's her fault," Jess continued. "Actually…I think it's all his fault. What the hell was he thinking to bring his wife to a party where his girlfriend was?"

"I don't know." I sniffed. "It was so stupid."

"Stupid is one word to describe it." He nodded then turned to look at the bricks. "I still don't see why YOU have to clean it." He turned back to me. "Let me have the cleaner and I'll get the bricks sprayed…get it soaking."

Without much thought, my hand moved to him.

He took the bottle and knelt down to spray the cleaner until the stains were covered.

"We'll let that soak a few minutes," Jess stood and looked back at me. "Ryle is making breakfast. He wanted to know if you could join us."

"What?" How did he go from bloody bricks to breakfast?

"We have four rodeos in the next three days. We thought we would start with a breakfast with our new landlady."

"Oh," I looked out at the bunkhouse then down to the bricks.

"We'll get those cleaned first." His hand rose toward me. "Let me have the hose."

My grip tightened on the nozzle making the water shoot out and hit the ground between us. We both jumped.

"Here…" He said softly and his hand slid over the top of mine as he stepped behind me. He pointed the nozzle to the bricks. "We can do this together."

His fingers tightened around mine making the water go off again. It splattered against the brick as it washed away the cleaner and blood. My mind went to Officer Mullins spraying the fresh blood off of the brick and grass. I flinched and stepped back but bumped into Jess' chest. His hand continued to spray as his other arm slid around my waist to hold me as my body began to shake.

So much blood...

"It wasn't your fault, it was his," Jess whispered to me. "We'll get this clean and you can move on."

It was if he had punched me in the stomach. My body convulsed forward as the tears rose through me in a tornado of emotions; guilt, anger, sadness, helplessness, and loss.   I began to sob.

The hose was dropped and he roughly turned me into his chest and wrapped his arms around me as I cried.

"Let it all out," He whispered. "Get it out...release it...clean your heart then you move on."

The sobs wracked my body but he held on, his arms tightening as he spoke.

"It's OK," He whispered and I felt his chin tuck into me and his arms tighten that little bit more.

I don't know how long I cried but when they began to ease I began to gasp for breath.

"You're OK," He said and released me just enough he could look down at me. "Just take deep calming breaths...with me..."

His chest rose as he took in the breath and I concentrated on it…matched his breathing to get mine under control.

My shoulders relaxed, lungs eased and body became calm again.

"There," Jess took a step back and looked down at me. "We let that go so now I'm just going to get rid of this."

Without hesitation, he picked up the hose and finished washing the cleaner off the bricks.

Although they were wet, it was easy to tell the stain was now gone.

My heart…my soul sighed and I closed my eyes to release the emotions and tension and the trembling stopped. The stains were in the past…I could move on.

Another quick cleansing breath and I wiped away the tears as my eyes opened.

Jess was coiling the hose as he walked it back to the side of the yard. He smiled a sweet understanding smile at me as he returned and picked up the bottle of cleaner and walked it to the outside garbage can. After tossing it in and closing the lid he returned to my side.

"Now, let's sit for a few minutes," He said it as if nothing had happened. "I have something to ask you."

"Breakfast? Yes…" I slid onto one of the patio chairs at the table and smiled at him.

"Well,…that's from Ryle…me too but not what I want to ask."

"Alright," I said tentatively.

He sat in the chair next to me and leaned his elbows on the table and looked at me. "If you would say yes…I would like to take you out for dinner."

I gasped in surprise, "Like a date?"

"Yes, a date."

"Jess," How was I supposed to turn him down after what he just did for me?

He leaned back in the chair and watched me a moment before his shoulders slumped. "You're trying to figure out how to say no."

"Oh, Jess," I sighed with an apologetic smile. "You don't want to date me. I'm too old for you."

"You're what? Thirty-five…six? I'm twenty-eight, that's not too old."

I chuckled and shook my head, "I have a 21-year-old daughter, that would have made me 13."

"Oh," He grinned. "But that doesn't mean…"

"Jess," I slid a hand over his. "You need to find a young lady that will love you and grow with you. Have kids…I'm not having anymore and you need that experience…that life."

He took in a deep breath and sighed, "Well…I guess if you had to say no."

"Thank you though," I grinned. "I'm very flattered you wanted to, but we're at different stages in life and you need that young love, babies, and growing together."

He nodded with another sigh. "It seems like everyone I grew up with is married and having kids. Here I am playing with horses and growing old alone."

I laughed and any tension left in my body dissolved.

"You're only 28! Besides, Ryle and I will be here with you so you won't be alone while you're waiting for your sweetheart to come along."

"That's comforting," He rolled his eyes with a chuckle.

I laughed again as the door to the bunkhouse opened; Ryle appeared carrying a box.

"Good morning!" He called out with a big innocent grin.

"Yes, it is," I smiled at Jess, silently thanking him again for helping me through my meltdown.

"I have pancakes and eggs…because that's basically all I know how to cook," Ryle laughed as he set the box down on the table.

"I'm the cook in the partnership," Jess added as he helped take plates and silverware out of the box. "If it was left up to him, we'd have cereal morning, noon, and night."

"We still do sometimes anyway," Ryle chuckled.

"I can cook, I would just rather be outside," I said as I flipped a pancake onto my plate.

Five minutes of slathering butter and pouring syrup then eating and Jess leaned back with a satisfied grin.

"Can I ask you something?" He asked.

"Sure," I answered and pushed my empty plate away.

"The brand on the gate and over the big doors of the stable is a circle with 3.3 in it. What does that stand for?" He asked.

I had been asked that question a thousand times and I loved telling the story…it always warmed my heart.

"The first time Uncle Austin and I roped together, we ran a 3.3," I answered.

"Only Masters and Corkill have run that at the NFR in 2009 and Kaleb Driggers and Junior Nogueira in 2017," Ryle huffed.

"True, but our run was years before theirs," I conceded with a smile. "When we ran together for the first time, he was showing me how to team rope and we used imaginary ropes, horses, and steer. When you dream, you best be dreaming of beating that world record."

"So, by naming it the 3.3 he was always dreaming of breaking that record," Ryle said with a bit of awe in his voice.

"Exactly," I said proudly. "This place was built for dreams and the dreamers."

"Well," Ryle said. "I can honestly say, I will never look at that brand the same again."

"Me either," Jess nodded. "Or this place."

"If every time you enter the box and you're looking to capture that magic moment of a 3.3 then you're always competing and reaching for that dream. It doesn't matter what anyone else does. Always shoot for the 3.3." I smiled at the pair. "That's my uncle's words said to me a thousand times and that's what led him to the world title."

"That's awesome," Ryle said seconds before his last bite of pancake was shoveled into his mouth. "My turn for a question." He said around the food making Jess and I grimace.

"Finish swallowing first," I chuckled.

He nodded and we waited until he dramatically swallowed the bite.

"Why do you always call him Uncle Austin instead of just Austin? Ryle asked.

"Hmmm," I leaned forward to rest my arms on the table. "I guess you don't know of my past."

"No," They both answered and their expressions turned serious.

"Well," I began. "When I was three, my father, Uncle Austin's brother, abandoned my mother and I. Then, when I was twelve, my mother took me to an arena where Uncle Austin was practicing with some friends and she left me there."

"She left?" Ryle gasped. "As in didn't come back?"

"No, I've never seen her since," I answered.

"Is she still alive?" Jess asked.

I just shrugged.

"Are they both still alive?" Ryle asked.

"I honestly have no idea," I answered. "After about a week with Uncle Austin I began to wonder…then we went to the first rodeo of the summer and I never looked back."

"You never looked for her?" Jess asked.

I shook my head, "No, I figured she left for her own reasons and she had the decency to leave me with a family member instead of at a hotel or gas station then I'd just leave her be. I didn't need her…or my father. I had Uncle Austin."

They both sat silent for a moment then Ryle spoke, "So, why do you still call him Uncle Austin?

I chuckled, "He made me start calling him uncle so the girls didn't think I was his daughter or a really young girlfriend." They both nodded and laughed in understanding. "My reason was that my father and mother abandoned me and I wanted people to know, and to remind myself, that I still had one family member that did want me."

Their laughter stopped and they both sighed.

"I was not the nicest kid before I moved in with Uncle Austin. I was a bully." I explained. "That's not an excuse for her but my life changed with him. There were no drugs…overdosing…or being left in an apartment for days by myself. When he told me that I had to have good grades and good morals to do high school rodeo, I changed because I found something that I absolutely loved."

"Rodeo…" Jess nodded.

"Uncle Austin," I corrected. "I loved rodeo but him taking in a twelve-year-old at his age?" I turned to Ryle. "You said you're 21?"

He nodded.

"Imagine your niece that you had only met a couple times being left with you…abandoned with you. What would you do?"

"Take care of her." He said without hesitation.

"He would," Jess nodded.

"I have no doubt," I smiled at the pair. "And that is what I saw in you two that made me offer this place to you. You're both a lot like him."

"Thank you for saying that," Ryle said.

"Yeah, thanks," Jess smiled.

"And thank you for helping me through a rough moment," I said to Jess then turned to Ryle. "And thank both of you for coming along at a time I needed to remember his dream and get that moving forward…moving on."

"Well, thank you for inviting us to stay here." Jess nodded. "Since we don't have to come up with rent and stable fees the first of the month we both took the next couple weeks off work so we could concentrate on all the upcoming rodeos."

"Three or four a week," Ryle added.

"Uncle Austin used to say, 'Every day you're not chasing your dream, you're jeopardizing your dream.' You guys just keep focused." I told them.

"We are," They said in unison.

A comfortable silence came over us.

"Well, you cooked, I'll clean," Jess stood and began stuffing the dirty dishes back on the tray.

"Want help?" I asked.

"No, just entertain Ryle and keep him out of my way," Jess grinned and walked away with the box in his arms.

"Let's move to the swing," Ryle said. "My mom used to have one like it but smaller."

"My uncle built it for me as a surprise when Jamie was born. He built it big so there would be room for more people on it. Technically the base is the size of a twin size bed."

We both sat.

"Where's Jess' dog?" I asked.

"He left him at his brother's place; didn't want him to mess with your cat and kittens."

That was thoughtful because I hadn't even thought of Rover when I asked them to stay.

"Tell me about Silas," I leaned back against the pillows as he pushed his boots to the ground making us swing. "How did you end up with that gorgeous pain in the ass?"

"You know who Chad Masters is?"

"Of course," I nodded. "NFR team roper…a header."

"Yeah…and he has this horse named Clint."

"Horse of the year," I nodded. "Silas is related to Clint?"

"Nah…Dexter, my sorrel with the wide blaze is. Clint is out of Son of Oak and Freddie's Baby Doll. Dexter is out of Son of Oak and a Dash for Cash mare."

"That's impressive but what does that have to do with Silas?"

Ryle grinned and looked down at his boots that were still keeping the swing moving. "The guy that sold me Dexter called Jake, a friend of mine, and told him about this palomino he had but he couldn't stand the horse because he was so damned touchy on the ground. He had bought it for his daughter for barrels but decided it was a better roping horse. He just knew the horse had the drive to be a champion but he didn't have time nor patience. Well…Jake already had a full corral so he called me." Ryle turned wide excited eyes to me. "Once I saw the horse and seen him work…he was only three at the time…I had to agree with the guy. Silas will be a champion. I have no doubt about that and I wanted to make sure I was along for the ride." He chuckled at his joke then shrugged. "I asked him to give me a week to get the money together which he agreed but I didn't get it."

"But you have Silas. Did he give you more time?"

"Nah," He looked back down at his boots. "He had four other buyers waiting for my time to run out." He sighed. "When I was twelve, I saw this truck I wanted when I got my driver's license. So I worked every job I could to get the money in the bank. The typical ones…delivering papers, shoveling stalls, legging up other people's horses, mowing lawns…that kind of stuff for a couple years," He smiled at me. "I bought the truck and it sat in my parent's driveway for 6 months before I could legally drive it."

"You sold the truck to get Silas?"

"Truck, clothes, saddles, boots, hats, old ropes, everything I had except Dexter." He sighed. "By the time I was done selling anything I owned and people would buy, I was still $3700 short. My only option at that time was to sell Dexter and try to make it with just one horse…but Silas was only three and I love Dexter."

"Damn," I sighed. This kid did have determination. His riding and roping had already impressed me but this sacrifice took it to another level.

"Yeah," He sighed. "My parents live pay check to pay check so they couldn't help."

"So how did you get it?"

His eyes glistened and cheeks turned red, "Marty, Pete, and Kade…they all three wanted to help so they split it up and wouldn't let me say no."

"Wow," I whispered. "They believe in you."

"Yeah," He barely got the word out as he nodded. After taking a couple breathes he continued. "Jess told me to go ahead and sell the truck because we had his outfit to use and we were a team. He also helped me get the night warehouse job." Ryle looked at me with a slight smile. "He was with me when I went to try out that damned palomino. The guy already had him caught and tied innocently to the fence."

I laughed, "The first inclination that the horse is a bitch to catch."

"Yeah," He laughed. "Only thing worse would have been if the horse had been sweaty and panting…but he wasn't. As soon as I put a boot in the stirrup and my butt on leather…I knew…and so did Jess." He looked at me proudly. "Between Dexter and Silas, we won enough the first six months to pay off Pete, Marty, and Kade. That was along with stabling the horses, feed, farrier, vet costs, apartment, and trying to help Jess with fuel."

"And of course there are all the entry fees." I nodded in understanding. "When did the third horse come along?"

"That's Gus…just got him this spring," He answered. "The job pays for my living expenses and stabling the horses but I was able to earn enough at jackpots over the winter that I could buy him."

"Why him?"

"That was my parents. They felt bad they couldn't help me get Silas so they were always searching the internet for a good deal on a horse. They knew what to look for and they found him in Wyoming at a cutting horse ranch that was selling off a bunch of horses they decided weren't going to work for cutting…kind of cutting rejects. Before the people even started posting the horses my dad called and asked if they had any with Son of Oak, Peptoboonsmal or a couple others I liked. They sent Dad the info and he sent it to me." Ryle turned and grinned proudly. "I pretty much had pick of the lot at that point so Jess and I drove down and I bought Gus and Jess ended up buying that big bay, Casper."

"Both young but they are coming along really well," I said. "They did great at the jackpot."

"Yeah…" He looked out to the bunkhouse as Jess walked out the door and made his way to us.

"We were just talking about your horses," I said to Jess. "Where did you get Warlock? What's his breeding?"

Jess huffed as he sat down. "I have no idea his breeding. A kid I went to college with called me one day and asked if I would go with him to look at a horse he wanted to buy for his wife. When we got to the place the couple had a handful of older horses in a pasture then this little black yearling in a corral by himself." He shrugged with a bit of a smirk. "I helped my friend choose one of the horses and as they were filling out the paperwork I asked the wife about the yearling. She said they bought a mare down in California with the promise she wasn't pregnant." His smile widened. "She was…had a late baby…August foal. They were pissed and called the previous owner. Although the mare was a quarter horse they had no idea who the sire was. They didn't even know she had been around a stud. His owners basically ignored him for the next year. Didn't even give him a name, they just called him 'the black surprise'. I asked if she would be interested in selling him." Jess grinned at me. "I bought that little neglected colt for $150."

"Oh, my Lord!" I gasped.

"They had put the halter on him a couple times but when I went in the corral to get him…it was like he knew I was saving him and was shoving his head into the halter. He'd never been in a trailer but he trusted me from the start and jumped right in. I thought it was a bit magical, hence the name Warlock."

"Oh, I love that," I grinned.

"We need to get the horses ready to go. Kade should be here any minute." Ryle said and stood. He smiled down at me. "It was nice talking with you this morning."

"You, too." I returned the smile. "Thanks for breakfast…and thank you, Jess, for helping me."

"Anytime," He nodded with a smile and turned away.

They started to walk away and I thought of everything Ryle had sacrificed to buy Silas.

"Ryle?" I called out.

They turned.

"What's Silas' breeding? Why was he so expensive?"

His smile widened, "He spent 3 months with Speed Williams and he's an own son of Frenchman's Guy and his dam was a daughter of Shining Spark."

My jaw dropped. "No wonder he's freaking gorgeous and smart. Speed is a fantastic header…and I have a brother to your Silas out in the pasture…my JW is out of Frenchman's Guy, too." I grinned.

"Nice!" He laughed and they walked away as heads turned to look out into the pasture where my horses were grazing.

The whole conversation proved to me that I had made the right decision to invite the pair to train here.

I leaned back in the swing and looked up into the sky.

"They are your type of cowboys," I whispered to my uncle.

I looked back at them just as their arms reached out for a fist bump then they pointed to each other with index finger out and thumbs up, like kids shooting a pretend gun, then they made the same gesture out in front of them. I'd never seen them do that before and knew it was something new. It was a bonding move…a move friends create and practice in private before sharing it with the world. Andrea and I had done the same thing when we were in our teens. We did a fist bump then made a fist with two fingers prancing in the air like they were horse legs. It was fun…it was something best friends shared.

I watched Jess and Ryle disappear into the barn and I pulled my phone out of my pocket.

"Lauren?" The female said in airy disbelief. "Is that really you?"

I grinned, "Yes, I'm relieved you haven't deleted me out of your phone."

She laughed, "Never! I haven't heard from you in a couple years so I hope you're calling with a good recommendation."

"Yes, they are a good recommendation but I don't want them to know I called."

I finished that call and made another…to another friend that was surprised and pleased to hear from me.

Twenty minutes after I ended the last call, I heard a whoop and a holler from the barn.

I leaned back in the swing with a satisfied grin to the sky…to my uncle.

CHAPTER TWENTY

I went into the house and changed quickly then headed to the barn. As I approached the barn I heard running hooves hitting the ground and a swear word echo across the property. I jogged through the barn and out the back to the corrals where Gus, Zeb, Dexter, and Casper were captured.

Jess was riding Warlock across the pasture with Ryle on foot swinging a lead rope and halter over his head just before he launched it at a running Silas. Another swear word rang out.

I chuckled and retrieved the pink bucket, grain, and the small rocks that helped increase the volume of the bucket being shook.

I walked to the gate to see Silas keeping a 15-foot pace in front of the walking Ryle. Jess was unhooking his lariat from the saddle.

Bucket in the air, I shook it and the grain and rocks rattled. Silas' head rose and without hesitation, he ran right at me.

"You damn horse!" Ryle shouted.

Silas ran into the corral and I quickly shut the gate. Jess rode up next to Ryle and looked down. They spoke for a moment then Ryle took off at a run to the corral. He was only halfway through the pasture when he started so it was a good distance.

Jess started trotting Warlock until they caught up with the huffing Ryle…the men grinned at each other then Jess took off at a dead run toward me and away from Ryle.

"No fair!" Ryle yelled as his arms swung dramatically as he tried to run faster.

Jess was laughing when he saw me and came to a halt just outside the gate. We watched Ryle run the rest of the way in.

"You weren't supposed to run…just trot," Ryle gasped for air. "That's what you said."

"And you believed me," Jess laughed and walked his horse into the barn.

Ryle and I looked at each other and joined his laughter.

This was going to be a fun adventure.

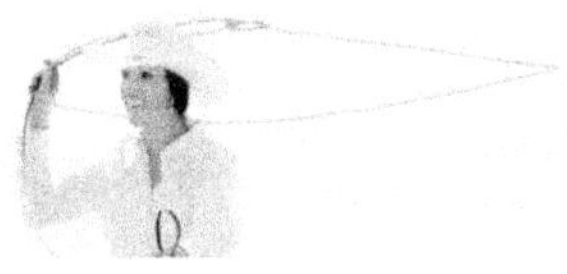

The horses were tied to the hitching post and the duffle bags were resting against the barn.

Ryle and Jess spoke over each other as they told me about phone calls they received. I just smiled and congratulated them.

My phone vibrated twice alerting me to Kade's arrival and I turned to the road to watch his truck appear.

Ryle and Jess nearly ran to greet him; their grins couldn't have been any wider.

Kade was returning their grins as he stepped out of his truck. Then he turned to me and the smile disappeared.

"You're not going to believe this!" Ryle shouted.

"Cactus Ropes called and offered to sponsor us," Jess announced with a laugh.

"And BioMane called too. They heard we use their product so they are sending us a supply." Ryle grinned. "For free! That's going to help us save for next year too."

"That's great!" Kade said. "Looks like your performance at the Stampede and Ogden got people talking."

"Unbelievable," Ryle said with the excitement making him shift from one foot to another.

"Best call Pete and Marty as soon as you're on the road," I told them. "They'll be pretty excited for you too."

"What a morning!" Ryle jumped as he turned toward the horses.

I looked at Jess as he turned to me. We shared that smile that hid a secret. I silently thanked him again for helping me.

He just nodded then turned to load the horses in the trailer.

I glanced at Kade and found him glaring at me again.

"I'm getting pretty tired of that," I grumbled to him and walked to the barn.

An hour after they left, I drove to my next counseling session.

"Good morning, Lauren," The counselor smiled. "You're looking well."

I huffed with a smile, "I have my moments."

"Considering a few weeks ago, I would say that's an improvement."

We settled down into the chairs and out of habit, my eyes went to the landscape pictures.

"What have you been doing to fill your time away from the office?" She asked.

"I've been hanging out with a few team ropers."

"Your uncle was a team roper."

I turned and looked at her in surprise. I had said nothing about my uncle to her.

"I did my research," She shrugged. "It helps me help you."

"I guess, but not everyone has an open history like mine."

"No, but this time, with you, it helps me understand you more since you haven't really been all that chatty in here."

We shared a humored smirk of agreement.

"You were quite the roper yourself." she said.

"Were…" I whispered and my eyes went back to the pictures.

"I have no doubt you still are. Are you hanging out with them or joining in the roping?"

"I've been working the chute and sled."

"At your ranch…the one your uncle built?"

"This last week…yes."

"But you're not roping?"

I didn't answer. It didn't have anything to do with Dave and his death so I saw no reason to.

"Your uncle used to hold a lot of clinics there and so did you after his death."

"Before I was abandoned with him, his whole goal in life was to make it to the National Finals Rodeo. After I came along and he was showing me how to rope, he realized how much he loved teaching and sharing so he combined the two…which is why he built the ranch…estate as some people call it."

"Before we talk about your parents…"

My eyes jerked back to her. "I have no intention of talking about my parents. They have nothing to do with me or Dave's death."

"This isn't just about Dave, it's about you."

"They are not in my life, they are not who I am…they have nothing to do with me." It was stated as fact with no emotion.

Her head tipped just a bit as her eyes narrowed. "You don't think that their leaving has anything to do with who you are now?"

"Of course, it does," I huffed. "If it wasn't for their actions I would not have had the life I had with my uncle and my daughter. I understand that and have left them in the past."

"Closed the door on them?" She asked with a lift of a brow.

"No door…just moved on," I said firmly. "And now we can move on from that conversation. They have nothing to do with Dave."

"Your daughter…?"

"Closed subject," I glared. "If you bring her up again, I will walk out the door and close your door behind me."

She stared at me a moment as if gauging my resolve. She must have decided it was impenetrable since she looked down at the tablet she had been writing on.

"So, you're coming into your uncle's life changed his life." She finally said with a glance up to me.

I took a deep breath and let it out slowly, my patients was beginning to fade.

"Yes, he became a teacher with not only his rodeo dreams but he wanted others to fulfill theirs, which included me and I did," I said. "He and his dreams had nothing to do with Dave so we can move on from that."

She huffed impatiently, "Lauren, we are here to help you. That includes the people that have had an influence on your life including your uncle and daughter."

I stood and glared down at her. "I am here because Patricia said it was mandatory to get my job back. I am here to get over Dave's death not dwell on my family."

"If you want your job back then we deal with all of you, Lauren. That's what will help you deal with Dave's death. Your uncle and daughter…"

I opened the door, walked out and firmly shut it behind me.

I wasn't even out of the parking lot when I received an email with an invitation for the next meeting; Wednesday at 10:00

When I had first entered her office I was lost and was there only because Patricia had said it was mandatory. But now? I was stronger with my goal in life reset…it did not include going back to work for the mortgage company. I had started there to fill in the time after my husband had left…then Jamie. I had no more time to fill. I had no desire to go back to the office that I envisioned Dave haunting and all those co-workers that had witnessed his death looking at me as if it was my fault.

My finger hovered over the decline button for the meeting but I didn't push it, I tossed the phone on the seat instead.

Friday morning started with a call from Ryle. I was standing in the middle of my group of older horses assessing their hoof conditions.

"Great job last night," I answered the call with a smile.

"Thanks," His voice was full of the morning gravel from a long night of no sleep. "Third and in the money."

"In the money is always good."

"True…but I want to ask you something and just want you to say 'sure no problem'."

I laughed, "Yeah, that doesn't happen without my knowing what the question is first."

He chuckled, "I have been trying to keep up with my Facebook page for my family and I want to post a few pictures I took in your arena but you said I couldn't post anything so I wanted to make sure it was alright before I did…because I don't want to upset you…"

"You've got a good morning ramble going on." I teased.

"Yeah," He chuckled again. "Is it OK? I promise I won't post any of you unless you agree…like the one at the jackpot of the 6 of us. Can I post that one?"

"None of the blue dress."

"No…the one in Star."

"I don't know…" I said hesitantly.

"I sent you a friend request so I can tag you in the pictures so you can see what I post…that way you can tell me to remove it if you want me to."

"I haven't been on Facebook for over a year."

"Please Lauren? I'm really proud of staying at your place and really want to share the pictures with my family and friends."

"Oh, Ryle…" I sighed.

"What would it hurt?"

Jamie might see it…or Andrea…but they had written me out of their lives so they probably wouldn't see them anyway. So, what would it hurt?

"Alright," I finally relented.

"Yes! Thanks! Don't forget to go accept the friend request so I can tag you…like in right now because I have a few to post."

I shook my head with a sigh, "Alright, I will. Now, go rope."

He chuckled as I ended the call.

I hit the Facebook icon on my phone and went directly to the friend requests. To my surprise, there were a couple dozen waiting for me to respond but I just accepted Ryle's and Jess' since it was there too then closed down the program. Damn, team ropers.

Pete and Marty came over to ride each morning and I fixed lunch for them the three days the other men were gone. Pete assisted me all day Saturday while the farrier worked through the fourteen horses. It was great spending time with him…and my horses again.

Once Pete and Marty left Sunday morning, I filled my time with paying bills and computer work. It needed to be done but I didn't want it to take me away from the arena when the ropers were there.

It was 1:00 in the middle of the night when the horse trailer and men returned but I still went out and helped them. They were tired…all three of them. There was no doubt they would be sleeping in on Monday morning.

"Kade," I said as they were unloading the horses.

"What?" He sighed impatiently.

I hesitated with my request but said it anyway. "Unless you have to be home tonight, why don't you stay in one of the rooms in the bunkhouse? You can anytime you want. There are plenty of stalls for your horse."

He stared at me a moment as his shoulders lowered, "Thanks…I'll take you up on that."

He unloaded his horse and followed Ryle and Jess into the barn. All three men disappeared into the bunkhouse as I walked back to the house and right up to my bedroom. I glanced out the large window and not a light was on in the building.

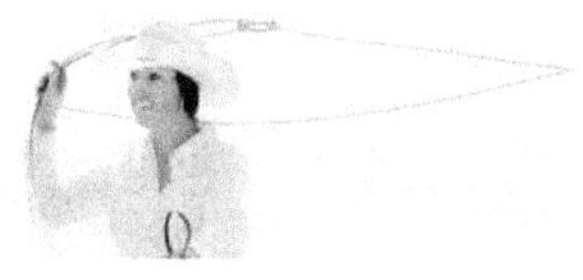

Pete and Marty wandered into the bunkhouse at 10:00 the next morning, by 11:00, Kade had left for a meeting, Ryle was sitting on his youngest horse in the header box while typing on his phone and Jess was riding his younger horse in the large round pen. Pete and Marty were off on another ride and I was mowing and enjoying the life growing at the ranch.

It was a laid back day leading up to the barbeque Sarah was putting on for Ryle and Jess.

Pete insisted on driving me to the party in his old orange Ford. I really wanted to say no but he looked so adamant so I relented.

When we arrived, Kade and Jess's trucks were already there parked down the drive by the pasture. Pete opened the truck door for me with a secretive grin on his face.

"What's that about?" I asked warily.

He didn't answer, he just tipped his arm out to me and I wrapped my hand around his elbow.

"You look beautiful in that white dress." He changed the subject. "And your hair all curly and pretty on top your head..."

I looked at him suspiciously. "Pete?"

He gave me a guilty chuckle and started walking to the side of the house.

The house was a long brick ranch house with a tall red gabled barn in the back. At least twenty acres set behind it with multiple fenced pastures. Dozens of roping steers wandered across a field while five horses were lying in the one right behind the house. I recognized Marty, Pete, and Kade's horses.

"Your horse is Barry, what is Marty and Kade's horse's names?"

"Clipper and Artis," Pete answered as he led me around the side of the house.

"Artis must be Kade's," I smiled and he nodded.

A brick patio set right behind the house with Marty standing at the chrome grill with Kade sitting at the table talking to him. A beer rest comfortably in both their hands.

"Ah! You're here!" Marty said loudly and within seconds Sarah was walking out the back door.

"So good to see you!" Sarah greeted me with a quick embrace.

"You too," I sighed. She made me feel so welcome.

"Now turn around," Sarah circled her hand around me.

"What?" I gasped.

"Just do as she says," Pete said and turned me around.

I heard the door open again and boots hitting brick.

"OK, turn back around," Sarah said with excitement in her voice.

Pete turned me again.

Jess and Ryle were standing side-by-side and looking at me proudly. They were wearing matching black shirts with their new sponsor patches attached. I had expected the Cactus Ropes and the BioMane, but I was not expecting the Circle 3.3 that was over their left chest.

"Oh," I gasp with tears rising. "You look so damn professional."

"That's what I told them!" Sarah was beaming at the two ropers.

"Sarah helped us," Jess grinned. "We have four colors. Pink for the 'Tough Enough' rodeos, white and a dark blue."

"We hope you don't mind we put your brand on them," Ryle said. "No one can support us as much as you are doing now."

"I just love it and Uncle Austin would be so proud," I nearly ran to them to pull them into a hug.

The rest of the evening was filled with laughter, relaxation, stories, and a bit too much alcohol for the pair.

When I rose from the lounger, all five men and Sarah turned to look at me.

"Well, since you wouldn't let me drive, now I need a ride home," I said to Pete.

"You in a hurry?" Sarah asked. "Any reason you can't just stay here for the night?"

"Baby chicks and kittens," I answered. "The horses could fend for themselves but I don't want to lose a chick because I was too lazy to go home."

"I understand that," She nodded and looked at the five men.

Ryle's eyes were a bit glazed from the alcohol.

"Jess and Ryle can stay here," Marty said.

"But I gotta put my horses away," Ryle frowned as one eyelid had problems staying up. "They'll get fat out there on all that grass."

"I promise to put them in the stalls for you." I smiled and he grinned crookedly.

Marty turned to Pete.

"I'm as good as I once was in driving during the day," Pete shook his head with a bit of a smirk. "But I wouldn't want to trust your life with my eyes at night."

I smiled, "I appreciate the honesty."

Pete's eyes twinkled in mischief and then turned to Kade. "Looks like you're the chauffeur tonight."

"I guess so," Kade sighed.

He had talked animatedly with everyone about the three days of travel and rodeos, even with me a couple times. He had been friendlier but still seemed guarded with me. His sigh that he had to take the time to drive me home was a bit irritating and I thought briefly about just calling a cab but I knew Marty, Sarah, and Pete would be upset with that. So, I just decided I wasn't going to let his attitude ruin the night and I just shrugged it off with a promise to myself not to get in this situation again.

"Thank you for inviting me." I hugged Sarah then Marty.

"You come over anytime," Sarah said.

"And I have an open door for you." We shared honest smiles.

"But what about the gate?" Ryle slurred with a big cocky grin.

"Gate too," I shook my head at him. As if he could be anything else, he was a happy drunk.

He leaned over to me and I could smell the whiskey on his breath, "I'm glad you came too." He tried to whisper. "It's nice seeing you all dolled up and out of the arena."

I laughed, "Dolled up? It's just a simple sundress."

"But the white is pretty with your hair all curly and piled on top your head," Ryle snickered. "Like an angel."

"And your shoulders are real pretty," Jess slurred then quickly looked away.

I laughed and placed a hand on his jaw to turn his head towards me. His eyes were a bit dilated and glazed over too. My hand slapped his chest lightly then came to rest just over his heart.

"You write that one down so you remember that line when you find that sweetheart we talked about. She'll like that one." I grinned.

"I agree," Sarah chuckled and looked at Marty.

Love shone in their eyes as they looked at each other.

"Oh, you know you have great shoulders," Marty huffed. "And some other great features I ain't saying to this crowd, but I'll show you in just a little bit."

We all laughed as Sarah blushed with a playful slap to his shoulder.

Without a glance or a word, Kade walked past me and jogged down the steps toward his truck.

I hugged Sarah and Marty then Pete held out an arm. I slipped my hand around his elbow and he escorted me to the truck where Kade was standing next to the door open.

"Someone taught you to be a gentleman," I teased.

He nodded to Pete. "Manners are a family tradition."

"Thank you," I whispered to Pete and squeezed his arm tighter.

"You be careful driving her home," Pete said to Kade as I stepped into the truck and Kade shut the door.

Kade huffed, "You know I will."

Pete smiled at me with a wink then turned away. I liked him…sure wished he was my grandfather.

I waved at everyone as we drove past the house then settle back into the seat.

"Do you want the window up or down?" I asked.

"Whatever you want," He said in a flat tone.

I glanced at him but couldn't tell if he was upset or not. Just another one of his moods, I guess. Well, that was his problem, not mine so, just to irritate him, I'd just keep pushing him.

"Ryle and Jess are both going to be a little hung over in the morning."

"Uh, huh."

I rolled my eyes and with a few pulls of a couple pins, my hair tumbled out of the curly bun and down my back and shoulders.

He glanced at me, or more specifically my hair, then turned back.

"Just getting comfortable," I said.

"Isn't it hair down and bra off?" He huffed without looking at me.

The comment surprised me. Not because he happened to mention my bra but that it sounded…playful. He'd never done that before. Well, I'd just play along.

"Who said I was wearing a bra?" I giggled softly.

He came to a stop at the light and turned and looked me right in the eyes. I could see the question but I just smiled.

"You SO want to look down and check right now, don't you?" I teased with a grin.

A mischievous light that resembled his grandfather's lit his eyes. He was quite the handsome man in his dark blue shirt and straw cowboy hat. He had a full day's growth of whiskers that gave him a rugged edge. My stomach fluttered a bit but I ignored it because he had always been distant with me. So, I just chuckled and leaned back in the seat.

The warm summer air from the open window caressed my skin and played with my hair. The stories and laughter of the evening ran through my mind as he drove. I smiled at what a happy group of people they were and I was very lucky to find them…or have Pete find me.

Laying in the arena, looking at the stars, and listening to the hoofbeats in the wind. I never would have thought that I could feel alive again.

"What was that for?"

"What was what for?" I asked and slowly turned to him.

"You sighed…a big sigh."

"Just thinking about what a nice night it was."

"It was," He nodded thoughtfully. "Marty and Sarah are pretty exceptional."

"As well as your grandfather."

"And you seemed pretty entertained with Jess."

"And Ryle" I nodded. Maybe, while it was just the two of us, it was time to confront him about his attitude toward me. "Even you tonight."

"Tonight?"

"Yes," I turned to look at him and try to judge his reaction to the conversation. "You haven't been very friendly towards me…right from the start."

"YOU weren't exactly YOU at first." He pointed out.

"Hmmm…true. So you didn't like me when I was down, but now that I feel better and you have a large private ranch to rope at? You like me now?" My stomach tingled in anticipation of his answer.

He stopped at the next stop light and looked at me, "I didn't understand your and Granddad's relationship to start with. There are a lot of people that try to take advantage of senior citizens his age. I've been concerned about that. It wasn't because you were down."

Silence as the light turned green and he started moving again.

The disappointment slowly took over as I thought of Andrea's jealousy and false friendship because of the ranch...then there was my ex-husband's betrayal. I turned and looked out the side window away from him.

He stopped at the next light.

"Lauren?"

I ignored him because I didn't want him to see the hurt in my eyes.

"Lauren, look at me."

His voice was low enough it intrigued me so I gave in and looked at him. The brim of his cowboy hat was just above warm brown eyes.

"There are arenas all over the place we can go rope; dozens of them." The light turned green but he didn't move. "We were content at the arena where we first met. We go to your arena because you are there."

Relief made my body relax back against the seat and I smiled at him. "Thank you."

His lip rose in a slight smirk, "And there is the fact you wrangled Ryle and Jess to come live there."

The wind gust into the window and tossed my hair in the air. I chuckled and tried to capture it again. The truck started moving.

"Heck of a wind storm coming," He said and looked out the window to the sky. "No stars out there."

"Best get Silas into the barn," I said. "That horse is hard enough to catch. He'd be a real bitch running in the storm."

He turned off the highway to the private drive to the ranch.

Another gust blew through the truck and I quickly rolled up the window as he stopped at the gate to key in the code.

"I'm so used to that just opening for me." I chuckled.

"Why don't you need to type in the code?"

"I have a transmitter in the front of my truck that sets it off."

"You have another one?" He grinned. "Typing in those 5 digits just drains me."

I laughed and relaxed back into the seat again and stared at my home. It wasn't very often I got to just look at it, I was usually driving.

I loved my home and the history behind it. Although it was late, it was still light enough to see the house, buildings, trees, and the horses and steer in the fields.

"Just drive to the barn, we'll get the horses in," I said.

"You think you can catch Silas?"

"He likes his grain and we just trap him in the corrals at the end of the barn."

"Since you're in sandals, you want me to do it?"

"I have boots in the tack room." I smiled at him while admitting to myself I liked this Kade…the one that seemed to like me. He made my stomach flutter and skin warm. "Thanks for the offer."

We slid out of the truck and the doors closed in unison then we slowly walked to the door of the tack room. For the first time, I felt comfortable with him and was sure the glares were a thing of the past.

I opened the door and stepped to the right where the boot case was tucked under the shelf. Due to spiders and bugs, I always kept them stored in the case. While I replaced the sandals with the boots, Kade gathered the halters and lead ropes. We turned and collided in the middle of the room.

CHAPTER TWENTY ONE

His hands were wrapped around the lead ropes and they came to rest on the outside of my arms to balance us. My hands were empty and came to rest on his sides…his very well-toned waist.

The heat between us was instant and I caught my breath as my eyes flew up to his. The warmth and intensity in his eyes made mine widen. He tilted his head just enough to invite a kiss. I was so shocked I stepped back as if he burned me then walked around him and out the door with my face flushed and pulse racing.

We said nothing as I dipped the bucket in the grain barrel and then we walked side by side to the back of the barn. Zeb was right behind the gate and his head rose in excitement as I walked through the doors. He trotted into the corral and Kade placed the halter on him as I let the horse have a few bites of grain for coming in so easily.

A gust of wind blew my hair around me and it flew into my face.

"I should have put it into a ponytail." I chuckled and brushed it out of my face.

He shrugged, "Sundress, boots, and hair blowing in the wind…that's sexy."

My body flushed again and I didn't respond more than pushing the hair behind my ears and looking out to the horses still in the pasture. All three of Jess' horses were on the far side of the pasture with Silas and Dexter closer and now looking toward the barn with heads held high. I dipped the bucket down to get Zeb's head out then lifted it into the air so the two horses could see it. They trotted into the corral.

I set the bucket on the ground and waited until their mouths were full of grain then slowly walked to the gate to close it.

Silas' head lifted and turned to me. From the lowering of his head back to the bucket, I knew he realized he was trapped.

"Sorry, big guy," I whispered and placed the rope over his neck then slid the halter up his nose.

"I'll get Zeb put away then come help with these two." Kade turned.

I slid the other halter onto Dexter then watched Kade walk away. The man was a pleasure to look at but I didn't even think he liked me…especially in any kind of romantic way. The moment in the tack room proved that wrong; the heat that raced through me proved I liked him too.

It was a bit…scary…but also skin tingling. The warmth from him and the feeling of my hands against his sides made my breath shake. I envisioned his chest, back, and abs when he took off his shirt to show me the tattoo underneath. Then there was his grin as he whipped the shirt over his head to the stripper beat.

I had to take a deep breath to calm my rising heartbeat.

But, what did he want? The thought of a one night stand was unsettling. The last thing I wanted to do was break up the dynamic of my team roping crew for just one night.

What did I want? Well…I wanted to touch him again. I wanted to feel that moment again of being so close to him and his inviting a kiss. It had been a long time since I had any interest in a man and I suddenly had a lot of interest in Kade.

Silas lifting his head brought me out of my musing and I kicked the empty bucket to the side and took a lead rope in each hand. I walked toward the barn with the horses calmly walking on each side of me.

Kade was approaching from the opposite direction. His eyes went to my boots then up the white flowing sundress and over to include the horses. A gust of wind played in my hair making it swirl around my shoulders. Surprisingly, he took out his phone and took a picture.

"What is that for?" I stopped.

"That's a vision to save." He shrugged.

The horses stood quietly as we stared at each other. The tightness in my chest grew and I knew I needed to face this now when it was just the two of us.

"What is this?" I asked uneasily.

"Just letting you know how I feel." He answered with a nod and determined look. "I've been patiently waiting for you to finish toying with Jess."

I gasped, "Toying with Jess? What the hell?" My attraction to him quickly turned to irritation.

"You…"

"I don't TOY with people," I growled.

His left eyebrow rose in surprise.

"Why would you even think that?"

"Because you are constantly joking together…and you touch him all the time."

"I do?" I huffed. "Jess and I have a friendship…a special one but not a romantic one…or flirty one."

My hands gripped the lead ropes of the horses that were standing quietly. I needed to stay calm. Without knowing about my meltdown on the patio, maybe it did look like we were flirting.

"Then…" He started.

"He helped me through a very rough moment." I interrupted. "Then we had an honest conversation about romance and…" I shrugged slightly. It wasn't any of his business what Jess and I talked about.

"So…you've never been interested in him?" Kade asked with narrowed eyes.

"He is a very good FRIEND," I said. "He will always be special to me."

Again, there was silence as we stared at each other. There was a lot of conversation within that silence that caused my skin to warm and my stomach tremble.

"You're willing to jeopardize the dynamic within our crew?" I whispered.

He slowly shook his head, "I've thought about it and came to the conclusion it wouldn't jeopardize anything."

I shifted my weight from one foot to another, "You sound pretty confident."

"I am."

"I've been through an awful lot the last year…especially the last month and I just don't think I could handle another loss…I don't want something temporary." I whispered and my heart compressed again. The heat rose up my spine.

He nodded in understanding, "I'm not looking for a one night stand and you are most definitely NOT a one-night stand type of lady."

I stared at him as my mind thought of all the good and bad outcomes. There were more good than bad but…

"What does it hurt to try one kiss just to see how it goes?"

"One kiss?" I looked at him anxiously. "Just one?"

"We start with one and go from there." His eyes warmed as he looked at my lips.

I looked at his in rising anticipation. They were full and surrounded by whiskers…very sexy. The heat created in that one moment in the tack room swept through me again.

The horses sidestepped and I tugged on the ropes to pull them back.

"An hour ago I didn't even think you liked me," I admitted.

"An hour ago I thought you were playing around with Jess. After hearing your sweetheart comment before we left the party tonight, I now know better and I'm not taking a chance of anything else happening before I let you know I'm interested…and…" He tilted his head to the side…all handsome and cocky like. "…I most definitely like you."

"Since when? You've never been friendly to me."

"At first I thought you were trying to swindle Grandad. Then when we came here, I realized you didn't need money so what could you gain from him?"

"Friendship," I whispered.

"I finally saw that the first night we were here and he became so adamant about coming back to check on you and found you crying by the fence."

That night seemed so long ago…not just weeks but months.

"He didn't tell me what it was about, he respects your privacy, but I realized he was trying to help you in some way."

"He did…"

"Then the morning we showed up and you were in that blue dress," He grinned. "That was something."

"You liked me then?" I gasped.

"I liked you after I realized you weren't trying to get something from Grandad," he said. "Even the day before when it looked like you were…homeless."

I smiled at the memory.

"But," He continued. "When you were in that blue dress…the light and happiness in your eyes as you sashayed out and called Grandad a smart ass? That was it…" He shook his head and sighed. "I was a goner."

"You still glared at me."

"Probably…just trying to figure you out…which I can't say I have altogether but I've watched you and have come to the conclusion you are a damn good person."

"I try…"

"Then, after the blue dress, I kept waiting for you to…I don't know…I guess heal but then you and Jess acted like you were together."

"He's just a friend," I repeated.

"I understand that now…which is why I wanted to talk to you tonight while we're alone."

"I think it's the first time."

"It is," He grinned. "So…now…I'm letting you know, I very much like you." The grin slowly faded and his eyes narrowed. "But, how do you feel about me? Do you like me?"

"Well…" I whispered and looked at him thoughtfully. "I always liked you because you adore Pete and you're so supportive of Ryle and Jess' dream…but I really hated the glares."

"And if I promise to never glare at you again?"

We stared at each other again; letting the silence build the conversation.

"One kiss? Just to see how it goes?" His brown eyes shone with hope.

"What if we don't like it?" I whispered nervously.

"What if we do?" Those inviting lips turned into an amused smile.

I shifted from one foot to another and looked into his eyes…they seemed sincere and honest. What would it hurt to try just one?

"Alright…" I started.

Three steps and his right hand slid around my waist and the left went to the back of my neck. He pulled me into a kiss that took my breath away from the moment it started.

There was no slow start, no intimate exploration, it was as if he had thought about it for a long time and was going to make sure this one kiss left me wanting more.

He had succeeded because I wanted more. My whole body rose in his arms to press our lips even closer together. My hands gripped the lead ropes tightly as I pressed them into his shoulders. I leaned into him…trying to get closer…and closer as the kiss continued.

The horses sidestepped again, yanking my arms and pulling my hands away from him. He must have thought I was breaking the kiss and he started to rise. I tossed the ropes out of my hands and quickly wrapped my arms around his neck to bring his lips back to mine.

I had never been kissed like this. His aroma was intoxicating…his body radiated heat…his arms were strong…his hands firm. This kiss was raw masculine desire. He tipped me to the right and lowered down into the kiss, pressing harder. Every neuron in my brain wanted more and my arms tightened…my leg slowly lifted to entwine with his.

A loud metal crash caused our lips to fly apart. My heels hit the ground as I gasped for air and pushed Kade to the side so I could look around him.

Dexter's muzzle was buried in a pile of grain from the overturned galvanized storage bin.

But the only thing I could see of Silas was his large golden rump and white flowing tail as he was running out of the barn and disappearing down the driveway.

The hardest horse on the planet to catch was running toward 2500 acres of belly high golden wheat. I was never going to be able to catch him but I had to try.

As Kade leaned down to grab the lead rope for Dexter, I grabbed a bucket, dipped it into the pile of grain, and ran.

Just as the palomino reached the hard packed gravel road, his hoof landed on the dangling lead rope and his head went to the ground and he started to stumble.

"Silas!" I screamed and ran faster.

Every injury ever known to a horse went through my mind as I ran. How in the hell was I going to tell Ryle that I injured…maimed…killed his beloved horse? The horse he had given up everything for.

Silas caught himself from falling and continued to run.

I sighed in relief…briefly. He jumped and flew into the field. He loped away as if he was a deer bounding across the field. He was celebrating his freedom!

"Silas!" I yelled again.

It had absolutely no effect on him as the wind carried the word away.

I was thankful for the boots as I ran into the golden wheat but it was nearly to my shoulders and scratched at my arms, knees, and thighs. Luckily, there was still enough daylight I could see which direction he was running. Terrifyingly, that let me see his head go down again, but this time his rump and all four legs went in the air then he disappeared into the wheat.

I broke his neck…all four legs…

CHAPTER TWENTY TWO

"Silas!" I screamed as I stumbled across the uneven ground while pushing the wheat out of my path. The bucket dropped from my hand.

"Silas!" My heart was pounding, my lungs full of the iron taste from over abuse.

This time his head popped out of the wheat as he began to rise. He was just feet away and I didn't break stride as I ran for his lead rope.

He rose just as I reached him which gave me time to get a good grip on the rope.

"You son of a bitch!" I gasped at him as my body shook in fear, relief, and overexertion. My body was not ready for sprinting down driveways and through fields.

I ran a trembling hand down all four of his legs and just started to have him walk around me when I heard it.

Hoofbeats in the wind made me turn to see Kade loping his bay horse across the field toward us. Damn…he looked like a western hero coming to save the damsel in distress. I didn't feel like that damsel anymore and I knew he didn't want me to be again but I'd let him 'rescue' me every day of the week.

I wanted him more with every stride his horse took. That vision was forever engraved in my heart.

"Is he alright?" Kade asked as he came to a stop then stepped out of the saddle.

"He seems to be," I said with a trembling voice.

We took a few minutes to walk him in circles and check for a limp then examine every inch of him with the light from Kade's cell phone.

"Step up on my horse and I'll ride behind you," Kade said as he turned to his horse to hold the reins.

The words brought a vision to my mind that I don't think he meant. My guilty eyes slowly rose to his and we shared a humored naughty glance before I walked to his horse.

As soon as I was settled onto the saddle, I took control of the reins and Kade rose and straddled the horse behind me. He kept control of Silas' lead rope.

"I'll follow the trail we just ran so we don't ruin any more wheat. You ready?" I asked and looked over my shoulder at him.

"I am," He said in a low voice. "But you had quite the run, maybe you should lean back and relax."

I giggled and did as he said. My whole body melted against him and a long slow sigh escaped me when I realized just how comfortable he was and how perfectly we melded together.

His hand rose and pulled my hair to the side then his lips touched the skin just under my ear.

"Son of a..." I exhaled and my eyes closed.

Two more light kisses down my neck and I was twisting in the saddle looking for those lips.

His arms tightened around me as our lips met.

As I kissed him, I thought of him riding across the field toward me. I twisted even more and tried to grip his neck to pull him closer. I thought of his love for his grandfather and his eyes shining when he laughed and his chest…covered with the tattoo…

His body jerked away from me and had me grabbing for the saddle horn to stay on the horse. The bay jumped to the side and I instinctively yanked on the reins to make him stop.

My heart jumped in my chest as I cried out.

"Damn…Silas!" Kade growled as he slid off the back end of his horse, landed on his feet, and pulled the lead rope to get the palomino's head up.

Silas looked at us with that "what?" look as he stood with his front hoof inside the bucket I had dropped and his mouth chewing on grain from the ground.

Kade freed the hoof from the bucket then turned and looked up at me. "We need to stay away from each other until this damn horse is safe in his stall."

"I totally agree." I gave him a nervous giggle. "I don't want to tell Ryle we killed his horse for just a kiss."

Kade grinned up at me as we started walking. "That wasn't…those weren't…just a kiss."

I smiled down at him and let him know I agreed…they were a beginning.

He walked in front of me as we made our way out of the field. Once we stepped onto the road, he maneuvered himself between the two horses. I looked down in time to see his hand rise up to mine. I slid my hand into his…warmth, strength, and caring. My grip tightened and my heart sighed. The walk to the barn ended way too soon.

When we reached the barn, I stepped off the horse and tethered him to the hitching post as Kade tucked Silas safely in his stall.

He did one more check down the horse's body to make sure he was alright.

"He's good?" I asked. "I'll call tomorrow and get the chiropractor out here as soon as possible."

"He's fine and that's probably a good idea," Kade stepped out of the stall, slid the latch across to lock it then turned to me.

Without hesitation, his arms went around my waist and he jerked my body to his. I wrapped my arms around his neck again and rose on tiptoes. Our lips met again. I could not believe this man that had glared at me for weeks was now kissing me…and with so much desire.

He turned to push me up against the stall door and leaned his body into me.

I felt his hand moving in my hair at the base of my neck and pulled him closer.

His hands roamed up my hips and rib cage…but he was still playing with my hair…then he tugged on my hair…with his hands at my waist.

I started giggling and lowered my heels to break the kiss.

"What?" He exhaled softly.

"Silas is eating my hair." I turned to look at the palomino who gave me that innocent "what?" look with a strand of my dark hair still dangling from his lips. I gently tugged it out of his mouth and back through the bars of the stall. "I think I need to wash my hair now." I giggled.

"Damned horse," Kade laughed and walked to his horse to pull the saddle off him.

I went to the tack room to change back into my sandals.

He brushed into my hip when he walked the saddle to the stand. I chuckled because it was completely on purpose. He bumped me with a wide hip swing when he walked back out to put the horse in the stall. I laughed and followed him out the door. I really liked this playful Kade.

He walked his horse into the stall and slowly closed the latch as his head and eyes turned to look at me. There was a question in his eyes. I returned his smile as I closed the large doors and waited for him. Outside it was dark with no moon or star sparkling in the sky. Only the driveway light between the barn and the house shone.

When Kade was at my side, I turned off the barn light and the darkness descended. This was the moment…if he went into the house with me…and kissed me like he did…there was no way I was going to want him to leave. He stood quietly as my mind raced. I could feel his heat and knew he wanted to kiss me again but he was waiting for me to make the move this time.

We were adults, both in our forties, had grown kids, and I had been married for 20 years. There was no one I had to report to. No one I had to justify my actions to…except, maybe, Pete.

"Kade," I whispered and placed a hand on his hip, curling my fingers into his belt.

"Yes?" His voice was low…sexy…and made my body tingle. It was dark enough I couldn't see his features, just the outline of his hat, neck, and shoulders…which was quite a sight in itself.

"I…if…I don't want to hurt Pete. I couldn't imagine if we…and it upset him."

A low chuckle rumbled from him.

"Why did you laugh?" I asked and my hand dropped from his waist.

"Lauren, there is absolutely nothing wrong with my grandfather's eyesight whether in daylight or at night."

"What?" I gasped then my mind played back the 'I don't want to trust your life with my eyesight' comment. "He lied?"

Another rumble as his hand moved to my hip and pulled me into him. "Yes, he did."

"But…" The reality started to sink in and I couldn't help but smile. "So, he sent us out here together…alone."

"Yes," His voice was full of humor. "He is a bit devious sometimes."

"But, you knew when he made the excuse," I pointed out. "You knew what he was doing and didn't say anything."

"Of course I knew and I wasn't going to turn down the chance of finally talking to you alone. I wanted to know if it was serious between you and Jess but I sure as hell wasn't going to ask him."

I chuckled and my hand went back to his hip with my fingers curling into his belt.

"And now," His hand slowly slid across my lower back and he pulled me closer to him.

I still couldn't see him but I could smell his musky cologne mixed with sweat and horse. Damn…standing in the dark next to a sexy man that radiated masculinity and smelled like horses, another moment etched in my heart.

"And now what?" I whispered and wrapped my arms around his shoulders.

"And now…you have to decide if you want more than that 'trial' kiss."

"We had more than one," I purred.

He leaned down to nuzzle into my neck. "So…I'm hoping you didn't hate it."

"The only part I hated was we kept having to stop," I admitted.

"So…do you want to go out on a date?" His voice was low…caressing…and hinted of humor.

"Well, we've been together nearly every day for the last three weeks," I whispered.

"Lots of meals in there too," He added.

"So, I think we have that part covered." I sighed and pulled away from him.

I took his hand and we walked toward the house.

"I believe you have animals to tend to." he said.

"Yes, if you'll check the chicks, I'll check the kittens and meet you at the door."

Our hands separated as we did our animal checks but they came right together when we walked into the dark house.

Only the porch light and a small light at the base of the stairs illuminated the house.

I turned into him and wrapped one arm around his neck and with the other hand, I traced over his shoulder where the longhorn steer tattoo would be.

"Do you want to watch a movie? Or maybe have a cup of coffee?" I sighed with a slight teasing smile.

He answered by capturing my lips again.

I melted into him and thoroughly enjoyed the taste of the kiss and the feel of his hands moving slowly from my hips and up my ribcage. His fingers spread out and massaged my back then made their way up. His left hand slid up under the shoulder strap on the sundress and his fingers moved across my bare skin.

I realized what he was doing and chuckled into the kiss; our lips moved just inches apart.

"Did you figure it out yet?" I whispered.

He chuckled, "No…I can't feel a band in the back and there isn't a strap…but it could be strapless."

"Or…" I bit his lip playfully. "The bra could be built into the dress."

He nuzzled into my neck, "So there is just the dress and…"

"Yes," I purred.

His hand slid to grasp mine. "Enough of this…we're going upstairs."

He pulled me down the hall and started up the stairs.

"Don't I have a word in this?" I teased.

"Just say no and we'll go back down," He continued to the landing at the top of the stairs and looked down the hall to the multiple doors. He turned back to me. "I didn't hear a no."

"Are you kidding? I want a closer look at that tattoo." I grinned and pulled him down the hall and to my bedroom door.

He laughed as the door slammed shut behind us.

I woke to fingertips tickling down my bare shoulder then gliding to the small of my back and pushing the sheet up and over my left butt cheek.

My face was buried in the white pillow with my dark hair covering me.

"I sure hope you're the cowboy I meant to come home with," I whispered.

I heard a deep chuckle and received a slap on the right butt cheek.

I giggled and turned my head then sat straight up gripping the sheets in front of me to hide my bare body. With wide eyes and mouth gaping, I cried out.

"You're not Ryle!"

I could not stop the grin and giggles as Kade laughed. Then he tackled me back on the bed.

It took an hour before we made it to the shower…and another half hour to get out of there.

With our fingers entwined and shared smiles we descended the staircase.

As my foot hit the hardwood floor, I heard a vehicle door slam.

I glanced out to see a white car I didn't recognize sitting in the driveway.

"Now who in the hell…?" I whispered.

"Who can get through your gate?" Kade asked.

"Only…" The happiness that had finally taken over dissolved. That fact was depressing and my mood plummeted. "It's my daughter, Jamie. I am going to apologize right now for whatever she says or does."

CHAPTER TWENTY THREE

"Well…damn…" He whispered. "That bad?"

I answered by squeezing his hand tighter and walked through the kitchen and to the back door where she was parked. She was looking back at the barn where I normally would be with the horses.

When I opened the door her head turned to the sound. Her long dark brown hair swirled around her shoulders and her brown eyes looked at me in surprise. In a white sleeveless shirt and blue denim shorts, she looked so at home and yet…so out of place. It made my heart hurt.

Our eyes met and there was no emotion shared until her eyes went behind me to Kade. Then a sneer and angry eyes looked back at me.

"He the cowboy of the night?" She snarled. "Which one of them is tonight's conquest?"

A cold fury raged through me. I let go of Kade's hand and walked right to her. My hand reaching for her arm caught her by surprise but not as much as my turning her and walking her back to her car.

"Mother!"

"Get out of here," I growled and opened her car door. "Get off my property." I pushed her into the car as Kade walked by and silently headed for the barn.

"Mother!" She fell onto the seat with her feet still on the ground and her eyes looking up at me in shock.

"I have no idea why you think you can come onto my property and talk to me and my guest that way but I won't have it." I stood with hands on hips, glared at her and let loose the words I had been holding back for the last year. "Look around this property, you self-righteous little bitch. This has been your home since the day you were born; you lived an extremely happy life here until you left for college. That's 21 years of running barefoot in the grass, loping horses in the fields, playing in the arena and in the barn. Parties and sleepovers with your friends, hours we spent in that swing, and the time you spent with Uncle Austin." Tears invaded her eyes but I wasn't stopping. "We spent thousands of hours practicing, thousands of miles traveling to shows and clinics together, and thousands of days filled with laughter and adventure. Why you threw all that away because of one incident just shocks the hell out of me."

"Incident?" She gasped; her eyes wide in disbelief.

"I'll apologize for where it happened but I won't apologize for one word I said." I took a deep angry breath and shook my head. "…not one DAMN word I said."

She started to climb out of the car so I placed a hand on top her head and pushed her back in. She landed with a gasp.

"I said get off my property," I growled. "As much as I loved you before, I cannot believe it came down to me having to apologize to Kade about you as we walked out the door."

"You what?"

"It breaks my heart you've turned out like this that I have to apologize to someone before introducing you, knowing that you're going to cause some kind of scene or be a bitch."

"I can't…"

"Exactly! You can't…so get off my property."

I leaned down and forcefully pushed her legs into the car.

"Mother!" She cried.

She was clear of the door so I slammed it shut and turned to the barn. Her car started when I was halfway there…the anger was diminishing. With every step, my heart rate increased until my chest began to ache. What the hell did I just do?

I didn't see Kade so I picked up a lariat and threw a loop at the dummy steer. Then I did it again and again. Each time was stronger but I missed with each throw.

I glanced at Kade when he walked out of the barn, but he was looking past me. I turned to see Jamie had backed out of the driveway and was sitting in the car on the road but wasn't moving.

"You alright?" He asked.

I dropped the rope to my side and looked up into his concerned eyes.

"Yes…no…just so…pissed," I finally sighed. "I'm so sorry."

Tires on gravel echoed as she began moving down the road and my chin hit my chest. His arms moved around me.

"I think I just lost my daughter forever," I whispered into his shoulder. "What the hell did I just do?"

His arms tightened, "She's not gone yet. She stopped again."

We held each other quietly waiting.

It was tires in the distance that finally broke the silence. The other four men were arriving.

"I'll go get the horses," He whispered.

We looked at each other and he leaned in for a comforting kiss then turned and walked back into the barn.

I turned to see if Jamie was still on the road. She was, she had just moved to the side so Marty's truck had room to pass by. It did slowly then turned into the driveway and to their normal parking spot by the barn.

All four stepped out of the truck with their heads swinging from Jamie's car to me.

Kade walked out of the barn behind me with the familiar heart soothing sound of hoofbeats following him.

"Who is that?" Jess asked as they approached.

"My daughter, Jamie," I answered with a calm voice that gave no hint of the turmoil in my heart.

"Why is she out there?" Ryle asked.

"Well," I said. "When she arrived and Kade walked out of the house behind me she made a very rude comment so I kicked her off my property."

There was dead silence as their eyes bounced between me and Kade. The implication was clearly there but they were trying very hard to decide if it was true. There was also the fact Kade had on the same clothes as at the party the night before.

"Yes," I looked out at Jamie's unmoving car. "He spent the night."

"In the bunkhouse?" Marty asked.

I turned back to see his dimples deepen.

"In the spare bedroom?" Pete asked with laughter dancing in his eyes.

I smiled at the two of them.

"On the couch," Ryle quipped.

"Probably fell asleep in the recliner watching TV." Jess grinned.

"You're just a bunch of smart asses, ya damn team ropers." I shook my head and turned to look at Kade. I wanted to kiss him but I don't think they were quite ready for that and I didn't want to change the dynamic of our group. I'd just save up the wanted kisses in the daylight and catch up to them at night.

Tires and gravel…I turned back to her car with my heart rising with hope.

My breath quivered as the car backed down the road until it stopped in front of the driveway.

There was a hesitation then my phone alert rang out. My hands shook as I pulled it from my pocket.

Text from Jamie: Mom, can I come talk to you?

I nearly cried to see the mom and not mother. There was hope.

"Saddle up, boys. I'll be back in a minute." I said as I walked past them.

Her car turned and slowly crept toward me.

"Boys?" Marty said. "Ain't been called that in a long time."

"Me neither," Pete's voice faded but I could hear them all chuckle.

Jamie didn't look at me when she stopped the car and slowly opened the door. I stopped a good ten feet from her to give a little space…comfort that I wasn't going to attack her again.

She looked to the back of the house, the patio, chicken coop, pasture, arena, then the barn where she hesitated. After a moment she looked out to the west pasture where my horses were trotting to the fence in excitement as the other horses were led out of the barn.

"Yes, I had a wonderful childhood growing up here," She whispered and finally looked at me. Her dark eyes were warm with memories. "I wouldn't trade it for anything and I honestly couldn't imagine not being able to come back here."

I didn't say anything, I let her talk this time.

"Mom, I don't want you to get angry again but…" She hesitated and bit her lower lip.

I remained quiet and calm but raised a concerned brow.

"I sat out there and all those memories came back to me and I…I just…I just couldn't come up with why it all went so bad."

I opened my mouth to speak but she raised a quick hand to stop me.

"It was Dad…I know that," She sighed. "But…I don't know why he did what he did." She looked out at the property again then back to me. "I thought we had a happy family."

"So did I," I said softly.

"Then one day it's gone…then last year happened…and we hadn't seen each other in months."

"More than a year…"

She nodded with a dramatic sigh, "I had to read in the paper and hear on the news what happened at your party. Then you sent me that picture of the baby chicks," Frustration radiated out of her. "I just didn't understand why and I just got so angry at it all."

"I was thinking of all the spring trips we made to the store to buy new chickens," I said softly. "I just wanted to show you I was thinking of you."

Tears sprung to her eyes, "I was so awful…what I texted back."

"Yeah…it hurt," I admitted. "And the other picture."

"You riding…team roping with them," She nudged her chin to the men that were now riding in the arena. "I was so angry…"

"Why would you think I was sleeping with any of them?" I asked. "What would make you even think that?"

"Dad…he said you had found someone else and I didn't know! I was jealous angry that you were moving on without me."

"You didn't want to be near me."

"I know, but…"

"I sent it to you to try to tell you I was moving on and trying to heal…to…" I stopped as my heart relived those days after the party. I had come so far…I couldn't slide back now.

"That's just it," She whispered and tears finally fell and she quickly wiped them away. "You were moving on…I was stuck…Dad was…well…frustrating."

"What do you mean?"

She looked out at the men riding then back to me with worried eyes. "Don't get mad."

"Alright…I've vented once today. I can contain myself now." I tried to smile but her anxiety worried me.

"When I was sitting out on the road, I called Dad and told him what happened."

I closed my eyes to hide the fury that took over me. My hands began to tremble and fingers curled in and out.

"I said don't get mad…there is a reason I did it."

I slowly opened my eyes and glared at her as I took a deep breath.

"I know, that no matter what I say, he won't tell me the truth." she said.

I silently agreed.

"But I also know that he would tell you or talk to you. I need to hear whatever happened from him and he won't talk to me."

"So what did you expect to happen?"

Her shoulders rose and teeth captured her bottom lip, "He's on his way here."

"What the hell, Jamie?" I gasped and felt the heat rise in my neck and pressure behind my eyes.

"I want you to have an honest conversation with him without him knowing I'm listening." She quickly added with a hint of desperation.

"Damn it, Jamie!" I growled to keep my voice low. "I didn't want to ever see him again."

"I know, Mom," She whined and bit her lip again. "I want to get back to us…to our regular life but I need the answers."

I lowered my head in defeat, "You're doing this for us…can't you just trust me?"

"Yes…but I think there is stuff that even you don't know about."

"Then what makes you think he will talk to me about any of it?"

"Because…for some reason…he is a bit of a jerk and likes to brag about things." She said with a guilty look. "He would want to gloat to you."

She had a point…he did like to be a jerk.

"You may not like what he has to say. It could be very upsetting…you really sure you want to hear the truth…no matter how bad?"

"Yes…we need to move on and be done with all the secrets."

"How long before he gets here?"

Her shoulders lowered in relief, "Four hours. He has to drive down from Pendleton."

"He living there now?" I asked in surprise.

"No, I don't know," She shrugged and her eyes went from me to the arena. "How long do they usually ride?"

"As long as they want," I said. "Ryle and Jess live in the bunkhouse so they are here when they aren't traveling. They just stayed at Marty's last night."

"I couldn't believe it when I saw that on Facebook," She said.

"I offered them the facility as a training center. I believe in them…that they'll go the distance."

"Oh…Mom," She exhaled. "Uncle Austin…he…"

"I know," I smiled in understanding and turned to watch the men riding.

"Which one is which and who was the one I was rude to?"

I turned to see her craning her neck to see the men.

"I'm not taking you over there unless we clear a few things up," I said.

Her eyes shot back to me, "I'm sorry about this morning. I don't know what I expected when I came out here but you kicking me off the property was not it."

"Then why did you come out here?"

"Just to talk, Mom…honestly…I didn't intend to be rude but he caught me by surprise. It was just another part of you getting your life back and…"

"Jamie," I huffed. "My life will never be back."

"Mom…?"

"My life before is done…gone…it died. I'm onto a new life that revolves around picking up the pieces and getting happy again. That's what those five men out there have done for me."

"I don't understand." She whispered.

"I lost everything and nearly faded into the dirt. Those men invited me into their lives to help me get my feet on the ground…to get all four hooves on the ground. I'm not there yet but I'm trying and they won't let me quit."

Tears rose in her eyes, "I'm so sorry, Mom. I truly am. Can you forgive me? Please?"

I looked into those eyes that I loved since before she was born and looked for any animosity, sarcasm, or underlining bitchiness but I couldn't see any.

"All this from me kicking you off the property?"

She took a deep breath, "That and shoving me back in the car. You've never laid a hand on me and I just realized how much you must be hurting…how much I hurt you for you to get that emotional. And…I just…it never crossed my mind of never being here again."

"The ranch?" I whispered and looked around the property my uncle had built, my ex-husband had coveted and my best friend had craved. "You only want to be here because of the ranch?" I looked back at her in rising heartbreak.

"No! Mom!" She gasped with wide disbelieving eyes. "Why would you say that? It's you I want back. Like you said, we had thousands and thousands of memories together whether we were here or on the road at races and rodeos. I love this ranch…it was my childhood home, built for us to have a fun wonderful life…which we did. But why would I want to be here if you aren't here?" She asked. "You give it life for me."

My own tears welled as she spoke and I had to wipe them away. "Thank you for that."

"Oh, Mom!"

She ran into my open arms and we held each other tightly…trying to squeeze away the last year.

I kissed her cheek, then her forehead then her cheek again. I pulled her in tight again and reveled in the fact she was back in my life. I just had to get through the confrontation with her father. What secrets were going to come of that?

CHAPTER TWENTY FOUR

"We'll face his secrets together…don't let him tear us apart again." I said earnestly.

"Never again, Mom," She pulled me into another embrace. "I'm never losing you again."

The metal chute clanging open drew her eyes back to the arena.

"Can I meet them?"

"Yes," I looked out to the riders.

The men were pushing the steers through the arena and into the alley. They all continued to glance back at us then to the steers.

When we walked hand in hand through the gate they left the steers and trotted over to us. They dismounted and looked to me.

"Jamie, this is the team roping crew that have been annoying me. Guys, this is my daughter." I smiled proudly.

All five grinned at her but Kade's eyes came back to me; silently asking me if I was OK. I just nodded with a relieved smile.

"Jamie, here with the sorrel, is Ryle," I decided he wouldn't appreciate it if I introduced him the same way that Marty had introduced him to me…as the young pup.

"You posted the pictures on Facebook," Jamie stretched a hand out to him.

"Yes, ma'am." Ryle nodded and shook her hand.

"Thank you so much," She grinned. "It was upsetting to see her roping without me but it pushed me to come home."

Ryle blushed and looked at me with a grin, "It took a lot of talking to get her to give me permission to post them."

"Well…I'm glad you did," She smiled brightly.

There was a brief pause as the two looked at each other.

"And this is Jess," I said loudly.

Jamie shook hands with him and they both looked shyly at each other then to me.

"And this is Marty. He owns the steers and is married to Sarah…a wonderful woman." I said.

"I look forward to meeting her," Jamie shook his hand.

"It's an honor to meet you," Marty's eyes sparkled then looked at me. "You two sure look a lot alike."

"Both really pretty," Jess whispered. His eyes opened a little wider as if surprised he said it out loud. He stared at me and didn't even glance at Jamie.

I wanted to laugh but contained myself.

"You look more like sisters," Ryle smiled shyly.

Jamie laughed, "We've been mistaken for sisters before."

"And this is Pete…he invited me to join their crew." I smiled warmly at him and his eyes looked at me proudly.

"Oh…thank you!" Jamie shook his hand vigorously, her eyes beamed happiness.

"It has been very interesting getting to know your mother," Pete teased.

I laughed right along with the other four men.

"And this is Kade," I said and grinned at him.

"I am so sorry!" Jamie shook his hand with wide apologetic eyes.

"It's OK…as long as everything is OK with you two now." Kade said.

"It is!" She beamed at me then turned back to him. "I cannot apologize enough…you just took me by surprise and I…" Her cheeks blushed red.

"Yeah," Marty nodded with a thoughtful look. "I'm sure Lauren was surprised when she found him asleep in front of the TV this morning."

Chuckles rang out as Jamie looked at me in confusion. Her eyes darted to a grinning Kade then back to me.

I rolled my eyes and smiled at her. "You'll learn real fast that these damn team ropers are nothing more than a bunch of smart asses."

They all laughed as Jamie grinned. Her eyes went back to the steer then to their horses. She turned and looked at me.

"We have time…" She glanced at the men then back to me. "Can I join you? Can I…?"

"Yes," Those damn team ropers and I answered.

She laughed again and the true happiness in her voice made my heart warm. "Can I ride, Marko?" She asked me. "Are you riding JW or BlueDoc?"

All five ropers turned and looked at me in anticipation.

"Of course, you can ride Marko," I answered with a sense of ease. "I'll be riding JW and maybe some with BlueDoc, too."

She looked down at her shorts then to the men. "I'll go change…I'll be right back."

She grinned at me again then turned and nearly ran out of the arena with her long dark hair bouncing down her back.

I looked back at Jess and Ryle who were watching her like she was a bowl of ice cream…or a new herd of fresh steers.

"Get your eyes back in your head," I said and they both turned with guilty wide eyes and flushed cheeks. "The last thing I need is my daughter hooked up with a damned team roper."

All five looked at me with brows raised and a tip of the head.

A devilish chuckle escaped me as I turned away to catch my horses for the first time in a month.

Kade followed me into the tack room.

"What did she mean by 'you have time'?" He asked.

I retrieved three halters and lead ropes then paused to look at him thoughtfully. There really wasn't a reason to lie to him.

"Her father is on his way here for a confrontation," I answered. "He's driving down from Pendleton."

"A confrontation?" He glared.

"She told him I kicked her off the property and asked him to come help."

"What the hell for?" He growled. "It looks like you two are fine now."

I shrugged, "I personally never want to see him again but he is her father. She wants to know what happened that led up to last year's catastrophe."

"What catastrophe?"

"The final court hearing for the divorce."

"That what came between you two?"

"Yes, she wants to know the truth and neither of us believes he will ever tell her the truth so she wants to hide and listen to him boast to me."

"And when he finds out she's there and it was a setup?" Kade's eyes narrowed.

"He'll just get pissed and drive away…hopefully never to be heard from again." I sighed. "Which will make my life better but break Jamie's heart."

"I'm not leaving." He said flatly and left no room for discussion.

"He won't talk with you here and it will just drag this issue out."

"Then he won't know I'm here either."

With that, he turned and walked out of the tack room. He was opening the front double doors of the barn as I stepped out and walked to the gate.

All three horses nearly knocked me over trying to get their noses into the halters. Evidently, they had missed roping and riding too.

Even though he was nine years old, JW was like a little puppy with me. I buckled his halter then tossed the lead rope over his back. We had spent thousands of hours together and I knew he would follow me out of the pasture and into the barn while I led the other two.

An engine roared to life and I turned to watch Kade drive his truck right into the barn. I presumed he had decided to hide it. Good plan, I thought. I wasn't worried about me physically but I wasn't ready to let him go. It could get very emotional for Jamie and having him there for support for both of us would be nice.

Another engine roared to life as I stepped through the gate.

Jess' truck then Marty's truck both started their way to the barn.

I looked at Kade who was walking toward me with a hand stretched out for a lead rope.

"What's going on?" I asked.

"They aren't leaving either," He smirked. "All three trucks and Jamie's car will fit in the barn."

Jamie's car started moving with Pete in the driver's seat.

"This is a bit of an overreaction." I sighed and handed him Marko's lead rope.

We waited at the side of the barn until all three trucks and the car were parked inside.

I slung the lead rope for BlueDoc over the hitching post and JW stepped in next to him.

Jamie stepped out the back door of the house in jeans, blue tank top, and her hair in a ponytail and sticking out the back of a 'Go Rope' baseball cap. I was thinking how beautiful and happy she looked and how much I had missed her the last 14 months when my phone vibrated twice.

"What the hell?" I reached for my phone.

My ex-husband was driving through the gate.

"Shit!" I looked up at Jamie whose arm was in the air swinging an imaginary rope then a quick throw…repeat. "Your dad is already here," I called out.

The grin disappeared and her hand froze mid-air.

I turned to Kade, "Leave the horses in the corral, maybe he won't notice the saddles. I'll try to distract him so you can get them off. Please, hide in the barn." I turned and walked toward the house. JW followed me as if he was attached.

"Mom?" Jamie cried out.

"Get in the swing," I pointed and she ran to slowly crawl onto the wide seat to keep it from swinging too much. She placed pillows toward the back to hide.

My truck was within twenty feet of the swing so I walked to it and lowered the tailgate as the sound of the car approached. I jumped into the back of the truck and opened the toolbox to pretend to be searching for something as he rounded the corner into the driveway.

My heart constricted at the sight of his cocky grin as he looked at me through the windshield. How could a person go from loving someone so much and wanting to spend your entire life with them, to hating them so much you wished they would just explode?

He stepped out of the car at least 20 pounds heavier than the last time I saw him in the courthouse. When we were married, he was very rarely without a cowboy hat but he wasn't even wearing a hat today and his dark blond hair was longer, almost touching the collar of his blue polo shirt. He was only an inch taller than me but much broader. He was still handsome…but inside he was ugly.

When he shut the door, I realized he didn't key in the gate code. I change the number every couple weeks so there was no way he would know it. My phone had vibrated twice which meant a receiver had opened the gate. He left the property two years ago and this was not the car he owned at the time. That son of a bitch!

The ire rose in my gut and my veins tingled in hatred. I jumped out of the back of the truck and walked right at his parked car that was within 25 feet our hidden daughter. JW was right behind me.

"That horse…" Blake started to say.

"Don't fucking mention my horse," I growled and walked past him to the driver's side of the car. I opened the door and popped the latch to open the hood. "You want to explain why you have a receiver for my gate on this damn car?"

He turned his back to the barn and I glanced to see saddles sliding off the horses. Not a person was in sight.

"Didn't see any reason to get rid of it," He smirked.

"Other than the restraining order keeping you away from the property and me?" I lifted the hood then reached down and removed the transmitter. Leaving the car hood up as I walked back to my truck and tossed the receiver into the open toolbox.

"That restraining order should have been issued the other way around." He glared.

"Problem is…" I gave him the cocky grin he always threw my way. "The judge wasn't as stupid or blind as you were hoping."

He shrugged with his eyes finally moving out past me and to the pastures, horses, and barns. "You still have a lot of horses. Anyone else here?"

I gave him a bland look, "You just scoped it out. Does it look like anyone else is here?"

His eyes swept over the property again then came back to me.

"You also didn't tell me about the property trust either," His hand reached out to my horse who stood between us.

"Keep your damned hands off my horse," I shoved his hand away and stepped between them.

"He's half mine."

I smirked, which I knew would piss him off. "No, he isn't…nothing here has ever been half yours. The Judge pointed that out to you."

"That fucking uncle of yours lied to me." Blake snarled.

"Guess he was a whole lot smarter than you ever gave him credit for," I chuckled…which I knew would piss him off too. His neck turning red said I was right. "Between Uncle Austin, the judge, and me? Well, you really should quit underestimating people."

He huffed, "You got the property because of the trust but I got you where it really hurt."

"What the hell does that mean?"

He grinned…knowing he had a secret that I hadn't guessed yet…Jamie was right.

His eyes went over the property again. It was quiet.

"Where's Andrea?" He smirked.

My eyes narrowed, "Home."

"Yeah, according to some mutual friends, she hasn't exactly been hanging around here since you got your boss murdered."

I tried not to flinch or react in any way but I could feel my skin moisten.

He huffed again with his secret dancing in his eyes.

"And where is our daughter?" He grinned again which made my stomach clench. "She called me in a bit of distress."

"That why you're here?" I asked. "Because I kicked her off my property this morning?"

"It's not yours…remember?" He lifted a brow. "It belongs to the trust."

I laughed coldly. His mentioning Andrea and Jamie had my anxiety up but I couldn't help but gloat back at him. "After the divorce was final and I was over 40, the property and everything that came with it is mine…free and clear. I guess you and that bitch wife of yours should have held out a bit longer."

His face turned red, eyes narrowed and lip snarled. I don't think I had ever seen him so angry.

"And there is that underestimating issue again," I smirked.

"Austin said the prenup was after twenty years of marriage." He hissed.

I shrugged, "Our married years didn't matter. It was the divorce itself that triggered the age factor." I chuckled. "You ever find it odd you had a prenup for our marriage with my uncle and not me? Guess he didn't trust you."

A low growl escaped him, "Yeah, well, now you may have this property and everything on it but I know it doesn't mean as much to you as your best friend and daughter did."

"Did?"

CHAPTER TWENTY FIVE

His secretive smile appeared again, "I've been working Andrea for years. I knew she was in love with Austin and took his death hard but she took a back seat to you during that time and ever since. Did you know they slept together?"

When I didn't respond he shrugged then continued.

"When we approached the twenty-year mark, I started telling her you were in love with Greg and I was feeling like you fell out of love with me. I kept telling her how unfair it was that she didn't get anything from her affair with Austin…that no one seemed to care that she was hurting too."

Wow, I did not see that coming but I kept myself from reacting.

"Bette and I saw her and Stan at dinner one night and 'accidentally' ran into them and invited ourselves to their dinner. I just kept telling them how much you had changed and to please give Bette a chance." He shrugged. "After last year's incident in the courthouse with you screaming and yelling, she began to believe it. I think the whole property trust thing kind of blindsided her and Jamie too…so I used that in convincing them that you had changed…you were keeping secrets." He looked around the property again and back to the house. "Pretty empty here by yourself without your daughter and best friend."

"So…that was your goal?" I asked guardedly. "To get your revenge by taking away the two things that meant more to me than the property?"

His grin was absent of the secret now.

"Yeah…been telling Jamie that you were screwing a couple cowboys way back when so I asked you to quit team roping…that way she would quit blaming me." He shrugged with a smirk. "She felt sorry for me, so I added you having an affair with a roper after she went to college and it drove me into Bette's arms."

"You know damn well I haven't slept with anyone but you," I growled. Damn, I hated this man. "So you think hurting our daughter helps your cause?"

"According to the call I received from Jamie this morning about you kicking her off the property…I'd say I accomplished that." His grin held pure pride in himself.

I thought of the moments in the arena after Andrea had walked away; the devastation, betrayal, and loneliness I had felt. How I had willed every breath to be my last. He had almost accomplished his goal. He had almost broken me but I would never let him know.

"You and that bitch wife tried manipulating me, the court system, then Andrea and worst of all, your own daughter."

"If I couldn't have the property or, to be more exact, the money so I could build my own life, then yeah…I was taking them from you so all you had was the property. That's what Austin wanted for you and that is what you got for cheating me out of what was rightfully mine."

I shook my head in disbelief, "Why? How did our happy marriage go so bad that you spent years manipulating everyone to get money?"

"Well, that's your fault." He said accusingly.

"Mine?" I asked in surprise.

"You took our daughter," He spat. "You refused to have any more babies then you took our only child and did nothing but barrels and break away. You were both in that damned arena or gone all the fucking time."

"You were with us for years and could have…"

"I'm not going to go sit around at a fucking barrel race waiting for you or being your damned groom."

"It's called supporting your daughter!" I huffed. "Millions of parents do it and I only started barrel racing because you talked me out of team roping." I pointed out in rising anger.

"Because you flirted with everyone."

"I did not! I just happened to know most of them and we were FRIENDS."

"They were only your friends to get at this place."

"That's just ridiculous," I said. "I don't believe that's the reason…there's something else."

He glared with his chest rising in growing anger.

"You stopped roping a couple years after Austin died…longer than that…Jamie was about twelve."

He didn't say anything so I knew I was on target.

"She and I won that district rodeo together…team roping…and we both won our division in breakaway. You didn't rope again after that."

His lip lifted in a snarl, "Do you know how embarrassing it is to have everyone tell me, as a grown fucking man, that my twelve-year-old and my wife were better ropers than I would ever be?"

I gasped in surprise, "You quit because we were good ropers? That's just stupid." I huffed. "Other than the fact that you SHOULD have been proud, we were both trained by a world champion roper! I was his training partner for over ten years, Dumb Ass. Of course, I was good and Uncle Austin and I trained Jamie." I shook my head in disbelief. How did I not know this? "You gave up years of being with your daughter at rodeos and races because you were jealous of her talent. You talked me out of team roping in the jackpots when she was nine or ten…was that because I am a better roper than you?"

"That was all the men you were flirting with. All those damned men wanted was to screw you, get rid of me, then take over this place."

"What the hell would make you say that?"

"Because that's what I was told." He snarled.

"By who?"

He hesitated…eyes narrowed…then his neck turned red again.

"Son of a bitch," I gasped. "That damn bitch wife of yours. She was married to George Masterson…the roper from Meridian." I laughed at the audacity. "She fucking manipulated you. That's where all this is coming from."

"She didn't manipulate me," He growled. "She just pointed it out."

"Bullshit!" I chuckled and his jaw clenched with the muscles twitching. "She started working you while she was still married to George. Once she saw that you gave into her will by stopping me from team roping then she knew she had you. The two of you got together 3 or 4 years ago, right after she and George got the divorce. Then you decided to wait until the twenty-year marriage clause was up in the so-called prenup so you could try to get me to sell half of everything or force me to buy you out."

We stared at each other. I knew I was right and he was beginning to realize his bitch wife had been manipulating him for years.

"I'm right and you know it," I gloated. "How does being manipulated feel to you? If she hadn't started working on you, way back when, then we'd still be happily married and you would still have an adoring wife and beautiful daughter and still be living here…with all of it and not just half."

When he didn't respond more than his nostrils flaring to go along with the jaw muscles twitching, I continued.

"Was the bitch wife worth it? Was she worth giving up the two of us?"

"You're nothing special," He hissed. "Alright to look at, decent in bed, but you'll never be more than an average 4D horse in a 1D world."

"Yes," I seethed as the heat rose in me. "You've told me that before. Did she feed you that line? She was a barrel racer before marrying George and that's more of a jealous vindictive woman thing to say."

His upper lip snarled which meant I was right again.

Then I smiled because he hadn't really mentioned the bitch wife, I had.

"Did she still stay married to you once she realized she wasn't getting half of my life? She just got the worst part?"

His eyes moved behind me…where the swing would be…his eyes widened.

I turned back to see our daughter standing next to the swing with tears flowing down her cheeks. My heart ached. I had truly forgotten she was even there. That's what my hatred for this man had done to me.

I turned back to tell him to leave. The back of his right hand hit me just above my ear which caused a ringing to go along with Jamie's scream. I gasped and started to fall backward but caught myself by grabbing JW's mane. I started to stand when Blake grabbed my shoulders and threw me to the ground under the horse who danced away with flying hooves.

"Dad!" Jamie screamed.

The shock of his assault changed to self-protection. I kicked at him as he leaned down to me with eyes blazing in anger. He gripped the front of my shirt with his right hand and his left was reaching for my braid when Jamie rushed to his side and pulled at his arm. He rolled his shoulder and pushed her making her stumble and fall behind him then he came at me again.

I lost all reason in my head as I screamed and kicked until his grip on my shirt released. I landed a few good kicks to his side and knees then scraped his cheeks two good slashes before he let go of me. His eyes rose toward the barn. He paused long enough Jamie hit him from behind and grabbed his arm; he pushed her so hard she fell back on the ground with a thud and a gasp.

Then I heard the thunder of boots hitting gravel.

Blake rose to his feet and turned toward his car but was stopped when Jess appeared to block his escape. Blake turned back to me but Kade was now standing in front of me with Ryle in front of Jamie. Their furious eyes and fighting stances made it very clear what would happen if he approached us. Pete and Marty appeared and helped me and Jamie rise to our feet.

No one said a word; JW's hoofbeats broke the silence as he walked up behind me.

"You said no one was here," Blake hissed.

"I just asked you if you saw anyone," I growled.

Pete's arm tightened around me. "The police are on the way."

"What the fuck?" Blake stared at him then turned back to his car.

Jess braced himself with a foot back and fists poised in front of him as if he was a boxer. "Come at me." He threatened with dark angry eyes. There was no doubt he was hoping Blake would try to get to his car.

Considering Jess was a good 3 inches taller, 50 pounds of muscle heavier, and twenty years younger, Blake did the right thing by stopping. Blood trickled from the gashes I'd left on his cheeks and his attempt to wipe it away caused red streaks.

Sirens started approaching and I fumbled for my phone…it wasn't in my pocket.

"Here," Ryle bent to retrieve my phone from the ground and handed it to me.

My trembling hands took it and I barely managed to remotely trigger the gate. Pete's arm tightened around me.

"It's all over now," He whispered reassuringly.

I just nodded and turned to Jamie. She fell into my arms and I held her tightly and squeezed even tighter when her body began to tremble. I glared at my ex-husband.

"I take it Bitch Wife divorced you." I snarled at him.

"She did," Jamie answered. "Right after the courthouse incident last year."

Incident…that was now the definition of a murder on my property and my screaming in the courthouse last year. I had no doubt this confrontation would become the next incident in my life.

The police car appeared on the road and turned down the driveway.

The officer that had washed Dave's blood off my patio appeared from the car. He slowly removed his dark sunglasses and tossed them back into the car.

"Thank God you're here!" Blake gasped at Officer Mullins. "These men have attacked me."

We all looked at Blake then Mullins who was looking at me.

"I have his DNA under my fingernails from his attacking my daughter," I held up my hands. "Would you like to see?"

A slight smile appeared from the officer's glare, "No, Ms. Connors, I believe you." He turned to Blake. "From the look on these men's faces…and you're not beaten to a pulp, I'd say she was telling the truth."

"I have something…" Jamie's voice quivered and she stepped out of my arms to walk to the swing. She returned with her phone in her hand.

We all silently waited until my voice echoed from her phone as Jamie handed it to the officer for him to watch the video.

"Was the bitch wife worth it? Was she worth giving up the two of us?"

"You're nothing special," Blake's voice answered. *"Never been much to look at, decent in bed, but you'll never be more than an average 4D horse in a 1D world."*

"Yes," My voice answered and my body wilted. What a horrible thing to have all these men hear. *"You've*

told me that before. Did she feed you that line? She was a barrel racer before marrying George and that's more of a jealous vindictive woman thing to say."

There was a pause and Officer Mullins looked up at me; my face blazed red in embarrassment as my voice continued.

"Did she still stay married to you once she realized she wasn't getting half of my life? She just got the worst part?"

Jamie's voice gasped then a surprised yell from me and a growl from Blake…then Jamie screaming "Dad."

Another couple minutes of sounds from the phone. Jamie returned to my arms as the tears fell again.

The officer stopped the recording then looked up at me. "The ambulance should be here any second. They'll check both of you over." He nodded to Jamie then his hand moved behind his back. Handcuffs dangled from his fingers as he walked to my ex-husband. "You're under arrest for assault of both women."

"There is a restraining order against him," Jamie turned with a stronger more defiant voice as her father glared at her. "He wasn't supposed to come within a hundred yards of Mom or this property."

"I was invited here," Blake argued.

The officer looked at me with a raised questioning brow…clearly showing he didn't believe him.

"Hell would have frozen over before I invited him to this place," I said.

"Well, we got you for that too." The officer pulled Blake along the car and opened the back door.

Blake turned and looked at me with a glare. All five of my team roping crew stepped in front of me and glared back at him. Blake disappeared into the back seat and the officer slammed the door closed.

The ambulance appeared and while they checked on my ringing ears and the lump on the side of my head, Officer Mullins talked to Jamie and had her forward the video from her phone to him and someone else at the police station. Ryle walked JW back to the barn and tied him up next to the other horses. Kade and Pete did not leave my side for even a moment.

CHAPTER TWENTY SIX

The ambulance left and the officer walked to his car then stopped and looked back. "Just so you know," He said to me. "There are a lot of good-hearted, beautiful 4D horses out there, but you're top of the line 1D, any day of the week."

I blushed with an embarrassed chuckle as he grinned and opened his car door.

As the police car disappeared, the energy in my body began to fade. I needed to sit down…recover…and hold my daughter.

As if she was reading my mind, Jamie took my hand and we walked to the swing together. With our arms wrapped around each other, we nestled into the pillows. All five men found chairs and placed them in front of us with Kade placing his chair next to me…which I appreciated. Other than holding my daughter, the only thing that could be better is if he had his arms around me.

"Thank you," Jamie said to them. "I never would have dreamed…when I asked him to come here…I just never…" Her voice trembled and a hand lifted to wipe away tears.

"Lauren?" Pete said.

We all looked at him.

"I'm glad you got a few claws into him," Pete nodded and I smiled. "Proud of you for helping your mom," He said to Jamie. "But I'm proud of you men for minding what I told you."

"It wasn't easy," Kade growled.

"What?" I asked.

Pete answered, "I told them not to lay a hand on him unless they had too. That way the jackass couldn't try to sue them and make the whole situation worse. And, all the damage to his face was from you…it's a greater statement than if we had all hit him like we wanted to."

I looked around at each of the men. By the looks on their faces, they all wanted to say what they wanted to do to Blake but they just glanced at Jamie then to another part of the ranch.

"Your horse sure does like you," Ryle broke the awkward silence.

"She was with him when he was born," Jamie answered and rose in the seat a bit. "JW has followed her like that ever since. Even in the house!"

"What?" Ryle sat straighter and looked at me accusingly.

I started chuckling.

"You let JW go in the house but you wouldn't let Silas?" He gasped.

"JW was only a yearling," I grinned.

"So…?" He started to say.

"Well, there was Uncle Austin's horse, Mitchum…he went in too," Jamie giggled.

While the other men grinned, Ryle shook his head at me, "And you wouldn't let Silas."

Jamie giggled again, "JW is special, he's one of Maggie's…well all of them are."

"All of who?" Kade asked.

"…and who is Maggie?" Jess added.

Jamie sat up in the swing and turned to look at me in surprise, "You haven't told them about Maggie?"

"No…we really haven't discussed the horses," I answered.

"SHE hasn't discussed the horses," Ryle said. "We've been wondering about them…especially why there are three draft horses with quarter horse foals nursing on them."

"Mom…Maggie is so special." Jamie said.

"I know," I smiled with a bit of guilt rising. "It is just that…well…I just didn't have the heart to ride this last month without…" Andrea, I wanted to say but didn't want to go into that discussion.

"Well, why don't you get your butt up and introduce us to this herd," Pete said and rose.

Jamie chuckled which made my body relax. By focusing on the horses, she wouldn't be focused on her father.

"Alright," I said.

All five men stood quickly and hands were out to help us stand.

Jamie chuckled and looked at me, "I like these guys."

"Yeah, well, you haven't spent enough time with them yet to learn any better." I grinned at them.

I looked out at Blake's car with the hood still up.

"I'll get a call out to the towing company," Marty said and lifted his phone.

I gripped my daughter's hand tightly as I walked to the pasture.

"So who is Maggie?" Ryle asked.

We stopped at the fence and I pointed to a bay mare that was grazing behind all the others. "That is Maggie, she was Uncle Austin's horse…she's twenty-two now. You know the great stallion Stoli My Heart?" I asked the men.

"Yeah…" They all answered.

"Well, he is out of Stoli and Maggie is Stoli's full sister." Jamie said.

"Whoa…Stoli was out of First Down Dash," Jess exhaled. "That's impressive."

"She was hurt so we don't ride her but we use her as a broodmare…sort of." I continued.

"What's sort of?" Pete asked.

"She can't carry a foal so we harvest three embryos from her each year and use the three draft mares as the recipients and they carry them for her," I answered.

"Any particular reason you use draft horses?" Ryle asked.

"We didn't always use draft horses. We've had other grade or quarter horses as surrogates but we came upon these three and their cycles were timed perfectly with Maggie's. They are just wonderful with very calm dispositions," Jamie answered. "Even though the foal's DNA belongs to Maggie and the stallion of our choosing, the calm demeanor of the mother helps keep the foals calmer the first couple of months. They are so friendly and easier to handle."

"Like JW," Kade said.

"Yes," I smiled warmly at him. "He has been my main roping horse for the last four years. BlueDoc is my barrel horse."

"Other than the three draft horses," Jamie said. "All the other horses are Maggie's foals."

"All of them?" Jess asked.

"Yes, and we've sent a number of them down to Texas for Ace and Taylor," I said.

"Who are they?" Marty asked.

"Uncle Austin's sons as well as my cousins," I answered. "They are 17 and 18 now and since they started in rodeo, they have always ridden a Maggie foal."

"They are Texas high school champions in team roping together and Taylor is in calf roping," Jamie said proudly. "Both already have full-ride college scholarships and Quincy, Taylor's horse, has been Horse of the Year the last two years."

"We have Maggie foals from 13 years old to those three foals." I pointed to the other pasture where the three golden Belgian draft horses were grazing with the three four-month-old foals; two light colored and one dark.

"Oh, Mom! How cute!" She took off walking to them then stopped about halfway.

The rest of us stopped behind her and waited to see what she was doing.

"Mom?" She whispered without turning around.

I walked to her to find her wiping away a tear so I slid an arm around her.

"What?" I whispered.

She turned tear-filled eyes to me, "I have always been involved with who we breed Maggie to and the foaling…first couple months." Her chin quivered. "Did you rebreed them?"

"Yes, to the stallions we talked about last year."

She stared out at the foals as her body began to tremble and more tears fell, "I can't believe he would do that to me." She whispered. "He didn't even care if he hurt me or not. He just didn't…I missed so much. WE missed so much this last year because of him…and that bitch wife."

"But we're together now." I squeezed her tightly and silently cursed her father.

"I don't want to go see the foals right now." She whispered. "But I'm a bit embarrassed."

I turned to see the five men waiting patiently.

"Let's get the horses saddled again and chase some steer," I said to them.

They immediately turned and walked to the barn.

"You going to be OK?" I asked her.

"Mom," She turned to me with wide eyes. "Are you OK? How is your head? Should you be riding?"

"Yes, fine and of course," I squeezed her tightly one more time then turned her to the barn.

"Which is your saddle?" Jess said from the tack room door.

I started to answer when I realized he was looking directly at my daughter…like I wasn't even there.

Damn team roper.

I saddled my own horse with a grin to Kade who was waiting at the gate for me.

I ran a hand down JW's shoulder then stepped up into the saddle.

"I'm looking forward to this," Kade said as we walked around the arena.

"To what?" I asked.

"To actually riding with you," He smiled. "Instead of you just sitting on a horse next to me."

"Or Marty leading me around," I chuckled.

"Yeah…that." He laughed.

I really wanted his arms around me…I wanted him to kiss me.

Jamie's laughter erupted behind us.

I closed my eyes and listened to every decibel of her laugh. My body relaxed as Pete's words came back to me;

"We're here to help you. Let us be that first hoof on the ground to help you get to all four." He had whispered.

I released a long slow breath then opened my eyes and looked for him.

He was standing next to his red roan horse, just getting ready to start up the mounting block. Almost like he knew I was looking at him he turned and looked at me. I smiled to let him know and he just nodded.

The second hoof was firmly on the ground.

The clanging of the chute opening brought me back to reality and I turned to see Marty pushing the steers out of the alley, through the chute, and into the arena.

"They've been sitting in the shade for the last hour napping," Marty said. "Let's push them through and wake them up."

Jess, Ryle, and Jamie trotted behind the steers with Jamie riding between the pair.

I pulled JW to a stop and watched them ride all the way across the arena.

"What's the matter?" Kade stopped next to me.

"They are both smitten with her," I said.

"Of course they are…she's a younger version of you," Kade huffed.

I turned and looked at him in concern. "I have this fear inside." I touched my chest. "I'm afraid she's going to come between them."

Kade turned and watched the trio then nodded. "Yeah…we just hope this works itself out."

"I would just die if…" I left the words unsaid.

JW was excited the first time we entered the roping box…first time in fifteen months. He pranced excitedly so I walked him out then back in. I waited until he calmed down then walked him back out.

"Score one," I said to Marty.

He pushed the lever and JW jumped as the steer bolted down the dirt.

"One more, please," I said and Marty grinned up to me.

"Who is more excited? You or the horse?" He asked.

"My heart is thumping out of my chest," I chuckled. "I'm trying to calm myself down."

"Just ride, Darlin'," Pete said from the side. "Don't mean you have to throw…just bust out."

I smiled at him then turned to my daughter in the heeler box. My heart swelled at the sight I had seen a thousand times…the sight I had prayed would return and now here she was as if the last fifteen months hadn't happened.

Her arm held the rope out to her side in preparation of the run. Her eyes filled with tears again as she waited.

I nodded to Marty and the steer bolted with JW and I following.

Muscle memory…my arm and body knew exactly what to do…so did my horse.

My heart was riding in my throat as I twirled the rope in the air. My whole body tingled in excitement as I threw the loop. It swirled around the horns then flew off.

"Damn," I growled. That was not a good way to show off to my team roping crew.

"Mom, we've talked about this," Jamie called out. "You have to at least give me a chance to throw!"

We looked at each other and laughed.

My racing heart was filled with joy.

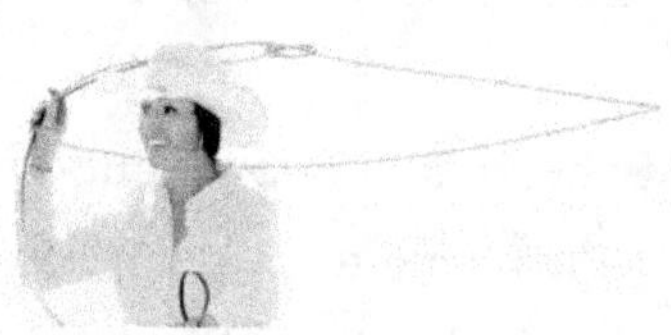

"You know I want you here," I whispered to Kade as we stood in the barn and watched the vehicles slowly moving out to the driveway.

"You need to be with your daughter," He said then pulled me into the tack room and shut the door.

Seconds later our lips met. It started in desperation of knowing we weren't staying together then it changed to enjoyment of just touching each other. It was still a bit bizarre to actually be kissing him.

His lips rose just inches from mine, "I wanted to do that all damn day."

"Oh, me too," I whispered. "It's been such a weird roller coaster day."

"I hate your ex-husband."

"Oh, me too," I sighed.

"I wanted to rip him apart but Grandad just kept telling me to keep my hands off him…to go to you."

"Thank you…"

"He reminded us that he wasn't just your ex-husband, he was Jamie's father…to think of Jamie. If anything happened she would be devastated and if we attacked him then it would just traumatize her more."

"Oh…" I melted into him. "Thank you all for thinking of her."

"She is a joy to be around."

"Yes, she is…thank you, I love her."

"She's going to have a rough night tonight when everything slows down and she starts thinking."

"Yeah…that's what I'm afraid of."

"Let me know if there is anything I can do." He whispered.

"There is…I need your arms…"

They slid back around me and crushed me to him as his lips found mine again.

Another five minutes of silent communication and we finally broke apart.

When we walked out the door, all five of them were leaning against the wall across the aisle from us.

"Checking to make sure the tack is in order?" Marty asked.

"Probably had to rearrange the bridles," Pete said.

"Dusting?" Jess grinned.

"Checking for mice?" Ryle smirked.

"Oiling the saddle?" Jamie grinned.

I rolled my eyes, "Damn team ropers! You've turned my daughter into a smart ass, too." I took a step then stopped and looked at their grinning faces. "No…wait…she's always been a smart ass."

We all laughed as Jamie looked at me with pure joy in her eyes.

CHAPTER TWENTY SEVEN

Marty, Kade, and Pete left, Ryle and Jess disappeared into the bunkhouse and I introduced Jamie to the chicks and the kittens. She played with them long enough it took us an hour to get in the house.

She stepped in the door and looked around.

"I've missed this place." She sighed.

"It's nearly five…what would you like for dinner?" I asked.

We cooked a vegetable stir-fry together then cuddled on the couch until dark then changed into pajamas.

I changed the bedding on my bed since Kade and I had shared the bed the night before…and the morning. That seemed so long ago.

Jamie and I cuddled in the dark and lay quietly for a few minutes before her whole body sighed.

"I'm so happy to be home," She whispered.

"I'm so happy to have you home."

"I don't understand Dad."

"He changed," I whispered and pulled her in tighter.

"I'm sorry about last year."

"Me too…I shouldn't have grouped you in with my tirade."

"I deserved it, Mom. I was awful to you and if you had given in? This place would be gone. Our home would be gone and that bitch would have won."

"She was very…" I tried to think of a word other than manipulative.

"You have no idea," Jamie sighed.

We lay quietly, both of us staring into the dark night.

"Mom?" She whispered.

"What?"

"I want to move home."

"OK…college doesn't start until September."

"No, I want to move home permanently."

"You only have a couple more months at Idaho Falls since you graduate in the winter."

"I know but I…"

"Finish there, Hon. With Ryle and Jess here I can come to visit more often."

"I can get online classes too and try and get any classes left scheduled on the same day so I can just go over once a week."

"You have rodeo practice and rodeos this fall."

"Just a couple…"

"We'll work it out so we can be together and not miss a day."

"I just borrowed that car from a teammate to save money. I'll drive over in the morning and get the truck and horses…everything."

"Do you want me to go with you? Marty and Sarah are going with Jess and Ryle for this five-day road trip to help with the horses."

She hesitated.

"It's OK if you need to do it yourself," I whispered.

"I want to say goodbye to everyone. It may take a day or two and don't want you waiting around."

"It's OK, Hon. Jess, Ryle, Marty, and Sarah are headed to Redmond tomorrow then to Idaho Falls the next day. "

"OK…"

"Why don't you get what you need to be done and then they can help you move back over when they are over there?   Kade has meetings the next couple days but we're all going to the Cambridge rodeo Friday night and the Emmett Saturday night."

"What kind of meetings does Kade have?"

"He's an architect. Jess is a night manager at a warehouse. He helped Ryle get a night inventory position at one of the other stores so they don't spend 24 hours a day together. Marty and his wife have a small ranch and he was a manager at a farm store before retiring."

"And Pete? Why did they all listen to him instead of…?" Her words drifted away.

"Pete is a retired attorney."

"Oh…makes sense," She said. "You don't think they will mind helping me move?"

"No…they are a great group of people and will be happy to help."

We lay quietly long enough I began drifting off.

"Mom?" She said softly.

"Hmmm?"

"I'm so sorry for today."

"I know, Hon, so am I, but at the end of this weird day the most important thing is we are back together."

"I know tomorrow is Wednesday, but before we leave, can we have a Sunday morning in the swing? I've missed them so much."

"Oh, yes…me too," I sighed contently.

"I love you."

I kissed the top of her head and pulled her in closer. Within moments her body relaxed into the bed and her breaths deepened.

I stared into the darkness and thought of my marriage…my husband who I had adored even though Uncle Austin didn't really trust him. Until the day Blake told me he was leaving me for someone else, I had been blind to his greed but from that moment on it grew until the final court hearing settling the financials of our divorce. The divorce was official two months before and he and Bitch Wife had married the next day. He thought it was a slap in my face. By then, after months of turning down his requests for me to sell the estate, I really didn't care. She deserved him…they deserved each other but they surely didn't deserve everything my uncle had built.

From the afternoon's conversation with Blake, I now knew why Jamie had begged me to give him money to settle out of court or even give him a portion of the back property that we only used for trail riding.

It wasn't until I was sitting next to the judge with my attorney asking me questions that anyone knew the truth. My uncle had placed everything into a trust under Charlene's name with me as the executor.

"Your honor!" Blake's attorney had shouted. "There is no proof that the trust is valid."

The judge turned to me with a bland look, "Are you smart enough not to bring a fake trust into the court?"

At that point, I knew he had not been fooled by Blake and his bitch wife.

"Yes, sir," I answered with a defiant nod.

The judge turned back and declared the estate could no longer be used as part of the bargaining.

"The horses are all in Lauren Harrison's name," Blake's attorney said. "The value is listed on page four."

There was silence as my breath caught and I stared at Andrea whose eyes were wide in disbelief. I had thought it was because of the request to sell the horses. Now, I realized it was because I had not told her about the estate trust.

"Mrs. Harrison," The judge said.

"I am not a Harrison," I said firmly but tried to keep the respect in my voice. "In the divorce papers, my name was changed back to Conners."

"Of course," The judge nodded. "So, Ms. Conners, do you have anything to refute the claim?"

"No, your honor," I said slowly as my mind raced on what to say. "They are…but…"

I paused while staring thoughtfully at him. There was no emotion on his face but his eyes were pleading with me.

"Well, Ms. Conners?" Blake's attorney said with an 'I got you' tone.

I turned back to look at him then to Blake who was sitting with shoulders rising and lowering as he took deep angry breaths and his eyes told me he would take every horse he could.

Knowing how much Maggie's foals meant to Jamie and after all the years of living on that ranch, I was just astounded at his bitterness.

"Ms. Conners, if you have nothing…" The judge started.

I quickly turned back, "Ask him how much he paid each month to live on the property and help support his daughter."

The judge's left eyebrow rose just enough that I noticed but no one else could have seen it.

The judge turned to Blake, "How much did you pay to live on the property?"

Blake's attorney turned to look at him but found his client with chin dropped in disbelief.

"Ask how much he spent the twenty years and one day we were married for food and provisions for himself and his daughter," I said.

The judge repeated the question to a silent Blake but to a muttering attorney.

"Ask how much he had to pay for fuel that he pumped from the tank at the ranch," I said and the judge repeated it as he started writing on his notepad.

"Ask how much he paid for the medical bills for the birth of his daughter, her appendectomy, and her broken arm from a fall from one of those horses he wants me to sell." I stared at Blake who sat quietly with eyes flickering between me and the judge.

"Ask how much he paid for the company truck he was driving until the day he walked out on me and his daughter."

"Mother!" Jamie whispered harshly.

I turned to the judge, "Ask him how much he spent on my wedding ring or even the wedding itself."

"Your Honor!" Blake's attorney stood but he was clearly shaken.

"I get the point," The judge said to me with a bit of a smirk. He turned to Blake and his attorney. "I've done a bit of calculation here and looked at the cost of renting or buying a house to provide for your child…and the stabling and feeding of your and your daughter's horses and let's go with three different new vehicles over the twenty years and one day of the marriage. Then there is the fuel and insurance."

"Your honor," Blake's attorney said.

The judge's right hand rose to stop him from talking which he did immediately.

"Mr. Harrison?" The judge said.

"Yes?" Blake answered.

"Did you have a job the twenty years and one day you were married or did you work for the estate?" The judge's pen was poised over his notepad and his eyes fixated on Blake.

Blake took a deep breath then exhaled softly as he realized he was about to lose everything, "I had a job. I am a manufacturing manager at JR Simplot."

"That pays well," The judge mumbled as he wrote on this notepad.

There was silence in the room as we all watched the judge. I occasionally glanced at Jamie but not once did she look at me; her face was red and hands clenched tightly in her lap.

I looked at Blake's bitch wife. Her lips were pursed in a thoughtful twist as she stared at the back of his head. I had thought she was only there for the money and her pensive expression confirmed it.

"Let's just go with $2000 a month for twenty years and not consider the one day for now." The judge said and he had everyone's rapt attention. "Twelve months…twenty years…that's a total of 240 months…at $2,000 a month that calculates to $480,000."

I felt my whole body tremble in hope. The value of my horses was covered. In my heart, I knew they were safe.

"New trucks…insurance…" The judge looked at Blake. "You want me to keep calculating to see how much you owe the Conner trust?"

Blake's jaw clenched as he shook his head to the judge.

"You will receive the written decision which will state that Ms. Conners owes nothing to Blake Harrison. No portion of the livestock nor property were ever Mr. Harrison's so all property, horses included, that are on the estate and are in Ms. Conners' name are hers."

I exhaled in relief and looked at Jamie and Andrea. Jamie had her head down and Andrea had a smile of support.

The judge rose as Blake's chin dropped to his chest and his attorney leaned over to whisper to him.

I nodded to the judge and silently thanked him with my eyes then turned to my attorney. She was grinning.

The judge walked to the door in the corner of the room and disappeared through it.

I stood with a cocky grin and looked at my ex-husband as if he was nothing but a pile of manure I had to clean out of a stall.

"Mother," Jamie exhaled dramatically.

I ignored her and looked back at the bitch wife who was now leaned back against the wooden bench seat with her slender legs crossed. Her pale blonde hair was in a bob to her shoulders, her skin pale as if she hadn't seen the sun in years and her blue 'innocent' eyes moved from Blake to me…they changed just enough I knew she was pissed and defeated.

"You can have him, Bitch," I huffed. "All that work for nothing." From the narrowing of her eyes, I knew she took that just like I meant it; she was nothing more than a whore out for money.

"Mother!" Jamie gasped but I heard Andrea chuckle.

"You fucking bitch," Blake growled and stood abruptly. His hand shot out to a glass that was on the table and he threw it at me before his attorney could react. I ducked in time that it just breezed above my head. There was a loud crash on the wall behind me to go along with the loud gasps from Jamie, Andrea, and my attorney.

"Blake!" His attorney yelled.

The judge stepped back through the door that had not closed prior to Blake's outburst.

The room went completely silent.

"Mr. Harrison," The judge growled.

Blake glared at him in complete open contempt.

"Would you like to press charges?" The judge asked me.

"Not this time, I just don't ever want to see him again," I said while staring at Blake.

"I agree it would be best," The judge said. "I'm granting you a lifetime restraining order." He turned to Blake's attorney. "Mr. Harrison is not allowed within a hundred yards of the Conner Estate or Ms. Conners."

Jamie gasped, Andrea chuckled, Bitch Wife's hand covered her eyes, both attorneys shook their heads in disbelief and my ex-husbands face turned red with nostrils flaring.

I smiled politely at the judge and the court secretary then waited for them to leave. I heard the click of the door closing and turned to the man I had once pledged to love until death. We were staring at each other; eye to eye and full of bitterness.

"I can't believe how stupid you are." I taunted.

"Mother! Stop!" Jamie stood from the bench.

"Stop what?" I huffed. "I've had to put up with this jackass…"

"Mother!" Jamie literally stomped her foot…and that…pissed me off.

"You're still defending him?" I shook my head. "Did you not just witness what happened?"

"He was upset…" She started.

"No, he was pissed because all the scheming the two of them have been doing against me for the last three years just blew up in their faces and they walk away with nothing but each other…which they deserve!" My voice had risen with each word.

"You could have given…" Jamie started with desperate eyes going to her father.

"Jamie!" I screeched. "He's been working for over twenty years and he didn't have to pay for anything. How much do you think he has in the bank? He has plenty to take care of himself…he just doesn't want to. He's a damned leach!"

"Mother…" She huffed.

"Jamie…open your damn eyes and see what's right in front of you!" I said. "They don't want to work for anything…they just wanted everything in my life handed to them."

"They just wanted…" Jamie started.

"THEY Jamie! THEY!" I screamed at her. "THINK about that. They screwed around behind my back while your father and I were still married…for years!"

"I understand you're hurt and bitter from that," She said.

"Oh my God, Jamie!" I dramatically rolled my eyes. "You think by not giving him money… horses… property… is because I'm BITTER about them having an affair?"

She nodded slightly and my body trembled in anger.

"Wake up! Open your damn eyes and don't be so ridiculously gullible! You're more intelligent than that!"

Jamie's eyes opened wide in disbelief, her face turned red as she looked at her father, his bitch wife, the attorneys, and Andrea.

"I should be thanking that damn blonde slut for getting him away from me." I declared.

"She's not that way," Jamie whispered.

"JAMIE!" It was said with complete disgust at the top of my lungs.

Her eyes turned defiant, "You're not…you aren't…I want nothing to do with you!" She turned and ran out of the room.

I swung around and shot daggers at my ex-husband. The motion was so violent that Blake and his attorney took a step back. Bitch wife was cowering behind them.

I ignored the attorney; he was just doing his job.

"You became the lowest creature that ever roamed this earth because of that blonde slut," I growled at Blake. "I don't know how you could possibly even think of taking Maggie and her offspring from us. The only thing I can think of is jealousy…you're bitter and jealous of Uncle Austin and everything he had from his talent to his personality. You can't accept the fact that you'll never be half the man he was and you've just proven that to everyone in this room."

"The FACT is…" Blake growled. "…no one could compete with the relationship between the two of you!"

"YOU JACKASS!" I yelled with the veins in my neck enlarging and tightening. "YOU didn't have to compete with him for the last sixteen years because he was dead!" I took in a deep shaking breath. "You started the affair long after he died."

"And you still pine away…"

"BLAKE! He was my family! The only family I had before you and Jamie came along. I would have been pining away for you two also!"

"Austin…" He growled.

"Don't you blame him for your insecurities, adultery, and growing stupidity when it's your damn fault. Man the fuck up and admit it. I've put up with your persistent jabbing at my life, and I've had enough. If you cross that restraining order, I will prosecute you to the full extent and put your selfish, cheating, growing ass in jail."

"So, Jamie was right," He sneered. "It's all because of the affair."

I laughed…loud and a bit deranged.

His expression turned from self-riotous to embarrassment. He obviously realized it wasn't because of the affair, it was just about him and that I really didn't want or like him anymore. For a man like him, that was a huge hit on the ego.

"Let's go have a drink," Andrea said.

I turned my back on Blake and our past and walked out of the room with head held high.

It wasn't until I drove down my driveway and Jamie's truck wasn't there that I began to worry. Every day for a month I woke up thinking she would call, text, or drive into the driveway. Then, the realization came over me, I knew she meant what she said.

Andrea kept telling me that someday Jamie would be back and she was right…I just never would have dreamed that Andrea would be gone when it happened.

My arms tightened around my daughter and I closed my eyes to the very long day.

CHAPTER TWENTY EIGHT

We were both early risers, it came from having so many horses to feed before we could start a normal day. Jamie was in her room showering and getting ready for our Sunday morning on a Wednesday and I was standing in the kitchen filling our bowls with fresh cut fruit and yogurt. Having already taken my shower, my hair lay down my back and bare shoulders and I was dressed in a long jersey summer dress. The dress was blue and white striped and nearly reached the floor.

I heard footsteps down the stairs and turned to see my daughter in her matching blue striped dress, hair cascading down her back, and a wide happy smile gracing her beautiful face. But, one thing had to change.

"Honey," I chuckled.

"What?" She asked innocently.

"You must go capture the ta-tas."

"But, Mom," She stopped with a petulant sigh. "They like being free."

"Honey, we are no longer alone on the property."

"Oh!" Her cheeks turned red. "I forgot."

She turned and made her way back up to her room…I heard a humored little giggle as she climbed the stairs.

I couldn't help but laugh.

We made ourselves comfortable on the swing, sitting at the opposite ends with our feet together in the middle. Pillows were fluffed for comfort and a tray sat to the side with a carafe of coffee and the bowls of fruit. We each cradled a coffee mug in our hands as we smiled at each other.

The air was already warm, blue sky full of white puffy clouds, and there was quiet…peace.

"Tell me about your year," I said then took a sip of coffee and listened to her talk of classes, rodeos, practice, flirting boys, and bitchy girls. I took in every word while watching her expressions change.

"Did you call Andrea?" Jamie asked with a thoughtful look.

"No," I sighed. "She left here a couple weeks ago stating she didn't want anything to do with me again."

I gave her a shortened version of the fateful conversation. I did not mention the fact Andrea had slept with my uncle. There really was no need for her to know.

"She'll come around, Mom," Jamie looked at me with encouragement. "Just like I did."

"Well, Hon," I said softly. "I'm not sure that I want her back in my new life."

Jamie's jaw dropped in shock.

"I am rebuilding my life and my uncle's dream," I said. "I'm going to move forward…move on."

"But…I love her," Tears brimmed her eyes.

"I know, Hon. And just because she's not in my life doesn't mean she can't be in yours…just like this last year when she kept checking in on you."

"You knew about that?"

"I know her well enough that she loves you like a daughter and would make sure you are OK."

Jamie sighed with a slow nod, "I struggled at the rodeos this year. She and Coach really helped me get through them."

My heart ached that I wasn't there for her. "Well, between your coach at school this year and me at home…you're going to kick ass your final year."

We grinned at each other as the excitement of the upcoming rodeos began to grow.

The door to the bunkhouse opened with Ryle and Jess walking out. They walked toward the barn until Jess looked back to the house.

I waved them over to use them as a distraction so I didn't have to talk about Andrea.

"Sure glad the ta-tas are captured," Jamie giggled softly.

The two men brought patio chairs to the swing and sat next to us. Both were smiling happily between the two of us.

"I want to thank you again," Jamie said to Ryle. "If you hadn't posted all those pictures on Facebook I don't know how long it would have been before I got brave enough to come home."

"You're more than welcome," Ryle said. "We've really enjoyed coming here and getting to know Lauren."

Both men grinned. I knew they were thinking of the aromatic ride back from the jackpot.

"She wouldn't let me post the best one though," Ryle said with an accusing glance to me.

"What's that?" Jamie asked curiously.

"Blue dress?" Jess asked with a grin.

"What blue dress?" Jamie asked.

Ryle turned to me, "Can I show her?"

I nodded with a laugh, "Yes."

He not only showed her the pictures, which made her laugh but showed her the video.

"Here," I said to Ryle and tossed him my phone. "Take a picture of us."

My daughter and I leaned toward each other in our matching dresses, hair flowing loosely, coffee cups wrapped in our hands, pillows surrounding us, and the blue sky and puffy white clouds adding to the image. Tears were fighting to rise at the pure happiness of the moment.

He took the picture then looked down at the result.

"Great picture," Jess said as he leaned over Ryle's shoulder.

I took the phone back and Jamie and I giggled at the happy image as I made it the background on my phone.

"Just to remind myself this is real," I whispered to her and sent the image to Charlene to let her know.

My phone alerted me to Marty and Sarah arriving. I was overjoyed to introduce Jamie to Sarah and they all readily agreed to help Jamie move home. Pete, in his old orange Ford, was the next to arrive.

I couldn't wait to get Jamie's horses home; all three Maggie foals. Sparrow was a smoky buckskin gelding, Tigger, a red and white paint mare, and Mister, a dark bay gelding.   She had refused to leave any of them behind when she left for college and she took great pride in telling the group about her little herd.

I couldn't help but watch her closely as they all prepared to leave. I had missed her so much and could still barely believe she was home. It was all I could do to keep from crawling into her car when she finally drove away. The rodeo crew was next to drive away leaving Pete and I alone in the driveway.

"So," Pete smiled. "What would you like to do?"

I turned and grinned, "Oh, we're going riding."

I sent a quick email to cancel my counseling session. I received an email in return with another session scheduled the first of the week.

Pete and I spent the next two days working with my younger horses and going for rides. That was all the counseling I needed.

We were just releasing the foals back into the pasture with their mothers when I received a text from Jamie.

Text: Put in notice on apartment, they already have it rented. I have reserved a smaller less expensive one for September through December.

Thursday afternoon, I received a text from Sarah as Kade drove in the driveway.

Text: Got your girl. Apartment is empty. We'll pick up the horses in the morning when we head home. Your daughter is an absolute delight.

I couldn't help the excitement in my heart and the proud grin spreading across my face as I looked up at Kade.

His smile grew as he walked to me. He was so damn handsome and I was so glad the glares of the past were gone. Every step he took toward me my body tingled in excitement knowing that his arms were going to wrap around me and his lips would be on mine.

How did I get so damn lucky?

Just as we were settling in for dinner, I received a series of pictures from Sarah. Each picture was of Jamie, Ryle, and Jess together; loading boxes in a truck, Jess and Jamie laughing at Ryle trying on one of her flowered cowboy hats, and one with all three sitting on horseback watching the rodeo.

Text: They have become inseparable.

The worry of Jamie coming between them still rest in my heart but there was nothing I could do but hope.

Late Friday morning, Pete and I were arriving back from a ride on his Barry and my Marko when the trucks and horse trailers arrived.

I squealed in excitement which made Pete laugh. I so enjoyed that old man.

We all left that afternoon for our quick trip to the Cambridge rodeo. It was an enjoyable time with my daughter, Sarah and those damn team ropers.

So much fun that when I rose the next morning, I was very surprised to find Jamie and Jess in an argument in the driveway. They and Ryle had traveled together in Jess' truck leaving us "older people" in the truck hauling the horses.

"You know I'm right, damn it!" Jamie yelled at him with hands on hips and face flushed.

"No, you're not," Jess countered. "I'm his roping partner, not his father."

"You should be looking out for each other," Jamie spat.

"If he wants to leave with a girl, I sure as hell am not going to stop him." Jess huffed. "And why the hell do you care? You jealous it's not you?"

"Oh, my Lord!" Jamie stomped a foot. "Of course not, he can do whatever he wants. Just not with that pink haired twit."

Well, my fear of her coming between Jess and Ryle dissolved. Instead, her mother hen instinct had kicked in.

Jess grinned, "What was wrong with her?"

"She's a damn buckle bunny," Jamie answered with a glare. "He needs to stay focused on his goal and she's the type to lead him astray."

Jess' grin broadened, "How do you know he'll let her lead him astray?"

I walked up next to them and Jamie looked between us.

"Because," Jamie huffed. "I know her and I've seen what she has done to other cowboys."

"And you think Ryle is gullible enough to let her do…whatever you think she is going to do to him?"

She huffed again, "No…he's just…he was so taken with her and her damn pink hair."

"Pink hair?" I asked.

Her 'full of attitude' eyes turned to me. "She has straight blond hair down to her shoulders. Very pale blonde except for a pink strand down the side. Ryle made a comment to her about the pink so she gave him her flirty damn giggle and showed him that when she moves her hair it reveals a layer of pink hair hidden underneath."

"Oh," I nodded. "I've seen that technique before. It's pretty cool."

"Mom," Jamie huffed. "It's just like one of Greg or Stan's fishing lures. It's bright and shiny and attracts the fish until he bites it and she yanks him out of his world."

Jess and I looked at each other then back to Jamie.

"I'm sorry, Mom," Jamie said with a scowl. "But you connected with Dad while you were in college and he took you away from your dream of riding in the college finals."

"Jamie, that was you…getting pregnant and having you. Most of the time, I think it was well worth it." I said and Jess' chuckle made her glare at him again. "I may not have fulfilled that dream, but I was pretty damn successful with the other ones."

"But that shouldn't happen to Ryle because of her," Jamie grumbled. "That damn hair…"

Jess smirked, "Well…I have to agree. He most certainly liked the pink, but would you feel better if you knew he wasn't with her last night?"

Jamie's eyes widened, "Jess, she was hanging all over him when YOU made me leave him behind."

Jess shrugged with a grin and Jamie's lips rolled into a tight line. Damn, she was pissed.

"But HE wasn't hanging onto HER," Jess pointed out. "He isn't rude enough to shove her away. He would have waited for an opportunity to just get away from her."

"You think he didn't go with her last night?" Jamie gasped in disbelief. "Where was he then and why would you insist we leave?"

Jess sighed and looked between the two of us. "Alright, I'll tell you, but you have to promise not to let him know that I did."

"Tell me what?" Her eyes narrowed.

"Promise," he said.

"I promise," I said lightheartedly. Now I was really curious.

We both looked at Jamie who exhaled impatiently.

"Fine, I promise." She huffed.

"There is a barrel racer that he knows and, as you put it, they are both focused on their goals. When they end up at the same rodeo together, they hook up."

"What?" Jamie gasped.

"She was there last night and he stayed with her in her trailer." Jess smiled. "Neither wants a firm relationship at this time but they…"

"We got the picture," I held up a hand to stop him. It wasn't the first time I'd heard of that type of arrangement.

"Why didn't you just tell me that?" Jamie exhaled dramatically. "Who is it?"

Jess shook his head, "I'm not telling you. Most people don't even know that they know each other and they want to keep it that way to stay out of all the drama."

Jamie stared at him and I could see her body relax.

"Fine then," She turned and casually called back over her shoulder. "Let's rope before we have to leave for Emmett."

Jess and I looked at each other.

"She's a mixture of a roper and a barrel racer," I warned with a chuckle.

We followed her to the barn.

For me, the Emmett rodeo was the total opposite of the Snake River Stampede. I was looking forward to the night and not once did Kade and I make it to the bleachers. Once we walked down to talk with Ryle and Jess we never left. Breakaway ropers, team ropers, and barrel racers were everywhere and I knew most of them. I talked until I nearly lost my voice.

"When do we get to come to play in your arena again?" Dillon Holyfield asked.

"Yeah, I've heard a lot about it and want to come rope," Robert Murphy added.

"I've been there," Jeff Flenniken said proudly. "I want to check out the trophy room again. You guys should see it." He said to Robert.

"What trophy room?" Phoenix Everano asked.

"Lauren is the niece of Austin Conners and she has his trophy room at her place," Cody Hill told them.

"Really? The World Champion?" Robert turned back to me. "I'd love to see it."

Letting Ryle and Jess move into the bunkhouse was moving forward with Uncle Austin's dream. It was just the beginning. Now was the time to keep it moving. "Well, we'll have to set a date…you guys here for the Caldwell rodeo in a couple weeks? Come out and rope that morning."

The word was out and the arrangements set; the dream was moving forward. I looked proudly at these ropers, all dreamers and true cowboys. Their energy and nods of agreement confirmed I was doing the right thing. My uncle would have liked these cowboys.

Kade's hand gripped mine tighter. I looked up at him to see a big grin of support. I squeezed his hand in return.

I turned to Jeff, "I just read in the Team Roping Journal that you're on track to win the PRCA Rookie of the year for heading; so proud of you. Congratulations to you and Jake for winning the Elgin Stampede."

"Thanks, Lauren, been working hard at it." He grinned back. "Jake's going to be bummed he missed seeing you."

"Well, you guys come out anytime. We rope nearly every day." I said.

Ten minutes later, I was surrounded by breakaway ropers and in a conversation with Jamie, Rylee Potter and

Janey Reeves. Jamie was scrolling through her phone for future competitions she would have time to enter.

"Your horses in shape?" Rylee asked.

"Very," Jamie answered. "I've spent the summer riding all three nearly every day."

"Good, then let's get you going. There's still time to get you in the Pendleton roping the Sunday after the roundup." Rylee said then turned to me. "And you, too."

I laughed, "Horses are in shape but I haven't competed in over a year."

"You have over a month," Janey grinned. "With your experience, I doubt you even need that much time to get yourself ready."

"Mom! You're doing it with me!" Jamie declared and looked between me and Kade.

The thought of competing again caused my stomach to swirl and heart race. Kade seemed to notice as his hand squeezed mine in support.

"I'll think about it." I finally sighed.

"We need to warm up," Rylee stepped up into the saddle. "You'll be there." She grinned at me then the pair rode away.

"Oh, Mom," Jamie smiled at me. "I have missed this so much."

"Me, too," I wrapped my arms around her. "Me, too."

As we embraced, I couldn't help but think of Andrea. I couldn't remember a race or a roping without her…there was a hollowness in my heart.

"Sure glad you could come to the rodeo with us," Pete huffed with a grin as we met at Marty's truck.

Marty and Sarah were in the front and I rode between Kade and Pete in the back. Jamie was riding back with Ryle and Jess…or at least Jess.

I held Kade's hand and leaned my head on Pete's shoulder.

"Have a good time?" Pete whispered to me.

"Yes, so very much." I sighed. "I cannot thank you enough."

He leaned his head on mine and patted my free hand.

It was a peaceful ride home.

CHAPTER TWENTY NINE

It was early in the morning on Sunday when I rose. Kade wasn't in the bed with me so I took a quick shower and dressed in preparation of riding all day. I jogged down the stairs expecting to see my handsome man but he wasn't there. Disappointment sparked as I walked to the coffee maker.

There was a movement out the window. Kade was sitting in the swing with his phone to his ear. By the time I walked through the back door, the phone was resting in his lap. He turned and smiled at me.

I sighed into his eyes and my body tingled in anticipation of his touch…even though we had just spent all night entwined in each other's arms.

Without a word, I slid onto the seat next to him so we were facing each other as I lay into his arms and our lips met. It was a long slow kiss as we enjoyed each other and the warm sunshine filled morning. My fingers slowly slid up his arm, neck then up to play with his hair. His fingers traced over my hip, down my legs and back. Slow, tender touches and kisses, my heart sighed as I finally leaned back to smile at him.

"Good morning," He whispered.

"And to you. You were up early."

"My son is on Texas time and forgets I'm not." He chuckled. "He had big news and couldn't wait to share."

"Oh! Something you can share with me?"

Kade nodded, "He and his girlfriend eloped yesterday and she is pregnant."

"What!?" I gasped and fell back away from him in horror.

"What the hell, Lauren?" He huffed. "What's so bad about my son expecting a child? He's young, but so was I when my daughter was born. I'm pretty happy for them."

"It's not your son becoming a father," I gasped. "It just means you're going to be a grandfather!"

"Well…yeah," He said warily.

"That means I'm sleeping with a grandfather!" I gasped with wide horrified eyes. "And it's age appropriate! I'm old enough to sleep with a grandfather!"

We stared at each other a moment before I finally couldn't hold back the grin.

"Damn, Lauren," He laughed. "Well, I'm not that elderly yet…we have about 6 months. So let me show you just how young I am." He pulled me back into his arms and thoroughly kissed me until I didn't feel old…more like a teenager making out.

My phone alert buzzed twice letting me know Marty and Pete had arrived.

I leaned back and giggled at his wide mischievous grin. How in the world did this man come into my life? How could I be so lucky?

With a sigh, I slid off the swing and held out a hand to him. Our fingers entwined and we silently walked toward the barn.

When Marty's truck came to a halt, Jess and Ryle walked out of the bunkhouse.

"You tell 'em I'm coming…and hells coming with me!" Jess yelled.

Their laughter echoed across the ranch making my heart warm.

"You're a daisy if you do," Ryle yelled.

What a pair.   It was obvious they had watched Tombstone before heading to the barn. We were going to be listening to movie quotes all damned day…and I looked forward to it.

Jamie was nearly trotting across the patio of the house.

"Are you gonna do something? Or just stand there and bleed?" Jamie yelled out.

They turned with wide grins.

"We'll be your huckleberry," They yelled back.

We all laughed. It was a good start to the day.

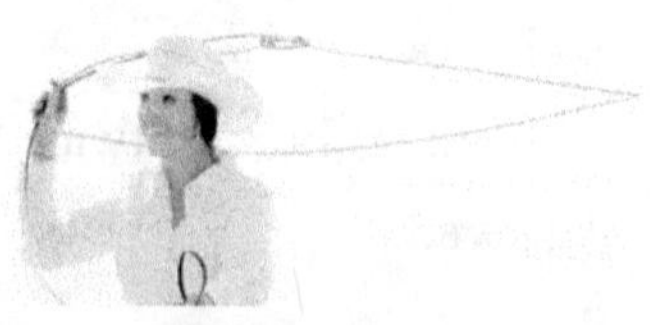

I coiled the rope and attached it to my saddle before stepping down. Loosening the cinch I turned to see Pete walking his roan horse toward me.

"I'm headed in to grab something for everyone to eat," I told him.

"I can help." He said and tied Barry up next to JW.

His arm tipped out to me and I happily slid my hand around his elbow.

"Your daughter is a delight," he said.

"I agree, most of the time. She does have her bitchy moments."

"We all do."

We glanced at each other and chuckled.

"What was your son like when he was her age?"

"Most of the time he was an upstanding young man," He turned and looked over his shoulder then looked at me, "At times, he was a bit of an asshole."

The laughter erupted from both of us. He told me some of the worst moments as we prepared the hoagie sandwiches and bowls of chips.

"Does Kade know these stories?" I asked as we walked back to the barn with boxes full of lunch.

"Some of them," Pete's eyes twinkled mischievously.

I chuckled, "I won't say a thing."

As we neared the barn, I could hear Jamie's voice and it wasn't pleasant.

"And there she is…" I whispered with a smirk to him.

"Oh, Lord, Jess!" Her voice rose.

"What?" Jess's voice was full of exasperation.

I stopped and took a step toward their voices. They were standing in the aisle face to face and Jamie's hands were back on her hips.

"I'm just months away from graduating with my business degree with an emphasis in Marketing. I started a business two years ago where I help some friends with their small businesses and create a business and marketing plan for them."

"You did? That's awesome." he said.

"Yes, it is," She growled.

I turned to Pete and rolled my eyes, "Like I said…" I whispered.

Pete chuckled softly.

"Then what did you "Oh, Lord" me about?" Jess asked.

"You just asked me if I needed help calculating the angle I should take to a barrel when I have a short arena entrance compared to an open arena." She huffed.

"Yeah…" He said cautiously.

I looked at Pete and we both had our eyebrows high in surprise.

"I've calculated it myself for years," she said. "I can do math."

"I didn't say…" Jess started.

"If you can figure out the D calculations in a 5D race then that would be impressive." She challenged.

"I haven't ever wanted to do that," Jess said softly. "But…"

"Do what?" Ryle asked innocently as he walked up behind them.

"Do the D math at…" Jamie started.

"Calculating the D's?" Ryle interrupted. "I can do that."

"You can?" She huffed in disbelief.

"Sure," Ryle quipped. "There is my favorite 34D, and then 36D and 38D isn't too bad either."

It took all I had to contain my laughter but I heard Pete squeak a little.

Ryle looked up at Jess with a wide smart-ass grin.

"Don't forget the double D's." Jess drawled through a smirk.

Jamie's eyes were wide as she stared at Ryle's grin. Her lips were rolled together but her chin was quivering.

"Oh! Yeah, the double D's!" Ryle exhaled as a hand went over his chest. "As in 34 double D's? Oh, Lord, help me."

Jess was staring at Ryle with a chuckle rumbling through him.

Ryle's eyes widened as he looked at Jamie who was frozen in place except the chin quivering. "You know, if you ever need help calculating the D's, I will always be there for you."

I snorted as the laugh burst from Pete. Jess's hand came up over his mouth to try and cover his grin.

Jamie was now biting her lip as she stared at Ryle.

"Smart ass," She finally gasped. "You are such a smart ass, you damn team roper." She turned away and walked out of the barn as the giggles finally erupted from her.

She looked at me with tears of laughter in her eyes as Jess laughed and Ryle looked at everyone with wide innocent yet mischievous eyes.

I turned to Pete with a grin. "Let's take these to the tables behind the chutes."

"She's an absolute delight," Pete sighed as he hoisted the box and turned away with a chuckle.

I sat across the table from Kade. All day I had wanted to touch him. Just to touch his hand or his arm or even sneak a squeeze of his butt cheek. I had also watched him every time I was at the back of the group and I knew no one could see me. His fingers as they gripped his rope, the tan skin of his arm, the length of his denim covered legs, and the love in his eyes when he looked at his grandfather…it all combined into one perfect cowboy. I was very lucky and I could hardly wait until I could touch him, kiss him, and wrap my arms around him.

It was almost dark as we led the horses to the barn. I'd managed to ride at least four of mine throughout the day but I had left JW to last. I took my time removing his tack then slowly brushing down his tan hide. As I ran the brush across his back I glanced up to see Kade watching me. Our eyes connected and we smiled. It was that knowing smile…that 'I want you' smile. My whole body tingled in anticipation.

I walked JW back to his pasture and passed behind Kade as he stood next to his horse. My fingers slowly crossed Kade's back pockets as I walked by. My heart raced.

Jess and Ryle were walking into their bunkhouse as I shut the gate to the pasture. Marty waved and stepped into his truck. His engine roared to life as I walked back into the barn. I could hear the gravel give way to his tires as he drove away.

Jamie and Pete walked out of the barn.

"We'll see you inside," Jamie said as Pete held out his arm to her and her hand wrapped around his elbow as they walked away.

"OK," I said softly and stepped into the tack room to hang JW's halter onto the rack.

I shut the door to the tack room and looked down the aisle of the barn for Kade. He wasn't there so I closed the large double doors.

When I turned back, Kade's arm wrapped around my waist and jerked me into him. The kiss was fierce. Pent-up desire burned through both of us as he pushed me back against the doors. My hands roamed over as much of him as I could touch.

He pulled back just enough he could speak with his breath caressing my lips.

"This not touching during the day…?" He whispered.

"Oh, it's done," I rose on tiptoes to seal the kiss again.

After another breathtaking, heart racing kiss, his lips slowly moved down my neck.

"Kade…I want you." I exhaled.

"Yeah, but if we go in the house Grandad and Jamie…it will take forever to get upstairs."

I leaned back and looked up into his eyes that were burning in desire.

"Just outside this door is my living quarters horse trailer." I smiled.

He grinned and took my hand to lead me out the smaller side door and to the trailer.

"Is it locked?" He asked as his hand reached for the door lever.

"I don't think…"

The door popped opened.

He turned and pulled me into his arms and into another firey kiss. He fell back onto the trailer floor with me on top of him and we chuckled. He rolled so we could both wiggle our way into the trailer and pull the door closed. I was removing my shirt and racing to the bed as his boots hit the floor. I crawled up onto the bed, closed the windows and pulled the curtains closed.

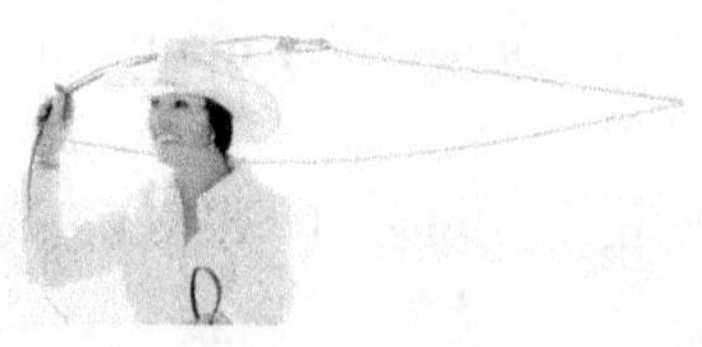

"I've really enjoy working with these foals with you. It's been a long time since I've been around anything but calves." Pete grinned from across the back of the three-month-old colt as he slid off the halter then patted him on the shoulder. "This one is dark grey…looks like bluish grey underneath."

"Could be blue roan," I walked the yearling I was leading through the gate and back to the pasture. "Maggie is Stoli bred. We've worked with many different stallions to find the magic match. They all turn out spectacular so we've decided it's Stoli Magnolia, AKA Maggie, that is the magic mare. We also experimented with colors to get different than bay and sorrel. My gelding BlueDoc is from Okanagan Blue off the Promised Land Ranch. He's a firecracker."

I removed the halter from the colt but he didn't leave; he just rubbed his head over my shoulder and snuggled his nose into my neck.

"They're pretty mean." Pete chuckled.

"The combination of Maggie's natural disposition and the gentleness of the three draft mares is wonderful. They are calm on the ground but willing with heart when in the saddle and they are very athletic."

I turned back to him and the air rushed out of me…his hands were gripping the fence as his body was slowly falling to the ground. His eyes were closed tightly and his face was ashen.

"Pete!" I screamed and ran back to him as I pulled my phone out of my pocket. I had hit 911 before reaching him then dropped the phone in the dirt as my arms dipped under his shoulders to help him to the ground.

I could hear someone talking on the phone and yelled out my address and screamed for them to hurry.

He was unconscious as he collapsed over my legs and pinned me to the ground.

"Pete!" My hand went to his chest. I could feel a heartbeat and wanted to cry in relief. "Pete!"

I had to lean back and stretch with the tips of my fingers to reach the phone.

"Are you there?" A man's voice asked.

"Yes…hurry. My friend Pete just passed out. He's 78 but good health."

"We have an ambulance on the way."

"I have to hang up the phone to remotely trigger the gate open."

Without waiting for a response I ended the call and opened the gate.

"Please be OK, Pete." Tears streamed down my face as my hand went to his nostrils…I could barely feel his breath. My hand went over his chest to feel his heart…to concentrate on each beat…just as the sirens pierced the air it began to slow down. I pulled him in closer and prayed.

CHAPTER THIRTY

As I rode in the ambulance with Pete, I called Kade.

I stood in the waiting room looking out the window into the sky as I waited. Kade's truck screeched to a halt in front of the hospital and I turned to him as he ran through the glass doors.

"Anything?" He yelled down the hall as he approached.

"They haven't said anything to me," I answered. "Maybe they will to you since you're his grandson."

He turned to the reception desk. I was right behind him.

"If you'll go back to the waiting room, I'll ask the doctor to come out and talk to you." The receptionist said then turned and disappeared through the back door.

Kade's arms wrapped around me as I told him what happened.

"I need to call my parents," Kade sighed and pulled out his phone.

We held each other as he talked to his dad with a promise to call back as soon as he knew anything. For ten minutes we waited for the doctor. Kade had just taken two steps back to the receptionist when the doctor finally walked through the door.

"Mr. Weston?" The doctor asked.

"Kade Weston…Pete is my grandfather." Kade answered.

"I'm Dr. Green and your grandfather is stable." He said.

We both exhaled in relief.

"What happened?" Kade asked.

"He's awake but a bit groggy. His blood pressure was very low and so was his blood sugar level. His heart rate is strong now but due to his age, we're running tests and I would like to keep him overnight to make sure both have time to level out."

"Yes, of course," Kade nodded. "Can we see him?"

I was overjoyed he said we…but the doctor shook his head.

"Just you for now until we get him to his own room…it will be a while." The doctor looked at me. "I'm sorry…we just…"

"It's OK, just let him know I'm here." I took Kade's arm. "Go to him…I'll call Marty and the rest of the crew."

Kade turned to follow the doctor then quickly turned back to kiss me, say thank you, then walk away.

I wanted to latch onto him and go back but I refrained. I needed to call make the calls.

After the two men disappeared behind a closed door, I slowly sat back down in the waiting room chair. I stared at my phone and tried to remember where everyone was. Jamie had left early to go riding with Rylee and her mom on their ranch. She was hours away in New Meadows. Marty was home, and Ryle and Jess were…where?

My phone alerted me to a missed call and a message. It was from the counselor's office. I had missed my appointment and if I wanted to go back to work I needed to reschedule.

I ignored it and called Marty with a trembling hand.

"Hello Darlin'," Marty answered.

I smiled at the joy in his voice then sighed that I had to destroy it.

I told him about Pete.

"He's OK then?" Marty asked.

"The doctor said he is stable but they are keeping him overnight for observation."

"Alright," Marty sighed. "As soon as Sarah gets back, we'll come over."

"OK," I whispered.

"You doing alright, Darlin'?"

"Just numb," I said honestly.

"Where's Jamie?"

"With friends, I'll call her after I call Ryle and Jess."

"OK, we'll be there soon." Marty ended the call.

I looked at the door Kade and the doctor had disappeared behind.

They had been in my life for only a month and now I couldn't imagine life without them.

I closed my eyes to try and contain my emotions before I called Jess then Jamie.

The nurse appeared to take me to Pete's room before the crew showed up. I wanted to run but I had no idea where I was going so I walked fast trying to encourage her to walk faster.

When I saw Kade standing in a room between a wall of windows and the end of a white-blanketed bed I nearly broke into a run. He was looking down at the top of the bed which was blocked by a curtain. My heart was racing, skin moist, and stomach bubbling.

Kade's eyes moved to me as I neared the door and the smile that spread across his face calmed my nerves.

I hesitated at the door, not sure what to do. My eyes questioned Kade.

"Come on in," He whispered.

I stepped slowly into the room and peered around the white curtain.

Pete was leaning around the curtain to see me. The bed was sitting straight up so he was sitting normally and not lying back as if frail. His dark tanned arms, neck, and face where a huge contrast to the white sheets. His blue eyes and the long white mustache that dropped down his chin seemed to stand out.

But he looked healthy again.

"Oh, Pete," I nearly cried.

"I'm just fine," He said and held out a hand to me.

I fell into the chair next to his bed and gripped the hand tightly. Kade stepped in behind me with a hand on each shoulder.

"I'm sorry for scaring you, Hon," Pete said.

"Scare me hell, you terrified me," I teased nervously.

"He needs to eat healthier and make sure he has plenty of water," Kade said.

"So no more fried fatty café food," I told him.

"Ah, damn," Pete exaggerated a sigh.

"Did you get ahold of the crew?" Kade asked.

"Yes," I nodded. "They are all on their way here."

"I need to make some business calls," Kade said to his grandfather. "You'll be in good hands until I get back, but I'll be right down the hall."

"I'll take care of him," I nodded and tried to smile to reassure him.

Kade leaned down and kissed me…our first public display.

When he walked out of the room, I turned to Pete.

"I'm sorry I terrified you," He lowered the head of the bed into a reclining position so I slid in next to him with my legs the length of the bed and my arms tucked between us. His arm wrapped around my shoulders and squeezed.

"You OK?" I whispered to him.

"Just fine," He sighed and I felt his whole body relax.

We lay quietly a few minutes before either of us spoke.

"I don't want you to die," I whispered to him. The threatening tears made my voice shake.

"I don't particularly want to die either," He chuckled softly. "But, I am 79 so it's not too far away."

"Not today, 79 or not."

"They always say 'age is just a number'. Pretty much lived by that."

I smiled into the room, "Almost 80 and still team roping nearly every day."

"I didn't say I was almost 80. I said I was 79." He grumbled.

We both chuckled then lay quietly again as I played back the afternoon we met…his leaning over the seat of his truck to look through the passenger window to me.

"I don't know what stars aligned for you to end up at the stop light and stopping me," I whispered. "But I sure do thank heaven it happened."

"I don't know that it was stars aligning or Berry being foolish."

"What's that mean?"

"Well, I'm going to tell you the truth and I don't want you to get mad at me."

"What?"

"That morning I was reading the paper while eating breakfast and I read about what happened at the party. About an hour later, I went to the ranch store to buy some knew reins since Berry stepped on his and broke one. I saw you in there and you looked, and probably felt, like the whole world was ganging up on you."

"Yeah…" I sighed.

"I followed you out of the store then to the first stop light. You were slumped over the door as if you were becoming part of it and you just sat through the green light."

"You didn't honk or anything?"

"No, the car behind me did so I waved them through. I was about to get out of my truck when the light turned green again and you started moving, so I followed you to the next. You sat through the green light again so when it turned red I pulled up alongside you."

"I had no idea," I whispered. "And now, thinking about it, that's a two-lane road. How did you get up alongside me?"

"No one was coming so I just pulled in that lane."

"Why would you do that?"

"Because I'm old enough and been around the block enough times to know that your life needed intercepted," he said. "I knew you hadn't roped in years so I thought maybe it would help if you got back to something your late uncle taught you."

I gasped, "You knew who my uncle was before you came out to the ranch?"

"Yes, just me, the others didn't. I used to go out there and rope when he was in town."

"I didn't recognize you."

"I had a full head of black hair and a full beard," He chuckled. "I shaved it off when too much grey got in there. Hell, half the people I knew didn't recognize me."

"Oh, I want to see pictures!" I chuckled. "I can't thank you enough; you stinky old goat."

"I think that was supposed to be sneaky."

"Have you ever been around goats? They are stinky, not sneaky." I smiled.

"After that trip home from the jackpot in Star, you're the one that should be called stinky."

We both laughed. When it faded, we lay silently listening to the quiet of the hospital again.

I closed my eyes to the fear that coursed through me as we waited for the ambulance. What could have been scared me. I couldn't imagine this man…this selfless life saver being gone.

"No matter what the tests say, you're coming home with me," I whispered.

"You going to put me in the bunkhouse with those two boys?" He asked.

I wanted to cry that he didn't argue.

"The guest room is downstairs. It used to be Uncle Austin's. You can move in there."

"That would be an honor."

Again the stillness of the night took over and we lay quietly. Within moments his chest rose in deep breathes as he drifted into sleep. His arm relaxed around my shoulder.

Listening to the rhythm of his breathes it wasn't too long before I drifted to sleep too.

When I woke, Pete's chest was rising and lowering in stronger, deeper breaths. A blanket covered me and Kade was sitting in a recliner across from me. His head back, lips parted slightly, and body occasionally twitching as he slept.

I stared at him…from the tip of his head to the Romeo shoes that covered his feet. A white button-up shirt and blue jeans were in between. In my mind, I pictured the tattoo that covered his arm, chest, and back. Then the wide muscular back and the fine hair that covered his toned chest and stomach. He was all kinds of good to look at and better yet, be around.

The man made me feel strong, safe, and in control again. How did I get so lucky?

"Thank you, Lauren," Kade whispered as I keyed in the security code to the house door.

He was holding a large box of his grandfather's clothes. Pete was trying to lift a box out of the back of the truck but Ryle and Jess weren't allowing him to lift anything.

"You've thanked me a dozen times," I smiled at Kade then looked out as Jess physically turned Pete from the truck and gently pushed him away.

"I tried to get him to move into my place but he just refused. I work from an office in my house and he didn't want to interrupt my business."

"Son of a bitch," Pete growled as he stomped up the driveway. "I ain't no invalid."

"Granddad, they are just trying to help," Kade said.

"Just pushing me around," Pete glared.

"Pete?" I said softly and both men turned to me. "They do it because they care. Would you rather they not care about you?"

His glare turned to resignation, "Just get in the house."

I chuckled at him and with a quick glance to a pleased Kade, I walked into the house.

It didn't take long for the contents of the back of the truck to be sitting on one side of Pete's new "apartment". The room was big enough for a king size bed and dresser on one end and a chair, sofa, end table, and a television on a stand on the other side. He had a large private bathroom with Jacuzzi tub and separate shower. A set of French doors led to a private deck out to the backyard.

"This is one hell of a setup," Kade smiled at his grandfather. "She should be charging you rent."

Pete lifted a brow to him then looked over at me. "I SHOULD be paying you rent. When my house sells…"

I slipped an arm around Pete's waist and hugged him. "I'll just trade room and board for companionship and your stories."

"Oh, I can do that." Pete chuckled and returned my embrace.

Jamie walked in the room with a box in her arms and Jess and Ryle nearly tripped over each other to help her carry it. She just giggled and let Jess take it out of her arms.

"I put fresh bedding on this morning," Jamie told Pete.

"Cindy, the house cleaner, will come to dust and vacuum and we'll take care of the rest," I added.

"I can still take care of myself," Pete huffed.

"Of course you can," I grinned and picked up a box from the dresser and handed it to him. "But I wanted to give you a house welcoming gift."

"Damn it, Lauren," Pete grumbled. "Take it back…I don't need more from you."

I smiled at him with eyes twinkling, "This is more for all of us than it is for you."

That piqued his interest as his eyes narrowed and he set the box on the bed. He slowly lifted the top off and looked into the box…then started chuckling.

"What is it?" Kade asked.

Pete lifted five new shirts out of the box. All were western, short sleeve, snaps instead of buttons, and plaid.

Everyone laughed.

"I peeked at your size at the hospital." I grinned.

"I was waiting for the day one of his shirts just dissolved off his body they were so old." Ryle chuckled.

"Were? Still are you young pup." Pete grabbed the color of his shirt and shook it.

"I think it's as old as you are," Jess teased.

"Not quite but close," Pete nodded and took the teasing as easily as he gave it.

I picked up a box of my uncle's items that I was moving to his trophy room.

Neither Jess nor Ryle offered to help. I looked at both of them in amusement then looked at Kade. He chuckled and took the box out of my arms then followed me across the hall to the room.

"Either one of them say anything to you about her?" I whispered to him as I opened the door.

"No…not a word, but I will talk to them." he said.

When I stepped through the door my eyes swept around the room; taking in all that it held.

I immediately knew something was wrong.

CHAPTER THIRTY ONE

My eyes went to the line of buckles from the National Finals Rodeo.

I must have made some kind of noise because Kade's head jerked over to me.

"You OK?"

"That's not the buckle," I whispered as a hollow emptiness spread into my stomach and lungs.

"What's not?" He turned and looked at the wall.

I walked to the display of buckles and my hand went to the leather box that normally held my uncle's championship buckle.

"This is not the buckle…this is from Calgary," I turned to Kade with my stomach starting to hurt and tears rising to my eyes. "Someone switched the buckles."

"Switched? Why the hell would they do that?" He asked as he stared at the buckle. "Where did this one come from?"

I walked over to the empty frame on the wall. "Here…" I whispered and had to take a deep breath to hold back the tears. I turned to Kade. "Someone stole his championship buckle."

I leaned against the leather sofa that sat in the middle of the trophy room. I had not left the room once I called the police and only Jamie had come in to join me. She was at my side, our hands grasped tightly together. Everything was inventoried from memory and I knew the buckle was the only item missing.

"They separated everyone," Jamie whispered.

"What?" I turned to her.

"They separated all the men and they are being interviewed by the detective." she said.

I stood and turned to her in confusion. "Why? None of them would have done this."

She shrugged, "Standard procedure, I'm sure. They wouldn't be doing their jobs right if they didn't."

"I guess…"

Detective Malone walked back into the room. There was a deep frown creasing his brow. "Lauren, I would like to talk to your daughter."

"Go ahead," I leaned back onto the couch and tightened my grip on her hand.

"Alone please," he said.

"Why? You think my daughter stole the buckle?" I shook my head at the sheer thought of it. I wasn't impressed with him the first time we met and it wasn't getting any better.

"It's my understanding that the two of you were separated for more than a year." His shoulders rose.

"The men just told you that?" I asked in surprise.

"I read the report from your ex-husband's attack a couple weeks ago and it was stated there." He answered. "In the report, your ex-husband stated that Jamie had called asking for help when you kicked her off the property." His eyes moved between us as if to gauge our reactions.

"That was my idea," Jamie said.

"It was a ruse to get him talking about our marriage," I stated flatly. "Which WE won't be discussing because it has nothing to do with my uncle's buckle going missing."

"It didn't go MISSING, it was STOLEN." Malone scowled.

My stomach clenched and I could feel my temper begin to rise. "My daughter has nothing to do with its disappearance. It's been in this room since she was eight. What reason would she have to take it?"

His look to me was pure impatience and it pissed me off…I glared back in return.

"You have spent the last 14 months apart due to a family rift and when she comes back it suddenly goes missing."

"That's ridiculous," Jamie huffed. "That buckle belongs in this room. I have no reason to take it."

"Revenge…money…college is expensive…" He started.

"Oh, that's just stupid," I stood with hands on hips. "Our relationship is perfectly fine and she has a generous college savings that pays for all her needs."

"I also have a small business," Jamie added as she stood next to me and glared at the detective. "I don't need money and as I said before, THAT buckle belongs in this room."

Malone stared at her a moment then turned to me, "Have you been in this room since the day your ex-husband was here?"

"No," I answered.

"When was the last time you were in the room?" He asked.

"A few weeks ago," I answered. "The day I offered Ryle and Jess to move into the bunkhouse."

"Besides you two, who has been on this property since that day? Anyone that would have access to the house?" He asked.

I was relieved he had moved on from accusing my daughter of theft but a sickening lump slowly grew in my stomach.

"The five men outside, Marty's wife, my housekeeper, Cindy, and my ex-husband," I answered.

"How long has Cindy worked for you?"

"Fifteen years," Jamie answered. "She would not steal the buckle either."

"No…she would have no reason or inclination to," I added.

"From the report, your husband did not enter the house before or after the confrontation?" He asked.

"No, he did not," I answered.

"And you're sure no one else has been on the property since you last saw the buckle?" He glanced at the empty frame. I had moved the Calgary buckle back to where it belonged.

"As you know, I have a gate that requires a code to enter unless you have a transmitter on the car," I answered.

His brow rose in interest. "Who has the transmitters?"

"Jamie, myself and a friend; you met her the day you came out for Dave's death at the party…Andrea, but she hasn't been here since," I said and Jamie's hand gripped mine tighter. "When the code is entered, a camera takes 2 pictures and sends them to my phone." I was going to tell him about the images from the second camera but stopped. Keeping my expression calm, I squeezed Jamie's hand in return.

"We'll need copies of those files," He nodded thoughtfully and his eyes narrowed as he looked at me. "You saw no one else come onto this property?"

"No," I shook my head slowly.

"Well, that leads us back to my original conclusion." His shoulders squared as he stood taller.

"I did not take the buckle." Jamie huffed in irritation.

"I'm sure you didn't," He nodded to her with a slight smirk before turning back to me. "We finished our interviews with the five men and will have to complete back…"

"They didn't take the buckle," My stomach clenched again with the heat from my temper rising up my spine and to my neck.

"They are the only logical conclusion," He said gruffly. "You have clearly stated that it wasn't you two or the housekeeper…therefore it leaves us with the five men outside."

I took a deep breath and slowly let it out as the heat rose into my cheeks and eyes.

"Those men would not take that buckle," I said through clenched teeth.

His body braced as if for battle, "It did not just disappear and another buckle move into its place by itself."

"They would not do that to me," I huffed.

"So, you're saying after 14 years of that buckle being in this room with no problems, just weeks after those men come onto this property…and no one else…the buckle vanishes. Sometimes, Lauren," He said as he began to turn toward the door. "It's the person you least suspect."

"Do not…" I started.

He disappeared through the door as if I hadn't spoken. I took a step forward but Jamie's hand tightened in mine making me stop.

"Mom?" She whispered with tears brimming her eyes.

"What?"

"Dad had a transmitter and he had been here…not driving from Pendleton…he was here so fast…" Her voice trembled. "Do you think he…?"

I looked back at the open door then back to her and whispered. "My phone would have alerted me if he had come through before that day."

"You don't always catch it though," She reminded me. "He would know how to time it when you were sleeping or working."

"True," I admitted with a deep breath. "The system keeps the images until I delete them. I'll send the files from the coded alerts to the detective then we'll review the files from the second camera once he leaves."

"You don't think we should tell him about the second camera?" She asked softly.

I looked back at the door, "No…he's going to be focusing on the team ropers…we'll review it first…then…maybe…"

"Depending on what we find…"

I turned back to her and nodded, "Yes, but now we have to go see what trouble that detective is stirring up."

But he was already gone when we walked out of the house.

All five men were sitting at the patio table; deep frowns were over concerned eyes as they turned to us.

All five stood as we approached.

"Lauren," Pete started.

I held up a hand to him.

"No matter what Detective Malone says, I don't believe any of you would do this to me," I said.

Shoulders lowered in relief.

"Do you want us to move?" Ryle whispered anxiously.

"Why would I want that?" I gave him a smile to hopefully quell his nerves. "Like I said, none of you stole the buckle."

"I don't want to leave you two here alone if someone is breaking into your house," Marty said as he looked at Ryle then back to me.

I looked at him thoughtfully then to my daughter and slowly moved around to the other men.

"Ryle and Jess are in the bunkhouse, Pete is in the house in his room now, and Kade is with me and across the hall from Jamie," I said. "We're not alone."

A quiver shook my heart as a memory from four weeks before flashed through my mind. Lying in the arena dirt I had been so alone, so broken and lost…but no more.

Tears rose and I knew my eyes were shimmering from the concerned expressions of the men looking at me.

I looked at Pete. "I'm not alone." I whispered to him.

"No, you're not," His voice was full of compassion and understanding. "And we'll make sure you aren't until this mystery is resolved."

I took a deep breath and looked at Kade…just his standing next to me made me feel stronger and the look on his face was full of the same compassion as his grandfather.

I shook off the melancholy and looked around at the crew.

"Aren't you supposed to be preparing for a rodeo or four?" I asked Ryle and Jess.

"Jerome, Homedale, Hermiston, and Omak," Jamie said from behind me.

"Well, there is no sense sitting around waiting for a shoe to fall," Marty said. "Let's go catch some horses."

I smiled my thanks to him, "Jamie and I have some office work to get to then we'll be out."

"Which horses do you want?" Ryle asked as his body rose in anticipation.

"BlueDoc," I answered with an appreciative smile.

"Sparrow," Jamie answered.

"Smoky buckskin," Jess said. "I'll get him for you."

Both men turned quickly and walked away. Marty and Pete hesitated then followed. Kade walked to my side and with just his eyes, he asked me if I was alright.

"I'm fine," I whispered and leaned up to kiss him lightly and ended up hesitating to take in his warmth. With a sigh, I leaned away. "We'll be out in just a few minutes."

"Alright," He looked between Jamie and me then walked away.

Jamie's hand took mine as we stood and watched the five men walk to the barn.

Not one of them would purposely hurt me. They would not take something that meant so much to me.

My eyes wandered from one man to another.

"They would not hurt me," I sighed.

Halfway to the barn, Kade turned and looked back. When he saw us watching, he stopped and our eyes connected.

"They wouldn't do anything to hurt me," I whispered to Jamie.

"If you truly believe that, then why do you keep saying it?"

CHAPTER THIRTY TWO

We started with the coded camera files from the morning I invited the men to move into the bunkhouse. At first glance, I didn't see anything unexpected. I sent the folder to the Detective.

"Alright," I smiled. "You want to see a really good one of them?"

"Of who?"

I turned and looked at her with an 'are you kidding me' smirk.

She blushed with an impish grin.

"This picture is from the morning after they took first Friday night at the Snake River Stampede." I clicked the file.

The rugged unshaven faces of the pair of ropers appeared on the screen looking at the camera. Their eyes sparkled, grins wide, and the happiness just radiated from them.

"Oh," Jamie gasped. "They are so handsome."

"Yes, they are."

We sat quietly looking at the picture.

"Mom…I don't know…you do…do you think that it is possible that one of them would have taken it?" Her voice shook as she stared at the image.

Ryle; the 'pup' sold everything he had to buy his star horse. Moments like that could easily have led him to theft to get the horse but, instead, he sacrificed everything. He knew what the buckle represented…the dedication and sacrifice it took to get one. No, Ryle would not have stolen it.

My eyes went to Jess just as the printer began to click and hum. Jamie had hit the print button and I just chuckled.

Jess was a man with compassion, tenderness, strength, and fortitude to approach a woman on the brink of losing her mind. His helping me wash Dave's blood off of the bricks so I could move on with my life, then holding me as I broke down? No, Jess would never tear me apart.

"No…I know in my heart they did not." I answered and glanced at her.

She was staring at the print of the two men.

I clicked on the folder that held the images from the hidden camera in the trees. There were duplications from the other file so I copied those files into the hidden camera file then sorted by date. I removed all images that were taken at the same time and those where I was in the driver's seat. Then the images that showed the house cleaner, Cindy, were deleted. It only left a couple dozen images in the file.

I looked at Jamie's image the morning she appeared back in my life. Tears were in her eyes and the look of fear. It made my heart hurt so I deleted it and all other images with her in the driver's seat. Only three images remained.

And we found the unexpected that we missed in the first folder.

"There's Dad," Jamie pointed to the image.

"And there he is again," I sighed as the disappointment and the anger rushed through me.

"That one's from the day I invited him…but when is that one?" Her voice shook.

"A couple days before."

"In the time frame the buckle was stolen."

I pulled up both images so they were side by side. In the first image, Blake's expression seemed a bit lost. Nothing but pride and cockiness radiated from the second image.

"He couldn't have gotten in the house," I said.

"Then what was he doing?" She whispered.

I shook my head with a sigh, "I don't know."

"Do you…should I…ask him?" She looked at me with a mixture of fear and sorrow.

"No," I slid my arm around her shoulders and squeezed tightly. "Malone will see it in the folder I sent him. We'll let him deal with it."

"OK," She whispered.

I went back to the folder and pulled up the third image. Only an arm could be seen. Someone had parked and walked close enough to trigger the camera.

"When is that one?" Jamie asked.

I looked at the date and kept myself from reacting. It was the date and time Molly and Ethan Armstrong had come to the property.

"It's…well, Dave…my late boss…his kids."

Jamie turned with wide eyes.

"They came to see where their father died but I wasn't home. I came over the hill and they were parked there trying to decide if they really wanted to see it."

"Did they?" She whispered.

"No, we spoke for a moment then they backed out and drove away."

We were quiet a moment, both staring at the arm. Then Jamie slowly turned and looked at me.

"Mom? Are you OK from what happened?"

I took a deep breath and slowly released it. Was I OK yet? The 'incident' did not consume me as it had before. The guilt did not consume me either but I don't think I would ever be OK with it…I had just moved it to the past.

"The memory is just there now," I sighed. "I don't know that it will ever totally be gone but the team has helped me through."

"Did they find his wife?"

"They tracked her to the Mexican border. I just imagine that she's on a beach somewhere and her kids can go down and see her…be reunited with her."

It was her turn to put an arm around my shoulders and squeeze. "I wish I could have helped in some way."

"Ultimately, it led you to coming home so we'll just focus on that."

We hugged then turned back to the image.

"So…this has gotten us nowhere to prove that the team ropers weren't involved," I said.

She leaned back in the chair and looked at me, "You're sure with Ryle and Jess but what about Pete and Kade?"

"They would have nothing to gain," I said without much thought. "Pete invited me into this group but he has a nice house and is an ex-attorney so he seems to be financially set. Besides, he was pretty focused on helping me…he's not going to do something to knock me down again."

"Kade wouldn't risk you," Jamie nodded. "So that leaves Marty and Sarah."

"They wouldn't."

"More, Mom," she said. "Pete and Kade are understandable and you gave me your heart for Ryle and Jess."

"They wouldn't have a reason."

"That doesn't…it's not…," She sighed. "Detective Malone said sometimes it's who you least suspect."

"I don't suspect them." I closed the folder and turned off the computer. "I don't see anything to show Malone from this camera."

"Alright," Jamie stood. "Let's go rope."

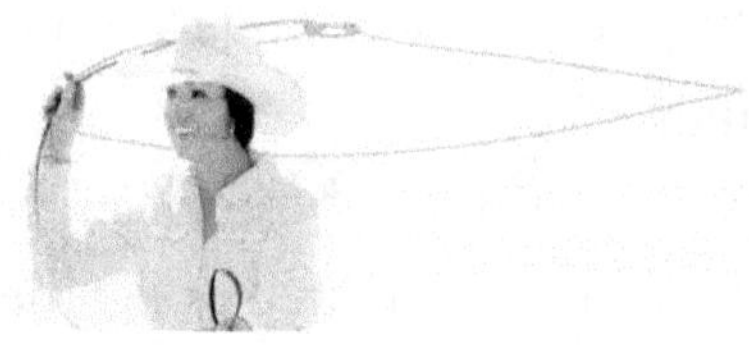

My eyes opened into the dark bedroom. I watched the shadows on the ceiling from the moonlight dancing through the trees.

"Are you alright?" Kade whispered.

I was lying on my back with him on his side and cuddled into me. His armrest gently across my abdomen.

"Well," I whispered. "I'm not sure whether to be flattered you're so attuned to me that you woke up when my eyes opened or if I should be creeped out because you were lying there staring at me at 2:00 in the morning."

I waited for his chuckle but it didn't come.

"You didn't just open your eyes," He said softly.

"Really? What did I do?"

"You flinched hard enough to wake me then gasped, then after a pause, you opened your eyes."

"Oh…I'm sorry," I whispered.

"Don't be sorry. What were you dreaming about? Your boss?"

"No…the day Uncle Austin died." I stared at the shadows. "I haven't dreamt of that in years."

"Do you want to talk about it?"

"I don't know…I guess…I just don't know why that would come up now."

"Finding the buckle missing today may have triggered it."

"Yeah…I guess."

"Tell me and maybe we can figure it out. How did you find out about the accident?" He whispered.

"Andrea and I were in the kitchen and Jamie was outside roping a dummy. I got a phone call asking if I was related to Austin Conners. I told them yes, I was his niece, but he wasn't home yet, he'd be here in an hour…he was driving back from the Roy Rodeo. They asked if his wife was there and I told them she was flying in from Texas and would be at the ranch about the same time. Then I asked what it was all about and he asked if someone was at the house with me."

Goosebumps rose on my arm the same as they did when the man on the phone asked me that question. Kade's arm tightened around me.

"I told him yes…what was this all about? He told me that Uncle Austin was involved in a three-vehicle collision. He was pulling a five horse living quarters trailer and someone in a car tried passing him on a hill just before a curve. A semi-truck driving the opposite direction came around the corner and didn't have time to react. The car tried to get back into the right lane but the semi clipped it and sent it into the driver's side…into Uncle Austin. They believe he was killed instantly…so was the guy in the car which was smashed…unrecognizable between the two trucks. There was a kid…a groom about eighteen riding with my uncle. When the three collided it sent the horse trailer in front of the semi and they rolled. The groom was killed and the semi-truck driver was killed…four horses killed. The only one that survived was one horse…she was the last horse into the trailer and when it rolled the back ramp was ripped off and the horse was thrown from the trailer…with massive injuries."

"Maggie, the mare in your pasture."

"Yes," I nodded into the darkness. "I remember sitting down and just visualizing the accident…over and over like I was watching TV or something."

"Where was Andrea?"

"She was in the kitchen staring at me because I wasn't talking but she knew something was wrong. When I asked the man on the phone if he was sure that my uncle was dead, Andrea dropped something in her hands…it broke…shattered. I turned to her and she looked sick."

"Did she say anything?"

"Yes…she said 'that wasn't how it was supposed to be'."

"That's odd."

"Yeah…I didn't catch it then or really…never. I just dreamt that memory. In the dream, she kept saying 'No, he isn't. It doesn't end like that.' Then she stared at me for the longest time while I asked about the mare…where she was…I needed to go to her. Then Andrea left."

"She left you alone?" He asked in surprise.

"Yeah…just me and Jamie. I put her in the truck and we drove to the clinic where they had taken the horse.

Jamie had no idea about the accident, just that a horse had gotten hurt. She was six. I was so shocked…numb…I couldn't think straight. All I could think of was the horse. When I got there, they asked if they could put her down and I just about lost it. I just screamed 'No! You can't kill her." It was like they were asking me if they could kill my uncle. Jamie started crying which kept me from totally going insane. I told them to fix her…keep her alive…do whatever they had to do.

"I was in the waiting room and could hear people crying. Most everyone at the clinic knew Uncle Austin and the word was quickly spreading. Jamie had fallen asleep in the chair while we waited. So I just…sat alone with her sleeping at my side and people all around me crying."

"Charlene?" He whispered.

"They met her at the airport and drove her and the boys to the clinic. The sheriff kept the boys outside…clueless since they were only 3 and 2. She came into the clinic…just inside the front door and she couldn't see me. She screamed my name as loud as she could and they hurried her back to the room I was in. We just hugged…didn't talk…didn't cry…just held each other until the veterinarian came out and told us about Maggie's injuries. They were severe, she would be scarred, never be a performance horse."

"Charlene didn't think of putting her down either?"

"Absolutely not…how do you put down a horse that survived something like that? She was the lone survivor…she was my uncle's calf roping horse…raised her from a yearling. He had ridden her and placed second at the rodeo. He was so pleased with her performance. How could we put her down? They told us when she healed she wouldn't be in pain but because of the missing muscle in her hindquarters and the scars on her legs she couldn't go through training. They said light riding but that was it." I sighed…a deep deep sigh from my soul. "We stayed at the clinic the whole night…with the mare…just praying she would survive…and it was a way for us to delay the inevitable…the truth…the reality that my uncle…her husband was gone."

"Andrea didn't go there to be with you?"

"No…I didn't see her again until the funeral."

"After all the years of friendship…her knowing him most of her life…she didn't help console you?"

I shook my head. "Her husband said she came home and told him what happened then she took the kids to the river to fish and swim. She was escaping reality…is what she told me later."

"I find that odd. She should have been there for you."

I shrugged, "Now that I know about the so-called affair, looking back and remembering what she said, I just don't think she got over Uncle Austin even though she was married and had two boys at the time."

"*It wasn't supposed to end that way*…so she thought they were still going to get together?" Kade asked softly.

"I guess?" I whispered. "After the dream and telling you about it, I'd say yes. She was just waiting…maybe for him and Charlene to break up."

"She was holding onto the dream still. Of them being together and with his death her dream ended."

"*And it wasn't supposed to end that way.*" I sighed again. "I had no idea she was still obsessed…or in love with him. I thought it was just a schoolgirl crush…like I had with Greg."

"Austin wasn't here all the time, yet she still came here."

"I don't know why…maybe to keep the connection until he divorced."

"She could have just waited until the divorce then reconnected. She must have loved coming here."

I shrugged slightly and sighed, "I thought so…but she…I don't know. I thought we were friends. We'd known each other for a couple of years before I went to live with my uncle."

"You were 10?"

"Yes, and we got into a lot of trouble; picked on kids, disruptive in class…we were a two kid wrecking machine in school; which probably has to do with why my mother abandoned me."

"But you changed when Austin came into the picture. How did Andrea handle that?"

"Not well when I kept refusing to do anything. I told her that my uncle wouldn't let me rope or travel with him if I got in trouble. She threw a tantrum in the library…throwing books and ending up in the principal's office. It was her first time there without me."

"How did she handle that?"

"She ignored me for a couple weeks…until he came to the school and she met him. Then she understood and became my friend again…so I thought."

"Did she see him all the time?"

"No…next to never until she had her driver's license and could come over."

"Then why wouldn't she be your friend?"

I stared at the ceiling, watched the shadows dance, and thought of all the classes we had together, tests we studied for, football games we went to, proms, and we were both on the basketball team. We had so much fun…laughed all the time…I never once doubted she was my friend.

The crushes started when Uncle Austin threw the 1st annual summer party. It was his way of relaxing during the storm of rodeos. It was the first time he and Greg had met. They were only a few years apart but became good friends. While they talked and laughed into the night, Andrea and I had sat on the opposite side of the patio and watched them. The crushes were born that night.

If I married Greg then we would be sisters-in-law. If she married Uncle Austin then she would also be my aunt. We thought that was hilarious.

Six months later, Greg and I had our make-out session and my crush disappeared. I thought Andrea's had too. Evidently, I was wrong.

"Lauren?" Kade whispered.

"Hmmm…?"

"Why wouldn't she be your friend?"

"She was…I know…but I don't understand when it changed. It had to be after we were out of school…onto college."

"I didn't know you went to college."

"Rodeo scholarship, TVCC." I sighed. "Two years in and I met Blake…three years in and I was married, pregnant and off the team and out of school."

"Tell me one of your fondest friend moments with her." He said softly and played with a strand of my hair.

I smiled into the darkness, "Always the best was a race we went to in Lewiston at the 49'ers arena. We woke in the morning to cloudy skies and as the race started it began to rain then turned to an absolute downpour. Still saddled, we stood with our horses inside our horse trailers for about an hour waiting for it to stop."

"Just you and Andrea?"

"No…Jamie was there too. She was 9 and there were a couple other friends." I giggled at the memories. "We decided to move the horses into other trailers and have a party in mine. My trailer has the walk-thru into the living quarters so we…six of us plus Jamie…ended up setting up a table in the back of the horse trailer and played cards; poker, of course. We taught Jamie how to play 5 card draw while the wine glasses and bottles were pulled from the cupboards." I sighed and smiled at the ceiling. "It was one of the funnest days we ever had at a race and we didn't even run…they canceled it when the arena became a lake."

We were quiet a moment then he whispered.

"What does that have to do with Austin?"

I stared at the ceiling, "Nothing, I guess."

"So, tell me another story."

"Alright…there was the rodeo in Nampa. Jamie and I breakaway as well as barrel race but Andrea only races. When the chute opened and the calf took off, I was about to throw when the calf turned then stopped dead in his tracks right in front of us. JW tripped over him and went down…we rolled with me under him. The people watching said Andrea barely touched the fence as she flew over it and was at my side almost before the horse was off me. A dozen cowgirls joined her…then the medic."

"Were you hurt?"

"Sore," I nodded into the darkness. "JW and I both went to the chiropractor and masseuse after that."

"So…scaring Andrea…her reacting so fast…what does that have to do with Austin?"

I sighed, "Nothing."

"Tell me one more."

I chuckled, "That would be the time we broke down coming back from a rodeo in Pocatello. That long damn straight stretch. We just had the three horse slant that time and not the living quarters since it was supposed to be a day trip. It was just Andrea and me this time. It was 2:00 in the morning and we had no idea why the truck stopped…it had almost a full tank. A trucker stopped and asked us if we had help coming. We said no so he radioed into the sheriff's office to get someone out to us. He left and, since it was such a nice evening, Andrea and I lowered the tailgate on the truck and waited. A white van shows up…one of those old ones with the side windows blackened out." I chuckled. "We decided right away that it was a serial killer so we jumped off the tailgate as the man stepped out of the van."

"Who was it?"

"I have no idea," I laughed. "But he was in a damned clown suit."

"Seriously?"

"Yeah…he was a clown for birthday parties and such and was going home from a late party and didn't take the time to change clothes. He'd taken off the wig but was still white face, huge red lips, blue stars painted around his eyes, and what hair he had was sticking straight up."

"Scary," Kade chuckled softly.

"It was…scared the hell out of us…he was a serial killer clown going to kidnap, torture, rape, and murder us at 2:00 in the morning on the side of the road. We got in the truck, locked the doors and no matter what he said we wouldn't open the door or even crack a window until the sheriff showed up. We opened it for the sheriff and popped the hood for them. The clown worked on the engine then had the sheriff tell us to try to start it. It started and the second the hood was lowered we got out of there while we were laughing…crying…shaking…laughing more. We told that story for years."

"How was Austin involved in that one?"

"Other than the fact we were both wishing he was there to protect us? Nothing…"

"And you have dozens of more stories." He whispered.

"For each year we've known each other."

"Which, I believe you said, was 32 years."

"Yes," I sighed.

"I'm just going to round the math up to thousands of memories that don't include your uncle."

I stared at the shadows dancing on the ceiling. It was still dark out with just the moon lighting the room and we were still whispering.

"All three stories you told me had nothing to do with this place."

My lungs tightened…tears began to rise.

"Your stories and thousands more are of two friends having fun…or getting terrified together."

"Kade…" My voice trembled.

"She went through a traumatic time too with Dave getting stabbed. Everyone there was traumatized. It took you weeks to recover."

"It's my fault…" A tear slid down my temple and into my hair.

"No, it's not." He whispered and gently wiped away the trail of the tear. "Maybe she was feeling guilty too. Maybe she realized the same as you did…that if she had told you about the divorce then the chain reaction that led to Dave's death wouldn't have happened."

When a shaking sob escaped, he rolled me into his chest and tightened his arms.

"The day he was here, Blake told you that he had been manipulating her for the last couple years."

"Yes," I shivered. "But we had the thirty years before that and she should have known."

"I can't answer for everything…you'll need to talk to her again…"

"No," I whispered and shook my head. "No…I can't."

"Lauren…you need to…."

"No, I can't," I closed my eyes tightly as the wave of tears began to rise inside me. I buried myself farther into his chest. "It's that…it's…I just miss her so much. I miss my friend…and…it nearly killed me once…I can't do that again."

His leg slid over the top of mine and pulled them into him while his arms tightened around me. I was thoroughly encased in his strength.

"You were alone last time, Sweetheart. We're here for you now and so is your daughter."

My shoulders began to shake as I fought away the tears.

"Let them out, Lauren. Let it all out." He kissed my forehead softly. "It's OK, it's just me and you…trust me, Sweetheart."

The emotion in his voice melted my last reserve. I had been holding back the loss of Andrea for weeks. The tears fell out of me like a raging river.

His arms held me close, his leg tightened around mine, he whispered to me and occasionally kissed my forehead until the tears stopped and I drifted off in exhaustion.

I woke to a chill across my eyes and forehead. My hand went to my face and found a damp, cool cloth covering them. Kade's warmth was not at my side and I could hear the shower turn on.

Our whispered conversation played in my mind. I would think of Andrea later…whether I should contact her or not. It was Kade and his willingness to talk me through my dream, my past, his holding me, whispering, kissing. I couldn't remember the last time I had felt so…comforted…safe…and loved.

Slowly, I pulled the towel from my face and looked at the ceiling. The shadows had given way to the morning light.

I was falling in love with him. It wasn't a youthful love like I had for Blake when we got together. He and mine and never grown to a deep love…just a comfortable love…until it went bad.

With Kade, it was deep. As deep as the love I had for my uncle and for Andrea.

With the realization I was falling in love him that much, made me realize I still loved her just as much. That's why I hurt so terribly bad. I had loved Andrea more than I had ever loved Blake. Her loss, her betrayal, and jealousy was worse than losing my marriage.

I did need to talk to her again. I sighed as that slight flicker of hope lit in my heart. Kade was right. I had my team roping crew and my daughter to support me…to love me if Andrea didn't anymore. Two solid hooves on the ground…that was better than before.

I sat up in the bed and listened. The water was still running so I stood and walked into the shower to join him. I let him know just how much his being there for me in the middle of the night meant to me.

CHAPTER THIRTY THREE

Our first morning with all four of us in the house was a bit reserved. Kade was outside getting his truck ready for our drive to the rodeo. I walked down the stairs to voices in the kitchen and was surprised to see Pete and Jamie sitting at the table drinking coffee.

"Mom!" Jamie called out the second she saw me. Her voice was full of surprise.

"What?" I huffed.

"Pete has a flip phone!" She laughed.

"You're kidding me?" I gasped and Pete gave me a sheepish guilty grin.

"It's simple and easy to use." He shrugged.

"No wonder you've never responded back to pictures or texts I've sent you." I laughed as my phone rang and Detective Malone's name appeared.

"The detective," I whispered and walked to the front window. I took a deep breath before answering, "Hello."

"Lauren, Detective Malone here."

"Yes?"

"Just giving you a quick update. We're finishing the background checks on the men…"

"They did not take the buckle." I growled.

"We're doing our job," He stated flatly. "We also reviewed the files you sent and found a second visit from your ex-husband."

"Yes, I saw that too and no, I did not see him or even know about it until we saw the image."

"That was why I was calling and to let you know I will be meeting with him this afternoon to discuss his visit."

"I'm anxious to hear what he says."

"I'll call after the meeting."

I ended the call and slid the phone in my pocket then turned to tell Jamie about the call. She was walking out the door as Marty was walking in.

"Good morning!" I smiled. "I'm looking forward to the rodeo tonight. I haven't been to the Hermiston rodeo in years."

"Glad to hear that, Hon." His voice was reserved and his eyes did not have their normal twinkle.

"What's wrong?" I stopped and internally prepared myself for another blow.

"I just need to talk to you about something."

"Alright…" I said cautiously.

"I know the detective is…"

"Does this have to do with the buckle?" My spine straightened.

He nodded his head with a deep sigh.

"You did not take it and you do not need to 'talk to me' at all," I said firmly.

"Well…yeah…I need to explain something."

"No, I do not want to hear it. If we haven't already talked about whatever you want to talk about then I don't need to know it just because Detective Malone thinks you guys had anything to do with the buckle. I know you didn't."

"Now, Lauren," He sighed. "It's going to…"

"No, Marty," I huffed. "Now…let's get on the road."

I walked to the door before he said another word and held it open for him to depart the house so I could lock it behind us.

He hesitated and looked at me thoughtfully.

"Marty, let's just go and have fun." I smiled at him although my stomach had soured. Between my dream, the phone call and now this, my head was beginning to hurt.

He just nodded and walked out the door.

Jess and Ryle had already left with horses in tow, so I rode in Kade's truck in the front seat with him, while Jamie rode in the back seat between Marty and Pete.

"This is going to be a good day," I said as Kade turned off my road and onto the highway.

"Yes, it is!" Jamie said excitedly. "It will be a late night back though."

"Well, they are backtracking the other way tomorrow to Jerome," Pete said. "Then back to Hermiston then Homedale on Saturday then all the way to Omak for Sunday."

"They are going to be so tired on Monday." I smiled. It was a life I missed; long road trips, middle of the night stops at truck stops for snacks, and too few hours of sleep between rodeos.

"Good thing they get along so well," Marty said. "Been that way since they met a couple years ago." He said to Jamie. "Met at a jackpot and they've been friends since and will be for years to come; like me and Pete. Lauren? Did I ever tell you how we met?"

"No," I chuckled. "Were you drawn together like they were?"

"Oh, Mom," Jamie groaned. "That is so corny."

We all laughed.

"That's how they told me." I turned in my seat and grinned back at her.

"So how did you two meet?" Jamie asked.

"Well," Marty started. "When I was younger, before buying the store, I worked for this ranch down south. After two months of working for him and not getting a paycheck I confronted the owner and he fired me and kicked me off his property."

The energy drained from my body and my headache increased. I turned to look out the window with my stomach trembling in rising anger.

"What the hell?" Jamie gasped.

"Kind of what I thought," Marty said. "So…when I knew he was gone, I went back and collected some tools that would cover the cost of what he owed me."

"Oh…" Jamie whispered.

"Now, I know it was wrong but I was young, stupid, and really pissed off," Marty explained. "I would never allow or recommend anyone do that but…"

"What happened?" Jamie asked.

My neck tightened in anger to the point I could barely move my head. My arms crossed in front of me to try and hold in the emotion. My body slowly lowered in the seat.

"Well, the cops showed up and took back the tools and I was arrested," Marty said. "I heard of this roper that was also an attorney so I called him."

"Pete?" Jamie asked.

"Yep," Marty nodded. "Pete represented me and got me off with trespassing since all the tools were returned and also got me a paycheck from the man."

"Wow…so it worked out," Jamie said.

"Well, like I said, it was stupid, I regretted it and wouldn't even think of doing it again but I ended up with a best friend out of it." Marty said.

"Good thing you were a roper," Pete chuckled.

My stomach and head ached. My jaw was clenched and I stared out the window the rest of the way to the rodeo. The harder they tried to get me to join a conversation, the more my anger rose.

When Kade parked at the rodeo grounds, I stepped out of the truck and walked away. I needed time to breathe and get my body to relax. There was plenty of time before the rodeo so I made my way through the crowd toward the rodeo office.

I found her just outside the door.

"Crystal?"

She turned to my voice and her smile was wide and welcoming, "Lauren! I haven't seen you in ages!"

We embraced and I felt a little bit of my past and history come alive then we talked for ten minutes with barely a breath.

"I have to get back to work," She finally sighed.

"Next time you're down, come out to the ranch for a burger and bottle." I grinned.

"Caldwell rodeo is right around the corner and I'll take you up on that."

"Great, but right now I have a couple ropers I'd like to talk to. Any way you could sneak me in past security?"

"Oh, no problem."

We walked to the back and right through the competitor's gate.

"Thank you," I hugged her again. "And I'll see you next week."

"I'll be there. Have fun!" She waved and walked away.

I made my way through the trucks, trailers, and riders. I recognized a lot of the riders but didn't make eye contact; I was focused on finding Ryle and Jess. I needed their excited energy to lift my spirits.

I found them just outside of the warm-up arena standing next to Dexter and Warlock. Much to my surprise, Jamie had already joined them. As I neared, I could see a pair of cowboys with wide grins and long strides as they approached the trio. I stopped just close enough I could hear the upcoming conversation but was just to the side so they didn't see me.

"Jamie!" Both cowboys called out.

A new Charlie 1 Horse straw cowboy hat covered her hair that flowed down over her shoulders and down her back. She wore a dark navy short sleeve western shirt that was tucked into tight Wranglers. She was adorable and the smile that widened as she turned to the two cowboys warmed my heart.

"Ahhh!" She cried out and threw her arms around the pair.

Jess' back straightened and his eyes bore into the back of Jamie's head. Ryle was grinning and nearly bouncing in his boots.

"It's so great to see you!" Jamie laughed.

She turned back to Ryle and Jess. "Guys this is Brady Portenier and Roscoe Jarboe; bull riders extraordinaire." She looped her arms through the bull rider's arms. "Brady, Roscoe, this is Ryle Jaspers and Jess Corday."

"Team ropers," Roscoe stretched out a hand to Jess then Ryle. "Seen you ride. Congratulations on the Stampede."

Ryle's grin widened as they all shook hands but Jess' shoulders rose and he just nodded…his expression was grim.

"Thanks, how do you know Jamie?" Ryle asked.

"We were in 4H and high school rodeo together," Roscoe said and laid his arm across Jamie's shoulders and pulled her into him. She just giggled with a wide grin and wrapped her arms around his waist.

"We went to Nationals too," Roscoe added. "That was one hell of a trip."

"So much fun!" Jamie grinned. "I was so proud of you making the NFR! Bull rider Rookie of the year!" She nearly squealed in excitement. "I was screaming at the television each night you rode."

Roscoe just laughed.

She turned to Brady. "I was in St. Paul last year when you won and nearly screamed myself out of the stands. I wanted to go back and talk to you but I was with a bunch of drunk girls."

Brady grinned, "Jamie…bring cowgirls back to greet me; drunk or sober."

Her laugh rang out and Jess' back straightened even more as he stared at her.

After a few minutes of talking, Brady and Ryle started a conversation while Roscoe slid his arm around

Jamie's waist then slowly pulled her away from the group as they talked. Jess' stare could have set the man on fire.

I decided to ease Jess' stress and stepped forward toward the group.

"Well, look who you found," I said loud enough Jamie and Roscoe could hear me.

"Lauren!" Brady and Roscoe called out.

Brady walked to me to shake my hand but Roscoe kept his arm firmly around my daughter.

"Damn, you two are lucky to be hanging with Lauren and Jamie," Brady said.

"Not just hanging," Ryle grinned proudly. "We're staying at Lauren's ranch."

"In the bunkhouse?" Roscoe said and seemed to turn Jamie away from the group so he put himself between her and the team ropers.

The lowering of Jess' head and narrowing of his eyes said he understood what Roscoe was doing.

"Yeah!" Ryle said cheerfully. "We get to rope every damn day."

"And with Lauren as a coach," Roscoe said. "She is the best. I live by her mantra from high school."

"One bull at a time, one barrel at a time, or one calf or steer at a time." Brady, Roscoe, and Jamie recited.

"Don't worry about the next one, focus on the one in front of you," Jamie added and looked at me proudly.

That, filled my heart.

"Yeah," I smiled at Roscoe. "I'm sure all those years living and learning from your dad didn't hurt either."

"Oh, yeah," He nodded proudly.

The trio's history made Ryle grin and Jess snarl.

"Are you riding at Caldwell?" Jamie asked the bull riders.

"My hometown rodeo?" Brady nodded. "Yeah, we'll be there."

"Why don't you come out to the ranch for a pre-rodeo get-together?" Jamie asked excitedly and looked at me to confirm the invitation.

"Really?" Brady turned to me.

"Absolutely, we'd love to have you join us," I said with a smile and a quick glance to Ryle and Jess. Jess just stared at me while Ryle was nodding.

Roscoe was looking at Jamie with a wide grin, "We'll be there. What's your phone number now and we'll make arrangements?"

As Jamie recited her phone number with Roscoe typing it into his phone, Jess turned to his horse, stepped in the saddle and rode into the warmup arena.

"Yeah, we got to warm up." Ryle said and turned to his horse. "It was great meeting you two and we'll see you next week."

"Where you headed after this?" Roscoe asked.

"Jerome tomorrow, back here Friday then Homedale Saturday, then off to Omak," Jamie answered.

She and Roscoe had their arms back around each other.

"Well, we'll see you in Omak," Brady said.

"Oh, fun!" Jamie laughed. "We can watch the suicide race together."

"That's a date," Roscoe said and hugged her closer.

Ryle's brow went up in surprise as he looked at Jamie then, as he stepped into the saddle, he inconspicuously looked out to Jess.

"Good luck, tonight," Ryle said and rode away.

"Are you going to Omak, too?" Brady asked me.

"No, too many horses at home." I smiled. "But we'll see you two next week at the ranch?"

"Oh, we'll be there," Roscoe nodded and squeezed Jamie one more time before he finally stepped away from her and toward Brady.

"We'll see you next week," Brady said to me then turned to Jamie. "We'll see you Sunday."

"I'm so looking forward to it." Jamie grinned and waved as they walked away.

I stood and stared at my daughter and wondered if she was completely clueless as to what just happened.

As she turned away from the bull riders her smile faded into a glare as she turned to look out at the team ropers. OK, she knew exactly what happened.

Her body seemed to rise and eyes widen. I turned to see Jess riding out of the warmup arena at a lope and right at her. I walked backwards to my original hiding spot.

With the horse still moving, Jess stepped out of the saddle as if he was a calf roper. They came to a halt within feet of Jamie. Her head tilted back to look up into his eyes.

As hard as I tried, I couldn't hear what he was saying to her but she smiled and nodded then he reached out and her hand rose to his, their fingers entwined. She rose on tiptoes as he lowered to kiss her gently then they parted almost as quickly. He lifted her hand to his lips as they smiled at each other.

"Hmmm," Came a voice from beside me. "Who knew?"

I slowly turned and looked into dark eyes that danced roguishly.

"You know," I told him. "I have been so proud of you over the years, but putting an end to that cat and mouse game so quickly and so sneakily…it's better than your rookie of the year award."

Roscoe laughed, gave me a hug, and walked away with a swagger.

I found the other three men sitting in the bleachers next to the chute. I sat on the end with Kade and Pete between myself and Marty. Although my mood was much better, I was still a bit pissed at the man. He should have honored my request instead of trapping me into his confession.

Jamie joined us as the grand entry began. She grinned the whole night without saying a word about her and Jess.

The pair of ropers came in second, Brady rode his bull to second place, right behind Roscoe.

It was no surprise that Jamie rode home with Jess and Ryle.

CHAPTER THIRTY FOUR

Ryle was loading his horses into the horse trailer with Marty and Pete supervising him…whether he needed it or not.

Jamie and Jess were walking his two horses out of the barn. Kade had left for an appointment with an out of town client and wouldn't return until late at night.

I was kneeling next to the kittens that were just getting adventurous enough to wander out of the dog house.

The detective's name flashed on the phone just before it began singing.

I truly did not like the man but hopefully, he had an answer to Blake being on my property.

"Hello?" I answered.

"Lauren," he said.

"Yes, did you talk to Blake?"

"We talked to him but he wouldn't talk to us so I have no answer for you."

Damn, I knew that would make Jamie want to talk to him.

"But, I just wanted you to know we believe we know who the person is that took the buckle."

"How did they get on my property?"

"You invited him."

"If you tell me it's one of my friends again, I'm going to scream bloody, fucking, murder."

There was dead silence for a solid minute before he spoke again.

"We're collecting the last of the evidence and will be making an arrest today."

"Do you have the belt buckle?"

"Not yet…"

"And are you going to say one of my friends stole it?"

More silence.

I ended the call and looked back to the barn and the four men and my daughter.

I had initially said no to going to the rodeo so Jess and Jamie would have time together without me. But, if the detective was going to make an arrest then I wanted to be with my crew at the rodeo to protect them. I had no doubt the detective would try to make it as public as possible and where better to make an arrest of stealing a World Champion's golden buckle than at a rodeo itself. Tonight was in Jerome which was only 2 hours away then they traveled back to Oregon where the sheriff had no jurisdiction. If he was going to make a move it would be tonight.

I glanced at the playful kittens one more time then stood to walk out to the group.

"Mom, we wish you were coming with us," Jamie sighed with a slump to her shoulders.

There was true joy and love in her eyes that made me happy and I didn't want that diminished. What if they arrested Jess?

"I was just thinking I would change my mind and go with," I said.

Her eyes lit with happiness. There…that made me feel better. The four men seemed just as delighted.

"Well, Kade will be happy you're not staying here by yourself overnight," Pete said thoughtfully. "I am pretty happy about that myself."

I grinned at him, "You have any idea how many nights I have stayed here by myself?"

"And how many of those nights were with a thief hanging around?" Marty quipped.

My anger toward him had diminished overnight and after a discussion with Kade after we fell into bed. Marty was only trying to prepare me for something the detective was sure to throw at me. This way, I wouldn't be surprised when I was told.

I smiled at Marty, "There is no winning this battle."

"Nope, so let me help you with your bags." Ryle grinned.

A half hour later, I was packed, a very happy Kade called, and I was stepping up into the back seat of the truck to ride between Marty and Pete. Since it was Jess' truck, it just seemed fitting the three younger ones got to sit in the front. I was perfectly satisfied with my two older cowboys. They regaled us with more roping stories as we drove to Jerome.

I didn't know whether to go to the bleachers with Marty and Pete or go with Jamie, Jess, and Ryle. The competitor area was set to the back and more remote so it wouldn't be as public if the detective showed up. The bleachers, however, were very public so I joined the older pair on the bleachers; tucked safely between them and with my feet setting on the bleacher in front of us.

"Missing my grandson?" Pete smiled.

"Not at all," I lied with a chuckle.

The rodeo grand entry started but I hardly saw it. My eyes constantly roamed the aisles and what I could see of the competitor's arena. Ryle was on Silas for the night and it was easy to keep an eye on the flashy horse. I constantly searched the faces for Detective Malone.

"From the sounds of it, you're going to have a full arena next Wednesday before the rodeo," Marty said.

"Yes, so I want to pay you for use of your steers for the crowd that is coming," I said.

"You don't need..." He shook his head.

"Yes, I do." I interrupted. "It's one thing if it's just the seven of us, it's another when you add another twenty riders. We'll have to use your whole herd instead of a dozen at a time."

"Alright, we'll work out a fair deal," he said.

"I also need to buy some calves for breakaway." I added.

"I have an in for those," Marty said. "Just let me know how many."

"Will do," I said and turned to Pete who was holding the day sheet. "How deep in the lineup are they?"

The sooner we could leave the better.

"Fifth team, then we'll head out." He answered. "You in a hurry for something?"

"No," I whispered and looked in the distance to search for Silas.

"Then why is your leg bouncing like you want to run out of here?" He asked.

I stopped my leg and turned guilty eyes at him.

"Maybe I should go to the bathroom before the team ropers are up." I chuckled and stood. It was a simple way to disguise my nervousness.

I walked behind the bleachers and stood quietly watching the crowd. My phone started ringing and I sighed in relief it was Kade and not the detective. I wanted to hear his voice.

"Hi, Handsome," I answered with a smile.

"Lauren," He said in a low tone.

My heart sunk.

"No," I sighed as my stomach clenched.

"Yep," He exhaled heavily.

"I came to Jerome in case he came here."

"Well, he came to me instead," Kade growled.

"I know you didn't steal it."

"I'm glad. I really have no reason to take it or jeopardize us."

Us…it was such a small word but it meant so much…my heart ached.

"Did he arrest you?" I whispered.

"I'm at the police station about ready to go back. He gave me one call first. Probably thought I was going to call an attorney but I wanted to talk to you."

"Oh, Kade," I wanted to cry, scream, and run the detective over with my truck.

My phone beeped letting me know I was receiving another call. I lowered the phone to see the detective's name.

"He's calling me right now," I said.

"Yeah, he said he would be back after he talked to you."

"I can't believe this is happening! Why did he arrest you? Why would he think you did this?"

"Evidently they got a tip and searched my truck."

"So?"

"It was tucked under the driver's seat."

"No…" I gasped. "How did it get there?"

"I have no idea," Kade answered. "Malone just walked back in. Don't tell Grandad. I'll talk to him when they get back tomorrow night."

"Alright," I nodded with tears of anger rising. "They are driving straight through the night tonight to go back to Hermiston." I reminded him.

"Yeah, it will be late tomorrow night, but, either way, he'll be upset I didn't tell him tonight."

"By the time they get back, we'll have answers," I said. "I'll have them drop me off at the ranch…are you going to be able to come home tonight?"

"No…"

The anger was rising through the shock.

"Oh, Kade," My voice shook.

"The detective just said to tell you that we'll be able to discuss this in the morning."

"The damn coward doesn't want to talk to me right now," I growled.

"Yes, I do believe you are correct." There was a slight hint of humor in his voice. "And I need to go now."

"I'm so sorry this is happening," Everything in me wanted to go to him.

"We'll work on the answers tomorrow." he said. "But tonight, you can at least rest knowing the buckle has been found and can be put back where it belongs."

"I'm not going to be able to rest."

"Well, do the best you can. Goodnight…"

"Goodnight…" I whispered and lowered the phone to end the call.

The hum of the crowd jolted me back. I looked at all of the happy faces as I tried to calm the anger rising through me.

There was nothing I could do besides make sure Pete and the rest of the crew remained clueless. Taking a deep breath I exhaled quickly then made my way back to the bleacher between the two older men.

"Just in time," Pete said. "First team is about…well they are running."

I glanced out at the pair as the heeler's loop trapped the steer's legs. Horses turned and the judge's flag dropped; 5 seconds flat.

"Damn," Marty huffed.

"Set the target," Pete nodded.

I searched the area behind the chutes. I could just make out a Silas' golden hide and Casper's grey. I could barely see the two cowboys and Jamie was nowhere in sight.

I wrapped my arm around Pete's and squeezed tightly. His hand patted my arm and we quietly watched the next four teams enter, throw, and ride out.

Ryle and Jess rode into the arena and backed into the boxes; black cowboy hats and shirts with the sponsor patches displayed proudly.

"They look sharp," Marty said.

"Very professional," I smiled.

Casper wasn't as still in the box as Warlock so Jess had to turn him a number of times before he held still. He turned to look at Ryle.

Ryle rolled his shoulders, then held his arm back with rope dangling over Silas' rump. He waited as the steer fought in the chute then finally became calm.

He nodded.

The steer bolted from the chute and made his run only to be stopped by Ryle's lariat tightening around his horns. Jess' loop trapped their target's legs with Casper scooting to a stop and Silas turning to complete the run; 5.5 seconds.

"Into second," Pete nodded.

I relaxed my arm that had tightened around his. For 5.5 seconds I had been lost in the excitement and now the reality of Kade being arrested rushed back. I kept myself from sighing, crying, or reacting any more than smiling for the pair of ropers.

We remained seated until the team roping completed then rose as Jess and Ryle were announced as taking second place.

"Still twelve hundred in the bank," Jess grinned as we approached the trailer.

"Pays for a couple entry fees next year," Jamie said proudly.

"Or gas, or food, or feed, or truck repairs…" Ryle chuckled as he replaced the bridle on Silas with a halter then tied him to the trailer.

The palomino turned to look at me and my hand reached for him. I stood running my hand down his nose and neck as Ryle removed the saddle off his back then brushed him down.

I watched my companions as they made preparations to leave and tried to come up with an excuse to have them drop me off at the ranch before they continued to Hermiston. It had to be something that was logical and wouldn't make Jamie want to stay.

My mind was blank until we were on the road and halfway back to the ranch. Then the idea hit.

"Well," I sighed dramatically. "I just remembered I have the vet coming in the morning to check the pregnant mares."

"Really, Mom?" Jamie turned. "You didn't say anything."

"That's because I just remembered." I lied. "It's too late to call and cancel so you're just going to have to drop me off."

"You want me to stay and help?" Pete asked.

"No, you're going to the rodeo as planned." I told him with a smile. "I can handle this by myself, I have for years."

"But not with someone breaking into your place," Marty said.

"I will be fine," I said. "Whoever it was is long gone and besides, I've been alone many times the last couple weeks while the buckle was gone."

"But…" Jamie started.

"No, you're all going to the rodeo as planned. I wasn't originally going so I was going to be home by myself anyway until Kade returned," I argued.

"Oh, that's right," Pete said. "That makes me feel better."

When Jess turned down my long driveway, the reality of Kade's arrest swirled my stomach.

"Just drop me off at the gate and turn around," I said. "I want to walk the rest of the way."

"Lauren," Pete grumbled.

"I'm just feeling a bit nauseous so I want to clear my head and stomach with the walk," I argued.

"No bubbles?" Ryle asked with a grin.

The other men laughed and Jamie looked at them in confusion.

"No, you smart-ass," I couldn't help but smile at the memory.

"What's that mean? What am I missing?" Jamie whined.

Jess stopped and turned the truck before the gate as Ryle told Jamie the story of our return from the jackpot.

My daughter snort-laughed at least twice.

"Mom!" She looked at me with wide sparkling eyes.

I just shrugged, "They fed me."

"We didn't!" Marty and Pete called out.

I just laughed as Pete opened his door and stepped out. He held out a hand to help me out of the truck. He was such a gentleman and he was going to be so mad at me when he found out the truth.

I gave him a hug then stood at the gate and watched the trailer lights disappear over the hill.

I keyed in the code and stepped through the gate then slowly made my way down the long driveway. I just wished it was light enough that I could see the ranch instead of just the bit of driveway the outside light illuminated.

The sky was full of sparkling stars and I stopped halfway down to look up at them. Those millions of people that I had imagined when I was lying in the arena had a different light now. They all had friends and family surrounding them and now I did too.

I inhaled to take in the evening air and listened to the night. There was no wind so I could hear crickets calling out but it just added to the peace. If it wasn't for the fact that Kade was sitting in a cold dark cement cell I could have enjoyed it. I promised myself that he would be free the next night and we would go for a midnight walk and enjoy the peace together.

I took another few steps and stopped again. The night I lay in the arena and the days after had also been quiet and I had been alone just as I was now. But the difference was knowing my friends and family were a drive away or a call away. The quiet had been so isolating then, it was comforting now.

The sun was barely peeping over the distant trees when I walked down the stairs. I'd barely slept, was cranky, and wanted to rip the detectives head off because there was nothing I could do until after 8:00…if even then.

I stopped in front of the large picture window that faced the road and on the other side was the wheat field. In the distance, I could see the farmer's tractor making its way around the parameter as he began harvest. That would create even more dust than normal. I stepped out the front door of the house and walked to my right to make sure the windows on this side of the house were closed. They would get the thickest layers of dust.

Going back toward the side of the house by the driveway I checked the kitchen windows across that side and around the corner to the back. The dog house turned cat house was tucked into the corner of the long wall and wide porch. The swing was to my right but I passed by it to make my way to the kittens.

Slowly and quietly, so I didn't disturb them, I sat down in front of the open door and peered in. Momma kitty was nursing her babies. I stretched my legs out in front of me and leaned against the base of the porch. I'd wait until the kittens were full then see if they were ready to play.

I set my phone on the ground just outside the opening and ran a hand around momma kitty's head. She purred softly which made me think of Andrea. She loved cats.

I thought of the middle of the night conversation with Kade. I missed her…terribly bad and I didn't want to leave our relationship with her walking away in anger and me melting away in the dirt. I needed closure with her and if I was going to call her, now was the time to do it while everyone was busy. Except for Kade, who I was sure that damn detective had placed in a cell overnight. Ooh, I hated that man.

With the phone still lying on the ground between me and the kitty house, I pushed the button until Andrea's phone number appeared. Even though it was early, I knew she would be awake…we had always been early risers.

My finger hovered over the 'call' button…my stomach tightened and hand trembled.

Momma kitty mewed and stood. For the first time since sitting down, I got a look at all the kittens. One was missing.

Momma cat mewed again as I mumbled, "What the hell?"

I turned to look for the kitten outside of the house and saw a movement on the swing.

I gasped and my finger lowered to the call button on the phone.

Sheila Armstrong was slowly rising from the swing; she had a grey kitten in one hand and a butcher knife in the other.

CHAPTER THIRTY FIVE

"What the hell are you doing home?" Sheila growled.

"Sheila!" I gasped as my body tingled in shock. "What the hell are you doing here? The police have been looking for you."

I said it loud enough that hopefully Andrea had answered the phone and heard it.

"And that would be the answer to your question." She huffed and sat back down on the swing…perched on the edge as if ready to run at any moment.

Her hand gripped the ten-inch butcher knife tighter.

"What…?" I exhaled in disbelief.

"You left last night," The hand with the knife moved to the kitten cradled in her lap. The tips of her fingers played with the kitten's fur while the blade hovered over her arm. "Why the hell are you back?"

"It's MY house," I said defensively. "What the hell are you doing here? Why in the hell do you have a knife?"

She shrugged slightly and waved the knife in the air, "Because I don't like guns and I just don't feel safe without the knife." She smirked. "Remember? Police are looking for me?"

"How long have you been here?"

"Just before you let those men move into that building," She waved the knife toward the bunkhouse. "Sure glad the dog didn't come with them. That damn thing kept growling at me that first day."

"That was weeks ago!" I gasped. "How? Why? You're supposed to be in Mexico! They said Chula Vista."

I wasn't really sure what to do with that knife firmly in her grip. I was nestled in the corner in front of the dog house and side of the patio with my legs splayed in front of me. It would be awkward to rise but I wasn't sure if I should. The phone was currently blocked from her view and I needed to keep it hidden.

"I figured that had worked," She huffed. "I overnighted the phone to a friend that gave it to a friend of a friend and they put the battery back in, turned it on, then off again." She shrugged slightly. "They did it a couple times as they neared the border then destroyed it."

"Well, it worked, but why here? How?"

She tapped the sharp edge of the knife along the arm of the wooden swing. No doubt she was leaving marks and the idea of that just pissed me off but I had a feeling if I said anything about it she wouldn't really care and I wasn't really sure of her mental state.

Her blonde hair hung to her shoulders. She was dressed in blue slip-on shoes and a peach-colored sundress. It was not the dress she wore to the party.

"I don't understand," I finally said. "How have you been staying here?"

Sheila shrugged again and looked down at the kitten in her lap, "Well, the first night was in the loft in the barn, then while you were gone, I ventured out to look around and found your horse trailer that has the camper in the front." She smirked at me. "Been living in it ever since."

"But…I was in there the other day." My face flushed when I thought back to Kade and I being in there…on the bed.

"Yeah," She chuckled. "You nearly caught me then. You wouldn't have this time except I didn't know you were here. I thought you left."

"I did," I nodded. "But I came back late last night…I had other things…" I stopped. She didn't need to know about Kade being arrested.

"Well you ruined my morning," She sighed and looked back at the barn.

I quickly looked down at the phone but the screen was black. I had no idea if anyone was on the other end.

My head shot up when she started to turn back.

"I didn't hear you walking or I'd been out of here…hidden again."

"You've been here all along? But they looked for you…dogs and everything."

"No, after the party I made it to a road before the police got here and hitched a ride out of town. Was gone for a couple weeks then came back."

"Why come back?"

"I ran out of money…didn't know what to do so I came here where it all started…or ended for Dave." She looked out to the patio; her tone was wistful and shoulders relaxed. If it wasn't for the knife in her hand, it would look like we were still at the party having fun. "I have sat here many hours and thought of that day…that moment." Her head slowly turned and her eyes were narrowed. "That damn recording…that ruined my life. According to the news reports, you did that."

"Yes," I said softly. "But I didn't sleep with him…I wasn't the one having the affair and I didn't play the recording."

"So you're going to lay the blame on everyone else for killing my husband?"

My eyebrows rose in surprise, "You were the one that did that."

The knife tapped harder against the swing but she looked calm. "If you hadn't recorded it…"

I shook my head and waved away her words with a hand.

"There are so many 'ifs'," I said loudly to stop her. "You have no idea how many, but it doesn't change anything."

"You're right…" She nodded and took a deep breath…the knife became still. "I can't change anything. I can't reverse time and bring him back to our heartbroken kids."

She stood, letting the kitten fall to the ground without a thought. It mewed and quickly trotted its way back toward me. I slowly leaned forward and shuffled him safely into the house next to his mother with a glance to my phone. There was no indication that it was on.

"I am sorry…I told them that." I said softly.

"Yes…I saw you talking to them." She had been looking at the patio…at the grill where she stabbed Dave but slowly turned and looked at me. "They brought me clothes…"

"They knew you were here?" I gasped. "That's why they were here?"

"Yes…we decided this was the safest place. Who would think I had come back? I was in a comfy little trailer to stay until we could get money together so I could leave the country."

"All that time in the trailer…"

"Yes, pretty quiet here most of the time but the drama last week? Scared the hell out of me when all the cops showed up. That tall good looking man showed up one day and walked around like he owned the place…then the cops!"

"That was my ex-husband," I said. "What did he do?"

She shrugged, "No clue really. He disappeared behind the locked door in the barn for a while then came out and drove away. I was sure as hell surprised when he arrived again and he attacked you and all the cops showed up."

My stomach ached at the possibilities of what he did in there. "He didn't go to the house?"

"No…I don't know that it would have done him in good. You're pretty damned good at locking up the house when you leave. I tried but couldn't get in until I tried it while you were busy slutting around with the men."

"I wasn't slutting around with them," I grumbled.

"No…just the one," She turned back to the patio. "First, I thought it was the tall one you were sleeping with but turned out to be the sexy cowboy with the tattoo."

"How did you know he had a tattoo?"

Her laugh was low but humored…to herself anyway.

"Did you forget your sex romp in the trailer last week?"

My stomach turned, "You were in there?"

"Yeah," She huffed. "Like I said, you nearly caught me then. I just barely got into the bathroom when you two fell in. I thought you were going to go at it right there on the floor."

"You watched?" I gasped in disgust.

"No…never been into that. Dave asked me about that once but it wasn't my thing. But, I did end up listening to the whole thing…and I admit I peeked in once."

I thought of our 'romp' as she put it…the words…the moans…the gasps…

I thought of Jodi and the 'oh' sounds she made on the laundry room recording. It was the first time, in all these weeks, that I had thought of her and how she felt with all those people hearing her panting and begging for

Dave to move 'harder'. How mortifying for her! I needed to apologize to her.

"That tattoo was sexy and boy was he all over you."

"Enough!" I growled and started to rise.

"Just stay down there." She took a step toward me with the knife clenched tightly in her hands.

"I can't. My legs are falling asleep and hurt." I lied and wiggled to a kneeling position.

"Don't get up." She waved the knife in front of her. Her voice was growing in panic. "I need to call my kids and have them come to get me." She was less than 10 feet away when she jabbed the knife toward me. Her eyes were wide. "Son of a bitch…I shouldn't have told you they helped me. You'll tell the police…I can't have that. You're not taking them away from me too."

"I didn't take Dave away from you." I reminded her. "I didn't have an affair with him…which didn't take him away from you either. YOU did that by stabbing him."

"That stupid son of a bitch!" She yelled with spit flying from her mouth. She looked a bit deranged with the knife flailing around, her face scrunched in anger, and feet pacing back and forth.

She changed in a split second. She was calm…then horrified…and now she looked like a crazed maniac.

I suddenly realized I should be scared for my life. Kneeling on the ground in the corner by the doghouse, I was trapped. She could be on me before I had a chance to move.

"Why in the hell would he have a fucking affair with that twit…that bitch?"

I took a deep breath and placed a hand on the edge of the dog house so I could at least brace myself to rise quickly if I got the chance.

"Well," I said with a soft tone to try to get her to calm down. "To be fair, Jodi isn't a twit or a bitch."

She stopped her pacing and turned to glare at me.

"She's a very successful business woman that had just gone through a divorce and was dating a handsome executive that said he was divorced."

I had no idea if Sheila would take that as good or bad but I just felt the need to defend Jodi after what I put her through. Besides, I needed Sheila to blame her husband.

Sheila stood completely still and lowered her head enough that she was basically looking at me through her eyebrows.

"He said he was divorced?" Her voice was almost inhuman.

"Yes," I nodded. "I've known Jodi long enough to know she would not have an affair with a man she knew was married." I took a leap of faith to hopefully talk Sheila down from her psychotic ledge. I needed to place the blame back on her husband. "Had Dave had an affair before?"

Her head rose enough she was looking at me down the bridge of her nose. "Once," She finally said. "He said it was a mistake, he'd never do it again, and he was mortified it had happened in the first place. He swore it wouldn't again."

"But it did," I whispered. "He did which drove you to become enraged and…"

"That's not why I was enraged…that's not why I tried to hurt him the way he was hurting me." She whispered as her shoulders lowered; that switch again from crazed to calm.

"You were just trying to hurt him? Not kill him?" I asked softly as if sympathizing with her.

"No," She shook her head slowly and her eyes were a bit glazed. "I was furious he screwed her…there at the party. I was embarrassed everyone heard it…knew he cheated on me. I was confused as to why she and I were both there…until I realized that was my fault." Her eyes widened and she nodded as if trying to convince me. "I surprised him by inviting myself at the last moment. He was already in the car when I just grabbed my purse and came with him…he didn't know."

"He should have taken you somewhere else…he could have made an excuse," I said.

Her mood switched again with a wild…wicked…laugh. "An excuse?" She laughed again and I shivered. "After screwing her, he joined me at the grill and whispered in my ear that I should make an excuse to leave and go to our favorite hotel and get ready for him. He was going to bring me a surprise and we were going to have an afternoon of sex…and love." The last came out a bit desperate as if she added it as an afterthought.

Jodi had said basically the same thing. I wondered if he was going to try for a three-way with them.

"But that's not why I got mad." Sheila continued.

"Then why?" I asked in surprise.

"Because…because he…" The skin of her neck turned red and it slowly rose to emblazon her cheeks. "He called her his 'little flower'."

"What?"

"That's what he has called ME," The knife waved in the air again. "That was ME!" She screamed. "He fucking called her his 'little flower' and I exploded inside. All I saw was white…then red…I wanted to run to get away from him but when I turned I saw that fork and wanted to hurt him. He killed my heart…he killed me." Her voice shook and tears fell.

"So…those three words are the reason he died?" I shook my head in disbelief.

"Yes," She whispered so low I barely heard her.

The knife slowly lowered to her side and her shoulders slumped.

"I didn't know he died…I didn't expect him to die. He was the father of my children. I had no idea the fork would go in him…into his heart. I'm not very big…I'm not strong enough for them to go into him." Her eyes fixated on me. "If you hadn't recorded it…I wouldn't have heard those words…and…you took him away."

"No, I…"

"You took my man away from me so I decided to take yours away."

I stared at her blankly.

"When you two were in the trailer," She whispered. "In the middle of all your moaning…what he was saying…those words…that you were sexy…soft…addicting. They were so…romantic." Her eyes were glazed, her voice raspy. "I didn't get romantic words…I got sex words. 'My little flower' was the only romantic thing he called me." In an instant, her eyes went from lost and hazy to angry and psychotic. "He called her that and I..." Her shoulders rose and she glared at me. "So I came up with a way to take your man away from you."

"The buckle?" I gasped. "You had the buckle?"

She looked at me in surprise then laughed again. "Yes…I took it just to hurt you. I knew the way it was displayed that it meant a lot to you. So I took it not really knowing what I was going to do with it. Then after that romp in the trailer…listening to his words to you…I knew. But how did you figure that one out?"

I took that leap of faith again…maybe if she thought she had succeeded, "Kade was arrested last night for stealing it. That's why I came home. So I could deal with that this morning."

Her shrill of a laugh rang out again. "So if I hadn't planted the buckle, you wouldn't have come home, and I'd still be hidden. How fucking funny is that?" She waved the knife in the air then lowered to lean her hands on her knees as the laughter continued.

I started to rise from my kneeling position.

Her head flew up, knife stretched toward me…then with wide glazed eyes. "No!" She screamed and I froze for a breath then slowly lowered back down to my knees.

"I told you about my kids." Her voice was high and breathing increasing. She was just on the verge of gasping for air. "I can't have my children hurt anymore than they already have been."

"I won't say anything," I promised. "They aren't part of this…they are innocent as far as I am concerned.

Her eyes narrowed, "That's what I thought of your daughter too."

"What? Jamie?" I felt like she had punched me.

She nodded with a slight sneer. "I stood in the kitchen…match lit and slowly moving toward the curtains." Her eyes went up to the house. "I was going to burn this place down and make you pay for what you did."

I stared at her in disbelief.

"I saw the picture of your daughter…well, the pictures," She huffed. "My children have suffered for what you did. They are innocent…so is your daughter so I blew out the flame for her. I wasn't going to destroy her home." Her eyes narrowed. "You will not hurt my children anymore. I won't let you."

"Sheila…it was Dave. It is his fault this is happening." I whispered.

Her eyes came back down to me as her spine stiffened.

"Yes, you are right." She admitted with a nod. "If he didn't have the affair…if he hadn't taken the chance with both of us at the party…if he hadn't screwed her then come to me…but if you hadn't recorded it I wouldn't have heard his words…to HER."

She lunged with knife high and aimed right at me.

CHAPTER THIRTY SIX

I fell forward then rolled back toward her legs. I heard her scream and rolled onto my back to face her attack but she was down on the ground…rolling with someone on top of her.

I scrambled to my feet as Andrea rose with the knife in her hand and tossed it toward the house.

"NO!" Sheila screamed again and with that lightning speed her leg swung up toward Andrea's head hitting her hard and knocking her away.

Sheila rolled onto her stomach and desperately crawled away like a scared spider. She started to rise to run when both Andrea and I tackled her from behind. Hair, arms and legs were everywhere as we fought with her.

Sirens blared in the distance.

"The gate…" I gasped as I tried to sit on Sheila's legs to make them stop moving.

"I left it open." Andrea panted.

She was facing me with her butt on Sheila's back, right between the shoulder blades, and her knees on the ground with her calves holding Sheila's arms into her side.

Andrea gripped Sheila's wrists and held them to the ground.

I faced Andrea with my butt sitting on Sheila's calves trapping her legs to the ground.

The woman wasn't going anywhere.

I glanced up at a wide-eyed, red-faced from exertion, Andrea.

"We need a piggin' string." She grinned.

Oh, how I have missed this woman in my life.

"Eh, you weren't good at tying those goats." I teased.

Two police cars flew by the house and turned into the driveway.

Andrea laughed and her eyes went behind me as the police officers stepped out of their vehicles.

"Looks like you two have this handled," Officer Mullins said. "But I'll take her from here."

Sheila's body melted into the ground so the officer gave me a hand to support me as I stood. He placed a handcuff on a crying Sheila's wrist as the second officer helped Andrea stand.

Andrea and I stepped back and watched as they finished handcuffing her, lifting her to her feet then officially telling her she was under arrest.

They placed her in the back of a car then turned to me.

"You OK, Lauren? Need a medic?" Officer Mullins asked.

"No…I'm fine." I inhaled deeply then exhaled trying to relax. "She didn't do anything until just the end there but she missed me with the knife."

"Yeah, we were listening," Officer Mullins nodded.

I looked at him in surprise.

"I called 911 on Cory's phone," Andrea said to me then turned to the officers. "He's my son…then I put mine on speaker so they could hear everything. They're on the seat of my truck…just down the road. I ran here so she didn't get spooked."

"Then dispatch patched it through to us so we could hear what we were getting into." The shorter officer said.

I exhaled in relief, "So I don't have to go over everything and tell you why we tackled her?"

"No ma'am," Officer Mullins said. "There will be some detectives come out and gather evidence and check out the trailer she was in."

"Kade!" I gasped and walked to my phone. "I have to call that jackass detective to let him know about the buckle."

"They already know. That's one of the detectives on his way here." Officer Mullins said.

Andrea was standing behind them, fingers buried in her back pockets and eyes looking at the ground then back to me. Her lower lip was caught between her teeth. Her eyes asked me, 'What should I do?'

"How long before they get here?" I asked.

The sound of tires flying over gravel echoed and we all turned to see the detective's car with Kade's truck right behind him.

I watched Kade as he pulled in with his eyes searching for me. When his met mine I smiled to reassure him I was OK. He nearly ran to me and engulfed me in his arms. Safe…he made me feel safe and my whole body relaxed against him then started trembling.

"You're OK?" He whispered.

"Yes, Andrea tackled her away from me," I answered.

"Andrea?" He stood back in surprise and looked behind me. "She was here?"

"She is here," I said and turned to see her walking toward the back of the house which led to the road and ultimately her truck down the road. "I'll be right back," I told him and jogged to follow her.

I have no doubt she heard me approach but she kept walking when she hit the gravel road.

"Thank you," I said and kept pace next to her. The truck was parked off the side of the road halfway to the gate.

She just nodded and kept walking, "I was shocked to see you were calling me but pretty terrified when you asked her why she was carrying a knife."

We walked silently for a full minute…both unsure where to start the conversation.

A horse whinnied in the pasture and we both looked out to it.

The team roper's younger horses, Gus and Casper, were calling out to each other.

"I saw them on Facebook," Andrea said of the horses. "That Ryle guy posted a picture someone had taken of all of you at a jackpot." She smiled slightly. "I was surprised you were back to roping; surprised but very happy."

"Honestly, at that point, I was just sitting on the horse." I said. "I didn't start riding until after Jamie came home."

"She's back?" She asked in surprise. "As in really back?"

"Yes," I smiled. "She moved home last week and will finish school here."

"Where is she?"

"She went on the road with a bunch of damned team ropers."

The police car with Sheila in the back drove by us. We both watched as they passed. Sheila's head was down, chin to chest.

We walked silently until we reached the truck and as we had a million times we slid into it and slammed the doors at the same time.

She started the engine and slowly moved forward toward the house.

Being in her truck was so familiar yet had never been as awkward as it was now.

She turned into the driveway and continued past the group of people to the barns. I could see Kade watching and for a moment our eyes connected. No matter what happened, I wasn't alone anymore…he was there…Jamie was there…and the rest of the crew would be there for me too.

Andrea stopped the truck behind the bleacher and we both stepped out. I was very surprised she walked to the arena gate but followed her through and into the middle of the arena where we had last spoken.

"Why here?" I asked.

She finally looked at me with a bit of a smirk, "I asked you that same thing when we met after the party."

"Yeah," I huffed. "Why did you ask me that?"

She looked around the arena again, "Why here?" She took a deep breath and let it out slowly. "Let's get the secrets of the past out before we talk about the now." She turned and looked at me. I nodded with my body tingling in fear and hope.

"Here?" she said. "Because this is the spot where Austin and I decided to end our relationship."

"Greg said it was just one time. That's not much of a relationship."

She shook her head as if the weight of the world was on her shoulders, "He only saw the last night…after we decided to stop. But we just couldn't walk away without…I guess…saying goodbye."

Her voice quivered and she looked at me with glistening eyes. "All these years later and it still…I wonder if we truly did the right thing."

"You said it was my fault."

"It was..." She said and her eyes went to the fields as if in the past. "But not the way I said it that day. He didn't tell me not to tell you, he suggested it and I agreed."

"Why? Why keep it from me?"

"Because we weren't sure how you would take it. You were eight months pregnant."

"Then why did you start the affair?"

She turned and looked back at me with narrowing eyes. "It wasn't an affair." She said coldly. "After the first, kiss we both realized there was the possibility of so much more…of a true future."

"Then why did you stop?"

"Austin hurt his hip when you were seven months along."

"Yeah…the fall with the colt he was training."

"So he couldn't compete and stayed here to recuperate, be with you and get this place built. I was staying here for you."

"So…it lasted two months?" I gasped in surprise.

"The first month we spent a lot of time together…flirted when you weren't around and when you and Blake went to his parents for a weekend it was just me and Austin here for three days…and well…there was this moment and we suddenly saw each other differently. "

"You hid it well."

"I don't know about that," She shrugged. "You were just busy with Blake and Jamie. We'd try not to be alone but there were moments we couldn't help it."

"I don't understand why you didn't let me know that something was going on."

She sighed, "Like I said...even to this day...21 years later...I wonder if we did the right thing. We didn't tell you...and we stopped...because...what if it didn't work out and we ended up hating each other? You would be in between us, with a new baby and husband."

I stared at her a moment and thought of what our lives would be like if they hated each other...but I really couldn't imagine either one of them hating anyone. But, then again, I never would have believed I would hate Blake as much as I do now.

But what would our lives had been like if Andrea and Uncle Austin had become a couple? It would be the three of us...and Blake...raising our families here together. Holding events together...fulfilling dreams together.

"I don't know..." My head swirled in confusion. "I don't know what I would have thought back then, but now? I kind of wished you had tried to...but I love Charlene, Taylor, and Ace. I couldn't even imagine our lives without Stan and the boys."

"Yes," Andrea nodded. "I love them too."

"But...I also love the thought of you and Uncle Austin..."

"Yeah...me too," She smirked. "Like I said, even 21 years later I don't know if we made the right decision."

"But...you loved each other?" I asked but I knew, now, that they truly did.

"Until the day I die," She whispered with sad eyes looking back at the house.

"But not enough to really know?"

"I think we did know…I knew but I doubted him…which I shouldn't have. But, what I do know, is that we both LOVED you and wouldn't do anything to hurt you. So we stopped and he left for Texas for a couple weeks, until right before Jamie was born. Then he married Charlene and I met Stan. We didn't marry people we saw as second best. We married people that we wanted to spend our lives with…if not with each other. That was the hard part and well, that's it." She sighed.

"So…that's it," I asked hopefully. "There's no more secrets?"

She stared at me a moment then slowly nodded her head, "Yes, there is one more."

"I don't want any more secrets between us," I said. "No more."

"Alright…I agree."

"Then, what is it?"

"I know what your mother's letter said."

CHAPTER THIRTY SEVEN

"What?" I gasped in disbelief.

"Austin told me so if you ever needed to know and he wasn't there for you that I would be able to tell you the truth."

"When was this? During your aff…relationship?"

"No, years after," She answered. "Right after Taylor was born. Austin and I were sitting in the swing and I was cradling Taylor and he was holding Ace while you were riding with Jamie. Stan, Blake, and Charlene were in the house sleeping in. Austin mentioned how life changes once a decision was made. He still wasn't sure we made the right one but neither of us could deny the love for Ace and Taylor, Cody and Seth. And of course, Stan and Charlene."

"That was five years after Jamie was born. And he still wasn't sure?"

"We weren't sure…I had doubted it through the years, thinking we should have tried no matter the outcome. But who knew what the future would hold for us? His death? Well…"

"It wasn't supposed to end that way." I finished for her.

She looked at me in surprise.

"I remembered that the other day," I explained. "That's what you said when I got the phone call."

"Yeah…it wasn't supposed to end that way."

As heartbreaking and emotionally confusing as it was, I understood that part of the past now.

"How does my mother's letter fit into this?"

"We were rocking the boys in the swing and he told me what it said…for you…so you would know if he couldn't tell you."

I stared at her a moment, "Why didn't he just tell me?"

"You said you didn't want to know…you were happy that she had the decency to leave you with Austin so she could just carry on with her life without you."

We stared at each other in silence while the memories of that day played out in my mind. The surprise she had left me, then the bit of joy that went through me that I didn't have to be around her friends or be left alone in the apartment anymore. Then there was the elation that I got to stay with him and ride horses and rope steer.

"Do you want to know or do you just live life knowing that I know?" She asked.

"My life will not change no matter what the letter says," I said.

"No, it won't."

"So, it doesn't matter if I know or not."

"I don't know that I agree with that," she said. "I think you will always carry that question within you."

I thought of my call to Charlene looking for answers. Maybe Andrea was right. She knew me better than any other person.

"Alright," I nodded. "I agree with that so…what did it say?"

"That is was mine and Austin's fault that she left you," Andrea said with a steady voice as if she had practiced making that announcement to me many times.

My brows rose in surprise then as I thought of her words I nodded.

"Honestly…since we were terrible kids before she left and we were in trouble a lot, I can understand why she would use you as an excuse but Uncle Austin? How in the hell could she blame him? I'd only met him once or twice before that day."

"It was that day," Andrea said. "She came back and sat on the bleachers and watched the two of you rope."

"NO way…!" My jaw dropped in total disbelief. "We didn't see her…that's a lie."

Andrea shrugged, "How would she know that you were roping?"

I huffed and shook my head.

"She said neither of you even saw her…that you were so immersed on what you were doing…him teaching and you learning…that you didn't know she was there."

From the moment my uncle and I had stepped into the arena, nothing else in the world had existed for me. I had to admit that she could have been doing jumping jacks on the bleachers and I wouldn't have noticed her.

"Well, that's probably true then," I admitted out loud.

"So she left you with him."

"That's it? She could have just moved me away from you," I growled in rising anger. "And to leave me with a man she didn't know? I'm damn lucky he was the man he was and not some damn pedophile."

"I agree," Andrea said softly. "…and no, that's not all."

My back stiffened in preparation for the answer.

"She didn't want to be a mother, had never wanted to be a mother…she tried but couldn't do it anymore." She looked at me with apprehension, as if gauging my reaction and not wanting me to be hurt.

"Now THAT I believe," I sighed and a bit of the anger started to subside. "That is the reason I have told myself the last 30 years. I pretty much knew that…she told me that to my face dozens of times."

"And to tell you everything, I tried finding her."

"What the hell for?"

She shrugged with a bit of a smirk, "Curiosity really; but there was one little problem that stopped me."

"What?"

"You have your father's last name and they were never married so I have no idea what her last name is."

I smiled slightly, "Funny that you know everything about me but you don't know that."

"What is it?"

I tilted my head and looked at her thoughtfully, "Well, since I know you'll try to find her, and I don't want her to be found, I'm not going to tell you."

Andrea grinned, "Yeah…I tried a couple times to inconspicuously ask you her full name but you always changed the subject on me."

I just shrugged.

"But, what does it matter?" Andrea asked. "What does it matter if she is alive or dead? What does it matter if you have brothers and sisters?"

"Half…they would only be half."

"So," She smiled slightly. "You've thought of that."

"Yes," I admitted. "I have, but it doesn't matter if they exist or not."

"Then why not just find out? There was that itch of what the letter said…"

"And it doesn't change my life or really tells me anything except she was at the arena but that really doesn't matter either. She left me with a man she didn't know. She left me no matter the consequences to me."

That was what had bothered me all these years. Not that she left me but that she had left me with a virtual stranger.

"You may not have known him. It doesn't mean she didn't." Andrea argued.

I looked at her thoughtfully; my lips rolling into a thin line.

"What does it matter? Give me her last name. Let's look it up right now and get the past out in the open."

"What does it matter? You think I would contact her if she is alive? Ask her why?"

She stared at me a moment then shook her head. "No, I don't think you would ever contact her. You know the reasons she left you so there isn't anything she could say to make up for what she did."

She was right. I had no inclination to talk to my mother. It really didn't matter if she was alive or dead…because she had been dead in my life for thirty years.

"So, you want to know," I smirked.

Andrea gave me a one shoulder dismissive shrug, "Yes, I'm curious if she is still alive."

"She would only be fifty-nine."

Andrea just stared at me, "The principal called her Oliva Conners even though she never married your dad. So I know her first name and I know your father and Austin were raised in Boise."

"They met there…yes…" I said thoughtfully. I wasn't curious about my mother. I had no feelings for her other than being thankful she didn't leave me on the side of the road. I wanted to believe she knew my uncle before dropping me off but that too really didn't matter. In my heart, I truly did not care about the woman. "Olivia Louise Baker."

Andrea's hand went to her pocket and pulled out the phone. I stood silently and watched her fingers tap on the device.

"Other than this, is there any other secrets?" I asked.

"No, not from my side." She didn't stop her research. "But you have one I want answers for."

I heard the gate swing open and turned to see Kade walking into the arena and across the dirt. He was carrying two chairs and two bottles of water.

I smiled at him and was pleased with his relieved smile. Andrea's head rose to look at him then lowered again.

Without a word, he set the chairs down, handed me the two bottles, then winked before turning and walking away.

I sat in a chair and stretched my legs out in front of me while I opened the bottle of water. With her head still looking at the phone, Andrea slowly sat in the chair and leaned back.

She stopped tapping and read for a moment before speaking, "Her obituary says she was married for 21 years and no children were from that marriage but she had one daughter and one granddaughter in Idaho."

She was dead and had recognized that I was alive and knew about Jamie...nope, still didn't matter to me.

"She lived in Macon, Georgia and died in a boating accident."

Andrea slid the phone back in her pocket and looked up at me.

"Now we know and the past is the past." She opened the water and took a drink while looking for my reaction.

Knowing about my mother still didn't make a difference in my life but Andrea did.

"What secret do I have from you?" I asked.

"Why didn't you tell me about the property trust?" She answered. "Having gone through the years before with all the court hearings with you and all the insane requests he was asking for, why did you not tell me?"

"I told Uncle Austin and Charlene that I would never mention it unless I absolutely had to."

"Not even to me?"

"No," I shook my head slowly. "If you had known when you had the accidental dinner with Blake and bitch wife would you have said something to him?"

She sighed and looked at me pensively, "Well, I'd like to say no to that but I couldn't 100 percent guarantee it. He was pouring on the 'poor him' routine pretty heavy."

"But, just so you know since Blake knows…"

"What? You've talked to Blake?" Her eyebrows rose in surprise.

"Yeah…this first though." I nodded. "Once I turned 40 and the divorce was final, the property reverted to me free and clear."

She gasped then laughed, "Oh, that had to piss him off."

"It did but what I didn't tell him was that I converted it back to a land trust in Jamie's name…and mine."

"Does she know?"

"Nope, just you and me…and the attorney."

"What if something happens to the two of you? What then?"

"It goes to Taylor and Ace."

She nodded in agreement, "I miss those two."

"Me, too." I took another drink of water then set it down into the dirt…squishing it down so it didn't tip over. "So, the past is in the past…no more secrets, so we talk about the now."

Her eyes went out to the pasture and began to glisten.

"When I heard their voices…Jodi and Dave, I knew what you had been worried about when you asked me to stay after the party. I didn't know that YOU had recorded them until Greg, Stan, and I went into the house. When we heard the screaming we went to the back door and saw Dave on the ground and you were reaching for the phone. I knew then and I was shocked that you would do that."

"Just the outside of the door and just so I would know for sure who it was," I said defensively.

She nodded but continued to look out at the pasture.

"Greg immediately blamed himself and I spent all day trying to tell him it wasn't his fault. Stan went and got Jodi so she wouldn't be alone and we…it was terrible…so much guilt. I started getting angry with you for recording it and it just escalated. Every time I had to tell them it wasn't their fault it became your fault…to me, not to them." She looked down and stared at her boots as she spoke. "I was so damn angry that Greg was hurting and that Jodi had been manipulated so terribly bad that she felt like a whore. She shouldn't because she sure as hell wouldn't have slept with him if she knew he was married."

I nodded in agreement but her eyes were still on her boots.

"I got angrier every time you texted me and by the time I came over here I was livid at you. Then you were out here…" She paused and took in a shaking breath. "Your driving Jamie away, not telling me the truth about the trust, then being here…where I lost Austin because of you…I just…" Her eyes finally moved to mine as a tear slid down her cheek. "It was too much and you became the target of all that anger."

I had no words to say to her. I couldn't console her and say it was alright because it wasn't. She nearly killed me in the spot we now sat.

"I can't take back what I said but I can say it wasn't your fault. That day, on the drive home, my mind raced with the words I had said. I realized that if I had told you Greg and Jodi were divorced you wouldn't have recorded the door." More tears fell. "Then I realized that it was my fault Dave was dead because I didn't tell you."

"It wasn't your fault," I whispered. I imagined what it was like for her at the time…by herself and taking on the guilt. I had to wipe away my own tears.

"If…"

"There are a lot of 'ifs'," I shook my head. "So many…"

She nodded and wiped away the tears. "A thousand times I picked up the phone or drove down the highway to apologize to you but I just couldn't get myself to do it. I couldn't get myself to admit out loud that it was my fault until Stan confronted me after the Stampede."

"I can't imagine that went well."

"No…not well at all." She crossed her legs at the ankle and leaned an elbow on the arm of the chair. Chin in hand, her eyes looked out to the pasture again. "I told him the truth…that I had blamed you and had been lying for weeks."

"You told him about Uncle Austin?"

She didn't answer right away and her expression didn't change.

"No," She finally whispered. "Austin is dead and I saw no reason to hurt Stan over what would never be. I love Stan, always have; maybe not as much as I loved Austin but enough to want to spend the rest of my life with him."

"Some secrets are best kept unsaid," I sighed. "Blake and Greg know you slept together but not about the romance…so it's just the two of us."

Her eyes slowly moved to me in silent question.

I shook my head, "I love Stan too. There is no reason to hurt him."

"Thank you," She whispered.

"Blake admitted to manipulating you for years, including telling you that I loved Greg. If he hadn't done that then you wouldn't have kept it a secret."

"And if Bitch Wife hadn't come into the picture and manipulated him then you wouldn't have gotten the job at the mortgage company to fill your empty time."

"So," I smiled at her. "We blame Bitch Wife for Dave's death."

She chuckled, "I'm good with that."

I took a deep breath and released the past as much as I could.

"Well," She sighed. "I guess it's a good thing you butt dialed me this morning."

"I didn't butt dial you," I huffed.

"Then how? Did your phone drop? How…?" Her eyes were wide in disbelief.

"I had your name up on the phone and was about to call you when she appeared."

"What? You meant to call me?" I could see the hope in her eyes.

"Yes, I had a dream the other night and when I told Kade about it, he convinced me that I needed to call you. I needed answers or we needed closure without the anger."

"Kade? The handsome cowboy that just brought us chairs?"

"Yes."

"And you two obviously are together." She smiled but it didn't really reach her eyes. It was if she was happy but also…not.

"Yes."

"So, you have a new man, Jamie is home, and you're roping again with a bunch of cowboys."

I just nodded.

There was silence a couple moments then she looked at me again.

"What were you going to say when you called? That your life had moved on and you didn't need or want…" She turned away as the words stopped.

"I was going to ask why, if you were only here for my uncle…why come here?"

She turned back to me, the seriousness back in her eyes. "I want to make something perfectly clear. Through the years, I did not come here for this place, Austin or the memories of him after he died. I came here for my best friend that is truly my sister and her daughter I think of as my own."

We stared at each other, eyes glistening as memories rose.

"If you were not here," She whispered with a trembling voice. "I would never come here again."

My heart sighed…I had no words so I just nodded.

"There is one more thing," Andrea said and rose to her feet.

CHAPTER THIRTY EIGHT

"What?" I asked cautiously and stood.

"I miss the horses," She smiled.

Without another word, we walked through the arena, past the barn, and into the pasture with my older horses.

"OK," Andrea said as she walked straight to Maggie. "One more thing I want to explain to you." Her hand slid down the horse's neck.

"What?"

She turned and looked at me, "Austin purchased Maggie when you were pregnant with Jamie."

"Yes…"

"When you were gone to Blake's parents, he and I had traveled to Bellevue to look at a sister of the great Stoli."

"You were with him?" I gasped.

"Yes."

"That's why you tried so hard to buy her after his death?"

She nodded and smiled at the horse as she ran her hand down her back then over her large hip…to the scars down her leg.

"Yes," she said. "I wanted to hold onto that weekend because it was all we really had."

JW was at my side, pushing against my arm for attention so I softly caressed down his neck.

"I can't help but think that I would have loved our life with the two of you together," I finally said out loud.

"The life we could have had," Andrea smiled slightly with a glance to me.

"Andrea?" I stood away from JW and looked at her with full sincerity in my heart. "I truly am sorry that you never had a life with him. That I didn't understand at the time of his death and console you, too."

"But, you did," She sighed. "You just didn't realize it. During and after the funeral…during all the tributes that were filmed…during the two weeks in Vegas…you included me in everything."

"You were part of his life, you were all of mine."

Our tear-filled eyes met.

"I hope that you can forgive me," She whispered. "It wasn't your fault; your boss's death or Austin and I not choosing to live our lives together. I can't take away the words I said…but they were said in confusion, anger, and guilt. I hope you can understand…"

"Yes," I stepped to her with my arms open.

She ran into the embrace and we tried hard to squeeze the last month out of our lives.

When we walked out of the pasture, I realized there was a relief in my heart but I still felt disconnected from her.

Kade was on the phone as we approached the house. He looked between us then stretched out the phone to me.

"Jamie," he said. "I apologize if I was out of place by calling her but I thought she should hear it from us rather than on the news."

"Thank you, I agree," I smiled and took the phone. "Kade this is Andrea, Andrea…Kade."

I lifted the phone and turned away.

After talking for five minutes convincing Jamie and the crew to stay in Hermiston, Stan drove down the driveway with their two boys next to him. As soon as the truck stopped, the doors burst open.

I glanced at Kade and Andrea. They were still in the same spot I left them and I wasn't even sure they had said a word to each other.

"Alright," Jamie said on the phone. "Group consensus is we'll stay because Kade and Andrea are there with you."

"Good," I sighed in relief. "Stan is here now too."

"Great, BUT," She said loudly. "We will be headed your way as soon as Ryle and Jess rope so take a nap because we're waking you when we arrive and we want the whole story."

"Tell them to focus and I'll see you tonight," I told her then ended the call.

I turned back to find Stan right behind me. His arms wrapped around me into a strong embrace.

"You OK," He whispered.

"Yes,"

"You and Andrea talk things out?"

"Yes,"

"You need time to process everything?"

He was a wise man, I thought as I sighed. "Yes,"

"We won't stay long then." He said as he stepped back. "I talked to Greg and Jodi and told them what happened. They send their love and would like a call when you're ready."

"Alright, thanks."

After five minutes of awkward introductions and conversation, Andrea left her truck behind and rode with Stan home.

The moment their car disappeared down the driveway I turned into Kade's arms and wrapped mine around his neck. We held each other tightly.

"You sure you're alright?" He whispered.

"Tired…" I admitted as my body relaxed.

"Did you sleep last night?"

"No, did you?"

"No."

He stepped away and led me back into the house and to the sofa. Within minutes, we were sleeping in each other's arms.

His arm twitched under me. My head lay on his chest. I felt his lips on my forehead, his arms tightening around me then silence; his heartbeat easing me back into sleep.

"I feel like I've been drugged," My voice was low and full of sleep as I sat up. I glanced out the window and my tired eyes widened in surprise. "Either we're having an eclipse or we slept all damn day."

"With you in my arms, I could stay here all night…or week." He said softly.

"Well, that was romantic," I turned to look into his eyes that were barely open.

"But, I need a shower," He continued.

"Well, that sounds inviting," I stood and walked across the room and toward the stairs. I could hear him scrambling off the sofa and wide footsteps following me.

It was the large jetted tub that we spent the next hour in before we made it to the shower, then the bed.

We woke to my phone alert telling me someone was at the gate.

"What time is it?" Kade sighed.

"One o'clock in the morning."

"Here we go…"

We dressed quickly and made it out the door just as the back of the horse trailer was opened and Jamie was jogging to the house.

"Just a warning," She whispered to us. "Pete is REALLY pissed."

"Yeah…" Kade nodded. "Knew he would be."

"Oh, yeah," Jamie smiled at me. "We stopped and picked up Andrea."

My senses jolted awake, "What? Why?"

"I wanted to see her and thank her so I called her and she said her truck was still here so we picked her up." She answered as she took my hand and pulled me out to the group.

Ryle and Jess stopped at the back of the horse trailer, their horses at their sides and their somber eyes looking at Pete. Marty was leaning against the trailer with Andrea next to him. They were quiet and watching Pete too.

It was odd seeing her there with my crew. I pushed down the thought that she was intruding in my new life and turned to Pete who was standing in the middle of the driveway, hands on hips, and glaring at us as we approached.

"You know exactly how we were going to take this," Pete growled at me.

I just nodded with a lump in my throat.

He turned to Kade, "You ever pull a stunt like that again, I'll whoop your ass just like I did when you were a kid."

As humorous as it sounded, no one laughed.

"You got it?" Pete glared at him.

"Yes, sir," Kade nodded.

Pete turned to me, "I'll give you this one, but not again. I'll whoop your ass, too."

"Yes, sir," I whispered and squeezed Kade's hand.

"Now," Pete glared. "You OK?"

"Yes," I nodded.

In an instant, his eyes changed to love, compassion, and worry.

I rushed into his arms, "I'm sorry."

He patted my back and nodded. "We move on now, let's get the horses in the barn then find a place to sit so you can tell us the story."

Marty was the first to the barn and he pushed open both doors. Jamie turned on the lights illuminating the length of the brick aisle and the wood and iron stalls. Jess and Ryle led the four horses to their stalls.

Chairs, bales of straw and anything that could be used as a seat was placed in a circle in the middle of the aisle. The doors were left open to let the gentle warm breeze flow through.

Once everyone was settled, I held Kade's hand as he spoke of his arrest then I told them of my conversation with Sheila that concluded with Andrea tackling her.

I turned to Jess, "In the morning, go get your dog."

"What?" He asked in surprise.

"That day he was sitting in the truck looking back at the trailers? It was her he was growling at. We'll watch out for the kittens." I said.

"You got it." Jess nodded.

"I didn't realize last week when I shut the curtains and closed the window in the trailer that I had checked them a couple weeks ago and they were closed." I said to the group.

"When does the buckle come home?" Andrea asked somberly.

"I didn't ask," I answered. "I'll call in the morning."

"But she saw Dad?" Jamie whispered. "The first time?"

My eyes went to the locked door just inside the barn doors. "He went in there."

All eyes moved to the door.

"What's in there?" Ryle asked.

Jamie and Andrea turned to him in surprise then they looked at me.

"I haven't been in there in months…just didn't have the heart for it." I shrugged.

"I'm sorry, Mom," Jamie sighed then bit her lip. "But…what would he have done?"

"You think he might have destroyed anything?" Andrea asked.

The men's eyes shifted between the three of us.

"Well," I took a deep breath. "We will just have to look and see."

I stood with the whole group standing and following me to the door.

I keyed in the code and turned the doorknob but just opened it inches before freezing. My heart was racing with what he might have done. How was Jamie going to handle her father betraying her again?

I turned and looked at her, tears slowly slid from her fear filled eyes.

"Look around you, Hon," I whispered. "No matter what we find, they are all here for you."

Jess stepped in behind her and slid his hand into hers as her eyes wandered from person to person.

"OK," She whispered.

I opened the door and switched on the light.

CHAPTER THIRTY NINE

At first glance, everything was the same as the last time I had walked through the doors. Andrea, Jamie, and I slowly wandered the room looking for anything missing, damaged, or changed.

"Are you kidding me?" Ryle cried out.

"A saloon?" Marty gasped.

An elaborate western bar ran down the left side of the room. A large mirror graced the wall behind it and sitting underneath the mirror were rows of drinking glasses and bottles of alcohol. During the rodeos my uncle and I had attended, vendors were shooting old-fashioned photos; the type that makes you appear from the 1880's. We had taken a number of them through the years and they were framed and placed on the wall to each side of the mirror. Jamie, Andrea, and I had added to the collection ever since. The whole wall looked like it could have been in an old western movie.

The other three walls were covered in action photographs of myself, Jamie and Andrea through the years. Gold buckles, trophies, leather engraved rope cans and bags, framed prints, ribbons, and other awards.

Trophy saddles were in each corner including mine and Jamie's national high school champion saddles.

A dozen tables with chairs and barstools, that had been purchased from a western movie prop house, set around the room.

"Damn," Jess exhaled.

"I never even thought of it," Kade said with wide eyes as he looked at me.

"Thought of what?" I asked.

"I knew you were pretty successful in your roping career…and barrels, but I never wondered where your awards…trophies were." He answered as his eyes moved to a large canvas that was the center of the wall across from the bar. It was set so it was what was reflected in the mirror behind the bar.

"That canvas…" He said and the group gathered in front of it.

"The Pendleton 4th of July barrel race," Andrea told them. "Jamie and I had it made for her after she won."

"BlueDoc?" Pete asked.

The blue roan horse's legs were stretched out in front and in back of him giving the illusion he was flying. Black cowboy hat, black hair flying loose behind me over a black long sleeve western shirt I was leaning forward just to the spot I knew gave the horse freedom of shoulder movement allowing him his widest stride. It was a powerful image but adding to it was the intense stare I had to the finish line. My mouth formed a growl as I encouraged BlueDoc to run as fast as he could.

"Whoa…" Ryle exhaled in disbelief.

"You won?" Jess asked.

"I did," I nodded with a flush over my skin at the memory. "We set up the large pattern in the back pasture so we could condition and train to it."

"They won Sandcup and Barrel Daze a couple times, too," Andrea said. "Finished first two years in a row with state Brand Four barrels and went to finals twice."

"You should see the videos," Jamie said proudly.

"Yes…" They all called out.

"Later," I chuckled. "We added all these as a marketing tool for the clinics we've held over the years."

They slowly moved around the room.

"Mom?" Jamie whispered.

I turned to see a puzzled look.

"I don't see anything missing or destroyed." she said. "What do you think Dad did?"

"I don't know…" I answered. "Honestly, Hon, unless he tells someone, we may never know."

"Should I ask him?" She asked with lips rolled into a grimace.

"No," I decided and said firmly. "We just let it go."

"You sure?" She asked.

"Yes," I smiled. "We just move on."

"OK…" She sighed.

"You went to Vegas? To the World Series Team Roping?" Jess asked and pointed to the image on the wall.

"First in the #12 the year after I was born." Jamie grinned. "Second the next year in #11 and third the following year in #10."

"I had a great coach and partner for the win," I said and pointed to the photograph which showed my uncle and I standing in front of our horses and grinning into the camera.

"Reno World Series Qualifier Champion, too," Andrea added.

"ICA Breakaway Champion three years in a row, then a couple more," Pete pointed to the pictures on the wall.

"A couple Reserve Champion, too, with Marko," Jamie said. "And, she was also the champion in barrel racing a couple years ago with BlueDoc."

"OK, note that Jamie is in a lot of these too…and Andrea." I said.

"Here's Mom and I winning the team roping together." Jamie waved her hand to the picture.

"You race or rope?" Marty asked Andrea.

"Never competitive roping but barrel raced. Although I've never been the caliber of these two," Andrea answered. "I'm fine with being in the 2D or 3D where these two are always in the 1D unless they are training a new horse."

"The D's?" Ryle grinned and looked at Jamie.

"No, Ryle," Jamie laughed.

"What?" Andrea asked.

"I help with calculating the D's." Ryle said with the most serious expression I had ever seen. "34D's, 36D's…" He looked at Jess then Jamie. "I do like the double D's too."

Andrea watched Ryle with a stunned expression. She looked at me, silently asking if he was serious. When I grinned she turned back to him.

"I once knew a girl that was a 34 triple D," She told him.

Ryle's jaw dropped, he dramatically fell back against Jess as his hand went to his chest.

"You HAVE to introduce us," He begged.

Andrea shrugged with a smirk, "Well, she is in her forties now and nursed three kids, so they may not be where they were when I knew her."

"Eeek!" He cried out in horror as his hands fell to his knees.

"Yeah, probably," Andrea crinkled her nose and nodded.

Everyone burst out laughing.

My stomach swirled and my heart sighed. She suddenly seemed a part of the group and was no longer a trespasser.

I stood back and watched everyone move around the room as Andrea and Jamie told them stories. In the midst of a burst of laughter, the third hoof hit the ground. I looked at Pete as tears filled my eyes.

CHAPTER FORTY

The morning of the Caldwell rodeo, I stood at my bedroom window and looked out at the ranch. There was just a hint of briskness in the air which would warm to a perfect day in the eighties. Blue sky with puffs of white clouds in the sky and sunshine; a day every horse person dreams of.

The chickens were wandering in their outdoor enclosure and the kittens were playing in the grass under the swing. Jess and Ryle were walking their younger horses out of the pasture and to the barn with the border collie, Rover, trotting happily behind them. Pete and Kade were just sitting down at the outdoor patio table with cups of coffee in their hands.

I watched Kade as he leaned back in the chair, stretched out his legs and crossed them at the ankle. He wore his well-worn boots, Wrangler jeans, a white short-sleeve western shirt. His cowboy hat set on the table allowing me to see his thick hair, wide jaw, and expressive eyes. I sighed at his handsomeness. How lucky was I?

I turned from the peaceful sight and pulled my best Resistol straw cowboy hat from the hook on the wall and walked to the full-length mirror and set it gently on my head then pushed it a little tighter.

The reflection in the mirror was of a woman I hadn't seen in years. Dark brown cowboy boots, dark Wrangler jeans, a white shirt decorated with a dozen sponsor patches, and the hat that covered my black hair; the long loose braid fell down my back. This woman had been lost to a manipulative woman, betraying husband, confused daughter, and her best friend who was ultimately her soul mate in life.

I thought of the moment I first met Pete. He leaned over the seat of his old orange Ford and looked through the window.

"Hey!"

He had called out, his eyes sparkling and grin wide.

"Aren't you Lauren Conners? Didn't you use to rope?"

"I am and I used to." I had answered.

I looked at the reflection in the mirror again as I stood straighter, shoulders back, chin up.

"I am Lauren Conners," I said to the image. I had just lost myself for a while but I was back and… "I AM a roper." I smiled at the woman in the reflection. There was pride, happiness, strength, and confidence in her stance.

"I am Lauren Conners and I am a roper," I said loudly and proudly then turned away.

I jogged down the stairs and wide strides took me to the back door. Jamie had joined the two men at the patio table. They all three turned as I stepped out the door.

"Oh! Mom!" Jamie gasped. "I haven't seen you like that in years!"

"Damn, Darlin'," Pete grinned as he stood. "I have to admit, seeing you like this, is even better than the blue velvet dress."

I laughed as my eyes went to Kade as he stood. He just stared at me, his chest rising as he took a deep breath; his hand covered his heart.

"Good morning," I smiled.

Pete stepped forward and tipped his arm to me.

"Oh, no, Granddad," Kade said and stepped in front of him. He offered me his arm. "Today, it's my honor."

My heart melted at his words, the look in his eyes, and his touch as I wrapped my arm around his. This man just kept stealing my heart.

"Well, Jamie?" Pete said.

"Of course!" She laughed and her hand took his arm.

As we walked back to the barns, I looked out at the property. The broodmares and foals had been moved to a back corral to make room for the horse trailers and trucks that had started arriving the night before. Horses were already tied to trailers and people moving around as they prepared for the day.

I had locked the driveway gate open so people could come and go as they needed and Marty and Sarah were arriving with their horses.

The day before we had installed another chute in the warm-up arena that was now a breakaway arena. The larger round pen would be used to warm-up as well as the pasture that normally held Ryle and Jess's horses. Silas had been trapped the night before and stalled for an easy capture. Today the rest of the horses were also stalled.

Barrels had also been placed in the pasture for anyone that wanted to practice.

"How many people do you think will be here?" Pete asked.

"Well, we personally invited a dozen and word spread so…really…who knows?" I laughed.

Two hours later, I stood at the top of the bleachers and looked out at the property. At least twenty riders were team roping with Marty working the chute and Pete removing the ropes from the steer in the stripping chute for those that had caught. Sarah was working the chute for at least a dozen breakaway riders. Kade was working the stripping chute in that arena.

Behind me, on the driveway, were the dummy roping steer and calves with kids and adults throwing their loops. Crystal, Jamie, and Jess were talking while they watched Ryle help Crystal's son rope a dummy steer.

The saloon doors were open that led to the table and chairs behind the roping chutes. Stan was at the grill next to the doors and Andrea was walking out a tray of snacks to place on the tables. She laughed at something Marty yelled out to her then she threw a bag of chips at him. She was a great hostess.

I took a number of pictures to commemorate the day Uncle Austin's dream came back to life.

A familiar truck parked next to my horse trailers, and even more familiar grins beamed from the front seat. I turned to look at Jamie and Jess. She was waving at Roscoe and Brady who had brought along Garrett Tribble, Denton Fugate, and Trevor Kastner. Jess's hand slid into her other hand. I chuckled. Jamie had told me the cowboys had all got along fine at the Omak rodeo. They had all had fun watching the suicide race together but now there was no doubt Jess was letting Roscoe know how things stood.

A car I didn't recognize pulled into the driveway and drove around the multitude of trucks and trailers. It stopped next to my truck at the house. I watched curiously to see who it was and was shocked to see Aubrey Olsen the therapist I had seen after Dave's death.

She stood at her car and looked around the property. I wondered what she had expected to find instead of what she was seeing. Her head turned to me so I waved and received a wave in return as she started walking toward the bleachers. Wanting her to see everything, I remained where I was so that she had to climb the bleachers and stand next to me.

"Wow," She smiled. "This isn't what I was expecting."

"And what was that?" I asked.

"I'm not really sure, I guess I was expecting that lost woman I had first met living on a desolate ranch. Not this strong woman in front of me and all this action. I was a bit worried about you when you stopped coming to therapy," She admitted.

I looked out at the arenas full of horses, riders, and the family on the sidelines that came to play.

"This is the therapy I need," I said to her.

"I can see that," She smiled. "And I'm very glad you found it."

We stood quietly a moment watching the action before she turned to me.

"I'm not even sure I should ask," she said.

The only people on the bleachers were on the bottom bench. No one could hear us so I turned to her, "I regret what happened to Dave but it was not my fault. It was his because of his actions and it's Sheila's fault for her actions."

"Good…good…" She sighed.

"Thank you for working for me and helping," I said.

She huffed, "I had hoped I was helping but I had my doubts."

"You did. I needed someone to talk to even when I didn't say a word, you were there." I sighed. "That's what I needed then…just someone there for me."

"I'll be there anytime you need but it looks like you have it all under control."

"When I looked in the mirror this morning, I saw the strong confident person I once was."

"But?"

"But, even then, when I was at the top of my game, there was still something deep inside that seemed…" My voice trailed off.

"What?"

I turned to her and looked into her eyes to see sincerity and the desire to help so I turned back and waved a hand out to all the people.

"This…it's here now, like it was in the past but deep inside is the fear…I was abandoned by both my parents and then my uncle was taken from me. My husband left me then for a while my daughter and best friend were gone."

"What are you afraid of?"

I turned to her with the strong confidence revealed to her and anyone else looking and not the abandoned girl inside me. "I have no idea."

"Then come into the office and let's talk it through," She said.

"I don't know…" I sighed and looked out at my daughter to Andrea then Kade. I had them now and all the team ropers, why was I even talking to her?

"Lauren, there is no shame in getting help. The shame comes from not getting the help you need to be able to live the full life that you deserve."

I just sighed.

"It may only take one session to talk through your fear," She said then smiled. "Unless you just sit and look at the pictures on the wall again."

"I may need to bring you some new ones," I smiled.

"I'll let you get back to all your guests," she said. "But I am going to send you an appointment request, then you can decide."

"Alright," I nodded.

I walked her to her car then turned back to my guests.

I stood in the team roping arena with Cody, Dillon, Robert, Phoenix, Jeff and a half dozen more ropers surrounding me. Dillon was telling us a story when I saw Kade walking toward the group. He smiled at the ropers as he casually walked up next to me and slid an arm around my waist with a hand dipping into one of my back pockets.

He leaned down and whispered in my ear, "Just so you know, it's not about letting all these ropers know you're my girl, but I just had a desire to touch your butt."

We both giggled.

I walked behind the bleachers to check on the group throwing at the dummies. They were happy and having fun so I walked into the barn to the saloon. It was empty of people except one teenager sitting at the table that held three photo albums of rodeo and race photos. He wasn't looking at the pictures he was playing on his phone. He didn't even look up at me.

"What's up?" I asked.

"Nothin'," He mumbled as he continued to play.

"Why in here instead of in the fresh air with everyone else?"

"Don't know how to ride or rope but my brother wanted me to come with him," he said. "Came in to look at the pictures of the pretty girls."

I chuckled, "Well, thank you."

His eyes finally rose to me and he smirked, "Nice pics. That big canvas is pretty cool."

"Thanks, again."

His hand flipped from his phone to the albums. "How come there are pictures missing?"

"There are?" I slid onto the chair next to him and flipped open a cover. The first picture was missing. I knew that it was a picture of Jamie holding her saddle at the High School National Finals. I continued to flip through only to find more pictures that had been of just Jamie were gone. All three albums had pictures of her missing.

So, her father had trespassed onto the property and came into the room for pictures of his daughter throughout the years. I little of the anger I was holding for him began to subside and I knew the relief that Jamie was going to feel. It was about his love of her. I didn't want her thinking of her father today, so I'd wait until tomorrow to tell her.

I pushed the books away and stood, "Why don't you come out with me and we'll find you something you'll enjoy…in the sunshine."

"Like what?" He set the phone down and looked up at me.

"What do you like?"

He shrugged.

"Well, do you like to cook?"

"Sort of…depends on what it is."

"A friend of mine, his name is Stan, is a grill master and he'd be happy to have some help."

"You sure?"

"Yes, come with me."

He stood and followed.

"What's your name?" I asked.

"Ryan."

"It's nice meeting you Ryan, I'm Lauren Conners."

"Yeah, figured that from the pictures."

I smiled, "It was nice of you to keep your brother company."

He shrugged again as we walked out the door next to the chutes. "I like going to rodeos and stuff with him. I just like the bull riding though."

I chuckled as my eyes wandered through all the cowboys and cowgirls.

"Any your favorite?"

"J.B. Mauney, Silvano Alves, Jess Lockwood…"

"Nice selection," I nodded. "You know any local riders?"

"You mean like Roscoe Jarboe and Brady Portenier?"

"So you know them?"

"I don't know them, know them, but I do like watching them."

"Well, while you were in there playing on your phone, those two and Trevor Kastnor, Denton Fugate, and Garrett Tribble are out here."

"No, fucking way!" He gasped and his eyes widened as they searched the crowd.

"You stick with Stan and they'll come to you."

"Cool!"

A half hour later, I saw Jess and Roscoe walking together in front of the barn and disappearing behind it. I stood and stared…what the hell were they doing? I was about to search for them when they appeared carrying the large training barrel on stands used to teach bull riding. We had used it for a few clinics held for the high school rodeos.

They placed the practice barrel in the round pen that had soft ground. Trevor threw a bull rope around it and within minutes, Ryan was grinning as he sat on top of the barrel and six bull riders showed him how to ride.

"Don't you think it's time to show everyone how it's done?" Pete asked as he handed me the reins to JW.

I couldn't help but give him a hug before taking the reins.

"Lauren! Me first!" Kim Grubbs yelled.

It had been years since I had roped with her and I was more than happy to back into the box across from her.

I spent the rest of the morning in the team roping arena. After lunch, I saddled Marko and Kim and I rode with the breakaway ropers.

"What do you think, Mom?" Jamie turned to me.

"About what?"

"Weren't you listening?" She gasped with wide eyes.

"No, Kim and I were talking," I answered.

"Rylee was just saying that the Pendleton race in September is also an American rodeo qualifier," Jamie said. "She's putting in for it so we should too."

"We?" I grinned with the spark in my stomach again.

"Janey has already qualified," Rylee added.

Janey leaned around Rylee, "It would be one hell of a trip to Texas with you two with us." She grinned.

My heartbeat increased as I looked between the three of them.

"You could do team roping too, Mom." Jamie grinned.

"You could, too," Kim said to Jamie.

"Both of you together!" Rylee added. "A mother-daughter team kicking ass at the American would be pretty cool."

"Oh!" Jamie shouted. "And you have to find a qualifier for barrels. You and BlueDoc would kick some of that ass too."

I dramatically rolled my eyes.

"That would put you in line for the All Around, too," Kim said.

"Yeah, you could give that Trevor guy a run for his money," Jamie laughed. "You know he would love it."

"No doubt," I nodded.

I huffed in a bit of disbelief at the thought but also the inkling of the challenge rose in my heart. I nudged Marko out into the arena then backed him into the box.

Holding the rope up and back in preparation for the run, I let myself briefly imagine that I was in the AT&T Stadium in Texas running in the richest rodeo in history. My heart raced and stomach clenched. For a brief moment, I could swear my uncle was standing at the chute telling me I could do it. I closed my eyes then looked down at the chute. It was Ryle standing there grinning at me.

I looked out at Pete sitting on his horse and holding the judging flag up in preparation of my run. He was looking at me proudly. There was no way he could know what we had been talking about, but there he was encouraging me with just his smile.

I looked at Ryle, the calf then nodded.

It wasn't just a nod to open the chute.

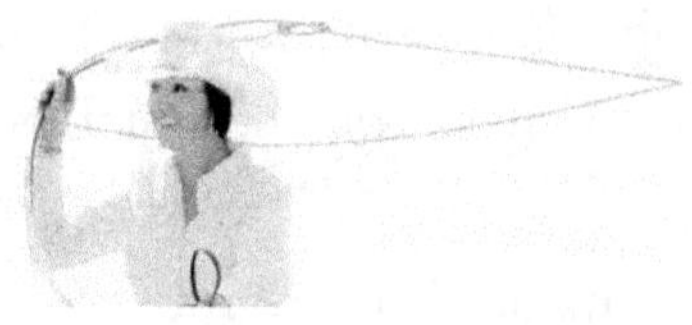

The last guest was turning out of the driveway as Ryle and Jess loaded their horses into the trailer to make their way to the rodeo.

"Did you tell them, Mom?" Jamie asked with a grin.

"Tell who what?" I chuckled at her. The smirk I gave her let her know I knew exactly what she was talking about.

"Mom…" She huffed then turned to the five ropers, Andrea, Stan, and Sarah. "We're going to run at one of the American qualifiers and try to get to Texas next February."

They all turned with excited grins. It was Pete that began nodding.

"You best nod," I told him. "Because you're riding with me in the team roping."

"I'm too old for that," He shook his head with a laugh.

"No, you're not," I slid my arm around his and squeezed. "You're never too old or young for this one."

"We're trying too," Jess said and looked at Ryle. "We've signed up for a qualifier in October."

Kade turned to Marty, "I'm not getting left out. Are you?"

Marty shook his head, "Nope, you got a partner."

Marty turned to Andrea with a raised brow.

"Oh, I'm going," She said with wide eyes. "I'll be the best damn groom any of you have ever seen."

"This is going to be so much fun!" Jamie squealed and everyone nodded in agreement.

"Let's go rodeo," Jess told Ryle.

The next morning it was just my five team ropers, best friend and daughter left on the property but there was an excitement in the air. The challenge of a new goal had settled over all of us.

The competitive fire coursed through me as I tightened JW's cinch then lowered the stirrup.

"Hurry up, Mom," Jamie called out as she rode her smoky buckskin, Sparrow, into the arena.

I didn't answer any more than a quiet chuckle.

I glanced over JW's back to see her ride in next to Jess who was already on Warlock. Their hands stretched to each other and they rode around the arena together with Ryle on Silas next to them.

The fact that Jess had asked me out on a date would never be known. How awkward would that be?

I chuckled as I turned to a movement to my left.

I sighed. It was Kade walking his horse toward me. He made my heart melt every time I looked at him but as he neared his eyes were thoughtful.

"Hi," I smiled at him.

He stopped with his bay horse at his side.

"There is something I want you to know," he said.

"What's that?" I asked and leaned against JW's shoulder.

"There are times that I just want to close my eyes and listen to your voice but I can't because when you're near me I can't help but take in your beauty. Not just your eyes, your nose, or your lips, but also the beauty of your heart. Moments hit me so hard that I can barely breathe for the fact that I am the one to touch you, kiss you, and have you in my arms at night. Like yesterday, when you walked out of the house, I was speechless because I knew we were seeing the real, true Lauren Conners for the first time. I began falling for you the day you wore the blue dress because of your sass to Granddad then every day since, but that moment yesterday, of meeting you for the first time, I realized that you were the perfect, imperfect woman for me. You are the most stunning woman I have had the honor of meeting. I had no prouder moment then yesterday when you took my arm…the world stopped at that moment as I walked with the most giving, loving, true woman that has ever walked into my life. I look at you and wonder, 'How can I be so lucky'?"

He smiled, "I just thought you should know."

With that, he and his horse disappeared on the other side of JW as they continued to the arena.

With my heart pounding and a gasp of disbelief escaping me, I closed my eyes as that fourth hoof hit the ground so hard it made my legs tremble.

When my eyes opened, I looked for him. He was walking around the end of the horse trailer, with his red roan at his side nipping at a treat he was feeding him. Pete smiled at the horse then his gaze lifted to me. His eyes held pride and joy.

This man had saved my life. He didn't have to stop me on the road. He didn't have to invite me into his life. But he did. Where would my life be if this man had not taken that moment to reach out to a stranger to help? Where would my life be if those damn team ropers hadn't fought so hard to help a lost soul?

Tears filled my eyes as Pete walked to me.

"I will love you until the day I die," I whispered to him.

His eyes shone, "Only my wife has said those words to me."

"And she did."

He nodded with a loving sigh, "Yes, she did." He took a breath. "We have four hooves down now, Darlin'?"

"We do," My voice shook.

"Well, what do you say to chasing a steer?"

"Well, why not? I have nothing better to do."

He tipped his arm to me, my hand slowly slid around his elbow. With a smile of shared love, we led our horses to the arena to start our new dream.

ABOUT THE AUTHOR

I grew up in the world of Shetland ponies. I would ride and pretend I was in the rodeo and not at a pony show.

I didn't purchase my first "big" horse until I was 21. That horse (Nan) was also 21 and pregnant with Jetta. Jetta gave birth to Libby when she was 18. Jetta passed away at 25. Libby was bred to a gorgeous palomino which gave me Miss Kit. So, I have had the pleasure of owning four generations of mares.

I am also the author of The Tagger Herd book series and a photographer. I use my own work as the cover of the books. Through the writing of the Tagger series, I have met many wonderful people. In the last few years, I have added district and high school rodeos to my photography. It's one way of getting into the arena I had dreamed of since I was a child.

 I enjoy my world of photography and horses with my family, two horses & dogs I named Tagger and Morgan.

www.ingramcontent.com/pod-product-compliance
Lightning Source LLC
Chambersburg PA
CBHW070925100726
47908CB00001B/107